CR_____ORY!

"Mallory w_____egend."
—_____Book Reviews

"Fresh and a_____hose who love historical
romances will_____ws Today

"Outrageously_____a poignant
moments, High_____ughter and
tears."
—RT Book Reviews

"A humorous and lively novel . . . you will want to pull an
all-nighter to read."
—Louisa's Magical Romance site

HIGHLAND FLING
"Lively and fun . . . delightful characters and an original
approach . . ."
—RT Book Reviews

"Have a rollicking good time with Mallory's latest."
—Booklist

"A wild time travel ride . . . This is a winner . . . a romantic
Back to the Future."
—Harriet Klausner

"I laughed and cried . . . and finished the book with a
smile. Then I ran out and looked for more of Ms. Mallory's
works."
—Gina Duvall, Paranormal Romance Reviews

"Griffin is a wonderful hero . . . I couldn't help but fall a
little bit in love."
—Reviewers-Choice.com

Dangerous Love

"So young," Jake murmured, "still so innocent, aren't you, in spite of your efforts to appear otherwise?"

"Lieutenant—" Torri said uneasily.

"Jake," he corrected. "From now on we are Jake and Victoria to one another. We have a hard job ahead of us. There's no place for formality here."

Torri stared at him, unable to take her eyes from his. "My friends call me Torri."

"Torri." He said the name as if he savored the sound. "I like it."

"Jake, tell me what you're doing here."

His mouth tightened and his fingers suddenly slid from her face up into her hair. Swiftly he bent his lips to hers. Torri felt the desperation behind his touch, and without understanding his need, she responded with equal passion, curling her arms around his neck. Suddenly Jake pulled away, and Torri saw something akin to shock in his eyes. Then she watched as his face shifted back into the smooth mask again, cutting her off, efficiently separating them.

"I came," he said softly, "to kill a man."

Other *Love Spell* books by Tess Mallory:

Tess Mallory

Jewels of Time

LOVE SPELL   NEW YORK CITY

To my children: Erin, Heather and Jordan—
the laughter, the sunshine, and the joy of my life.
Thanks for believing in me. You are my heart.
I love you always.

LOVE SPELL®

October 2009

Published by

Dorchester Publishing Co., Inc.
200 Madison Avenue
New York, NY 10016

ISBN 10: 0-505-52249-7
ISBN 13: 978-0-505-52249-8
E-ISBN: 978-1-4285-0755-5

Visit us online at www.dorchesterpub.com.

ACKNOWLEDGMENTS

My love and thanks go out to all those many friends and family who believed in me and helped make this book a reality, but especially to my husband, Bill Mallory; my best bud, Jan Miller; my sisters, Cas Measures and Jewell Dean; my father, J. T. Casler; and my mother, Alpha Casler.

Also thanks to Laura Lightner, Tom Thomas, Shannon Story, Cerelle Simmons, Linda Reeder, Janice Zimmerman, the Bitkowers, dear friends in Kerrville and Weatherford, and of course, the Sunday night Acorn-heads.

A great big thank you to my agent, Natasha Kern.

To all others I would like to mention, God bless you and thanks for believing in me.

Jewels of Time

Prologue

K'meron smoothed the front of the strange gray uniform with both hands, then cast a questioning glance at his companion.

"Are you sure this is authentic?" he said. "I don't want to take a chance on anything going wrong this time."

The dark haired woman beside him shook her head. "The Council researched the accepted dress of the period right down to the last buttonhole on your double-breasted coat. I did the finishing work myself."

"Look out, T'ria," he cautioned, "you might have actually done something that could be interpreted as domestic. No telling what that might do to your reputation if word got around."

In response to his sarcasm her gaze shifted from admiring her handiwork, to a quick search of his face. "We're counting on you, K'meron."

He smiled. Her words were edged with the familiar sharpness that had provoked them into some violent arguments in the past.

In the past, he thought, the smile turning cold and sardonic.

The young woman watching him frowned. "Are you sure you can go through with this?" she asked, her tone doubtful. "After all—"

His eyes narrowed. "I've claimed the right. Are you opposing that claim, T'ria?"

She shook her head, her short, dark curls moving savagely

against her cheeks as she looked away, her eyelashes shadowing her expression.

Amazing, K'meron thought, gazing down at her. If I didn't know better, I'd think she *cared.* But that would mean she had a heart and, I know better than anyone, she's the original ice lady.

"No, I don't oppose your claim." She glanced up at him, her blue eyes haughty. "Just make sure your feelings are quite clear in the matter *before* you go. Be very sure. You won't get another chance."

One corner of his mouth drew up in reckless challenge. "Is that a threat, my sweet?"

She glared at him. "Yes, *my sweet,* it is."

"I know what I'm doing, T'ria." He leaned closer and tilted her chin, his thumb caressing the side of her face. "It's only you who doubt me."

"You've failed before."

K'meron dropped his hand to his side, anger building inside him. "You know why. Some of those times I ended up in the wrong time periods and then I tried to make it to 1863 and ended up in 1847." He glanced away.

"The job still could have been done. This is twice you've used that as an excuse."

"The time before last the target was five years old," he said in disgust.

"Sentiment has no place in our organization, K'meron," the dark-haired woman said softly. "Surely you've realized that by now?"

He lifted one eyebrow. "Sentiment? Let's get something straight, *Commander.* I don't kick puppies, I don't torture kittens, and"—his mouth twisted in derision—"I don't kill children. If I end up too far back again this time, and find my target is still just a child, I'll make the same decision I did before."

T'ria's gaze swept over him as if weighing his words and

their implications. "I'll do you a favor," she said. "I won't repeat that to the others."

"Awfully good of you." He laughed harshly. "What in hell do you think they can do to me, T'ria? Kill me? That's rather a moot issue, wouldn't you say?"

T'ria backed away from him and gestured toward an object on the slick, translucent, tiled floor. "Then take your weapon. Go and prove my doubts are foolish."

K'meron leaned over and picked up a long scabbard, withdrew the brass-hilted sword and released an admiring whistle. "How did you get your hands on this?"

"Never mind. You don't have to know everything, only what is necessary, remember? We agreed the less we all knew—"

"Forget it." He buckled the scabbard at his waist. "You seem to think I'm continually pumping you for information, T'ria. It's called paranoia."

She frowned at him again and drew herself up stiffly. "Are you ready?"

He reached inside his gray coat and drew out an oddly shaped pendant attached to a golden chain around his neck. It was studded with variously colored jewels.

"Goodbye, T'ria," he said softly.

"I've been wondering . . ." She hesitated and the harsh lines around her mouth faded into a sudden vulnerability. "Why did you make the claim?"

K'meron stared at her for a long moment, his jaw tense; then he shrugged. "At least I won't be waiting around wondering when it's going to happen. Or maybe I just don't want my murder on someone else's conscience. Not even yours, T'ria."

"K'meron—" she took a step toward him, her arms half-extended, then quickly lowered them.

He gazed down at her. "No sentiment, right? How does that old saying go? 'We who are about to die—'"

The momentary warmth faded from her clear blue eyes,

leaving the usual ice. She stepped back. "Goodbye, K'meron," she said, lifting her chin. "Serve us well."

He smiled again, not hiding his contempt. Placing his fingers carefully on two of the jewels glimmering on the pendant around his neck, K'meron gave the dark-haired woman one last penetrating look . . . and disappeared.

Chapter One

"It's not a necklace," the old man said. "It's a way to travel through time."

Torri looked into her grandfather's feverish eyes, then ducked her head, trying to hide the horror in her own.

So, Christine and Harry are right, she thought, staring down at the necklace in her hands. *Grandfather is crazy.* Her fingers tightened around the pendant, the golden edge biting into her palm.

No! They were wrong—she knew they were wrong. Then how do you explain this, her own honest nature whispered. Torri shook her head as if to dispel the traitorous thought.

Perched on the edge of an antique rocking chair she'd drawn close to his side, she turned and glanced out the wide, open window near her grandfather's bed. Virginia in the springtime. How she had always loved it, loved the sweet perfume of the honeysuckle and jasmine budding everywhere. This year it didn't matter. This year she didn't care.

She was tempted to lean out the window and tell the birds cheerfully chirping in the azalea bush to shut up; the roses to stop blooming. Torri didn't want the scent in the air to tell her everything was all right, when she knew her world was collapsing around her.

The worst of it was, she couldn't do a thing to stop what was going to happen, any more than she could stop the birds from singing, or the buds from opening their petals to catch the morning sun. Nathaniel Hamilton, her beloved grandfather, was leaving that day for the Sunnyside Sanitarium, and there was nothing in the world she could do to change that miserable fact.

She glanced down from the second floor window to the driveway below. An ambulance waited in front of the Hamilton mansion, ready to take her grandfather away. Torri had been prepared to do something desperate to keep them from taking him, but now, after this alarming statement about the necklace, could she be so sure Christine hadn't been right all along?

Even if her aunt was right—if her grandfather was as crazy as a loon—Torri still didn't want him sent away. She could care for him herself, allowing him to stay in his own home. Sunnyside Sanitarium! How hypocritical the silly name, when in truth the place was nothing more than a rich man's mental institution.

"Grandfather, you're tired," Torri said, taking his hand and stroking it gently. "The competency hearing was so hard on both of us. I know finding out that Aunt Christine was the driving force in getting you sent to that awful place was a terrible shock to you."

The old man's face sagged and he lowered his gaze to the quilted coverlet. "Yes," he agreed, "yes, it was a shock. My son's wife. If Jeremy were alive—well, for the first time I thank God he isn't." He shook his head. "I don't understand why Christine did this. I've always been more than generous with her." He lifted querulous eyes to his granddaughter's. "Why, Torri? Why did she lie? Why did she tell the judge that I tried to strangle her? I don't understand."

Torri closed her eyes, remembering the horrible courtroom drama that had seemed to suck the very life from her once vital grandfather. She saw him, again, on the witness stand, Christine's lawyer firing one question at him after another until he was so confused that his hands began to tremble. He had collapsed, right there on the stand. She had screamed and run to his side. If she lived to be a thousand she would never forgive Christine for that one awful moment when she had feared her grandfather was dead.

Torri opened her eyes and tears trembled on her lashes. "I don't know, Grandfa," she whispered, using the childish name she'd given him years before. "Of course, her witnesses were hired, and that psychiatrist was bribed, but I swear to you," Torri leaned toward him, forcing a cocky smile, "you won't be in Sunnyside long enough to get sick of the wallpaper!"

A slight smile quivered around the old man's lips. "That's great, darling," he said, patting her hand, "I'm sure it will be daisies or something equally nauseating."

"I mean it." Torri tossed her hair back from her shoulders. "We're not licked yet. I'm going to find the best lawyer in the country and fight this thing. I would've done it before; I just never dreamed Mr. Bennington would fail."

"Poor Arthur. He felt so badly about the outcome, but he's getting old, like me." He glanced up at her. "Forget about another lawyer. Christine controls your trust fund now, child, until your twenty-first birthday."

"That's only a year away, Grandfa—but you won't have to wait that long, I promise you." She spoke slowly and deliberately. "I'm going to get you out of there—no matter what I have to do. I can get the money. I can—I can"—she cast around in her mind desperately—"I can hock this necklace! If the jewels are real—"

"No, no!" he cried, thrusting out one hand to cover the necklace and sending himself into a coughing spasm. Torri held him until the seizure passed. He fell back against the pillow. "Never, never do that," he implored her weakly, "and never let it fall into the wrong hands—why, if it did, it could mean catastrophe! Time travel can be used as a weapon, my dear, never doubt that!"

Torri's lips parted as if she'd been dealt a physical blow, but this time she met his searching look and knew she could not hide the pain in her eyes.

"You don't believe me," he said, his bushy gray brows knitting together, his voice laced with disbelief. "You think I'm crazy, just like Christine, and your boyfriend Harry."

"He isn't my boyfriend anymore," she said in a choked voice. "Did you think I would stay with him after the way he tried to get me to testify against you?"

The old man's eyes burned with an unhealthy intensity. "Well, Granddaughter," he said with a sigh, "at least I can go happy in that knowledge. I knew you'd see through that smooth facade of his sooner or later."

"Grandfa, please, let's not talk about Harry."

"Never mind, then. And don't worry. You'll be meeting someone new very soon—just as soon as you use the necklace."

Torri hadn't thought her sorrow could go any deeper but it pierced her like an arrow. "Yes, of course," she said gently.

He grinned at her. "Humoring an old, crazy man, eh? But that's all right, I keep forgetting. You'll understand soon enough. Now, honey, look at the necklace, don't you recognize it?"

Dispassionately her gaze flickered back to her hand. Diamond shaped, the necklace's pendant was about three inches in length and two inches across. The metal was gold, or at least she assumed it was from the heaviness of the pendant and its long chain. Torri frowned. It certainly wasn't the kind of jewelry she would pick to wear. In fact, she thought it rather ugly.

In each corner of the pendant a different jewel sparkled: a ruby, a sapphire, an emerald and a diamond, all quite large. Real jewels? Torri had never been that interested in gems. She owned only a pair of diamond earrings and an amethyst dinner ring. Curiously, she turned the necklace toward the light.

Strange. They did look very different from any jewels she had ever seen before. The gems had clear-cut facets, as she expected, but inside . . . inside there seemed to almost be movement, as if under the hard crystalline surface the jewels were not quite solid.

In the center of the pendant an upraised, diamond-shaped button of gold made a curious addition to the piece. There was something engraved there, a design, but the etching was too worn to decipher. She had to admit, it was unlike any necklace she'd ever seen except—

Torri looked up at her grandfather with a quick smile. "Now I remember," she said. "It's the necklace in the portrait—the one the first Victoria Hamilton wore, isn't it?"

He nodded. "Your namesake. The one who disappeared for a time when she was about twenty and then miraculously reappeared. This necklace was hers. She married and the necklace was handed down in our family until it came to my father, then to me, and now, I pass it on to you."

Torri lifted the necklace and let the long chain dangle from her fingers, trying to think of something safe to say. "It doesn't exactly go with my wardrobe, you know," she joked, looking down at her stone-washed denims, and dark purple T-shirt topped with a paisley print jacket.

"It isn't exactly your style, I know," her grandfather laughed, then quickly sobered. "And this goes with the necklace." He groped around under the blanket and after a moment, drew out a small book. Bound in cracked blue leather, it looked as if it might crumble if anyone so much as breathed on it. The old man pressed it into her hands and she took it gingerly.

"This," he said, "is the first Victoria's diary. She recorded her adventure. You'll understand everything after you read this. It will tell you how to travel through time. Will you read it, for me, Torri-mine?"

The endearment sent a fresh wave of grief through her and brought more tears to her eyes. Torri bit her lower lip and looked away, blinking furiously, her heart crying out as the question of her grandfather's sanity seemed suddenly answered. "Yes, Grandfa," she began softly, "but I—"

"Victoria! Sugar, are you up there?" a lilting voice called up the stairs.

"It's Christine." Torri said flatly. "If she sticks her nose in here I'll—"

"Hide the necklace and the diary," her grandfather interrupted, "and whatever you do, Torri, don't let Christine have them. And don't tell Harry either—not that he would believe you!" He chuckled. "Wouldn't they have loved having *that* story to throw at me during the hearing."

"I won't tell them," she said, then leaned forward and pressed her face against his. A lump of sorrow welled up in her chest as she felt tears on his leathery cheek. *Damn Christine!*

"Listen," she whispered, "do you remember the day I came here?" she asked softly.

He nodded.

"I was scared and alone. Christine picked me up at the airport and said how foolish my daddy was to take my mother to the Middle East, how it was his fault their plane had crashed."

She leaned away from him, tears brimming in her eyes. Torri was surprised to find that, after all the years, it still hurt. She blinked the moisture away.

"I'm sorry I sent her to meet you," he said. "That was before I realized how vicious Christine could be. I was still distraught over losing my son. Nathan was a fine man." His eyes grew suddenly more weary. "One by one, they go."

Torri patted his hand. "Christine practically dragged me up the walk the day I came to live with you, remember? I had my teddy bear, Jasper, and I was holding on to him for dear life, trying not to cry. Then you opened the door."

A half-smile appeared. "And you took one look at my grizzly old face and it scared you half to death."

"Just about!" Torri teased, then sobered. "No," she said thoughtfully, "You picked me up and said that things would never be the same again, for either of us, but maybe we could go on together. And in that moment, I knew everything was going to be all right, somehow." She brushed the tears from her face with the back of her hand and laughed self-consciously. "And, you know what, Grandfa? Everything was. Because of you."

The old man's hazel eyes shone with pleasure. "The last fourteen years have been the happiest in my life. Only my time with my dear Martha can compare."

"Thank you." She gazed down at the jewelry he had given her, her tears clouding her vision. "And thank you for the necklace."

His joy faded. "It's yours—your birthright. But be careful. Always remember that you must use the necklace. Never let it use you."

Torri swallowed hard. "I don't understand what you mean," she said gently.

A slow smile crossed his face and for a moment, Nathaniel Hamilton looked like his old self, vibrant and alive. "You will, Torri-mine. I promise that you will."

Torri squeezed his hand, determined he wouldn't go to the sanitarium thinking she didn't believe him. "Okay, so I'm the proud owner of a time-travel necklace, only used by a little old lady in my family tree a few times to find out if Marc Antony really was the cutest guy in history." She was rewarded with an appreciative laugh. He squeezed her hand in return.

Suddenly Torri realized she was terrified. She'd heard of Alzheimer's Disease. Maybe this was the beginning of the dehibilitating illness. Would her grandfather one day soon not even recognize her—not know who she was? She fought the ache in the center of her chest.

"Torri," her grandfather said, "don't be sad—or afraid. It's going to be all right, I promise. Read Victoria's diary. It will tell you more than I can. And I'll be all right. Truly. You'll see that everything will work out just as God intended."

His kind expression changed to one of irritation as the sound of quick, no-nonsense footsteps echoed down the hallway. There was a brief silence in front of the door, then it was flung open.

"My, my, my, isn't this cozy?"

Christine Hamilton stood in the doorway with her hands on her hips. She was smiling, but the gesture never reached her cold blue eyes. Her dress, made from an elaborate flowered material, seemed to imitate the dresses worn by Southern belles a generation before, with its off the shoulder design and the frilly ruffle at the neckline. As usual, from the top of the wide-brimmed hat she wore, to the tip of her high heeled shoes, Christine was impeccably groomed. For a woman pushing over fifty her face was remarkably unlined, although Torri suspected most of her smooth, taut skin was the result of a surgeon's knife and not nature.

Her grandfather's soft dialect had always sounded natural to Torri, even though she had spent the first six years of her life in the Midwest. But Christine's caressing, syrupy drawl was a manufactured put on as far as Torri was concerned, and nothing could make her believe her aunt's voice was any less artificial than the woman herself.

"Victoria, darling," the woman said, patting her blond coiffure and allowing her false smile to widen, "what have you got there?" She walked over to take a closer look.

"Just an old book," Torri said, holding up the diary and using the distraction to gather the necklace and its gold chain more compactly into her fist.

Christine glanced over at Nathaniel Hamilton, obviously amused. "Oh, dear, is it a present?" She laughed, a condescending little laugh. "How sweet."

Neither of them responded and the blue eyes immediately

hardened. Her pouty bottom lip was thrust out just a trifle to show she was annoyed.

"We really must be going, Victoria. Come along now."

Torri felt her grandfather's fingers tighten around her hand, helping to hide the necklace. "Just another moment, Christine," he said quietly.

"For heaven's sake!" She strode across the room, the sugar-coating gone from her tongue, and acid in its place. "You act as if you're never going to see each other again." She flung the window curtain back dramatically and pointed down at the driveway below. "Those ambulance drivers are being paid by the hour, and I for one don't intend to pay them to sit around while the two of you have a nice long chat!" She turned and stalked to the door, pausing at the threshold. "I'm sending the attendants up with the stretcher!"

As soon as she was gone, Torri and her grandfather looked at one another, their gazes locking. He pressed her close to him in a final, private farewell. "Goodbye, Torri-mine."

She clung to him, her face buried in the shoulder of his robe. "Oh Grandfa, I çan't stand it. I just won't be able to stand it, knowing you're in that awful place, even for a day!"

"It's all right," he said, helping to shore up the brave front they had both so busily engineered earlier. "You'll come and see me—"

"Every day!"

"—and we'll still have our chess games, just like we always have."

"You ready, Pops?"

Torri spun around and glared at the two men standing just inside the door, a long stretcher between them. Christine came in just behind them, pulling on short white gloves. She returned Torri's angry look.

"It's time, Victoria. Stop this nonsense and act like you're twenty instead of six." She glanced over at the two men waiting and softened her voice slightly, as if suddenly aware she wasn't sounding like a nice, considerate aunt. "Believe me, sugar, your grandfather will be much better off at Sunnyside." She turned to the man beside her. "Mr. Jenkins?"

The attendant started toward Nathaniel, the expression on his face one of determination. With amazing agility for such an old man, Nathaniel slipped from the bed and stood, a challenging look in his eyes. The attendant hesitated.

"I am quite capable of leaving my home under my own power, Christine," Nathaniel said. He picked up the quilted robe lying across the end of his bed and began pulling it on, keeping his gaze locked on the man in front of him as if daring him to approach. Once Nathaniel had tied the belt he gestured to two suitcases in front of his closet door.

"These 'gentlemen,'" he made the word sound like an insult, "may carry my bags downstairs. Come, my dear," he beckoned to Torri and she hurried to his side, stuffing the necklace securely out of sight in her jacket pocket. His arm encircled her shoulder, the gesture lending her courage.

Torri lifted her chin haughtily as they passed by her aunt, glad that her grandfather had had the last word, had shown Christine he was still Nathaniel Hamilton and not some child under her control.

Her sense of triumph quickly faded as they walked down the hall, the echo of their footsteps ringing out like hollow voices, reminding Torri that life, as she had known it, was forever over. Fourteen years ago a secure life had ended abruptly with the death of her parents, and now it was happening again. But this time there would be no kind and compassionate Grandfa to help her pick up the pieces. Now Christine would be living in Torri's home and trying to run Torri's life.

It struck her then. She would be emotionally alone. Harry was gone, out of her life, just as she wanted him to be. She'd never had many close friends. Her grandfather had been her very best friend. Tears stung Torri's eyes and a sob slipped out before she could stop it.

"Easy," the old man whispered, "don't let her see how much you're hurting. She's like a shark. Don't let her see that you're bleeding, or she'll attack for sure."

Torri could feel him trembling and slipped her arm around his waist to steady him. Together they took the stairs one slow step at a time. She didn't lift her eyes until they had reached the bottom of the stairwell.

Why? Torri thought, a sense of panic flooding over her. Why did Christine do this? It's not like she'll be able to gain anything from managing the estate for a year. She can't touch my six-million-dollar trust fund, only what I'm sent each month, and that can't be that much more than the allowance Grandfa gives *her*. Torri glanced up at her grandfather. He was staring fixedly at something in front of him.

The stairwell was situated to one side of the front foyer, and the wall directly in front of the stairs contained the Hamilton portrait gallery. Her grandfather walked slowly over to the antique, framed pictures, his gaze roaming hungrily over the portraits which represented hundreds of years of his family's history.

Torri's glance followed his, as she watched him say a silent goodbye to the familiar faces. The larger portraits were arranged in a large circle, with the smaller paintings hung inside. She always looked at them in the same order. The one at the top was a large color portrait of Martha Hamilton, her grandfather's late wife. She had died before Torri was born. Torri had looked into the warm brown eyes many, many times and wished she could've known the kind-looking woman, the woman so dear to her Grandfa's heart. Next to Martha was Nellie Stephenson Hamilton, Torri's great-grandmother. She could see a bit of her grandfather in the portrait, mostly in the calm, hazel eyes.

Underneath Nellie was the portrait of Randolph Hamilton. Her grandfather had told her that Randolph had lived during the Civil War. Torri had always found his picture especially fascinating because he and her grandfather could've passed for twins.

There were a few others, people who had never looked all that interesting, then right in the middle was the portrait of the mysterious ancestor her grandfather had just been telling her about. Victoria, the time traveler. Torri smiled in spite of herself, then sobered. There was nothing to laugh about.

Family resemblances seemed to run heavily in the Hamilton family, for just as Randolph Hamilton had favored her grandfather, the first Victoria Hamilton was the spitting image of Torri.

Rose colored lips, exactly like her own, curved up in a mysterious smile. Was it because she knew something no one else had ever dreamed of? Torri wondered, then pushed the thought away in irritation. In the portrait, Victoria's hair, black and wavy like Torri's, curled around her face, ringlets spilling to her shoulders from the topknot, held by a beautiful pearl comb. Blue eyes, not green like Torri's, stared back at her, beautiful eyes that, like her own, tilted up at the corners. Clasped around her throat was the necklace Torri now had in her jacket pocket, safely hidden from Christine—the necklace that Grandfa claimed could turn a simple mortal into a time traveler.

Her fingers tightened around the small blue book her grandfather had given her. Oh Grandfa, she thought with a sigh, how did it happen? When did you start slipping away? She turned away from the portraits and gently led her grandfather toward the big double front doors of the mansion. The doors were open and the bright April sunlight cast a strangely cheerful light on the somber twosome as they walked outside.

A chauffeured limousine waited near the curb, behind the ambulance. Torri glanced up and saw Harry standing a few feet away, his arms folded across his chest. His handsome face seemed sterner than usual and a trifle impatient. That was odd, for Harry was the soul of patience. In fact, patience was one of his most endearing qualities. Dark, curling hair dipped over his forehead and he brushed it back with one hand, casting a resentful glance into the wind. His eyes were fixed upon her with a very strange expression. When he realized she was staring back at him, he straightened and tossed her a grin. Torri stiffened and lifted her chin.

What was he doing here? She'd thought she'd made it very plain the day before the hearing that it was over between them. She glanced back at him and in that brief moment of distraction, the two white-coated attendants pulled her grandfather away from her and hustled him toward the ambulance.

Hastily the men bundled him into the vehicle before Torri could even react; then, her heart pounding, she ran after them. Just as she reached the back doors, the driver slammed both of them shut in her face, but not before she caught the look on her grandfather's face as he sat, ramrod stiff, on the stretcher inside. The great courage that had seen them through the last few weeks of misery dissolved into a look of despair, and his hazel eyes reflected his resignation.

"No!" she cried, running forward and beating on the ambulance doors with both fists. "Let me ride with him! I want to ride with Grandfa!"

"Victoria! Stop it this minute!" Christine's hand came down on Torri's shoulder. She spun her around and started leading her forcibly over to the limo. "I will not tolerate this scandalous display of childishness again," she hissed. "Get into the car!"

"Really, Vicki," Harry drawled in a slow, lazy voice, "don't make a scene in front of the servants."

The ambulance pulled away from the curb and Torri watched it leave, feeling numb. All right, she told herself quickly. Don't fall apart. That's what Christine wants. We'll be there only a few moments after Grandfa.

Straightening her shoulders, Torri turned and walked to the limousine.

"Please, hurry, Victoria," Christine said irritably from behind her. "I have an appointment."

Torri turned slowly around and held her aunt's gaze for one long, icy moment, then without a word, climbed into the back seat where Harry was already waiting. Christine hurried in beside her and slammed the door.

"What are you doing here?" Torri asked Harry coldly.

"Why, baby, you don't think I'd let you go through this alone, do you?"

Torri tightened her jaw and when she spoke her words were very controlled. "I am not your 'baby' and I don't need you or want you here. I thought I'd already made that quite clear."

"Don't be so rude, Victoria," Christine scolded. "Harry's here to help, aren't you, Harry?"

They rode the rest of the way down the long driveway in silence. The sweeping drive led to the great iron gates at the edge of the estate's property and as they approached the gates, Torri felt a wave of longing twist deep inside of her. How had Grandfa felt, knowing he was leaving his home—all alone? Did he wonder, as she did, if he would ever again hear her slam the front door and run inside calling out, "It's me, Grandfa—Torri—I'm home!" as she had been doing for the last fourteen years?

She felt the tears push to the surface and took a deep breath. *Don't let her see you bleed.* Her grandfather's advice came back to her. Torri slipped one hand inside her jacket pocket and found the hard edge of the necklace. Somehow, touching it comforted her, even if the ridiculous story connected with it *had* seemed to confirm Christine's claims about her grandfather's insanity.

Torri stroked the edge of the necklace and tried not to think. The car began passing through the gates. Torri closed her eyes, fighting the flood of emotion sweeping over her, feeling faintly sick at her stomach. Then they were on the road and headed toward Richmond.

"Well, thank goodness that's over," Christine said cheerfully, settling back against the seat with a smug look on her face. "But I was happy to take care of things for you, even if it was unpleasant at times and led to some misunderstandings." She paused to pat her hair, rearranging one elaborate curl carefully. "I told Harry last night that if we couldn't keep Victoria from losing her fortune at the hands of a senile old man, well, we'd just better resign from the human race."

"I thought you already had," Torri said sharply.

Christine ignored her, pulling off her gloves, her voice trilling with self-satisfaction.

"Of course, I couldn't have done it without Harry. He was my right arm through this entire miserable experience." She smiled at him and once again Torri felt a painful twist in her middle.

Harry Kendall was an attractive, twenty-five year old investment banker whose future looked promising. Nathaniel had hired Harry as a financial consultant and as a matter of course, he and Torri had met. One thing had led to another and somehow, within six months of their meeting, they had announced their engagement.

Torri glanced up at him. Harry was beautiful, there was no denying it. His hair, always impeccably groomed, was so black there were glints of blue in it when the sun struck the glossy locks just right. His eyes, dark, velvet brown, always seemed to be smoldering with an inner fire—at least, they used to, when he looked at her. Yes, Harry was straight out of a magazine ad, his jaw solid, his chin firm. No idle rich kid, Harry Kendall had worked hard to get where he was. He was a self-made man, handsome, ambitious, perfect.

And Torri hated him. Hated him and Christine with their

perfect beauty and their smug expressions. Suddenly she realized the car had turned. Torri sat up a little straighter and peered over the front seat. The limousine was no longer following the ambulance, and was heading toward Richmond.

"The chauffeur took the wrong exit," Torri said to Christine. "He's going the wrong way."

Christine and Harry exchanged glances, and Torri had a sudden premonition.

"Why is the driver going away from Sunnyside?" Torri demanded.

"We aren't going to Sunnyside today, dear." Christine reached into her purse and took out a silver compact. She opened it and daubed a little powder on the end of her nose.

Torri stared at her in disbelief. "We aren't going? What do you mean? Do you mean to tell me you're sending Grandfather out there alone?"

That odd look between the two of them again.

"Now, Vicki—Victoria, you must understand we're doing this for your own good." Harry's voice was meant to be soothing, as if he were talking to a frightened child. "The emotional trauma of your witnessing his admission there, well, we decided it would just be too much for you."

"You decided! You!" She leaned forward toward the chauffeur. "Stop the car!"

The bald-headed man turned and looked back. To her surprise, Torri saw it wasn't their regular driver but a man she didn't know.

"Sorry, miss," he said in a gravelly voice, "I only take orders from the lady."

Christine turned to Torri, her face as smooth and hard as a china doll's. "Harry and I have already discussed this—at length. We aren't going to Sunnyside today and that is final. We have an important appointment and we both agreed—"

"You agreed?" Torri had never felt such blind, irrational rage. "And who, I would like to know, died and made you queen, Christine Hamilton? And am I to be one of your obedient slaves? Who in the hell do the two of you think you are?"

"I am your aunt," Christine said haughtily, her back rigid against the fine leather seat. "We might as well get this straight right here and now." Her tone hardened. "I call the shots now, little girl—do you understand?"

For a minute Torri thought she might either faint, or more likely, punch Christine in her silly little nose, but the dizziness passed and she managed to control her rage by squeezing the edge of the necklace in her pocket a little harder.

Don't panic, she commanded herself. You can get out to Sunnyside by yourself. But there's something more to this. Why is Harry here? What's going on?

"All right," she said, forcing a more agreeable note into her voice. "Then in that case, I'd like to go back home."

Again the exchanged looks between her aunt and Harry.

"Why sure, sugar," Christine said. "That's just where we're going."

"You mean we've just been going in circles?"

"Yes. We didn't want to cause a scene in front of the servants. We thought we'd take you for a little ride and explain things, then get back for our appointment."

Torri felt a sudden flicker of fear. "Appointment? With whom?"

"Reverend Frakes. He's waiting for us at the house."

Torri frowned. Reverend Frakes was the pastor of the huge, socially prestigious, affluent church where Christine was a member. Torri had never cared for the pompous man who seemed to be a pious caricature of what a man of God should be.

"What for?" she asked, narrowing her eyes.

Christine glanced at Harry, and as if responding to an unspoken cue, he smiled and placed one arm around Torri's shoulders, giving her a squeeze.

"I have a wonderful surprise for you, darling. We're on our way to be married. Isn't it great?"

Torri sat staring straight ahead, shocked into silence.

"Christine helped me set up the whole thing. This way we can avoid all the unpleasant publicity and have a nice, private honeymoon."

Alarm rang out clearly and loudly in Torri's mind. "This is a joke, right, Harry?" she said, forcing a laugh. "I mean, a joke in very poor taste, but still a joke."

"Baby—" Harry's handsome face turned suddenly petulant. "Do you think it's a joke that I want to marry you?"

"Harry, I told you, it's over. Finished. Finis. I am not going to marry you—not today—not ever!" Torri fought her mounting rage.

"I really must insist," Harry said, tightening his grip on her.

Torri went rigid at the sound of his soft, cold voice. "This discussion is over," she said, feeling more and more frightened. "Let me out of this car. I'm taking a taxi to Sunnyside."

Harry laughed harshly and Torri looked up, startled. She found herself gazing into the eyes of a stranger. Gone was the polite, well-bred banker who had always treated her with the utmost respect. In his place was a man staring down at her with undisguised hostility.

"No, my darling," he said, the sarcasm in his tone now unmistakable. "You see, I've invested a great deal of time and energy on you—not to mention money. I made the mistake of thinking your devotion to your grandfather could be undermined. I'm learning, too late, just what a determined young woman you can be. Still, nevertheless, certain aspects of my business have taken a turn for the worst and I find myself in need of immediate funds." He nodded in Christine's direction. "Christine promised me if I helped get the old man locked away, she'd help me tie up the little merger between you and me immediately, then petition for the trust fund your father left you to be placed under my authority."

"What!"

He shrugged. "After all, darling, the ordeal with your grandfather has quite unsettled you. I doubt you can quite manage your affairs anymore than he could. Who knows?" He cocked one dark eyebrow. "Insanity may run in the family."

"Harry!" Her cry was a hushed whisper. Torri blinked back burning tears. "*You* must be crazy if you think I'd allow this—this—farce!"

His brown eyes, always warm and tender when he had gazed at her before, now glittered with violence. "You are under the misapprehension, my darling one, that you have a choice. You and I are about to be married, whether you like it or not." His eyes narrowed. "And once it's done, you'll learn to do as I say—or I'll have *you* committed and you and your dear old grandfather can live together happily ever after."

In shock, Torri turned to Christine and met her aunt's self-satisfied, ice-blue eyes. "I'd listen to him if I were you, sugar. Harry's a very resourceful man. Very resourceful." She gave him a slow, fluttering wink and Torri saw Harry's grin widen into a leer. "And what have you got to complain about? Harry's the kind of man who can keep a woman very happy. I should know."

"Thanks, baby," he said in a languid voice, "I'm glad you think so."

All at once Torri knew the truth was even uglier than she had imagined. Christine and Harry were lovers—probably had been long before she ever met him. The whole thing had been a set-up. How stupid and naive she had been!

"I won't do it," Torri said, aloud, fighting for calm. "I'll simply refuse. You can't force someone to get married."

"Oh, but you forget something, sugar." Christine's tones were honeyed. "I told you, I'm calling the shots now. It's *my* money paying for Nathaniel to stay in that rather luxurious institution where he will associate with only the cream of society's crazies."

"It's Grandfather's money," Torri said, feeling very much like the little girl who, ten years ago, had tried to argue with her aunt about what a wonderful father her daddy had been.

"But *I* control his money now." Christine's gaze hardened. "Listen to me, Victoria, and listen good. If you don't cooperate and go through with this marriage without any trouble, I'll take your precious grandfather out of Sunnyside and place him in a state asylum. Do you know what that would mean?" Her long eyelashes swept downward and then up again as she watched Torri's face. "I don't think dear Nathaniel would do too well in such a place. No special treatment. No special private room. No special anything. He will be trapped in a nightmarish hell—and *you* will be responsible. Can you live with that?"

Christine leaned back against the seat and took a long cigarette out of a gold case. Harry hastened to light the slender tube. She blew a thin stream of smoke into Torri's face. "It's going to be hard enough on the old geezer to be the only sane one at Sunnyside, much less be tossed into a crowded state institution."

Torri stared at her, stunned. "You *knew*," she whispered. "You knew he wasn't crazy. You did this to get your hands on his money!"

"Brilliant deduction, my dear," Harry drawled.

"I'll tell the police—I'll get a lawyer—I'll—"

"You'll do nothing but sit back and enjoy the ride," her aunt said flatly.

The shock rolled across Torri's mind. She tightened her grip on the diary in her lap. So it was all a plot! Somehow Harry and Christine had engineered the whole thing to get rid of her grandfather and now—she felt a chill slide down her spine—to get rid of her? What would happen after the wedding? Would she have a convenient accident which would leave Harry in control of her money, free to marry Christine? Or would Harry do as he threatened and have her committed too?

How could this be happening? She'd been dating Harry for six months! They'd talked of spending the rest of their lives together. He had been the perfect gentleman, considerate, attentive, until his insensitivity about her grandfather had led to their split. He had never been this leering stranger who kept running his hand up and down the side of her arm.

Pushing the pain aside, Torri tried to think. Grandfa! she cried out silently. You were right. I should have listened to you. If only I could go back and change it all. I'd fight them harder, I'd get a better lawyer, do something to save you.

All at once she wished the necklace in her pocket really was a time-travel device. She'd go back in time, back before this crazy scheme ever got started and somehow keep Christine and Harry from destroying her grandfather's life, and her own. But it wasn't and she couldn't. She was trapped.

"Here we are, sweetheart," Harry said, his voice silky. "Reverend Frakes is waiting inside. I have the license in my pocket, along with a very expensive ring." He opened the door and held out his hand to her. "Come along, darling. I can hardly wait to start the honeymoon."

Torri swallowed hard and got out of the car. Christine and Harry flanked her. The chauffeur went ahead to open the door.

Someone help me! Torri cried silently. As if in answer to her unspoken plea, a large black bird overhead suddenly let out a tremendous shriek. Harry looked up in time to have his perfect, handsome face splattered with a disgusting, sticky white substance. He cursed and Christine groped in her purse for a handkerchief.

It all took place in a matter of moments, was only a brief

diversion, but it was all Torri needed. In that instant she saw her one bid for freedom. She whirled—and ran.

A shout came from behind her as Torri plunged across the manicured lawn and toward the dense forty acre woods that spread across the back of her grandfather's property. He had never allowed the woods to be touched. There was plenty of grassland on the other side of the thick woods—one hundred acres—and he had always insisted the woodland be left just as nature intended. As a result it was overgrown and almost impenetrable. But Torri knew its secrets, and now its secrets would be her salvation.

The sound of heavy footsteps caused her to quicken her pace. If she could just reach the big oak tree at the edge of the woods, there was a trail just behind it. Once inside the shelter of the trees with their vines and the tangled underbrush beneath them, Torri could disappear.

Her breath came more rapidly now and a sharp pain pierced her side. She had neglected her jogging ever since she'd begun dating Harry and was out of shape. Panting, she risked a look over one shoulder. Twenty yards behind her, two men had not given up the chase.

She stumbled suddenly and fell to her knees, dropping the diary. Too panicky to stop and retrieve it, Torri jumped to her feet and went on. She didn't realize the necklace had slipped from her pocket too until she had gone another five yards. Pausing for breath she looked back and saw it, glistening on the ground. Without hesitation Torri ran back for it. She couldn't leave it for Christine to find. Whether she understood or not, her grandfather had placed it in her care and specifically did not want Christine to have it.

Torri reached the spot and grabbed the necklace, the stones biting into her fingers, then turned to run again—only to find her way suddenly blocked by a man.

He had blondish-brown hair and gray eyes. He was handsome, but it was not his well-chiseled features sending a wave of astonishment through her, but his Confederate uniform—and rifle.

Torri took a step back from the cold eyes and clutched the necklace to her chest. A wave of dizziness swept suddenly over her. She fell to her knees. Torri had never fainted before, but she knew without a doubt she was passing out. Glancing back, she saw Harry and the chauffeur were almost upon her. The man in gray continued to stare at her, ruthlessness carved into his face. Who was he? A hunter—or one of Harry and Christine's men?

Torri darted a desperate look at the stranger and squeezed the necklace in her hand tightly. "Please," she said, "please help me."

He stared right through her, as though he couldn't see or hear her, then slowly, he lifted the rifle and pointed it directly at her.

Hysterically, Torri screamed and the sound reverberated inside her head as the world began to spin. The two men running toward her were moving in slow motion, like an old movie, then they began to spin too, picking up momentum, whirling faster and faster, until they, the strange man in the uniform, and the surrounding countryside turned into a bright blur of colors, a hazy picture which quickly dissolved into blues and greens, golds and grays.

Then the world turned upside down . . . and inside out.

Inside a dark, closed circle, Torri cried out soundlessly as she spun around and around and around.

Where am I? she cried, mouthing the words. What's happening? There was no answer. Her only sensation in the twilight world was the warmth of the stones beneath her fingers, the jewels in the necklace she held. The spinning quickened and Torri moaned aloud, as nausea coursed through her, but no sound echoed through the darkness.

After what seemed like forever, the whirling movement began to ease and she began a long fall in slow motion, down,

down, down—like Alice falling down the rabbit's hole, she thought in some still rational part of her mind. Then she couldn't think at all, as a gyrating black vortex sucked her into its center, absorbing her, gulping her down like a great black whale would.

Then there was stillness. Abruptly, Torri felt herself dropping through the air. She twisted, trying instinctively to break her fall. Instead, she landed hard on her stomach, her breath leaving her body in a harsh sound. The spinning stopped. Almost.

Gasping, dazed, Torri opened her eyes. A kaleidoscope of images danced in front of her. Woods. Smoke. Bright flashes of orange. Men running. Men shouting. Loud, explosive noises. They assaulted her senses in a dizzying mass of confusion. She struggled to her feet, and as she did, a searing pain darted across her brow. Staggering, she heard a piercing scream echo through her brain. Her strength was gone, her consciousness ebbing. So this was what it was like to die. Torri closed her eyes, and with a trembling breath, released herself to the blackness.

Chapter Two

Lt. Jake Cameron wiped his hands across his ragged uniform, ignoring the red stain left on the gray material, and clutched his rifle once again. He lowered his gaze from the woods and stole a glance at the bleeding body beside him. His jaw tightened in frustration. How the woman—woman! she was hardly more than a girl—had suddenly popped out of nowhere into the middle of the skirmish, he didn't know. It didn't matter. He didn't care what happened to her, what he did care about was that she had stopped the bullet he had meant for someone else. Once again, through no fault of his own, he had been denied the sweet success he sought.

"Stupid kid," he muttered, "what did you think you were doing?" He checked her wound again, a deep angry-looking crease in her left temple, and sighed. How badly was she hurt? he wondered. Did he dare leave her for someone else to find?

Her face was half-covered with blood and taking a worn handkerchief from his pocket, he wiped it. He hadn't had time to really look at her before, but now he tilted her head gently toward him.

This girl—woman—was so young. He frowned. What had she been doing here of all places, dressed in men's clothes? She should be home with her mammy, not traipsing around the countryside. His anger rekindled.

Checking her wound more closely, he decided it was, after all, just a graze and probably not serious. Head wounds bled a lot. He was more concerned about the knot on the back of her head. When she had fallen from the bullet, she'd struck her head against a rock.

He turned her head slightly and examined the swelling. Not good. Suddenly he was aware that he was stroking her long, dark hair. It was soft, as soft as a kitten's. He bent over her still form, his lips almost touching her ear.

"Wake up, kitten," he whispered, "time to go home."

The girl's eyelids fluttered open and two clear green eyes stared up at him in confusion. She was more than just pretty, Jake decided. With her black hair, heart-shaped face and huge, velvet green eyes, she was breathtaking. He drew his thoughts back into line.

"Are you all right?" he asked, careful to keep his voice low. There could be snipers still out there, waiting for a sound or a movement.

"Harry—Christine—Grandfather—" she opened her lips again, then her eyelids slowly closed.

"Great. Just great. Bring the whole family next time." Jake clenched his fist and cursed. He'd had Reed right in his sights. It would've been an easy shot, one that no one could question in the heat of battle. Now, because of a stupid female who didn't know any better than to walk into a fight, he'd lost the best opportunity he'd had so far.

"Thanks a lot," he said, glaring down at her unconscious body. "I'd like to find some way of paying you back for the mess you've made of things, but I guess the sooner I get rid of you, the better. Lucky for you I'm a gentleman."

Poking his head cautiously above the tall grass, Jake looked around the meadow, then toward the woods only a few yards away. He gritted his teeth and slung his rifle across his back. His voice was little more than a growl as he bent over her.

"I hope you don't weigh much, because if you do, I may just toss you into the nearest briar patch and leave you there."

Taking hold of both her arms, Jake pulled her to a sitting

position, then leaned forward and eased her over his shoulder. With a grunt he staggered to his feet.

"Just like I figured," he muttered, "you weigh more than you look." She really was a slight little thing, but his frustration and simmering anger was making him lash out at this new, unwanted responsibility. The woman moaned. Jake looked at her and saw the blood flowing more freely down the side of her face. Instantly a picture flashed into his mind, the picture of another bloody face, a face contorted with pain, and death.

Gently he slid her limp body into a more comfortable position as he cradled her in his arms. He took a deep breath and looked down at her. *So she was beautiful—so what?*

Suddenly Jake felt his anger ebb and he smiled. "Okay," he said softly, "let's go find you some help. I promise, I'll be more careful from now on."

He watched her eyes flutter and then shut again, her lips open and close like the petals of a rose. Something contracted inside him. Something long submerged and well controlled.

"I guess I won't throw you into the briar patch after all," he said, taking the first step of what might be a long haul to find a doctor. "Even though I'm positive that you, kitten, are going to be trouble with a capital T."

Torri floated on a hazy cloud of unreality. From time to time different faces and voices intruded into the peaceful dream world where she drifted. Once it was her grandfather's face, another time, Christine's. The vision of Grandfather spoke comforting words to her, but Christine hovered over her, threatening to send her to an insane asylum. Torri cried out in her delirium, then sank restlessly into sleep again.

Several times she dreamed of someone she didn't know. A stern looking, handsome man with unruly blondish-brown hair. Piercing gray eyes stared out of the mist around her mind.

The spinning had stopped at least, but a strange throbbing in the back of her head had replaced it, along with a burning sensation in her forehead. She felt as though she were being constantly moved, bouncing in a very peculiar way. It reminded her of when she was a little girl and her father would carry her into the house after she fell asleep in the car on the way home from getting ice cream.

"Daddy?" she said aloud, unsure why she was calling for her dead father. Strong arms tightened around her. Yes, she was being carried. "Where's Grandfa?" Torri asked, her eyes still closed. "Where is my Grandfa?"

"Shhh," a voice said back to her. "Just be quiet little girl, you'll be all right. I'm sorry, I'm really sorry."

Torri opened her eyes and looked up into the face of the man carrying her. It was Gray Eyes. "Oh, it's you," she said, having trouble forming the words. "Will you be here when I wake up?"

"Sure, kid, I'll be here."

She closed her eyes again and sighed. "That's all right then. Tell Grandfather I'll just take a little nap. You know, you shouldn't have been in our woods. You scared me."

"I'm sorry."

Torri heard his voice as if it were coming from a long way off, down a deep, narrow tunnel. What had she been saying? Something about the woods? She reached out to try and piece the fragile memory together but couldn't.

"Just hang on," his voice echoed around her mind, barely audible. "We're almost there."

Torri sank gratefully into darkness.

When Torri awoke, the haze clouding her thoughts had lifted and she could think more clearly. She glanced around, and was startled to find she was lying in a huge, antique four-poster bed, complete with feather mattress and downy comforter. Through the window at the end of the large room she could see the sun barely above the horizon. But was it coming up or going down? Taking a deep breath, she tried to organize her thoughts as her gaze wandered around the room.

All of the furniture was antique, and Torri thought, with a pang, how much her grandfather would have enjoyed seeing the beautiful old secretary in the corner, and the authentic pitcher and bowl on the cherrywood washstand across the room. Wallpaper with elaborate pink roses ran all the way up to the high, fourteen foot ceiling. The wooden floor was covered with pale rainbow colored fabric braided into a large rag rug. A rocking chair in the middle of the rug lent an air of quaint serenity to the lovely room.

Somebody's really into authenticity, she thought, then winced. I feel as if I've been run over by a truck. Where am I?

She lifted one hand to her forehead and felt a wide cloth under her fingers. A bandage. So, she had been in some kind of accident. Feeling a little anxious, she sat up slowly and looked down at herself. A beautiful nightgown had replaced her jeans and T-shirt. Her jacket was nowhere in sight. White linen sleeves with embroidered lace at the wrists lay cool and clean against her skin. It was not a hospital gown. This was not a hospital.

The last thing she remembered was running away from Christine and Harry. There was something else hovering at the edge of her memory, something about the woods, but it slipped away before it could solidify in her mind.

"This is very strange," she said aloud to the empty room.

A soft knock at the door made her jump. "C-come in?"

Gray Eyes, the face from her dream, appeared in the doorway. "Good evenin'," he said, his accent quite Virginian. "Excuse me, miss, but could I come in and talk to you just for a minute—before the doctor arrives?"

Torri stared at him. He was much older than she, and probably the handsomest man she had ever seen. Her heart did a rapid little dance before she commanded it sternly to stop being so silly. Just because he had beautiful gray eyes, long dark lashes, a nice square jawline, and really fantastic hair was no reason to act so ridiculous.

She nodded, then caught her breath in amazement as he slipped into the room and shut the door behind him. A double-breasted gray coat, well-worn from the looks of it, hugged his broad shoulders and tapered down to the yellow sash, dingy and tattered, tied around his waist. A long saber sheathed in a scabbard, hung at his left side, a holstered gun at his right. Gray trousers were tucked into black, knee-high boots.

He's wearing a Confederate soldier's uniform, Torri thought, her eyes widening. A Confederate soldier. As in the Civil War. Again she sensed there was something she should remember, something associated with that uniform, but she couldn't grasp it.

Feeling as if she had somehow wandered into the Twilight Zone, Torri lifted her chin and decided to put this—this intruder—on the defensive, just in case he was somebody dangerous.

"Who are you?" she said.

He raised an eyebrow and looked quietly amused. "You've asked me that at least a hundred times in the last two days. Concussions will do that to you."

Torri lifted her hand to the bandage on her head, feeling suddenly dizzy. "You mean, I've been here that long?"

"Just about."

She sank back against the pillow, feeling more and more confused. "And I have a concussion?"

An uneasy look crossed his face. "That's right."

"Have you been here the whole time?"

It was his turn to stare. "In here?" He laughed, the sound hearty. "No ma'am. In fact, if Hannah catches me here she'll skin me good. I've just been stopping by from time to time. After all, it was my fault and everything. I wanted to make sure you were all right."

"It was your fault?" She looked at his costume again. Of course this *was* Richmond, and there were many old plantations where scenes from the Civil War were re-enacted. Was it possible she had been taken to such a place? But for what purpose? His words sank suddenly into her mind and she struggled to sit up again.

"What happened to me? Where am I?"

"You'd better lie down." He crossed to her side and gently pushed her back. "I don't think the doctor wants you to sit up yet."

A distinct blackness flashed across her vision and she closed her eyes, then opened them. His face was still there, too close for comfort. "Please," she whispered, "this is scaring me. Please tell me who you are and where I am."

He hesitated, then smiled and straightened away from her. "My name is Cameron." He glanced down at the uniform he wore as if he was reminding himself of something and his smile changed into an expression that filled her with a strange foreboding. "Lt. Jake Cameron," he went on. "You're in Dr. Hamilton's guest room."

Torri could read the bitterness in his expression and wondered at the ill concealed cynicism she heard in his voice. Though he looked as if he were in his mid-thirties as she had noted, his eyes seemed much older, as though he had seen terrible things, perhaps done terrible things. She passed one hand shakily across her eyes and tried to concentrate on his words.

"Dr. Hamilton?" she echoed. Stranger still! No, just an odd coincidence.

"But why was I brought here? Did I have an accident? Is that how I got a concussion?"

He ran his hand over his face, which was covered with a slight growth of beard, then released his breath in a long sigh. "You don't remember anything, do you?"

"I remember being near my grandfather's house and—" she stopped, suddenly feeling that perhaps she shouldn't give away too much of what she did remember. "I remember—some—things."

"Well, you see, miss, somehow, I don't know how, you ran in front of me just as I was firing my rifle."

Torri's eyes grew round. "You mean you *shot* me?"

He cleared his throat and for the first time she saw the shadow of hesitancy in the cool gray eyes. "Yes, miss," he drawled, "that's what it amounts to."

"Please stop calling me 'miss,'" Torri said in irritation. "But I don't understand. Grandfather doesn't allow hunting on his property. What were you doing there? And—" she stopped, completely bewildered, then plunged on. "Why are you dressed in that uniform? What happened to Harry and Christine?"

"I'm sorry, I can't answer any of your questions. You can ask the doctor when he comes in." He cleared his throat. "But before he gets here I wanted to ask you something."

Feeling stunned, Torri simply nodded.

"You know, I really didn't mean to shoot you . . ." For the first time Torri noticed he held a gray slouch cap in his hands. He turned it around and around in his hands. Was he nervous? This big, muscular, confident man? He cleared his throat. "I know your family will probably want to report me to my commanding officer. I don't blame you, of course, I mean, even though I must remind you that you ran right into the middle of a skirmish, directly in front of my rifle—"

A sudden tightness around his lips made Torri suddenly aware that the pleasant words and good manners were just a cover-up. Lt. Jake Cameron was angry. At her? That made no sense.

"Anyway, you could get me in a lot of trouble, and, well, miss," his gray eyes sharpened as his voice took on a stilted politeness, "as one of the soldiers fighting in our gallant cause, I'm here to ask you not to do that."

Torri stared at the man. Was he insane? What did he mean—soldiers fighting? Had she been put into a mental hospital by mistake? That thought was especially frightening, given her shocking discovery of Harry and Christine's plans.

"Now you listen to me," Torri said, feeling terrified but determined to remain calm. "I don't know who you are or who put you up to this, but if you don't let me out of here I'm going to call the authorities!"

Jake Cameron's dark brows pressed suddenly together. The expression on his face clearly showed he didn't like her reaction. Torri ignored the strange look he gave her. "Where are my clothes? What have you done with them?" Her head ached as she tried to remember what she'd been wearing. Jeans, a T-shirt, a jacket—the necklace!

"What have you done with my necklace?" she demanded, the pounding in her head increasing with the volume of her voice. Maybe she had been mugged! Robbed and then kidnapped!

"Look." The good ol' Southern boy act was starting to deteriorate as his voice turned slightly harsh. "I don't know anything about any necklace. I'm sorry I shot you, but after all, I did carry you up here to the doc's. I could've left you to die. So don't—" he stopped himself and assumed a more polite attitude. "Please, don't say I stole something from you, miss. It isn't the truth." There was a touch of bravado in his voice, but Torri also recognized an underlying tension.

Her clarity of mind suddenly turned to confusion. The necklace. Grandfa had given her the necklace, but there was something else about it she should remember. Something important.

"What have you done with my necklace?" she asked again, clenching her fists, frustrated because she couldn't remember. "Tell me! Or I *will* accuse you of stealing my necklace—as soon as I can find someone who will listen to me."

"Here now," a strangely familiar voice said from behind her, "what's all this about?"

Torri glanced at the doorway, and her fear transformed instantly into relief. "Grandfather!" Torri clasped her hands together. "I can hardly believe it. Thank goodness you're here. But how did you get out of Sunnyside? Did . . ." Her words died away as the elderly man approached the bed and stared at her blankly.

Torri drew in a sharp breath. His eyes were blue. Grandfa had hazel eyes!

The tall, thin man had a receding hairline just like her grandfather. His eyebrows were the same bushy salt and pepper gray and his deeply lined face had the same slightly harsh look that often made people think mistakenly that Nathaniel was a cross old man. As she continued to stare at him, Torri noticed first one small detail in his facial features, and then another that made her realize he was not her grandfather at all.

The man exchanged a knowing look with a plump, black woman who had come in after him, then turned his attention to Torri.

"I am Dr. Hamilton," he said, "and this is my housekeeper, Hannah."

"I—I'm sorry," Torri stuttered. "You remind me, that is, for a moment I thought—"

"It's all right," his voice was gruff, just like her grandfather's. "You're suffering from a concussion, and things often seem confusing during recovery." He took a stethoscope from a black bag the woman handed him and adjusted the instrument around his neck.

"Mr. Jake! What are yo' doin' in here?" the black woman

said, her hand on her hips. She had on a long skirt that reached to the floor and her hair was tied up in a bandana. Another actor in a Civil War re-enactment? Torri wondered.

"I'm sorry, Hannah," Jake said, tossing her a rakish grin. "I was hoping you'd be up here. I just couldn't stay away from you any longer."

The woman went off into peals of laughter. "I think it's my apple pie yo' so fond of, Mr. Jake, not me!"

"Is this place some kind of tourist attraction?" Torri said, interrupting the little byplay.

Everyone stared at her. Finally Dr. Hamilton spoke. "I don't understand what you mean, but this is my home. I also use it as my medical office whenever the need arises. You were lucky." He gestured toward the lieutenant. "This young man saved your life. He carried you two miles before he saw the plaque on my front gate. If he hadn't gotten you here quickly you might've bled to death."

Torri felt a cold chill down her spine. To come so close to death through some crazy accident! Oh, everything was so mixed-up!

"Excuse me," Torri said, "but I still don't understand. Why did he bring me here at all? Why didn't he take me to a hospital? Please, if you'd just let me use your telephone—"

The sharp intake of breath at the foot of the bed caused Torri to turn in that direction. Jake Cameron no longer wore his polite look but was staring at her as if he'd seen a ghost.

Torri hesitated, then cleared her throat and tried again. "I'm grateful to you for helping me," she said to the doctor, "but my—" she hesitated. It wouldn't do to let him know she was virtually alone in the world. "My aunt is going to be so worried about me. If I could call her—"

Dr. Hamilton shook his head, the stern look in his eyes softening with pity. "Here now, just lie back and rest. Everything will be all right."

"But if I could just call . . ."

"Well now, just lie back and tell me where your aunt lives."

Torri did as she was told and closed her eyes. "She lives outside of Richmond, just a few miles from my grandfather's house. 721 Carver Lane."

"Richmond? I'm afraid you could call all you'd like, young lady, even shout, and she still wouldn't hear you," Dr. Hamilton chuckled. "We're five miles from Richmond."

"No, you don't understand, I—" Once again her voice faded. "If I could just use your phone."

The old man rubbed his hand across the lower part of his face. "You're just confused, young lady. You don't realize you're talking nonsense. Just lie back now and rest while I examine you."

"You're keeping me here against my will!" Torri said, her panic rising again. She threw back the cover and stood up, only to be met with a wave of blackness.

Jake Cameron caught her as she fell and picked her up in his arms, lifting her back onto the bed. When the room stopped spinning, Torri looked up at him and saw his previous anger had disappeared. His eyes were filled with what seemed to be a sincere concern—and a great deal of confusion.

"That was a foolish thing to do," Dr. Hamilton said, "and I wouldn't recommend you try it again."

She looked at the doctor. A new thought occurred to her. Had she been kidnapped by these people? Were they in on Christine and Harry's plan or was this something different? The newspapers had carried the story of her grandfather's incompetency hearing and that she was the heir to his vast fortune, making her a likely target.

Torri glanced at Jake Cameron. Maybe his story was a lie, entirely. Maybe she hadn't fallen backwards and hit her head. Maybe he had smacked her a good one when she wasn't looking. She lifted her hand to her head. The injury felt like a burn. Surely he wouldn't have shot her if he had been hired to kidnap her.

The lieutenant had wandered over to the window and stood staring out, his face looking suddenly harsh in the fading evening light. Torri could see the tops of trees through the window, so she must be in a second-story room. That was lousy luck, but after dark, maybe she could tie the sheets together and climb down. Or could she simply sneak out of her room and down the stairway? Would Jake Cameron be camped outside her door?

And why did the doctor look so much like her grandfather? Was that part of the plan too? Did the kidnappers intend for her grandfather to be blamed for her kidnapping? No, that made no sense! And where would they find someone who looked like her grandfather? The only other person she'd ever seen who looked like him was—Torri's eyes widened. The doctor bent next to her, adjusting his stethoscope, his craggy face very near to hers.

"Hannah," the doctor was saying, "light the lamp, please." The woman hurried to do his bidding. "Now, just let me listen to your heart," he said to Torri, "and then I have a few questions."

Recognition flooded over her. It's *him*, Torri thought, her heart pounding rapidly as he pressed the instrument to her chest. It's Randolph Hamilton, from the portrait in Grandfa's house. But it can't be. It can't—

All at once the elusive memories she'd been trying to retrieve, crystallized in her mind. *The necklace!* The necklace that her grandfather claimed the first Victoria had used to travel through time. Could it have—had it taken her through time? Crazy, insane idea.

But could it be—was it possible? Had she really gone back in time? Her gaze darted to Jake Cameron, and she scrutinized the now harsh set of his jaw, the unusual color of his eyes. All at once the rest of the memory returned. She had seen him standing at the edge of the woods during her mad flight from Christine and Harry. But if she had gone back in time, then how could she have seen him in her own time and—

Torri raised her hand to her brow, feeling her confusion increase. She could also feel a rising hysteria and she closed her eyes for a moment, willing herself to be strong. If it were true, if the necklace had brought her here, only the necklace could take her back. And the necklace was gone! She opened her eyes.

"He took my necklace!" Torri said, pointing at the lieutenant and trying not to sound panicky. Cameron lifted his chin and turned away from her. There was pride in the very set of his shoulders and all at once Torri felt very foolish for having accused him. She flushed and hurried on. "I mean— I guess he took it. Anyway, it's gone."

Dr. Hamilton glanced at the soldier, then back down at Torri, his compassionate eyes turning suddenly as hard and cold as blue glass. He was wearing a light tweed jacket and his hand dipped down into his pocket, then lifted, to reveal her necklace dangling from his fingers.

"Is this the necklace you're talking about?"

"Yes, I—" she stopped as Jake Cameron whirled around and took three long strides to reach Dr. Hamilton's side. Rudely he snatched the necklace from the doctor's hands and stared down at it open-mouthed.

After a moment of deadly silence the lieutenant looked up rather sheepishly into the stares of both Torri and Dr. Hamilton.

"I beg your pardon," he said, his voice once again smooth and genteel. He handed the necklace back to the doctor. "I was just so amazed to see—I mean, it's a beautiful necklace. Quite unusual."

"Yes," the doctor agreed, apparently accepting his apology, "it is unusual." He shot Torri an accusing look. "And it's been in my family for one hundred years. Three days ago, in the middle of the afternoon, while my housekeeper and I were out, someone stole it from my home."

It was Torri's turn to stare open-mouthed. His necklace. Of course. If she had gone back in time, the necklace would have existed during the Civil War and—she lifted her hand to her head again as her mind whirled with the possibilities.

Suddenly she felt incredibly dizzy. "You don't mean that you think I stole it?"

"Young lady, I don't know what else to think. There isn't another necklace like this in the whole world, I'll wager."

Dr. Hamilton turned away to talk in low tones to the black woman. Cameron moved to the other side of her bed, his gray eyes no longer showing any pretense of Southern chivalry. Her first assessment of him had been right. He was angry about something, and she had just done something to make him absolutely furious. As he glared down at her, Torri felt the overwhelming terror of her situation engulf her.

She turned to the lieutenant. "Please, tell me, what is the date?" she asked, her voice trembling. His dark eyebrows collided and the anger in his eyes shifted suddenly into something less hateful, but more suspicious.

"April 20th," he said.

"But the year," Torri said insistently, "what year?"

The man ran his hand through his hair, then slapped the gray slouch cap on his head, his gaze hardening once again. "It's 1863"—one corner of his mouth eased up into a cynical smile and the change from Southern gentleman to adversary stunned her—"as if you didn't know."

Dr. Hamilton turned back to her. "I'm sorry, my dear, I have no choice. This is a matter for the authorities. Tomorrow you should be well enough to be questioned by the sheriff."

Hannah stood behind him shaking her head mournfully, her eyes downcast. The doctor noticed she was upset and patted her kindly on the shoulder.

"Hannah, I don't need you any longer. Why don't you go and prepare some of your wonderful chicken soup to help this young lady get her strength back?"

"Yes, sir, Dr. Randolph," she said and quietly left the room, her large body swaying from side to side.

Torri leaned back against the pillow and folded her hands across her stomach, her gaze on the ceiling. Dr. Randolph. Then it was true. It had to be true. She felt the hysteria returning and commanded herself not to think.

Just lie here. Just lie here and think of nothing. "She's a nice lady," Torri said aloud, her voice slightly slurred.

"Yes, Hannah has a very gentle heart. She's been with me a long time." Dr. Hamilton's lips pressed firmly together. "And I never let anyone take advantage of her kindness. Now, young lady, there are some questions I'd like to ask you before—"

"No!" Torri shouted, then looked around as if wondering who could have made the outburst. Her mind clouded and her head was beginning to ache. "No questions," she said, closing her eyes. "No questions."

"Have you been experiencing a great deal of pain?" the doctor asked, his voice more gentle.

Torri nodded. "My head hurts." Her lower lip began to tremble and all at once she wished very much that Jasper were there. It was so silly, so childish to want her teddy bear, but she did. Sometimes, even after she had come to her grandfather's house and was happy there, Torri had taken Jasper out from under her pillow and held him. Alone in the darkness, she had cried for her dead mother and father. Jasper had comforted her.

More than anything at that moment she wished she could hold Jasper very tightly and cry until she couldn't cry anymore. But she wouldn't cry in front of this man who looked like Grandfa, but wasn't. And she wouldn't cry in front of this strange man playing soldier, even if he had saved her life, which was debatable. But to her abject humiliation, and before she could stop them, Torri felt tears sliding down her cheeks.

"There, there," Dr. Hamilton said hastily, handing her a glass of water and a creased paper filled with a white powder. "Swallow this and you'll feel better. I suppose it's a little too soon for questions. Just go back to sleep, young lady, and tomorrow will be soon enough. May we at least know your name?" The wrinkles at the corners of his eyes deepened. "I'm sure you'd rather be called by your name instead of 'young lady'."

"My name is Torri," she said, wiping the tears away with the back of her sleeve. "That is, my name is Victoria, Victoria Hamilton. My friends call me Torri."

"How interesting," the doctor said, rubbing his chin with one finger, "that we have the same last name. My grandmother's name was Victoria."

He gave her a searching look, then glanced down at the necklace still in his hand. He shoved it into his pocket and turned to open the door behind him. He gestured for the lieutenant to leave first. The younger man hesitated, looking at Torri as though he wanted to say something. Finally he tossed her a warning look she didn't understand, and walked out.

Dr. Hamilton followed him, then paused in the doorway as he looked at her, his expression deadly serious. "Rest tonight, but tomorrow, Victoria Hamilton—or whoever you are—I will expect answers to my questions."

Torri waited until the house was quiet before slipping out of bed and creeping stealthily to the long window at the end of the room. Her dizziness had stopped, but she still had a bad headache. The housekeeper had checked on her several times in the evening and had brought her a bowl of hot soup and some fresh biscuits, but finally even the faithful nurse had slipped away to her own room. Now, Torri stood nervously glancing behind her, knowing this might be her only chance to escape.

She had succeeded, over the last few hours, in convincing herself that she had not done the impossible and traveled through time, but was either dreaming, was the victim of a bizarre kidnapping scheme, as she'd first suspected, or she had gone stark, raving mad. Any other possibilities she firmly refused to consider.

Carefully she raised the window, then stuck her head out and smiled. There was a balcony outside the window. It struck Torri as strange that there would be a balcony but no door from the room leading out on to it. Then she saw a flight of narrow wooden stairs running up the side of the house, reaching the whitewashed platform underneath the window.

It must have been added after the house was built, she realized, as a sort of observation deck. Oh well, it didn't matter. All that mattered was that it would make her getaway a lot easier than she had thought.

Quickly she pulled her head back in and started searching for her clothes. Hannah had hidden them well, for although Torri searched every drawer in the old dresser, and looked through the old wardrobe, she couldn't find her T-shirt, jeans and jacket.

Releasing her breath in a long, frustrated sigh, Torri walked to the window, then turned her back to it and gazed around the room.

"Now if I was Hannah," she said aloud, in a low voice, "where would I—"

Her words were cut short as a rough hand reached suddenly from behind her and clamped firmly over her mouth, while another seized her around the waist. Terrified, she fought her unseen attacker, biting and kicking as hard as she could.

"Hold still you little spitfire!" a familiar voice hissed in her ear.

Torri froze, then jerked her head to look back over her shoulder. Jake Cameron smiled down at her, his face shadowed in the moonlight.

"If I take my hand away, will you be quiet?" he asked softly.

Torri nodded and he lowered his hand from her mouth. As soon as the hand around her waist dropped, however, she spun around and kicked him in the shin.

Cursing roundly under his breath, he hobbled over to a trunk at the end of the bed and sank down on it.

"That'll teach you to come sneaking into someone's bedroom in the middle of the night!" Torri said in a hushed voice.

Cameron rubbed his injured leg and glared at her. His tone was equally low. "Why don't you just scream for Dr. Hamilton, like any well brought up Southern girl would?"

His words held a note of sarcasm that Torri didn't understand. "I will, if you don't leave."

"No you won't."

He stood and crossed to her side, limping a little. In the moonlight she could see his face quite clearly. Gone was the polite gentleman she'd met that afternoon. In his place was a man with dangerous eyes.

"You won't scream. You don't want the doc to come up here any more than I do. That might spoil both our plans."

Torri started to retort angrily, then bit her lip and simply glared.

"You did plan to escape tonight, didn't you, miss?" he said, in an exaggerated Southern drawl.

Suddenly Torri realized he hadn't been speaking in the

soft accent he'd used so effectively that afternoon, and a cold chill crept down her spine.

"What do you want?"

He gestured toward the window. "I've been out on that balcony trying to open the window without anyone hearing. Nice of you to solve my problem."

"I didn't see you out there."

He cocked his eyebrow. "I didn't let you see me."

"Look," she said, becoming frightened and trying to disguise her fear with haughtiness, "you'd better go before I really do have to scream."

"You're tougher than that," he said, moving a step closer. His nearness was unsettling and Torri swallowed hard. "I know that for a fact. I have to admit K'mer picks his agents well. I would never have suspected you—not with that innocent face. Too bad your concussion left you disoriented and you let the cat out of the bag."

Torri shook her head. "I don't know what you're talking about. Is this about the necklace? If it is, you and Dr. Hamilton are mistaken. It's mine. My grandfather gave it to me."

"Oh, I believe you."

Torri looked at him in surprise. "You do?"

"Why not?"

Torri frowned. His face was veiled in mockery, but there was something more there, something frightening in the set of his jaw, his lips. A gust of wind drifted through the open window and she shivered. His gaze raked over her and narrowed as if he was suddenly aware she was clad in only a thin nightgown. Torri took an involuntary step backward, crossing her arms over her chest.

"Here," he said roughly, reaching over and picking up a robe lying across the rocking chair. "Nights around here get kind of cold."

Torri slipped on the robe. "Thanks."

"Sure." Still the sarcasm. "Always glad to help out."

"Please," she said feeling too tired even to generate any anger toward him, "what do you want?"

The lieutenant leaned against the window sill, folding his arms across his chest. When he spoke, it was again with that deep Southern drawl. "Why, Miss Hamilton, I just wanted to hear the story of your life. It's been a long time since I met anyone half as fascinatin' as you."

She spun away from him, clenching her fists. "I can't believe this. I've lost my grandfather, I've lost my necklace—possibly my mind—and now I'm being held prisoner by a mad scientist and his leering assistant."

A low chuckle followed her plaintive words. "That's a pretty good description of me, but surely you don't really think Dr. Hamilton has ulterior motives, do you?"

She hesitated, then turned around. "I don't know what to think. All I know is a strange man comes sneaking into my room in the middle of the night claiming he wants to know the story of my life." She walked over to the door of the room and opened it. "Get out, Lt. Cameron, or whoever you are," she said flatly. "Get out now."

He crossed to her and leaned one hand against the door, forcing it shut. "All right, Miss Hamilton, I'll tell you what I want."

Torri felt her pulse quicken as he leaned closer to her. He smelled of tobacco and whiskey and for an instant she wondered if he was drunk. That might explain his strange comments, yet he didn't act drunk. His lips were scant inches from hers.

"I want to help you get away from Dr. Hamilton," he whispered.

Suspicion flooded her mind. Torri moved quickly away from him, back to the window. He followed, standing beside her, his gaze on her face. She kept her eyes on the brilliant round moon peering through the tall trees behind Dr. Hamilton's house.

"Why would you want to help me?" she asked.

He shrugged. "Maybe because I don't believe you stole his necklace. Maybe because I'm a nice guy." Torri tossed him a scornful look and he laughed. "Listen," he said, "if you had a telephone, who would you call? Or would it be all right if I just ran you home in my skimmer?"

Torri turned and frowned up at him. "Your what?"

"I mean . . ." a curious gleam lit his eyes as he said the last two words hesitantly ". . . my car?"

"Could you?" Torri said, deciding to overlook the fact that he was a smart-aleck and possibly a lunatic. She was desperate. "I'd be glad to pay you if you'd help me get out of here. You could just drop me off at a bus station or just anywhere in town!"

His gray eyes flickered over her. "I'll help you get home," he said, "but I'm afraid I can't take you in my car."

"Why not?" The sliver of hope that had sprung up inside her was quickly fading into apprehension.

One side of his mouth eased up into a mocking smile. "Because, Miss Hamilton, automobiles haven't been invented yet."

Chapter Three

Torri glared at him. "Damn you! You think this is funny, don't you? Well I think—" Suddenly a sharp pain stabbed into her temple and she swayed forward, feeling the blackness sweep over her.

He slipped one arm around her waist. "You'd better get back in bed."

"What do you care?" Torri said angrily, near tears. What was happening to her? What kind of crazy situation had she stumbled into? Too weak to resist, she suffered him picking her up as easily as if she were a feather pillow, then plopping her down on the bed's soft comforter.

She was crying now and the realization made her even angrier. Roughly she brushed the moisture aside and throwing her head back, met his gaze.

"You can tell whoever sent you here that you're doing a good job at confusing and scaring me. 1863—cars not invented—Confederate soldiers—" she started laughing softly, then shuddered and covered her face as her momentary attempt at bravado faded.

"No one sent me," Cameron said, "at least not to waste my time scaring little girls." He gave her another long, intense look. "If you are from K'mer, you're awfully good. Better than the usual trash he uses."

Torri lowered her head and covered her face again. Crazy. One of them was crazy and the terror was not knowing if it was she or this handsome apparition.

"What's wrong? Afraid I hit on the truth?" He sat down beside her and she shrank away from him.

"It doesn't matter," Torri said, her voice muffled. "If I'm not dreaming and not being kidnapped, then I'm crazy—I'm really, really crazy. Maybe it runs in the family."

"You aren't crazy and you aren't dreaming or being kidnapped or anything like that. We all go through this the first time: confusion, disorientation, not wanting to accept what's really happened." She looked up at him, amazed when he gently brushed a tear from her cheek with his thumb. "Do you have any idea what's happened to you, kitten?"

His compassion broke down the last defenses that were keeping Torri's tears at bay. A sob escaped first, followed by a flood of tears rolling down her cheeks. When he slipped his arm around her shoulders, she turned her face to his chest and cried, careful to keep the sound muffled. He held her close, then after a moment, she felt the warmth of his hand caressing her back. The gesture calmed her and somehow she managed to bring the torrent of sobbing under control.

"I'm sorry," she said, sniffling. "I'm okay."

"It's all right. You can cry some more if you need to," he said, for the first time sounding less than sure of himself. "Even I can't stand to see a girl cry."

Torri smiled at him through her tears. "You mean big mean Jake Cameron has a soft spot after all?" To her surprise, he didn't come back with a sharp retort, but instead glanced away, a sheepish look on his face. For the first time she noticed the shadows under his eyes. Lack of sleep? she wondered. Stress?

What a strange person, she thought, feeling once again mesmerized by his nearness. It was like sitting next to an open flame. He was the fire and she the moth drawn to it. She shook the foolish thought away. No, he was just an enigma and that was his mystique.

His dark eyebrows came together in concern. "All right, I'm willing to give you the benefit of the doubt."

About what? Torri wondered, then stiffened with his next words.

"Why I should, I don't know. If I had any brains I'd kill you here and now."

Torri glanced down at the gun at his hip and ran her tongue across her lips. He could do it too, if he wanted. He could carry her right out that window and—

"Don't worry," he chuckled, "I didn't carry you two miles to get you to a doctor to turn around and murder you in your sleep."

Torri shook herself mentally and decided to change the subject. "What—what did you mean—we all go through this the first time?"

"You didn't answer my question. Do you know what's happened to you?"

Torri stared up at him, unable to speak, fearful of what he was about to tell her.

He got up and strode across the room to stare out the window. "Afraid to tell me, eh? I don't blame you. The first time it happened to me I didn't want to believe it either." He ran his hand through his tousled hair. "I have to confess, this has really wiped me out. I mean, this is a bizarre coincidence." He shot her a look. "If it really is one. If it is, it's almost enough to make me believe in God again." His eyes narrowed. "If it isn't, I promise you, *you'll* start believing in the devil very soon."

Torri shivered, and he laughed softly.

Moonlight shone through the window and reflected in his eyes, turning them silver. Torri's trembling hand touched her throat. My God, my God! she cried out in her mind. What have I gotten myself into? Suddenly she was reminded of old movies she'd seen about werewolves, baying at the moon. Certainly this man could easily pass for some otherworldly creature. Impatiently Torri shook the ridiculous thought away and tried to concentrate on what he was saying.

"By some amazing quirk of fate, or trick of the gods, or hand of the Almighty, we have both been brought here, to the past, to the same place, to the same time." His eyes narrowed. "And it couldn't have happened at a more opportune moment."

Torri's stomach felt queasy. "What do you mean, to the past?"

His mouth lifted in a quizzical smile. "You know exactly what I mean. Face it, Victoria Hamilton, it worked. Oh, we never think it will, when we use it the first time, and when it does, we try and deny it until the only other answer is to admit we've gone mad."

Torri swallowed hard. "What do you mean?"

"Whether you want to believe it or not, today *is* April 20th, 1863." He leaned against the wall and folded his arms across his chest, a subtle challenge dancing in his eyes. "In case you aren't up on your history, America is divided into two factions, the North and the South, and is presently engaged in a great civil war."

With a certainty that took her breath away, suddenly Torri knew he was telling the truth; knew it even as her mind recoiled from the thought. *Grandfa's necklace.*

"That would explain your uniform," she said faintly. "But how did you know I was from my time? How did you know about the necklace?"

He paced the room, his hands behind his back as if trying to decide some weighty question. He stopped at the window and stared up at the moon again. "I'm not from this time either," he said quietly. "In fact, I'm from an even more distant future than yours. Now . . . why don't you tell me how you got hold of a TDA?"

"A what?"

"The necklace," his voice was soft, but held an underlying tone of authority. "Where did you get the necklace?"

"My—my grandfather gave me the necklace and," she swallowed hard, "he—he told me it was a way to—" she broke off and turned away. "No, I can't believe it. I'm dreaming. I have to be dreaming!"

He walked to the bed and his hand encircled her arm. "He told you it was a way to what?" She stared up at him, frightened, and he grinned. "A way to travel through time?" He dropped her arm and Torri could only shrink back, trembling, trying to absorb his words. "Well, it is, kitten. I just told you that. So why did you come back in time, Victoria Hamilton? For kicks?"

"No . . ." her voice trailed away.

"Be careful now," he said, his voice shifting again into sarcasm, "if you act too stupid I might think you're overdoing it, and that might make me suspicious again." His cynical smile broadened, the gesture never touching his eyes. "And don't think I'm not."

Torri didn't hear a word he was saying. "Travel through time." She echoed his words. "Then it's true," she said, and with that, she sank back into the pillows.

Jake sat down beside her, his expression doing another lightning fast switch, first to concern, then to suspicion.

"I really did it." She turned to him, her voice hoarse with fear. "But I didn't mean to. It was an accident. I was running—I was holding the necklace in my hand and—" Torri reached out and gripped his arm. "I want to go home," she whispered, then repeated the words slowly. "I want to go home."

The suspicion in his eyes faded again and Torri felt a great sense of relief as he nodded.

"Okay," he said, "I'll help you go home, if you really don't know how. But you'll have to trust me."

"Trust you?" Torri searched his eyes and found once again only an arrogant self-assurance.

He cocked his eyebrow. "The way I see it, you haven't got much choice. At least, I don't hear anyone else offering to be your knight in shining armor. Tomorrow morning, when Dr. Hamilton hauls in the sheriff, you're going to find you need all the help you can get. Besides, it works two ways—I have to trust you as well, which believe me, is not my first choice."

Torri bit back a sharp retort and considered his words. It was true. She needed someone's help. She was scared and not afraid to admit it. Coming here to 1863 had been a complete accident. Even if she could get the necklace from the doctor, she had no idea how to use it to get home again.

She sat up and drew her knees to her chest. "Okay, I'll trust you. So how do I get home? And by the way, will you please tell me where I am? And don't just say Dr. Hamilton's house."

"Where were you before you came here?"

"I was outside of my grandfather's house, outside of Richmond." She glanced up at him. "The doctor's my great-great-great-grandfather, isn't he?"

He looked at her, acting dramatically crestfallen. "You already figured it out?" A more gentle smile returned. "Did you figure this out too? You're home and don't even know it. You see, when you use the jewels, they send you to any time you want, but they can only send you back in the same space."

"I don't understand."

"Your grandfather's house is built near where I found you—in the woods—only in your time. In this time it doesn't exist yet. I took you to the doc's house which was about two miles away. When you get home again, check it out and see if there wasn't another house on your grandfather's property long ago."

Torri felt totally overwhelmed. "Yes, when I get home." She twisted her hands together, feeling strangely numb and bewildered. "I'm tired, Lieutenant. Would you please leave now?"

"I'm sorry, but we won't have a chance to talk privately tomorrow and there's a lot more to be said."

She heaved a sigh. "Listen, Lieutenant—"

"Call me Jake." He lifted one brow. "After all, I did save your life. That entitles me to something."

Torrie felt his steady gaze unnerving her again and she rushed on. "All right, Jake—whoever you are—this may be simple and reasonable to you but at the moment I'm a little overwhelmed."

"Tell me why you came back in time."

The sudden edge in his voice made Torri look up in surprise. Once again she saw a glint of something hard in his gray eyes. Something she didn't understand.

"I told you it was an accident."

"Then you didn't come back in time with any specific purpose or mission in mind?"

Torri hesitated as she remembered thinking that if she *could* go back in time she could correct what had happened to her grandfather. She bit her lip and saw the quick light of caution jump back into Jake's eyes.

"What is this, *Star Trek?*" Torri asked in irritation. The look on his face didn't change and she hurried on. "My grandfather gave me the necklace before he went into a sanitarium and—"

"Into a what?"

"Never mind. He gave it to me and told me a ridiculous story about how one of my ancestors used it to travel through time. I thought he was crazy." Torri felt a swift pang. "If I had known it would really work I would have—"

"Would have what?"

"Well, I sure wouldn't have picked the Civil War!" Torri

stopped talking. She didn't feel like exposing her plans concerning her grandfather to Jake Cameron.

"Why did you want to come back at all?" he asked flatly.

"I didn't want to come back *here!*" she said. "It was an accident, which by the way, was probably your fault!"

"My fault?" He gave her a puzzled look. "Why my fault?"

"Now who's playing innocent? You were in the woods near my grandfather's house. Don't deny it," she said hastily as he frowned and opened his mouth to speak. "You were wearing that same uniform and—" her eyes widened. "I was holding the necklace. I must have accidentally done something that activated it, and since I was looking at a Civil War soldier, the necklace brought me here. Is that how it works?"

He frowned. "Yes, thought transference works interactively with the TDA."

"What were you doing there?" Torri demanded.

Jake shook his head. "That's very strange. I haven't been to your time before. Cars, airplanes, television, right?"

She nodded.

"I guessed your era earlier when you mentioned the telephone." He shook his head again. "No, I've read about it but I've never been there." He grinned. "Or maybe I was for only a second. I've flicked into the wrong era several times."

Torri closed her eyes. "Please, I'm confused enough already."

Jake dropped the bantering tone. "So," he said quietly, "it was an accident. You didn't even know how to use the TDA."

"The what?"

"The TDA. That's what we call it. Short for Temporal Displacement Apparatus."

She hesitated, unsure whether she should tell him how little she really knew about the device. She didn't want him to think he had her cornered. The diary! Where was the diary? Grandfa had said the diary would tell her how to use the necklace! Had she taken it back in time with her? No, now she remembered. She'd dropped it during her mad dash into the woods.

Torri got up from the bed and moved toward the window. It was still open and the cool spring air drifted gently across her face, the smell of honey-suckle heavy and sweet. Torri shivered and drew the robe closer.

"What about you?" she asked without turning. "How did you get here? Do you have a necklace like mine? Is that why you looked like you were in shock when Dr. Hamilton pulled it out of his pocket?"

Jake watched her steadily as he answered her. "Yes, I have one just like yours. All of the TDAs look alike because they were all made at the same time."

"Who made them? How does it work?" Torri asked, feeling awed and slightly horrified. "I mean, is there a scientific explanation?"

"You said you were tired, remember?"

Torri sat down decisively in the rocking chair. "I've suddenly regained my energy."

"All right," he said, "I'll tell you." He started unbuttoning his coat, shrugging out of the heavy gray cloth. Torri stiffened.

"What are you doing?"

One corner of his mouth eased up as he glanced at her. "Don't worry, kitten, I don't rob cradles. Or haven't up to now." He stretched his arms above his head and Torri felt her pulse quicken unexplainably.

Jake Cameron was a big man, over six feet tall. His shoulders were broad and strong and as he stretched, his worn white shirt turned transparent in the moonlight, giving her a provocative hint of a hard, muscular body. Torri felt her face growing warm, her hands growing cold.

Jake lowered his arms and for a moment, as their gazes locked, something dark and smoldering burned in the gray eyes of the man Torri faced. Then it was gone, mockery in its place.

"That coat is pure wool," he said, "and I'm not as cold natured as some." He smiled and raised his eyebrow. "Disappointed?"

Torri wet her lips but stopped the moment she saw how his glance followed the movement of her tongue. "D-disappointed? I don't know what you mean," she stammered.

"That I'm not stripping down to ravish you." He moved toward her, slowly unbuttoning his shirt. "However, I could oblige you, if that's what you want. I don't usually get involved with women your age, but if your customs are different—"

"Stop!" Torri squeaked, holding up both hands defensively.

Grinning, Jake rebuttoned his shirt, and Torri felt a sudden burning anger. The man enjoyed making her look like a fool.

"Shhh," he cautioned, "you'll wake the house. You don't want them to find you entertaining a man in your boudoir, do you?" He leaned against the wall again, propping one foot up on the low window sill. "You know, in the South a lady's reputation can be compromised pretty easily, so you'd best mind yourself while you're here—none of your loose twentieth century morals."

Torri clenched her fists. "None of my—"

He cut her off. "Well, anyway, back to the subject at hand. The jewels in the devices came from a planet that was discovered when I was three years old." He stopped as he saw the disbelieving look on her face. "I know that probably sounds ridiculous to you, but remember, I live in the year 2417, which is more than four hundred years past yours."

Torri stared at him, her mouth dropping open. "Four hundred . . ."

Jake went on, oblivious to her shock. "Scientists discovered the jewels had amazing properties, involving the time/

space continuum which, correctly channeled, could result in time travel. You see, the jewels possess a curious kind of energy when combined with human energy. In a sense, the jewels are alive, almost sentient beings, and when they are worn by a human, they automatically re-pattern their own life force in synchronization with the life force of the human. In this way—"

"Whoa, hang on, time out!" Torri interrupted. "Are you making this up as you go along or what?" she asked incredulously.

His lips pressed together in a grim, straight line. "You don't want to hear it? Fine." He turned toward the window.

"Wait—I'm sorry," she said, "but you have to admit this is pretty hard to swallow. And would you please explain this in words of less than ten syllables? I'm not a scientist, you know."

The anger faded from his face and he nodded. "Sorry. I forgot that in your time women don't receive as much scientific training as men."

"I beg your pardon," Torri said, standing and facing him with her hands on her hips. She kept her voice hushed but her outrage was still evident. "I'll have you know that in my time there are women astronauts, women doctors, female nuclear physicists and—and—a lot more!"

From the pleased expression on his face, Torri realized she had let herself be baited.

"Excuse me," he said with an elaborate bow, "must have been a different century I was thinking of. Anyway, the jewels were a wonderful discovery—at first. The scientific world went nuts over the concepts and the possibilities." He stared down at the floor. "And I guess it could have been wonderful, but then everything went wrong. Everything always goes wrong when people are involved."

"What happened?" Torri felt as though the two of them were bound together by this bizarre conversation, linked for some purpose she couldn't imagine.

Jake sighed and turned toward the window again. Torri watched the silver moonlight strike his remarkable gray eyes. For a moment they blended together, two quicksilver lights, then he glanced back at her and the magic disappeared—but not the strange foreboding that continued to sweep over her every time she looked at him.

"The most brilliant scientists in the country developed a crude time travel apparatus using the jewels," he answered. "One was manufactured for each scientist."

"Why one for each scientist?"

He shrugged. "The scientists decided that they alone would take the risk of traveling forward in time. They had all agreed that the risk of traveling backward in time was much too dangerous. If one single moment of history were inadvertently changed, our own existence could be jeopardized.

"One by one they would try it, then determine if time travel held any worthwhile value for mankind, based upon the reports of those who returned—if they returned. If one didn't return, the next scientist had his own device to use. One of the scientists was something of a jewelsmith, and he shaped the devices into pendants. Each differently colored jewel had different properties, for use either in the time/space continuum of the past, or the future. Do you follow what I'm saying?"

Torri nodded, mesmerized.

"Each jewel represents a direction in time, far future, near future, far past, or near past. By pressing two jewels at once, you can gauge how far forward or back you want to travel. You must have been pressing some of the jewels when you saw me and that's how you ended up here."

"One of my ancestors, the first Victoria, disappeared when she was twenty," Torri said thoughtfully, "and then she miraculously reappeared."

Jake stiffened. "What do you mean?"

"I mean, maybe she accidentally went somewhere in time and by using the jewels correctly found her way back to her own time."

His easy chuckle surprised her. It was the first genuine emotion she'd heard him express besides anger. "She must have or you certainly wouldn't have the necklace, now would you?"

"Oh. Well, anyway, what you're saying is that I got here because I pressed two of the jewels when I was looking at your uniform, which made me think of the Civil War. Does it always work that way? Send you to the place you're thinking of?"

"Not always," Jake said, avoiding her gaze, "but almost always."

Torri decided she was too tired to try and find out what he was hiding. Her brows knit together. "How did my family come to have a TDA in the past? I mean, in my time and before? That necklace has been handed down in the Hamilton family for generations."

"I'll get to that."

Torri sat back down in the rocking chair. "Go on," she said at last.

"One scientist, named K'mer, volunteered to be the first to use the TDA."

"K'mer," Torri interrupted. "You said something about me being one of his agents. What did you mean?"

"That's what I'm about to tell you. K'mer broke the agreement and instead of going into the future, traveled to the past. He was gone for a day. When he returned, suddenly the comp-news, the vid-news, everywhere you looked, revealed that K'mer was the undisputed leader of the world. He had an army. They filled the streets, arresting anyone he believed was a threat to him. Of course the first arrests were those of the other scientists."

He turned away from her and Torri noted the knotted

muscles in his shoulders, his back. Obviously what he was revealing was a very painful memory. "All the scientists were taken away. Later the general public learned that K'mer had somehow gone back in time and usurped the government, but it was too late."

"I don't understand," Torri interrupted. "How did he do it?

"No one's really sure just how he managed it all, but apparently when he went back in time, he changed history in a way which gave him the political power necessary to become absolute dictator of Canamerimex when he returned. He began a war with most of the rest of the world. It continues to this day, with our young men and women sent to fight as soon as they turn sixteen."

"Dear God! Men—women—you mean boys and girls!" Torri gasped.

His fingers tightened into a fist. "Yes—children. The 'men' fight, the girls are sent to cook for them and keep their spirits up, if you know what I mean. They pass them around like—" he wiped one hand across his face and drew a ragged breath.

"But how could just going back in time give him such power?"

Jake paced the room, his hands linked behind his back. "First you have to understand exactly what kind of power a time traveler wields. A person who travels back in time, already knows what's happened—or what's supposed to happen—through the chronicles of history. If you can return to the past and use that knowledge to change history, then you can change the future." His gaze drifted off again to some unseen point in the darkness. "Power," he said again, his voice tight. "A terrible power, and K'mer used it to become our dictator . . . and to reduce most of us to being his slaves."

"Slaves . . ." Torri whispered. "You don't mean, really slaves?"

"Yes, I mean really slaves," His voice, laced with bitterness, cut between them. "He uses the TDA to keep the people in line, along with his very powerful army. Because, after all, he can always go back in time and wipe out your entire family, for generations past and future. Only a few of the TDAs slipped through his fingers before he outlawed them." He turned toward her. "Apparently one of them is yours."

"And you think I'm one of his agents?" she asked in horror.

"Let's just say you're a likely candidate for the part," Jake said. "After all, your apparent ignorance could just be a good act. If K'mer knows I've gone back in time and what I plan to do, he'll send the best."

Torri swallowed hard but refused to let his strange story frighten her. "Well I'm not K'mer's agent," she stated flatly. "So, how did *you* get a device, if he outlawed them, and how did I end up with mine?"

"The scientists still had their devices, at first. K'mer thought his show of force would cause his fellow scientists to automatically support him and aid him in his quest for control. In fact, he offered to share the power with them." He stopped.

"Well, what happened?" Torri prodded.

"Three of them did back him and have continued their research into the uses of the TDA."

"What about the rest?"

"Two of them died buying the others time." He laughed without humor. "Buy them time. Kind of funny, don't you think?"

"Hilarious." Torri shifted awkwardly in the rocker. The strange gleam in Jake's eyes had grown more pronounced and it frightened her. "Time for what?"

He suddenly whirled and began pacing again. "Time to escape *into* time!" he said triumphantly.

"Shhh," she cautioned, "you'll wake up the doctor."

He lowered his voice and stopped pacing. "One scientist, a man named H'lton went back in time and never returned. It's assumed he tried to find out what changes K'mer had made, and put them right. Since nothing ever changed in my time, apparently he wasn't successful. Either he stayed in the past, or died there. I suspect that scientist became one of your ancestors."

For some odd reason Torri wasn't surprised. "That would make sense. Our family line can be traced back to the first Victoria's father and no further. My grandfather was fascinated with genealogy and—wait a minute." Her mouth fell open in awe. "Her father gave her the necklace! But, Jake—I'm descended from her. Are you telling me that Victoria's father came back in time from the future and then became my *ancestor*?"

A rare grin lit his face. "Hard to figure out, isn't it? Welcome to the mixed-up world of time travel."

Torri shook her head as if trying to rid her mind of her confusion, but quickly stopped as her head began to pound. "What about the other scientist who escaped?"

A long, empty silence fell between them. Jake shoved his hands into his pockets and for a moment he looked younger, vulnerable. "He was my uncle. He escaped into the past too," he said at last, "but he came back. K'mer killed him, but not before he passed his TDA on to me." Jake stopped talking and took her by the hand.

Torri rose, facing him, aware of some subtle change between them. His gray eyes stared down at her, an unspoken question in their depths.

"I've told you the truth, Victoria, and I promise I'll help you get back home. In return, are you willing to help me?"

Torri realized as she stood beside him, she only came to his shoulder. It made her feel very small and helpless and she wasn't sure she liked the feeling. "H-how?"

"First we've got to get your necklace back. Dr. Hamilton

has it locked in his safe downstairs. You can't get back to your own time without it, and you can't help me without it."

"Help? What kind of help do you need?" she asked, half afraid to hear the answer.

He cleared his throat and to Torri's surprise she saw he was embarrassed. "I lost my TDA."

Torri blinked. "What?"

"When I came here, for reasons I won't go into, I had to become a soldier. That means I've had to fight in some battles. During one of the battles, I lost it."

He was still holding her hand and Torri drew away from him. She walked to the window. "So, you need my help, how interesting."

"And you need mine, don't forget that."

Torri swept him a look. "Do I? You've explained how the device works."

Jake rolled his eyes skyward. "Well, there are a few little things you might need a little help with. The sheriff is coming tomorrow." He moved to stand beside her. "I might be persuaded to back up any kind of story you might want to invent. Your necklace is locked away in the doc's safe—" he gave her an appraising look. "Ever do any safecracking?" She glared at him and he smiled. "I have. Also even though you may understand the concept of the TDA there are other things you don't know." He leaned one hand against the wall, the other cocked on his hip. "I'm not stupid, Miss Hamilton. I never lay down all my cards at the same time."

"Okay, okay," Torri grumbled. "I get the picture. You scratch my back, I'll scratch yours."

His eyes grew suddenly sultry. "Anytime, kitten. You just give me the word."

She rubbed her temple, thinking maybe it hadn't been such a good idea to hear all of this while suffering from a concussion. Glancing up at the moon and the stars she wondered if her grandfather was looking up at them too. No, he hadn't even been born yet, and yet, he had. A sudden thought surged into her brain.

Now that she knew the necklace really worked, once she got back to her own time, she could try to go back again, just a few months into the past, and keep her grandfather out of the sanitarium. A smile eased its way across her face. And Jake Cameron would help her. She turned back to him. Jake lifted both eyebrows and his eyes narrowed speculatively.

"I know that look," he said. "It means you've thought of something you want." He nodded. "Yes, something you want badly."

Torri started to tell him about her grandfather, then decided to wait. Once she had the necklace she'd be in a better position to barter, and Jake might be more willing to listen to the deal she had in mind.

"Yes, I do have something I want. I have something I want to change in history. If you'll help me do it, I'll help you."

"All right."

Torri's eyebrows darted up. She hadn't expected such an easy victory. "Just like that? You don't even want to know what I want to change?"

"Look—my mission is more important than anything else. Besides," his lips curved up in a cynical smile, "what could you want? To go back and make sure your best friend doesn't steal your boyfriend?"

Torri drew herself up to her full height. "Just how old do you think I am, anyway?"

Jake frowned and drew his hand across his unshaven face. "About seventeen?"

Torri's mouth dropped open. "I'm almost twenty-one!"

He shrugged. "Practically jailbait. What difference does it make? I said I'd help you, so have we got a deal or not?"

She nodded, furious but afraid to vent her true feelings for fear he would leave her to fend for herself.

"Great, then—"

"But how are we going to get the necklace?" she interrupted. "For that matter, how am I going to stay out of jail? By the way, why *does* Dr. Hamilton think I stole his necklace?"

Jake rubbed the back of his neck wearily. "Oh yes, a minor detail. You see, by coincidence—if anything is coincidence—someone actually did rob Dr. Hamilton's house during the skirmish in his woods. Naturally when he found a necklace just like his missing one—"

"Wonderful. Well?" she demanded. "How are we going to get the necklace back? Assuming I'm not arrested."

"Maybe we should tell the doc the truth."

Torri made a face at him. "Very funny. I'm sure if I go and tell him I'm his great-great-great-granddaughter from the future and I need his—I mean my—necklace back, he'll just hand it over." She slapped her hand to the side of her face. "But it *is* his necklace, that is, it was. It's the same necklace, isn't it, then—"

"Do yourself a favor and don't start thinking about it," Jake said seriously. "Time travel is full of paradoxes, strange mind-bending puzzles. Just concentrate on the here and now and I promise I'll get you back to the there and then."

Torri smiled in spite of herself at his quip. "But if someone stole the necklace, shouldn't we make sure the thief is caught? What if it isn't returned?"

Jake raised his eyebrow condescendingly. "Obviously it was, or it couldn't have been passed down to you, right?"

"Oh. Yes." She raised one hand to touch the bandage around her head.

"I've kept you up too long," he said, "get some sleep. We'll sort the rest of it out later. But remember, tomorrow the doc expects answers. You'd better have some kind of story and be ready to explain how you came into possession of his necklace."

"What should I tell him?"

Jake ran one hand through his hair in exasperation. "Don't

women in your century do any thinking for themselves? Think of something! I'm taking care of getting the necklace back."

"You haven't said how you intend to do that little thing."

One corner of his mouth lifted in a half-smile. "But I will. You just concentrate on your own end of the problem. I have great confidence in your acting ability. And now, kitten," his voice suddenly shifted back into the smooth Southern accent. "I'd better be moseyin' along."

"You do that well," Torri commented.

"Oh yeah," he said, "I can turn it on and off. And you'd better learn to as well, if you're going to claim you come from around here." He lapsed back into the drawl and exaggerated it until he sounded like Hannah. "I'd best be goin', Miss Hamilton, before I compromise yo' and ruin yo' reputation." His eyes sparkled suddenly with humor. "Yo' wouldn't want to have to marry li'l ol' me, now would you, sugar lamb?"

Torri felt the blush creep up her neck and knew in the bright moonlight he couldn't fail to see it. She tried to keep her tone light as she switched on her own version of Southern charm. She'd imitated Christine a million times behind her back.

"Not if you were the last man on earth, honey chile."

Jake chuckled. "That's what I thought." He picked up his coat and put it on, then moved to the window and sat down on the sill.

"Wait a minute," she said. "I got here by accident." Jake glanced back at her, his face changing to a mask of caution, his eyes narrowing as if he anticipated her next question. She met his stare without flinching and plunged on. "But you never told me what *you're* doing in the past."

Jake sat there in the open window, poised in the moonlight.

"That's right," he said quietly, "I didn't."

"Well?"

To her astonishment he picked up the end of her robe's belt and fingered the smooth silk. "This is pretty." He tugged on it. "Come down here."

Mutely Torri found herself obeying him, allowing him to draw her downward until she was on her knees in front of him. He lifted one hand to her face and brushed the back of it across the line of her jaw.

"So young," he murmured, "still so innocent, aren't you, in spite of your efforts to appear otherwise."

"Lieutenant . . ." Torri said uneasily.

"Jake," he corrected, "from now on we are Jake and Victoria to one another. We have a hard job ahead of us. There's no place for formality here."

Torri stared at him, unable to take her eyes from his. "My friends call me Torri."

"Torri," he said the name as if he savored the sound. "I like it."

"Jake . . . tell me what you're doing here in the past."

His mouth tightened and his fingers suddenly slid from her face up into her hair. Swiftly he bent his lips to hers. Torri felt the desperation behind his touch, and without understanding his need, she responded with equal passion, curling her arms around his neck. The kiss deepened and Torri felt a sudden wave of desire coursing through her, right down to her fingertips. Suddenly Jake pulled away, and Torri saw something akin to shock in his eyes. Then she watched as his face shifted back to a smooth mask, cutting her off, efficiently separating them.

"I came into the past," he said softly, "to kill a man."

Chapter Four

"Kill a man!" Jake was almost through the window when she stopped him. "Now wait just a minute," Torri hissed. "You can't drop a bombshell like that and then disappear." Her eyes searched his. "Are you kidding me?"

Jake stepped out onto the balcony, then bent over so she could hear him as he whispered, "I don't usually joke about killing people." One side of his mouth lifted in a mocking gesture. "I may be a murderer, but I'm not insensitive."

"Then you really mean . . ." her voice faded.

"I mean, I was sent here to set some things right for the people back in my time."

"You mean you came back to correct what that man—K'mer—did?" Torri asked. She leaned toward him, her hair falling over her shoulder, silhouetted against the robe. She didn't miss the shift in the direction of his gaze, nor the sudden heat in the depths of his cold gray eyes. For a moment their gazes locked, then the spell was broken as Torri rushed on, her voice trembling, but not with fear.

"That—that tyrant kept someone evil from being killed and now you've come back to—"

"Now wait a damn minute." Jake knelt beside the window, his face harsh in the moonlight. He reached in and pulled her the rest of the way through the window, onto the balcony.

Torri cried out softly in protest but hushed when she saw the anger mirrored in his eyes. He stood, dragging her up with him.

"Try and get this through your head, Victoria. Maybe the uniform and the Southern put-on charm have misled you into believing I'm some kind of honorable character—a knight in shining armor." He shook his head slowly. "Forget it. I'm here to kill someone, plain and simple."

Torri shuddered. To think she felt attracted to a person capable of cold-blooded murder. "You're horrible," she whispered.

He smiled, his teeth flashing, even and white. "Why thank you, ma'am." He released her and touched the brim of his gray cap. "We aim to please."

Torri felt a cold sweat beginning across her forehead. This changed everything. How could she possibly trust such a man? And yet, without him, could she ever return to her own time?

"You said you'd help me," she said. "Did you mean it?"

"Sure."

"Why?"

His eyebrow rose and his chiseled lips almost smiled. "You learn fast, don't you? Cultivate that cynicism, it just might save your life. I'll help you," he said, "because it will also help me."

Torri felt suddenly deflated. He was right. Somehow she had cast this man—this stranger—in the role of hero. She glanced up at him, her own eyes wary now. Apparently he was little more than a hired assassin. And she was supposed to trust him?

"You mean if you didn't need me, you wouldn't help me get back to my own time?"

"Oh, I don't know . . ." he ran his hand lightly up the side of her arm. His touch through the thin fabric sent a sudden warmth careening through her. "If I had time, I might help you anyway. If you didn't cause me too much trouble."

Torri snatched her arm away. "Lucky me," she said, her eyes narrowing.

Jake stared into her eyes for a long, tantalizing moment and Torri saw an astonishing interplay of emotions cross his face. She watched as desire changed to shock and she caught a brief glimpse of vulnerability behind his steel gray eyes. It was gone scarcely before she realized it was there, the cold mask once more carefully back in place.

"You didn't answer my first question," she said, the silence making her nervous. "Did K'mer keep someone from being killed in the past?"

"No," he said harshly. "I don't know what he did to change the past and I don't care. It's late. I've got to go." His eyes gazed down into hers but he made no move to leave.

She shook her head. "I don't understand. If you want to— to kill this K'mer person, what are you doing here in the past, trying to kill someone else?"

"Don't be ridiculous," he said, his voice hard. "If I could kill him in my own time do you think I'd be here, sacrificing—" he broke off but not before Torri saw the flash of pain in his face. His jaw tightened. "Unfortunately, it is impossible to kill him there. I have my orders and I intend to carry them out."

"And I'm supposed to trust you?" Torri felt her hopes sinking, along with her heart.

"Don't worry," he said, "as long as you have something I need, I'm your willing servant, Miss Hamilton." He swept his cap off his head and made her a mocking bow.

"I think I'd rather make a pact with the devil, thank you," Torri retorted. "I'll find my own way back, without your help!"

Jake turned rigidly away from her. "I'll help you get home, Victoria. I said I would and I meant it." He glanced back at her and smiled, the gesture transforming his face from stony indifference to sheer sensuality.

Her gaze dropped from his eyes to his lips. This is nuts,

she thought. *I'm standing here in the middle of the night with a murderer from the future and all I can do is wonder if he's going to kiss me again.*

He moved closer and Torri frantically tried to focus on the stars that glittered in the darkness beyond his right shoulder.

"Look at me," he commanded.

Hesitantly, Torri obeyed.

"Look, Torri," he said softly, "I know this is hard for you but you're going to have to decide right now, once and for all, if you're going to trust me or not. I can't help you if you don't. I can't take a chance on you turning on me or fighting me when I tell you to do something you may not understand."

"So I'm supposed to blindly follow your orders," Torri said, wishing desperately she could control the pounding of her heart.

"That's right. Without question." He tilted her face up to his, bringing his lips close to hers.

"Please, don't."

He seemed suddenly shocked at his own actions. "Forgive me." He ran one hand over his face. "I'm tired, it's late and here you are in front of me, your eyes as green as the Irish Sea, your hair—your hair is like ebony silk. Your mouth like the softness of a fawn." Jake moved closer. "I'm just a man, Torri, a very human man who has been without the warmth of a woman for a very long time." He gazed down at her longingly, then sighed and stepped away. "Again, forgive me. But I promise, if you'll just trust me, I'll steal the necklace out of Dr. Hamilton's safe and I'll take care of you."

The sound of a gunshot sent Torri screaming into Jake's arms. The momentum of her weight and the unexpectedness of her flight sent them both plunging to the wooden floor of the balcony.

"Sorry about that." A dry, laconic voice spoke from below them. "Didn't mean for it to go off. I guess I'm not used to handling firearms much any more."

Jake staggered to his feet first, pulling himself up to lean against the edge of the white railing. The furious look on his face changed quickly to one of disbelief.

"Dr. Hamilton?" He straightened, darting a quick, suspicious look at Torri.

"Well, don't look at me," she retorted, holding her head with both hands. "I don't know what's going on any more than you. Oh, my head!"

Jake reached down and helped her to her feet.

"Are you out of your mind, Doctor? Torri's injury—"

"I'm sorry. I really didn't mean for it to go off. Now, suppose the two of you come down from there and we have us a talk."

Torri looked nervously down at the older man who stood clad in a striped bathrobe tied over long flannel underwear. He held a long rifle in his hands.

"Nice weapon," Jake commented.

"Thanks," the doctor said, patting it like a favorite child. "It's a new Sharps. Can fire ten rounds a minute without reloading. You, for instance, could only get off one shot with that pistol you got there, then you'd have to reload. On the other hand, well, let's say I'd have the advantage."

"Point taken."

"Good. So the two of you were in on this together," Dr. Hamilton shook his head, "from the beginning. I'm disappointed. All right, come on down here. I'm taking the both of you to the sheriff right now."

Torri could see Jake's jaw twitch. Slowly he lowered his right hand from the railing of the balcony to hang perilously near the pistol in his holster.

"Jake," she whispered, her hands clasped to her chest, "no."

"I told you, kitten," he said softly, "I can't let anyone stop me, not even your great-great-great-grandfather."

"Stop right there, Lieutenant," Dr. Hamilton said. "Unbuckle that gunbelt and lay it down real carefully."

A dangerous smile stretched across Jake's lips, warning flickering in his cold gray eyes.

"Sorry, sir," he said, "afraid I can't do that. And if you try to shoot me, you'll find yourself vastly outmatched—in spite of your fancy rifle."

"Sure of that, are you?"

The moment hung frozen, as though it had been plucked out of time and left suspended while thoughts raced madly through Torri's mind. If Jake killed her great-great-great-grandfather, would it change something in her future? Had he already had his children? Probably. He was at least in his late fifties. But she knew, from her grandfather, that Randolph Hamilton had lived to be ninety-one years old. Surely killing him would have to change something in her family's future!

One look at Jake's determined face told her that it wouldn't matter to him, not one whit, if by killing this innocent man he killed her entire, unborn family. Jake Cameron was consumed with his mission. Everything and everybody else were just problems to be eliminated. Eliminated.

"Dr. Hamilton!" Torri cried, then blinked, startled by the passionate plea that had been wrenched from her. The man looked up at her and the expression in his eyes softened slightly. Wetting her lips, she plunged on. "This isn't what you think. Give us a chance to explain." Jake shot her a suspicious look, but there was no time to worry about that.

"I don't know what you're up to," he warned, his words too soft for the doctor's ears, "but be careful what you say or I'll have to kill both of you."

Torri swallowed hard as Dr. Hamilton walked to the bottom of the stairs, a puzzled expression on his face.

"I don't see what else I can think, young lady. This man shows up on my doorstep, says he accidentally shot you, then it turns out you're carrrying my stolen necklace. Now I find him here outside your bedroom window—where no respectable people of the opposite sexes would be this time of night—plotting to steal my necklace again!" His lined face deepened into a scowl. "There's nothing more to say."

"Oh, but there is!" Torri said, thinking quickly. She grabbed a handful of her robe and lifted it, hurrying down the stairway. Dr. Hamilton backed up a step. "Please, please listen to me," she implored him, holding out her hands.

"Dr. Hamilton," she said, "if we were trying to steal your necklace do you think we would be so foolish as to arrive on your doorstep with it?"

The older man rubbed one hand across his face. "I admit it doesn't make much sense." His eyes narrowed. "But I know what I just heard the two of you talking about. You were planning to steal the necklace again."

"Yes, yes we were," she said. Jake took a step forward, his hand on his gun, when Torri whirled around. "Stop it, Jake. You're not going to hurt anyone. There's no need. I'm going to tell Dr. Hamilton the truth and he—well, I know he'll understand."

Jake stopped at the corner of the balcony and in spite of himself, one corner of his mouth curved up in a half-smile.

Torri turned back to the doctor and clasped her hands together in front of her. "The truth is, doctor, that Jake and I are in love!"

A muffled expletive from the stairs caused her to turn and glare at the man smiling down at her now in amusement. When he raised his eyebrow suggestively, she felt her cheeks growing warm, and whirled around to face the doctor.

"You see," she went on, less sure of herself now with Jake's bemused gaze on her, "I am not from the South—I'm a Yankee." The doctor said nothing, just stared at her patiently.

She cleared her throat. "Jake's folks didn't want him to marry me and neither did mine, and let me tell you, Dr. Hamilton, they have made my life miserable ever since I told them I was engaged to a rebel!"

"I can imagine," Dr. Hamilton said dryly. Torri shifted nervously under his steady gaze. "Go on," he said, "I'm listening."

"Well, I wrote Jake and told him how awful Papa was being to me—locking me in my room, denying me food—and how he just had to come and rescue me."

"And being a chivalrous gentleman of the South, Lt. Cameron traveled north, into enemy territory and stole you out of your father's home?" The tone of the doctor's voice expressed his doubt more eloquently than words ever could.

"No," Torri said quickly, "I was afraid for him to come north of course, but I sent word—by a servant I trusted—for him to meet me near Richmond. I told my father I had changed my mind and would be a dutiful daughter and, once convinced, he allowed me my freedom again."

"Which you no doubt immediately abused by running away from your family and home to be with this scoundrel."

"Oh, he's not a scoundrel, Doctor, truly he isn't." Torri wrung her hands and puckered her brows in consternation. "He's the most wonderful man that ever was and I love him more than anything—anything in the world! Can't you understand that, dear Dr. Hamilton? Haven't you ever loved someone so much that you would give up everything, just to be with them?"

The man's face sagged suddenly and Torri was shocked to see the glint of tears in his steady blue eyes. The gun wavered.

"Yes," Dr. Hamilton murmured, "yes, I have loved someone that much." Torri released her breath explosively. The doctor's head snapped back up. "But that doesn't explain the necklace."

"We found the necklace," Jake said, his deep voice sending a tremor of relief through her. He was going to back her up—for what it was worth. "I met her outside of Richmond. I had arranged for her to stay with a friend of mine and his wife, but when we got there, their house had been burned and they were gone. I—I didn't know what to do."

Torri glanced back at him. What an actor! she thought. The plaintive note in his voice, the anxiety in his eyes, if she didn't know better she'd have believed him herself. A frown creased her brow. If he was such a clever liar, how did she know all the things he had told her were true?

Considering for the moment, in light of the evidence, that the time travel stuff was true, how did she know he was what he portrayed himself to be? What if he wasn't working on the side of good, but was, in fact, one of K'mer's men, come back in time to wreak havoc with history? She shivered.

"I decided to take her with me," Jake was saying.

Dr. Hamilton's face registered his shock. "Take her with you? Into battle?"

Jake grimaced. "I didn't plan it that way. I got her some civilian clothes—men's clothes." His gaze raked over her. "I didn't want to take a chance on anybody—well, you know what I mean. A woman who looks like her, you just can't take any chances."

To Torri's mortification, Dr. Hamilton was nodding in agreement. She pulled the robe closer around her throat and shot Jake a scathing look.

"Anyway, I had taken a leave of absence from my company and we hid out in the woods for a time."

"The two of you? Alone?"

Torri smiled to herself. Dr. Hamilton's shock was so sweet, so old-fashioned.

"Er, yes, it was necessary, you understand."

The doctor's blue eyes became like flints of steel. "We

shall discuss that part of your story in more detail a little later, sir."

Jake cleared his throat and for the first time Torri thought he was actually, genuinely uncomfortable and a little unsure of himself.

"He is my fiancé, after all," Torri said hastily, remembering the rigid Southern code of ethics.

"Humph. Well, go on."

"While we were hiding out, a skirmish started. We ran. I was trying to find a place to hide Victoria. We—we stumbled across two corpses—beg your pardon, Torri, honey"—Torri smiled sweetly in his direction—"two dead deserters. They'd been caught in the crossfire. They had a knapsack full of things they'd apparently been stealing from folks in this area. That's where we found your necklace." Jake moved down the stairway and slipped his arms around Torri's waist. She stiffened, then forced herself to relax against her would-be lover.

"So you just took it. That it?" Dr. Hamilton asked.

"No, no," Torri interjected, "we agreed we'd turn it into Jake's commanding officer as soon as we reached the camp, but in the meantime, well, it was a pretty thing." She lowered her long lashes and looked up at the doctor from beneath them, her lips curved flirtatiously. "I don't think any woman in the world could have resisted having such a lovely necklace, Doctor. I know it was wicked of me, but—"

"Supposing I buy this cock and bull story," Dr. Hamilton interrupted, "you still haven't explained the little conversation I overheard just now. You were planning to steal it."

Jake's head drooped and his rugged features were wreathed in shame. "I admit it, sir. I had planned to steal it. I didn't know what to do. I couldn't take Torri with me back to Jeb's boys—"

"Jeb Stuart?" Dr. Hamilton's voice registered his disbelief. "You're one of Jeb Stuart's boys?"

A boyish smile broke out across Jake's face and Torri watched in wonder. Either Jake Cameron was an Academy Award winning actor or this was something he was honestly proud of. Jeb Stuart. Torri wracked her brain. Oh yes, wasn't he a major or general or something of the cavalry, notorious for his raids on the Yankee camps? The men who rode with him were considered heroes and respected by North and South alike.

"Yes sir. Like I said, I couldn't take her back to camp with me—I'm usually gone on scout. I—well, sir, I felt desperate. I thought if Torri had that necklace, maybe she could sell it for enough money to get back home to Maryland."

"Jake!" Torri was amazed at her own ability to fall right into his concocted story at a moment's notice. "You said we'd use it to set up housekeeping here—that I could be near you!"

He turned her toward him and she almost pulled away. The heat was there, automatically, and she had to force herself to relax, to behave as an adoring fiancee being held in her love's arms.

"I'm sorry, darling," Jake said earnestly, "but I can't take a chance on anything else happening to you." He turned back to the doctor. "We were trying to get through the skirmish when she was hit. If anything had happened to her—" He wiped the back of his hand across his forehead. "It was crazy I know, and it was wrong, but, Doctor," his voice was a plea, "I didn't know what else to do."

The doctor stared at them both for a long moment. Torri could feel the sweat trickling down the side of her face. One of Jake's hands was still at her waist and his fingers tensed and untensed against the silk of her robe. Finally the older man rubbed one hand across his face and tucked the shotgun under his arm.

"Well, I know what I have to do," he said, a finality in his voice.

Torri glanced up at Jake fearfully, then back at Dr. Hamilton. The silence stretched between them as they waited for the old man to continue.

At last he nodded, almost to himself, as if settling the matter within himself. "All right. While this war is going on, and while Lt. Cameron is with his company, you can stay here with me and Hannah." He turned and started walking away from the two astonished people behind him, then stopped and glanced over his shoulder. "After the two of you are properly married of course."

And at that, Torri fainted.

When she regained consciousness Torri was in the four-poster bed once again. Her head was throbbing and she could hear voices downstairs, loud, male voices. Quietly she got out of bed and tiptoed to the door, easing it open. She could hear them quite plainly.

"I can't marry her now!" Jake's deep voice was booming. "It wouldn't be fair to either of us." Torri could imagine the exact color of his eyes: gray ice.

"How do you figure?" the doctor asked heatedly.

"Well, for one thing, I'm about to leave on a scout that will probably get me killed!" Torri could hear Jake pacing, his heavy boots resounding firmly across the wooden floor. "That wouldn't be fair to Torri—to marry me only to be made a widow."

"Then why did you bring her here?" Dr. Hamilton said suspiciously. "Outside you intimated that you more or less stole her out of her father's home so's you could marry her."

"I brought her down here so we could be together—period."

Torri could almost see the old man rubbing one hand across his wrinkled face, his eyes narrowed.

"Ah, I see. You didn't ever intend to marry the girl—you've been leading her on, is that it?"

"No, that's not it!"

Jake's frustration would have been amusing, Torri thought, if there hadn't been so much at stake.

"Then what is it? Looks to me like you're just a scoundrel, intent on having your pleasure and ruining a young girl's life—and don't be telling me you haven't had her, for I can tell by the way she looks at you that you have."

Torri blushed furiously in the darkness. Whatever could Dr. Hamilton mean? She didn't look at Jake Cameron with anything other than loathing. Of course, she had had to act like she was in love with him. Yes, of course, that's what he meant. She didn't know she was such a good actress.

"Maybe," the doctor was saying, "maybe I'd better just go have a little talk with Jeb Stuart. I'm sure he'd like to know that one of his men has dishonored a young girl."

"She's not a girl, dammit!" Jake exploded. "She's a woman. You act like I kidnapped a ten-year-old and ravished her!"

"Keep a civil tongue in your head, boy," Dr. Hamilton's voice was icy. "Now, are you going to do the right thing or not?"

"I always intended to," Jake said, each word clipped. "I just didn't think that now was a good time."

"Well," said the doctor, "when she's big with your child I reckon you'll think so. I read people pretty good, Lieutenant, and in spite of your reluctance, I don't think you're the kind of man that would want his child branded illegitimate."

Torri held her breath as she awaited Jake's answer. "No." His voice could barely be heard. "I'm not."

The voices lowered and continued for a few minutes more, then Torri heard a door open. Unable to contain herself any longer, she opened the bedroom door and slipped into the hallway. The stair landing was only a few steps down. She walked softly to it and crouched behind the carved wooden stair railings. Dr. Hamilton and Jake walked out of a room.

The two men shook hands gravely, and as Jake turned to go, she could see his jaw clamped in rigid anger.

Afraid of being caught, she hurried back to her room, and ran to the window, hoping to catch a glimpse of Jake before he left. She was treated to the sight of her hero walking down the long road leading away from the house without looking back. She was sure she'd never see him again.

Chapter Five

Torri walked toward the full-length mirror. The hoop under the rich ivory dress moved with her, rocking from side to side. She felt almost as if she were wearing an umbrella—a very uncomfortable umbrella. She pulled at the stiff waistline. Hannah had strapped her into this terrible contraption of linen and bone and she felt as though her ribs were being slowly crushed.

Torri stared at the reflection, wondering if it really was she, or if this was more of the TDA's strange magic. No, it was real. Familiar green eyes gazed back at her as she looked down at her wedding dress.

Since the night Jake had ridden away she had been confined to her bed, to regain her strength, the doctor said, but she felt like a prisoner. Jake had not returned, and for all she knew he had disappeared back into time, leaving her to fend for herself. Every day she had grown more and more anxious until last night she had burst into tears and demanded that Dr. Hamilton take her to the Confederate camp to look for her erstwhile rescuer.

Dr. Hamilton had simply patted her on the hand and told her to have patience, then handed her a delicate porcelain cup and suggested she have some more herb tea. Infuriated she had sent the cup flying across the room to shatter against the fireplace then spent the better part of the night crying into her pillow.

Never had she felt so helpless, so alone—so stupid. In only the few hours she'd known Jake Cameron, and in spite of the way he had treated her, she'd begun to depend on him. If it hadn't been so frightening it would have been laughable. Somewhere near dawn she had dried her tears and resolved to stop behaving like a hysterical schoolgirl. She would find a way to get the necklace herself and she would get back home to Grandfa.

This morning she had been awakened by a smiling Hannah, carrying a breakfast tray on which a fat stack of pancakes rested.

"Pancakes!" Torri had exclaimed. "And syrup!" Such luxuries, as she understood it, were few and far between.

"The very last of the molasses," Hannah said happily. "And you know about molasses, don't you honey?"

Torri shook her head as she watched the woman deftly cut the stack into neat squares.

Hannah leaned closer and said, conspiratorially, "Well, you can't have *mo'* 'lasses when you ain't had *no* lasses at all!"

Torri managed a weak smile as the woman slapped her thigh and chuckled at her own wit.

"Hannah," she said, with sudden curiosity, "are you a slave?"

"Why no, honey, I ain't no slave. Mr. Lincoln, he done set all the slaves in the South free they say, but Dr. Randolph, he set me free ten years ago." She rose awkwardly to her feet, then straightened her shoulders with pride. "I'm the housekeeper. I gets a salary, every week."

"I'm so glad," Torri said, relief flooding through her. She realized suddenly that she quite admired Dr. Hamilton, and if he had slaves, somehow she wouldn't have felt the same about him. But maybe Hannah was an exception. "Does he have . . . any slaves?"

"No, child, he sure don't. Don't you see how this old place is goin' ta rack and ruin? He don't get paid much o' nothing for doctoring, an' he can't raise cotton no more."

"Why not?"

"Dr. Randolph couldn't raise no cotton without slaves, child. If you was a Southern girl you'd know that. When you have to pay workers, why it ain't worth it to plant the crops!"

"Why doesn't he have slaves?"

Hannah shook her head. "Now that's a sad tale, Miss Victoria."

"Call me Torri."

"All right, Miss Torri."

"No, I mean without the 'Miss'. Just call me Torri."

Hannah put the fork she held down and stared at her, a shocked expression on her face. "Why, I couldn't do that!"

"Why not?" Torri asked.

"'Cause it wouldn't be fittin', me callin' you—"

"Why, Hannah?" Torri said softly. "Because I'm white? We're both free, aren't we?"

Hannah's mouth fell open for a stunned second. Then her face split into a wonderful smile. "I sure never thought of it like that, no sir, I sure never did."

"Well, think about it. You know, Hannah, my grandfather told me once that sometimes people only think they're free, but if they aren't free up here," she touched her temple, "they aren't really free at all."

She opened her mouth as Hannah chuckled and poked a forkful of pancake at her. Torri chewed thoughtfully. Her grandfather had been talking about Christine when he said that, how he and Torri should really feel sorry for Christine because she was in bondage to money and social position. After all Christine and Harry had done to him, she knew her grandfather still felt sorry for both of them. She shook herself out of her reverie.

"Tell me, Hannah, please. Why doesn't the doctor have slaves?"

Hannah hesitated a long time, then finally spoke. There were tears in her voice. "It's on account of his wife."

"I thought his wife was dead."

"She is. The way Dr. Randolph look at it, his slaves killed her."

"Killed her?" Torri placed her hand to her throat. "What do you mean?"

"He used to have slaves, honey, then one winter, the slaves all got the fever. Miss Amelia, she insist on helping the doctor treat them, and then she got it herself." She brushed a tear from her eye and her lips trembled. "Dr. Randolph, he loved that woman so much, when she die, I think he's gonna die, too. But he don't. He just set all his slaves free and devote himself to doctorin'. He told me, when he give me my freedom, 'Hannah,' he say, 'I knowed slavery was wrong, but I wanted to make money. Well, I got my money, but now I don't got my Amelia.'"

"That's so sad," Torri said, feeling her own eyes getting teary. "Here, stop feeding me," she said, suddenly realizing that she was allowing Hannah to act as a slave even while she was deploring the institution.

She fed herself, listening to Hannah's chatter, and suddenly began wondering why she was getting such special treatment. Usually Hannah brought her a tray, but didn't try to wait on her hand and foot. And breakfast had always consisted of oatmeal alone.

"We got to hurry, now," Hannah beamed, stirring more sugar into the cup of coffee.

It wasn't pure coffee of course, Torri had learned that much. Since the North had blockaded the Confederacy's coast, coffee was an almost unobtainable luxury. The coffee in the Hamilton household was Confederate coffee which was a concoction made from a few precious coffee beans ground together with corn or barley. The result was hot but less than tasty. Torri picked up the delicate china cup and sipped.

"Hurry? What for?"

Hannah stopped tucking the faded cloth napkin into Torri's nightgown and gaped at her. "You mean you don't know? You mean nobody ain't told you?"

She shook her head. The sight of the other woman's astonished face filled her with fear. "What?" She set the cup down and grasped Hannah by the wrist. "He's sending me away isn't he? Dr. Hamilton is sending me away or"—she swallowed hard—"he's turning me over to the sheriff."

Hannah's mouth shut with a snap, then a wide smile spread across her generous lips. "Oh honey, I didn't mean to scare you. Of course he ain't doing that. Don't you know Dr. Randolph's taken a shine to you? You remind him of his little granddaughter, the one who's family went out West. He set quite a store by her and he ain't seen her in oh, most five years now."

"Then, what is all this about?" She pushed her plate away and pulled the napkin from her throat. "Please, Hannah," she said softly, "just tell me."

"Why, darlin', don't look so scared," Hannah said, "it ain't nothing so terrible—though I would think Dr. Randolph woulda told you! You're gonna be married, child."

"Married?" Torri repeated the word in a hushed tone. "Who—who am I supposed to marry?

"Why, your sweet soldier-boy, who did you think? Come on now, honey, the sun is rising high and we got a lot to do 'fore six o'clock."

Numbly Torri had watched as Hannah sent for a large, wooden tub. Once in place, Hannah and a thin, older black man filled it with bucket after bucket of water.

The woman had provided a small bar of rough soap, a thin towel, and would have scrubbed Torri herself if Torri, flushed and nervous, hadn't pleaded with her for privacy. After the bath was complete, Hannah had reappeared with a corset, a pair of thin pantaloons and a lovely soft chemise.

Now, Torri stood gazing at herself, thinking that perhaps

the corset was worth the agony, given the wonderful things it did for her waistline. The dress itself was simple, made from a heavy silken fabric with a lustrous sheen. The high necked collar was trimmed with a froth of exquisite lace. The sleeves, long and slim, had pearl buttons, fastening the closure from elbow to wrist.

Torri could see that the dress was far from new, but had apparently been laid away with great care. Perhaps it had once belonged to the doctor's wife. Torri's long, dark hair had been gathered into a high knot at the crown of her head, a few long tendrils allowed to escape to brush against the soft ivory of the gown.

As Torri appraised her appearance, she was suddenly grateful to Hannah in a deep, profound way. Her mother had died when Torri was so young. She'd never had a woman fuss over her, tie ribbons in her hair. Maybe that was why she had been such a tomboy in her early teens. But at that moment, she had never felt so beautiful in her life. She was grateful for Hannah's hard work. Obviously, in 1863 there were no department stores where racks of clothes hung waiting for women to find the best bargains.

According to Hannah, there wasn't even any new material to make new dresses from. The 'damn Yankees' had blockaded the coast, keeping new supplies from reaching the Confederate capital. Hannah must have refashioned this gown for her during the long, interminable week while she'd been hoping Jake would return. The dress fit like a dream, thanks to the woman's talents.

There were other horrors of this war that her college history classes had never revealed. Hannah had told her yesterday morning, after a breakfast of thin oatmeal, about the terrible food riot that had occurred a few weeks before in Richmond. Torri had eaten the rest of her oatmeal gratefully, thinking that for the first time in her life she might know real hunger.

Oatmeal. You're standing here, staring at what is supposed to be your wedding dress and you're thinking about oatmeal.

A cold chill swept over her. Thinking about oatmeal and riots kept her mind from thinking about this travesty of a marriage. She'd never dreamed of this outcome. She'd believed that either Jake would come at night and steal her away, or else he would desert her completely.

I want to go home, she thought frantically. I want to go home. Things are just moving too, too fast. How can I possibly marry Jake Cameron?

Torri closed her eyes. She couldn't think about him now. If she did she'd go mad. The words held a familiar ring to them. The memory slid into place and she smiled. Scarlett O'Hara. *Gone With The Wind*.

"I'll think about that tomorrow," she whispered in a pseudo-Southern accent. Her smile disappeared.

Nervously she touched the handmade lace around her neck. This was crazy, ridiculous. She couldn't be forced into this. She couldn't—Torri bit her lower lip—she could. This wasn't her world, this was a world where well-brought-up women had few choices and women alone none at all. If she didn't marry Jake and get away from Dr. Hamilton, what would she do? What if Jake didn't show up? What if he left her to fend for herself?

Torri stared at herself in the mirror, suddenly aghast. What was the matter with her? She wasn't some whining baby to be coddled and sheltered by a man! Hadn't she stood up to Harry when he and Christine had begun the competency mess? Hadn't she thrown his engagement ring in his face, even though it had broken her heart to do so? She lifted her chin. She was a Hamilton. With or without Jake Cameron's help, she would survive. And somehow she would get back to her own time and help her grandfather. That settled, her thoughts turned back to the problem of her marriage.

If Jake did show up, then what? Strange, how different everything was only a little more than a hundred years ago, how rigid the standards of Southern society. Was it that way in the North too? she wondered. Her gaze shifted from the mirror to the long window. And how much more different would things be *four* hundred years *in the future*? What was Jake's time like? Was it really as bad as he claimed?

Torri shivered. Again the realization of his words swept over her. She couldn't believe he would really kill someone in cold blood. While he did seem a cold and cynical man, she sensed there was more to him than the dispassionate face he presented. Behind those cold gray eyes she thought she had glimpsed a vulnerability, a hidden anguish—or was she just unable to accept such a terrible reality?

Torri walked to one of the long windows and looked out. Staring out at the setting sun, she felt the nervousness in the pit of her stomach turn to fear. More than anything she wanted to be home, home safe with her grandfather. But even if she *could* go back, she wouldn't be going back to the life she had known.

Grandfa. What was happening to him? she wondered. Were they treating him kindly in the sanitarium? Did he miss her? Was he heartbroken because she hadn't believed his story about the necklace? What would he think if he knew that she had, indeed, used the necklace, as he had claimed she could? Would he be relieved? He had seemed to think traveling through time would bring her great happiness. What secret knowledge had he possessed?

Happiness. The thought brought a grim smile to her lips. Once they were married she would be under Jake's control—at least in the eyes of Southern society. It was hard to imagine, even for a moment, that Jake wanted the farce of a wedding any more than she did. Why he was going through with it was a mystery. He had said he needed her, but from what he had told her, he needed only her necklace.

She frowned. Since her concussion she hadn't been able to really think straight, but in the last few days she had become more clearheaded and had begun to wonder about some of Jake's story. Somehow she couldn't imagine that retrieving the necklace from Dr. Hamilton's safe would prove any problem to Jake Cameron. So, why didn't he just steal the necklace? For that matter, why did he even bother with her? If he were the kind of man he said he was, her needs wouldn't matter. He would tell her whatever it took to get what he wanted. Why, then, would he resort to marrying her? Why didn't he just take the necklace and run?

Maybe he already had.

Cultivate that cynicism. His words came echoing back to her. *It might save your life.*

Her mouth dropped open in sudden understanding. No, Jake didn't just need her necklace. Somehow he needed *her*. A new, hard look settled into the emerald green depths of her eyes as she gazed coldly back at her reflection.

All right. He needed her. Somehow she would use that knowledge to her best advantage. She would not help Jake, in whatever way he needed her, without forcing him to help her first.

"How lovely you look."

Dr. Hamilton's low voice broke into her thoughts. Torri turned. His blue eyes held a gentle light she'd never seen there before. Oh, she had sensed his kindness, but the tenderness mirrored in his gaze seemed almost as though it was for someone else.

She wasn't prepared however, when he crossed the room and kissed her gently on the cheek.

"Forgive an old man," he said quietly. "This was the dress my wife wore the day we were married."

"I thought it might be!" Torri said, touching the silken skirt with something akin to reverence. "Oh, Dr. Hamilton,

you shouldn't have—I mustn't wear this—it's too precious—
you don't even know me!" she finished guiltily.

"Don't I?"

His blue eyes twinkled and for a moment Torri had the
oddest feeling that she was gazing into her grandfather's
eyes. The moment passed and Torri managed to smile back
at him, wondering exactly how much he really did know
about her. And Jake.

"I—I don't understand."

"Neither do I, completely," he admitted with a chuckle.
"All I know is that ever since I first laid eyes on you I've felt,
well, I can't say for certain what I've felt. I knew you were a
lady—I truly felt that in my heart of hearts in spite of the
evidence against you." His blue eyes were perplexed. "And I
felt, somehow that I knew you." He shook his head. "I know
that makes no sense at all."

"Perhaps it does," Torri said softly. It was tempting, very
tempting indeed, to tell this kind man the truth: that she
was his great-great-great-granddaughter.

"Does it?" he said, scratching his head, obviously puzzled
by his own feelings.

"Yes, because after all, I'm—" she stopped, an icy knot
tying itself tightly across her middle. Two cold gray eyes,
chiseled into a sensual, granite-like face dared her, from behind Dr. Hamilton's wiry shoulders, to tell the truth. She
ran her tongue across her lips and cursed her sudden nervousness and the quick flush of color she could feel flooding
her face.

"Of course," she finished lightly. "Hannah said I reminded
you of your granddaughter, the one out West. That must
be it."

"Maybe, but—"

"Good morning."

Jake's flat voice broke into their conversation. Never had

Torri seen a man look so furious—or so fabulous. He wore a beautiful gray uniform that looked as though it had never seen any wear or tear. The one he had worn the day he brought her to the doctor's had been threadbare and almost ragged.

This uniform was clean and neatly pressed, the brass buttons shining in double rows down the front, the gold colored sash tied jauntily around his waist. His curved sword hung at his side and on his head was a rakish, broad-brimmed felt hat of Confederate gray. The entire ensemble was impressive and most attractive. There was something different, however, in Jake's face. He looked more gaunt and the shadows under his eyes were deeper. He looked tired, as though he carried the weight of the world on his shoulders.

For a moment Torri's gaze softened. This was the man she was going to marry. How strange. She'd thought for so long it would be Harry. Harry . . . her involvement with him seemed a lifetime ago. How poorly Harry would measure up to this magnificent specimen of a man. How broad Jake's shoulders were, how square his jaw and his eyes—

Torri stopped in her dreamy appraisal, as his steel gray gaze held hers disconcertingly. She blinked, astonished at the hostility she felt emanating from him. Quickly she banished the silly, romantic feelings she'd been entertaining. This man was a murderer, or would be in the near future. He didn't want to be with her but he needed her. Somehow the doctor had talked, or perhaps threatened, him into this marriage. The fact that she didn't want it either seemed to make no difference to the angry lieutenant in gray.

Wait a minute! Torri's mouth fell open slightly. Jake doesn't know I don't want to marry him. For all he knows, I was the one behind the doctor's proddings. He feels trapped.

So? Her tougher side demanded. And you aren't trapped? At least he knows how to get back to his own time—you don't! You need him and what better way to make sure he sticks around than to marry him?

Lifting her chin, she extended her hand to her intended husband.

"Good evening, Jake, darling," she purred, "how handsome you look."

"Good evenin' Lieutenant," the doctor echoed.

"My, my," Hannah's voice was filled with awe, "where'd you get them pretty clothes, Mr. Jake?"

Jake smiled lazily. "This old thing? Just a little something Jeb had whipped up for me."

"Oh!" Hannah suddenly gasped. "You ain't supposed to see the bride before the wedding! Don't you got no sense at all? It's bad luck for sure. Now get on downstairs with you, Mr. Jake."

As he smiled at Hannah, the coldness in his eyes shifted to warmth, and Torri found herself wondering what it would be like to be on the receiving end of a tender Jake Cameron. He loved to tease the old woman and seemed to have a genuine affection for her.

But he's a liar, a little voice reminded her. *You can't believe anything he says.*

And I'd better remember that, she thought dully.

"Why certainly, Miss Hannah," Jake drawled, turning sultry eyes on the overweight woman. "After all, I'll be seein' plenty of her after the ceremony, won't I?"

During the astonished silence he slipped out the door. Hannah broke the awkwardness by suddenly bursting out laughing.

"That boy!" she cackled. "Mind you, you're gonna have your hands full with him, Miss Torri. He's going to be a real loving kind of man. He—"

A loud throat clearing stopped her from going any further. "Hannah," the doctor said sternly, "would you please go down and tell the minister that we are ready to begin?"

Hannah, properly subdued, nodded and headed for the door, then turned and gave Torri a big wink.

Real loving man? Torri's eyes widened. Surely Jake didn't think, couldn't imagine, that their marriage would be a real one in the full sense of the word. She relaxed. No, of course not. He was a man with a one track mind: killing. He was doing this because he needed her—not as a wife but as—what? She didn't know, but she couldn't think of any reason sex would enter the picture at all. No, his little comment was just his way of making her uncomfortable.

"I'm feeling rather guilty," the doctor said suddenly.

Torri turned. She had forgotten he was in the room. "Guilty?" She smiled and lifted one hand to touch the side of his face lightly. "You've been wonderful. What could you have to feel guilty about?"

"I should've told you about today."

"Oh, that's all right. It was quite a surprise—not that I didn't know Jake and I were going to get married eventually, but—"

"Are you sure you want to marry him?" the doctor asked, his blue gaze worried. "I only did this because, well, because if my little granddaughter was in a similar situation I would want someone to make sure her honor was not treated lightly."

Torri's face softened, and for a moment she felt an overwhelming love for Dr. Randolph Hamilton. "Thank you," she said sincerely. "I do want to marry him."

"Even if he wasn't altogether willing? That's why I didn't tell you. I didn't want you to get your hopes up and then, come today, the man not show up."

Torri opened her mouth and closed it. What would be the proper response? She smiled again. "Oh, you know how men are, Dr. Hamilton—they always get cold feet before the wedding."

"Yes, yes, I suppose," he muttered, moving toward the door. He turned back. "Oh, one more thing."

"Yes?"

His mouth curved up in a crooked smile. "Mind if I give the bride away?"

Tears sprang into Torri's eyes. All her life she'd dreamed of the day her grandfather would give her away in marriage. She had often fantasized about how it would be. She often changed her mind about what she would wear or who she would marry, but she always knew the proud look that would be on her grandfather's face. Now, as she faced marrying a time-traveling killer, the pride on her great-great-great-grandfather's face was no different from what she had imagined Grandfa's face would show. God had given her that much, at least.

"Of course," she whispered, and with a muffled sob, ran into his open arms.

Chapter Six

The ceremony would be mercifully short. Jake had slipped the minister a gold piece before the doctor came down to insure it would be brief and to the point. He felt strangely uncomfortable about the whole thing, which was ridiculous. This was just another step toward his goal. After all, the necklace belonged to Torri and she had held it. The jewels were linked to her and her alone. He needed her, but he hadn't needed to marry her to carry out his plan. He'd only thought that it might make things slightly easier—especially if Torri really was who she claimed to be. According to his history files, twentieth-century women, though somewhat liberated, by and large still preferred a monogamous relationship sanctioned by the rites of their own religious affiliation.

Besides, the old man would have made good on his threat to go to Jeb Stuart. Something Jake couldn't allow. Jeb Stuart's respect gave Jake a great amount of freedom in the Confederate Army. He couldn't risk losing that freedom of movement for a moment. As their heated meeting had progressed that fateful night, Jake had realized that Dr. Hamilton wasn't buying his hesitation and that he was in danger of jeopardizing his mission by refusing to marry Torri. Damn the luck that had caused the woman to appear in front of him just when he had his first real chance at killing Col. Reed! If it *was* bad luck. He was beginning to wonder.

He had begun to give Torri the benefit of the doubt, had started to believe she wasn't one of K'mer's agents, but that was before she had set up this compromising situation. Her words on the balcony had saved them, but had also conveniently tied him to her, which no doubt suited whatever ulterior purpose she had in mind. His dying embers of suspicions had suddenly been fanned back to life as he rode back to camp that night, but he had resolved to go through with the wedding, just to see what her reaction would be. On the honeymoon he would have ample opportunity to sort things out.

Jake brought his thoughts back to the present. He turned his gaze toward Torri Hamilton and felt a sudden, heady mixture of desire and hate. She looked beautiful. No, she looked like a dish of frothy cream and he felt like a hungry alley cat. The smooth ivory dress fit her to perfection, showing off the tininess of her waist and the fullness of her breasts.

Her long, black hair flowed gracefully from a topknot to her shoulders, surrounded by faded silk flowers, left over from another, richer time. Her green eyes were lowered, demurely shaded by thick, dark lashes. It took every ounce of strength Jake possessed to keep from jerking her face up to his and crushing her lips against his.

Instead, he coolly slipped the plain gold wedding band— which had belonged to Dr. Hamilton's wife—on her finger, and when the preacher pronounced them man and wife, tilted her chin and dropped the kiss of a loving husband on her half-parted lips.

Desire coursed through him and he jerked back from her as though he'd been shocked. Torri, too, looked startled, as though she'd felt the current as well, then Hannah and the doctor were hugging her and Jake was shaking hands with the minister and it was over. After cutting the fruitcake that Hannah had been saving for the doctor's birthday next month and toasting the new couple's happiness with apple cider, Hannah spirited Torri away. The new bride reappeared a half hour later, looking bewildered and lovely in a dark gray traveling dress, trimmed in dark green, carrying a small valise.

"I don't understand," she said haltingly, from the top of the stairs. "I thought I was going to stay here."

"Of course," the doctor assured her, "but first, the honeymoon."

"Honeymoon?"

Jake watched the color drain out of Torri's face and felt an odd satisfaction. So, she hadn't reckoned on that part of the marriage. He frowned. That made no sense at all. K'mer's agents would do whatever they had to, at all costs, in order to assure their success. They all knew too well what K'mer did to failures. She couldn't possibly be squeamish about using sex to get what she wanted.

His frown deepened. In fact, he figured that had been her intent all along—to seduce him, lull him into a state of bliss and then kill him. Well, she'd done her job well, compromising him into this marriage, so why did she look faint? He lifted one brow speculatively as he gazed up at her. Was she scared? He frowned. She looked scared. But no, she couldn't be. Her delicate behavior had to be for the benefit of the doctor and Hannah. Sure. That was it. She had to carry out the fragile flower bit to the end. But her pallor was very convincing, he'd give her that. Face powder probably.

"W–where are we spending our honeymoon?" She addressed the question to the entire group, but her gaze was locked on Jake's face.

"In a secluded cabin, my love," he said, then smiled, delighting in the terror that seemed to leap into her eyes at his words. Of course—she was afraid he was on to her. She was afraid of what he might do to her once he got her alone in an isolated cabin. His gaze swept over her boldly and he winked. "Where we can be totally alone."

"But where?" The panic in her voice was growing.

Ah, she hadn't counted on this. Hadn't planned on being taken away from the security of Dr. Hamilton's home. Good. Very good.

"Jake has a friend who has a small hunting cabin," Dr. Hamilton interjected, turning anxious eyes in her direction.

Jake shrugged. "When your commanding officer says, 'Use my cabin', you don't very well turn him down."

"Jeb Stuart again?" Torri asked, her curiosity appearing to override her fear, then her tone went flat. "How very kind of him."

"Yes," Jake said, moving to stand near her, his chest almost brushing the front of her bodice, "you'll love it, darling."

With one, quick movement Jake swept her off her feet and into his arms. Torri squealed and with her outburst the minister, the doctor and Hannah laughed.

But as Jake carried a stiff, unyielding Torri out to the doctor's wagon, borrowed for the occasion, he glanced back. Dr. Hamilton was no longer smiling. His eyes spoke silent volumes. *Don't you hurt her*, they warned, *don't you hurt her in the slightest way*.

Jake smiled. Amazing. Dr. Hamilton didn't even know that Torri was related to him, but his instincts had taken over and he treated her as though she were his own daughter.

"Don't worry," Jake called, singling out the doctor for his reassuring words, "I'll take good care of her." He bundled her into the seat of the wagon, then looked up into her emerald green eyes, large with an unspoken question.

"Jake . . ." she began.

One side of his mouth curved up. "Congratulations, Mrs. Cameron," he whispered, "you got what you wanted." He swung himself up on the seat beside her in one easy movement. Taking the reins, he turned toward her. "Hope you're prepared to fulfill your vows to love, honor and obey." He leered at her. "I know I'm ready to cherish you."

The wagon started moving and Torri turned in the seat, as if desperate for one last look at Randolph Hamilton. Jake chuckled softly and headed the horses into the twilight.

* * *

Torri sat in rigid fear next to the man beside her. She didn't know what to say or what to expect. Surely Jake Cameron wasn't going to take time off from his all important mission to have a honeymoon with a woman he didn't even know. She glanced over at him. His face could have been carved out of stone, but his eyes, gazing at the distant horizon, were thoughtful. Summoning her courage, she managed a casual tone as she stared down at her hands, folded demurely in her lap.

"Well, that was quite a performance," she said, "thanks for agreeing to the wedding. I thought if I refused it would look suspicious."

"Yes, definitely suspicious." Something in his voice made Torri glance up at him. He was staring at her, his gaze raking over her. She felt a cold chill beginning at the base of her spine.

"What's wrong?" she whispered, then rushed on. "Oh, are you worried that I'll consider this a real marriage?" She laughed nervously. "Well, you don't have to worry on that score. I know you only did it to help us both out of a sticky situation."

"Did I?" He was staring straight ahead now, his eyes on the horses.

"Well, of course you did," Torri answered, her voice shaking slightly. "Now you can sneak back and steal the necklace and take me home—right?"

"I already have the necklace."

Torri gasped. "What?"

"While you were planning your trousseau, Mrs. Cameron, I was working late at night on cracking that safe. I've got the necklace in my pocket right now."

"But what about the doctor? When he discovers it missing, he'll—"

"By the time the good doctor checks his safe—if he ever does—we'll be long gone."

"So you never intended to take me back to his house?"

"Of course not."

Torri felt a rush of premonition. "Then why did you go through with this stupid marriage? All we had to do was sneak out and—"

"You forget," he interrupted brusquely, "I'm calling the shots. Trust me."

Torri swallowed hard. "I have no choice, do I?"

Jake scowled, returning his gaze to the road. "No," he said flatly, "none at all."

"All right, so we're married—but what are we doing heading off for a honeymoon?" Torri laughed nervously. "Let's use the device! Take me home." She placed one hand gently on his arm. "Please, Jake, you promised." He didn't answer and she shook his arm. "When will you take me home?" she demanded. His head snapped in her direction and their gazes locked. For a moment, Torri felt as if she couldn't breathe, so swiftly did the anger flood his face.

"Drop the act, will you? It's getting on my nerves."

Torri slumped dejectedly against the seat, turning away from him so he wouldn't see the tears in her eyes.

What did he mean? Belatedly she remembered his accusation that she was an agent from the future. A quiver of fear danced down her spine. If he believed that, perhaps he was bringing her out to this secluded hideaway to—

A shadow covered the wagon and Torri straightened, looking around fearfully. They had turned off from the main road—which was no more than a dirt lane actually—and were now traveling down a narrow trail. On either side, dense underbrush huddled at the base of tall trees which formed what seemed to be an impenetrable forest. It was growing dark and sounds of night animals and insects sent a new shiver of apprehension through her.

Looking up, she realized there was still a little light, but the many branches of the trees interlocked, blocking most of the last lingering rays of sunlight. The wheels of the wagon caught on rocks and dipped down into potholes, making the ride bumpy and rough. After one particularly violent jar, she was thrown against Jake. He quickly put his arm around her, clutching her to his side. Torri felt the heat between them, and looking up into his taut, flushed face, she knew he did too.

Oh God, she prayed silently, what is *wrong* with me? This man is probably going to *kill* me and I'm hoping he'll kiss me!

Her nervousness returning, she blurted loudly. "Where are we going?"

Jake pulled the horses to a stop and in one quick movement, jumped down from the wagon seat. Without giving her time to protest, he circled around and lifted her, slowly, letting her body slide down his.

Torri blushed violently as her breasts pressed against his broad chest and her legs came in contact with his muscled thighs. He held her, his arms tight around her, his hands hot against her back, his eyes smoky gray. The moment stretched between them, until, with a ragged breath, Jake moved her away from him and began to unharness the horses.

Torri sighed deeply, feeling shaken from their brief, intimate contact. "Where are we?"

"We're in the middle of nowhere, kitten." He led the horses a short distance away to tether them, then glanced up, his gaze traveling toward a steep incline behind them. "Up that path is Jeb Stuart's cabin. Our honeymoon haven. We'll stay there tonight, maybe tomorrow night too."

Torri's mouth dropped open. "But why?" she cried. "Why can't you just use the necklace and send me home?"

"It isn't that easy, Torri."

"Why not?" she demanded. "Because you think I'm what's-his-name's agent? Because you brought me out here to kill me, too? Just remember, Jake Cameron, you admitted to me that you need me. Don't think I didn't pick up on that double message. You need the necklace but you need me, too! So start explaining why you won't take me home or I'm walking!"

Their eyes met, then with a squeal of exasperation, Torri turned and started striding away from him.

Jake moved toward her with the speed of a jungle cat and frightened by the look of sheer fury on his face, Torri began to run. He was too fast for her, and before she had gotten ten feet, his arms closed around her waist like a metal vise.

"You're going nowhere, except up to that cabin." Jake growled, turning her in his arms and shaking her slightly. "And I haven't forgotten anything. Don't worry, I'm not going to kill you." He ran his hands up her arms.

"Why do we have to stay here?" Torri whispered, trying to ignore the way his hands seemed to burn against her skin, even through the cloth. Her heart pounded as his hands tightened around her upper arms.

"I already told you, sweet," he said, moving closer so that his breath brushed against her ear, "we haven't had our honeymoon yet."

Torri jerked away from his embrace and stared at him in horror. "You don't mean—" she broke off, his mocking, knowing smile causing the words to die in her throat.

"Oh, but I do, Mrs. Cameron. I intend for this to be a marriage in the purest sense of the word."

"Purest?" Torri's eyes narrowed. "You wouldn't have the slightest idea of what the word means. You spoil everything you touch—you—you murderer!" The expression she saw leap into his eyes as he took a step toward her was exactly that—one of murder. Torri screamed. From the bottom of her lungs, with everything she had, she screamed, hoping that someone, anyone would hear and come to her aid.

Damn! Jake gritted his teeth and clamped his hand over her mouth. She bit him twice and he tore a bandana from his pocket and tied it over her mouth, fending off her kicking and scratching as best he could. Then he dragged a blanket out from the back of the wagon and wrapped it around her. At least it helped cushion her furious blows, and kept her sharp nails from his face.

It was hard work, carrying her up the mountain trail, and he gasped as her foot wrenched free of the blanket and found its mark in the pit of his stomach. Thankfully, it didn't take him long to reach the cabin. Jake stumbled up the steps leading to the small porch and kicked the door open. Practically dumping her on the floor, he dusted off his jacket and stalked over to a huge, stone fireplace which dominated the small room.

"Take your clothes off," he ordered, kneeling down beside the hearth. "I'll start a fire."

"You're even worse than I thought," Torri said, her voice trembling. "I won't do it."

Jake looked up from the fire and watched as Torri struggled to stand. At that moment he felt the full impact of her beauty. Her eyes were blazing emerald, her heart-shaped face flushed, her bosom heaving against the snug restraint of her dark gray bodice. Wild and abandoned from the struggle up the mountain, her hair fell in tantalizing curls down her back.

He had fantasized, in the few rare moments he allowed himself the privilege of relaxing, of how it would be to slowly remove Miss Victoria's clothing and make slow and passionate love to her. He felt a quickening in his loins. Yes, there was nothing he would like better than to kiss Torri into reckless abandonment and join with her in a flight to physical ecstasy.

Gazing at her rigid stance, seeing the abject terror in her eyes, he knew it was not to be. She would not yield gracefully to the situation. If she were an innocent, she would fight for honor's sake—at least twentieth century honor as he understood it, love and all that rot—and if she was an agent she would fight to keep the power of the necklace for herself alone.

He roused himself, feeling dizzy. So it was getting worse. All the more reason to get things settled as quickly as possible. And it no longer mattered to him whether she was from K'mer or simply caught in circumstances beyond her control.

Abruptly Jake stood and crossed the room. He gazed down at the frightened woman, disturbed by the pain in her green eyes. He had seen enough pain to last him a lifetime. If he could have any wish it would be never again to cause another human being pain. He closed his eyes. Well, his retribution was coming, and very soon.

She's so small, he thought, as he lifted a dark curl from her shoulder, ignoring the way she flinched from his touch. She barely came up to his shoulder. He couldn't help but feel the actual trembling of her body as they stood, just inches apart. It was obvious she was terrified. His lips pressed tightly together. Or else she was a terrific actress. He wished he knew which. It would help him know how to handle this already precarious situation.

Acting on the natural instincts that had served him well for many years, Jake made a sudden decision. He would try to give Torri the benefit of the doubt—and see what happened. Not that he would let his guard down, even for an instant.

He released her curl. "Torri," he said, as he began to remove his gray coat, "I have my reasons for doing this. It is necessary."

"Necessary?"

At the horror in her eyes he felt a deep and unusual shame. He pushed the feeling away. Willing his fingers to obey, he began to unbutton his shirt. Her gaze followed his slow movements and he noticed she licked her lips once or twice. Out of fear, he wondered, or something else?

"Yes. Necessary. Besides, we're married, aren't we? That ought to take care of the moral issue if that's what's bothering you."

"There's a little more to it than that," she said haughtily.

Jake tossed the shirt aside and gently reached out to cup her face between his hands. She shivered at his touch, but didn't pull away. "There were a few little details I left out of our talk that night at Dr. Hamilton's," he said. "I'm sorry. This is the way it has to be, and like they say, you can make this easy, or you can make it hard."

Before Torri could speak, Jake lowered his lips to hers and kissed her. Suddenly she knew what that something she had occasionally glimpsed in his eyes really was—hunger, desperate and violent. She jerked her mouth away from his, but her gaze was frozen on his face, his sultry, heavy-lidded, seductive face. He leaned toward her again, his grip around her waist tightening.

No, Torri thought frantically. This cannot be happening! She twisted in his arms. He laughed and turned her around to face him.

Jake's lips descended again, but this time she sensed the hunger was under control. Gently he parted her lips and softened his kiss, caressing her mouth with a tenderness she had not expected. For a moment Torri felt paralyzed, as a delicious fire spread through her, licking at her skin in a warm caress, sending a tremor through her soul. She had her hands against his chest in an effort to keep him away from her, but it was useless. Jake crushed her against him, his lips moving to the hollow of her throat.

Somehow Torri's hands were no longer pushing him away but encircling his neck. As his mouth moved lower, she threw back her head to allow him to flick gently at her skin with his tongue and she shivered as new and foreign feelings flooded through her. She had never felt this way with Harry.

Harry's kisses had been either sloppy, or hard and brutal. Never had they stirred her as much as this murderer's.

Torri opened her eyes with a gasp. At her back she felt Jake's fingers deftly unhooking her dress. In moments it was puddled at her feet. He groaned deeply and made short work of the endless laces on her corset, then cast it quickly aside. The hoop and petticoats followed. Slowly, his gaze lingering on hers, he lowered his lips to the satin smooth skin curving above her low-cut, thin chemise.

As if she had been paralyzed, then suddenly released, Torri thrust his head away with her hands. He clutched her more tightly to him, and began lowering her to the blanket beneath them. His intent was all too apparent. Tears were spilling down her cheeks in earnest now, and Torri realized her only hope was to beg.

"Please," Torri whispered as he began unbuckling his belt. "Please, Jake, don't do this to me."

He stopped cold. Lowering himself beside her, he stroked her hair back from her face. Her eyes were clenched shut, as if braced for a blow. "Look at me," he ordered.

Torri opened her eyes. To her surprise, instead of the cold expression she had come to recognize and hate, she saw regret and self-loathing.

"Torri," he said, softly, moving one leg over hers, his chest pressing down against her. "I'm sorry. You don't know how sorry I am. Just let me make love to you. Don't fight me. I promise I'll be the most wonderful lover you've ever had."

"I've never had any!" she said through clenched teeth, her fear suddenly replaced with anger. "What conceit!" She spat the words out, struggling impotently against his weight. "You a wonderful lover? Don't make me laugh! You're a killer, an assassin—a murderer! All you know is hate. You know nothing of love. Now—let—me—go!"

"Sorry, kitten, but my whole world is depending on me."

"Depending on your doing *this?*" Her eyes were wide with disbelief. "You dare try to claim that this—this *rape* will help your mission?"

He winced but he didn't release her. "Yes. Listen to me."

Torri stilled as she saw something shift in his face. A tight, desperate look had replaced his determination. He was so near, his breath soft and warm on her lips. Torri shook herself and concentrated on the words he was saying. It would be so easy to yield to the fever she felt coursing through her veins. So easy. Fight, Torri, she cautioned herself. Remember—he's a liar.

"The jewels," Jake was saying, "always link with the wearer's lifeforce. Remember, I told you about it. It's a kind of symbiosis, a blending of mutual energies. This joining is what enables the wearer to travel through time. The problem is, only the *first* person who has the necklace becomes bonded to the jewels."

"But I wasn't the first," she protested, still paralyzed by the closeness of his body. "Someone long ago—"

He cut her off. "Once the owner of the jewels dies, or if he or she stops wearing the jewels for a long length of time, the jewels return to a state of readiness, until the next person touches them, allowing them to bond."

"You talk as though they're alive."

"In a sense, they are."

She struggled against him again, uselessly. The floor was hard and her back was beginning to ache. Torri sighed and for the moment, stopped fighting him. "So, what does this fascinating story have to do with me—with this?"

"I need your necklace."

"Why?"

"Because I lost mine, remember? I need your necklace in order to return to my own time eventually."

"I still don't understand any of this," Torri said in frustration. "I think the truth is I am at this moment sitting in a mental institution eating checkers and playing polo with my fruit salad—and I think you're in the chair next to me!"

He shook his head. "You aren't crazy. Don't you understand? I can't use your jewels to take me back to my own time, unless . . ."

Understanding dawned suddenly in her mind. "Unless you bond with me," she whispered.

Jake closed his eyes, the relief evident on his face. "Yes. You've heard the old saying, 'the two shall become as one?' "

"From the Bible," she murmured, "but it spoke of the beauty of a man and a woman joining together, not rape."

"It doesn't have to be rape," he said softly. "It can be an equal exchange of enjoyment—with a side benefit. If we make love, I become a part of you, your energy, your lifeforce. Then the jewels will accept me and I'll be able to travel back to my own time. I'll be able to help you get back to *your* time. Didn't you say there was something you wanted me to help you change—to fix? Do this and I swear, I'll help you." He gently drew his fingers down the side of her face.

Torri caught her breath. Grandfa. She had been thinking only of herself—her feelings of right and wrong—what about her grandfather? Could she refuse Jake? Did she dare? What would her grandfather advise if he were there? She knew without thinking.

"I will not barter with you," she hissed. "You already promised to help me on both counts!"

"Yes, I did, but things have changed." He ran one finger up the side of her jaw and Torri gritted her teeth against the trail of fire his touch left. "Listen to me, if you deny me my conjugal rights," his lips eased into a mocking smile, "then I'm afraid you must share in the responsibility of putting an innocent man to death."

"What?" Torri whispered.

"If I can get back to my own time, I have a plan that may be able to help my people without killing Colonel"—he stopped, then hurried on—"without killing a man in cold blood."

"Oh, now it's up to me to save this man from your gun!" Her voice was filled with disgust. "You'd say anything to get what you want. If you aren't going to rape me, then take me back to my own time—like you promised."

"No."

Torri felt the rage almost choking her with its intensity. "Liar," she hissed.

"You don't understand, Torri, because you don't know what I'm up against. I have to do this, with or without your cooperation. Can't you see that we have to set aside our own personal needs and do whatever is necessary to save the future? I want to make love to you, I want to be gentle and not hurt you," his tone changed, "but if I have to take you by force, I will, never doubt it."

"I don't," she said coldly, "and never doubt that it *will* come to that!"

"Dammit, Torri—"

"Wait! I have an idea. Take me back to my own time. Once I'm there, I won't wear the jewels, and after awhile, they'll be ready for someone else's lifeforce."

Jake shook his head. "I can't take the chance of—" he stopped and Torri knew instinctively he was hiding something from her. "I can't wait that long. I'm sorry." He leaned back and began removing his trousers.

"Wait a minute!" she said desperately. "Wait just a damn minute!"

Jake kept right on shedding his clothes and Torri quickly averted her eyes. "Believe it or not," she said, "I *am* concerned about the future, the way it is in your time—*if* what you say is true." She turned her gaze to his face, now only inches away from her own. "Unfortunately, I only have your word for it. If this is true, about the jewels, how do I know you aren't K'mer's agent? How do I know you're not the bad guy?" He began kissing the side of her neck and she shivered, fighting to remember what she'd been talking about. "D-did you really think I would just give in to you?"

Jake lifted his head and smiled. "Well, I did entertain the thought."

Torri's lips curved back at him, tight and challenging. "Tell me, Lieutenant, how does it feel to be a murderer and a rapist?"

Angrily Jake tightened his grip around her arms and moved suddenly against her, the heat of his body shocking through the thin barrier of cotton separating them.

"Why not, kitten?" he sneered. "Am I so repulsive? So disgusting? Is that why you start trembling every time I touch you? Is that why you look at me half the time like you're starving and I'm a slab of roast beef?"

Torri flushed and struggled against his grip. "You bastard! I'll never submit to you! If I tremble it's because it makes me sick to my stomach every time you touch me!"

"Damn you," Jake hissed. "Then have it your way. Fight me, kick me, claw me—I'm ten times stronger than you. Face it, Torri, you're just something to use, a pawn in the ultimate game I have to play."

Chapter Seven

Torri screamed, bringing her knee up savagely between his legs. Jake was momentarily startled by her assault, but blocked her attempt with one hard forearm while cutting off her cries by grinding his lips against hers. He wanted to punish her for her words, her protest, her complication of a very simple matter.

She fought him like a wild animal. Twisting and biting, she managed to bring one hand up to his face and ripped her nails against his skin. But in a matter of moments, he subdued her.

"I can do this all day you know," he said, "I'm twice your size and a bit stronger." He bent to possess her lips once again.

In spite of his words, Jake secretly marveled that a woman so small could have such strength. But he felt her weakening beneath him, tiring, and suddenly he stopped punishing her with his mouth. Suddenly, as she yielded to his superior strength, he lost himself in the mesmerizing sweetness of the kiss. She lay limp and still, beaten and weary. Jake felt another unfamiliar rush of shame, and crushed it. He had a job to do, dammit, no matter who got hurt.

He hadn't shaved since morning and his jawline was beginning to roughen with bristle. Belatedly he realized his beard had raked against her face, leaving it raw and pink.

"Sorry," he murmured against her lips, "I didn't mean to hurt you, Torri. I don't want to hurt you. I'll be gentle, I swear it." As he lowered his lips to the soft skin of her breast, he accidentally brushed the bristle against her throat. This time the bare touch of his rough face had a vastly different reaction. Her soft intake of breath and the corresponding rush of passion he experienced himself, gave him a sudden hope. "Just cooperate," he said softly, "enjoy this with me."

When she opened her eyes, he straddled her waist, then slowly tore her chemise all the way down to her waist, exposing the creamy whiteness of her skin. She squeezed her eyes shut as if she were about to face a firing squad, Jake thought in irritation.

He gently brushed the sides of his face against first one breast and then the other. He watched Torri bite her lower lip as if fighting to contain her moans of pleasure, but she continued to keep her eyes tightly closed. Afraid of losing the slight advantage he had gained, he moved back to her mouth, teasing her until she was moaning aloud. When he pulled away, her face was flushed, her breathing erratic.

"L-leave me alone," she whispered. "I-I hate you."

"I think I could change your mind, Mrs. Cameron" he chuckled, "and I think you know it too."

Jake frowned when she didn't answer his jibe. His frown deepened as he watched the subtle interplay of emotions across her silent face. Impatiently he leaned down to kiss her again. This time it was different. This time she had herself under some kind of rigid control. Challenged, he stopped being such a gentleman and turned up the heat. With one quick movement he tore the rest of her clothing away. The sight of her body very nearly sent him over the edge. She was like a miniature goddess, perfectly shaped, skin like alabaster, as beautiful as any statue—and just as cold.

An hour later, sweaty and writhing in frustration, Jake rolled away from her, feeling close to violence. No matter how he had teased and caressed her, kneading and massaging, kissing and tantalizing, she had lain there beneath him, silent, unresponsive. A statue indeed.

He threw one arm across his face as he realized that it wasn't going to work. She wasn't going to give an inch and if he was to join with her, he would have to take her by force.

"Dammit, Torri," he said harshly, "what can I do to convince you I'm telling the truth?"

"I don't know," she said, in a tight, angry voice, "but not this—not by raping me. It will only prove to me what I already suspect—that you are a vicious, cruel, ruthless man—someone just like this K'mer you speak of."

"Don't ever say that!" He was on his feet in seconds, glaring down at her.

Damn her! He wasn't telling her the truth about his need for the necklace, but damn her for suspecting as much! He had no intention of returning to his own time and pleading for Col. Reed's life. The truth was, if he didn't bond with a TDA soon he wouldn't be alive to carry out his mission. But if he told Torri that, she would certainly never yield to him.

Jake picked up her clothes and threw them at her, then grabbed his trousers from the floor and pulled them on, cursing roundly under his breath. To compare him with K'mer, scum of the universe, spawn of Satan—damn her to hell! It didn't matter that his world was in jeopardy—hell— that *her* world was in jeopardy.

She would have children some day, and her children's children would inherit the horror he lived in. He couldn't make her understand that it didn't matter what he wanted, what she wanted, all that mattered was his cause. All that mattered was doing what he had to do, and doing whatever it took to make it happen. If that meant lying, killing, raping . . . He stopped in his mental tirade and lifted his hand to his head. What had he become? Almost choking with shame, Jake pushed it away and got it under control. He had no choice. He turned to tell her so.

Torri sat on the floor, holding her torn chemise across her breasts, her face warm with the glow of the firelight. The flames danced in front of her, making shadows in the silence. Her bosom rose and fell as she watched him warily from beneath her lashes and Jake wanted to touch her all over again. The gentleness he felt toward her was something foreign, strange. It almost frightened him.

She was lovely, unlike any woman he'd ever known. Women in his century, in his organization, had little time for softness or caresses. Death was such a frequent companion in their line of work that only an idiot would get involved romantically. They had all lost so much that they lived behind emotional walls, constructed to keep the pain at bay. The thought of loving someone—and then losing that loved one—was something few were willing to chance. Certainly he never had.

Jake sighed and ran his hand through his hair again. She was looking up him, trying to act so cool, so tough, but he could see the panic in her eyes and the tension in her clasped hands.

I am a fool! he thought bitterly as he turned away. And a coward.

This wasn't his first attempt at killing Col. Reed. One time he'd appeared when his quarry was a five-year-old boy. He'd refused to kill him in that time period and again when he missed the mark and found Reed a fourteen-year-old. Other times he had missing his targeted time period completely and was now paying the consequences for his mistakes. His people thought him a coward for his compassionate refusal to kill Reed when he was a child. They had given him one last chance to prove them wrong. Torri Hamilton was his last—his only hope. And yet . . .

Jake leaned against one of the small windows and stared out through the dirty pane at the moon just starting to rise above the trees, feeling the certainty of his decision settle within him.

He would not rape her—at least for the time being. He

didn't relish having that on his conscience, along with all the rest of his crimes. At the thought of the melting sweetness he had just tasted and been denied, Jake drew a ragged breath, then tightened his jaw, and his resolve.

He would have to continue to fight his illness, and hope he could survive long enough to kill Col. Reed, Jeb Stuart's right-hand man. Of course, if his illness worsened and it appeared as though he wouldn't be able to finish his mission before he, himself, died, then he would have no choice. Torri Hamilton would become another sacrifice to the cause of the survival of the future.

His eyes narrowed as he watched her large, fear-filled eyes. Maybe he was a bigger fool than he'd thought. If she was K'mer's agent, of course she wouldn't let him join with her in order to use her device. Of course she would put up a fight and what better way to sucker him than to pretend to be a virgin.

He gritted his teeth. Yes, he was a fool, because even if she was an agent, he couldn't rape her. The Council was right. They should've sent someone else, someone tougher, someone smarter.

I may not be able to get smarter, he thought suddenly, *but I can get tougher.*

"All right," Jake said quietly. "Then let it be on your head."

"It's not my fault!" she cried.

"Fine!" he shouted back. "Have it your way! But understand this"—he whirled and stabbed one finger in her direction—"I am now convinced that you *are* K'mer's agent. This innocent virgin nonsense is simply a ruse to make me think otherwise. You don't want me to be able to use the necklace because that would ruin your plans, wouldn't it, dear wife? So be warned. From this moment on you are my prisoner, and I will treat you as such." He turned away and moved into a dark corner of the cabin.

"I am not K'mer's agent!" Torri cried, as the sound of

heavy objects being tossed aside echoed through the cabin. "Why won't you listen? I can't make love to a man I don't know, don't love and don't trust! And I don't believe what you say about my needing you to get home. I got here by myself and I can get back by myself!" She stuck her hand out, ignoring the fact that it was shaking. "Just give me my necklace and let me go!"

Jake reappeared suddenly out of the darkness and Torri recoiled. The firelight was reflected in his light-colored irises, giving him a satanic look.

Their gazes locked for a long moment. "Put on your dress," he commanded, then turned away from her again.

Trembling, Torri did as he said, leaving the back of her dress open when she couldn't reach the hooks. A log in the fire slipped and the flame shot brighter for a moment. Her hand flew to her throat as Jake moved back into the light with a rope in his hands.

"Turn around."

"No," she whispered.

Without a word, Jake spun her around, then encircled her wrists with his hand and began binding her wrists together. Once that was done, he shoved her to the floor and bound her ankles as well.

"Bastard!" she hissed.

Ignoring her sputtered curses he rose and strode to the door, slamming it hard behind him.

Time passed. Torri tried to calculate how long, but without a watch it wasn't easy. When she estimated he had been gone over thirty minutes, she felt a sudden terror. Surely he wouldn't leave her here, alone in the wilderness, tied up, at the mercy of wild animals, without food or water. Her heart began pounding and frantically she twisted her arms. Her movement only served to tighten the knot and she cried out from the pain as it cut into her wrists.

She searched the darkness for something, anything that could help her cut herself free. She could see nothing by the firelight except a few cans of beans Jake had tossed behind him, and a horse's harness. Then her gaze fell on the fire itself.

Perhaps, if she held her wrists against an ember in the fireplace . . .

Dragging herself close to the fire, Torri held her arms over one small burning log thrust slightly out of the fireplace at an odd angle. She gasped as the heat sent a searing pain up her arms. She could smell hair burning and it took all her strength of will to keep her wrists positioned over the flames. Perspiration began pouring off her forehead in rivulets. The pain was incredible but still she forced herself not to pull away from the flame.

She would be free! Jake Cameron would not do this to her! Suddenly smoke began pouring out from behind her, filling her lungs. Torri began to cough and felt a terrible pain shoot up her arms.

"Torri!"

Jake stood transfixed in the doorway, his arms full of saddlebags, a canteen, and blankets. He threw his burden to the floor and reached her side in two long strides. Jerking her roughly away from the fire, Jake felt, for the second time that night, like slapping her senseless. The pain in her eyes quickly changed his mind.

He bundled her into the blanket on the floor and smothered the flames that had been leaping up the back of her dress. He didn't know if he had been in time to keep her from being badly burned. Shaking uncontrollably, Torri was screaming and crying, frantically trying to get free of the rope cutting into her wrists and ankles.

"It's all right," he said quietly, "be still, Torri. I'll cut you free."

Still crying, she stopped thrashing and taking a knife from his pocket, Jake deftly cut the ropes binding her hands and feet. Torri cradled her arms across her stomach and curled into a fetal position as gut-wrenching sobs wracked her slim body.

Gently, Jake pulled her into his lap, and rocked her back and forth for a moment, making soothing sounds against her hair. When her sobs began to fade, he took one of her hands in his.

"Let me see," he said softly. He turned her arm over and blanched, not only at the sight of the bad burns, but at the red welts where the ropes had bitten into her fragile skin. He wrapped his arms around her, squeezing his eyes shut. "You stupid fool," he whispered, unsure if he was talking to her or to himself.

A ray of pink light struck Jake squarely in his left eye. Blearily, he opened both eyes to face the new day. A dark growth of beard now covered the lower half of his face and his mouth tasted of whiskey.

God, how he hurt. From the top of his head, down every nerve in his back, straight down the back of his legs to the bottom of his feet. He pushed thoughts of his own discomfort away.

He had treated Torri's arms as best he could, rubbing a salve he had made from a succulent plant that grew wild around the cabin on them and wrapping her burns in strips torn from her petticoat. The dress had been scorched, but the flames hadn't made it through the thick material to her legs.

She had wept for hours, as if the pain of the burn had evoked every memory of every pain she'd ever had; as though something had exploded somewhere deep inside of her, bursting the dam around her feelings and letting them pour freely for the first time in her life.

Jake had held her, allowing the ocean of emotion to roll over him, fighting the feelings stirring inside of him, feelings he had forgotten he possessed—compassion, fear, love. He had held her until at last, still sobbing brokenly, like a child, Torri slept from sheer exhaustion. After he had eased her onto a pallet on the floor, Jake had taken a bottle of whiskey out of his saddlebag and drunk most of it in an effort to numb his intense guilt.

What if he hadn't returned when he did? What if she had died? Staring down at the empty bottle beside him, squinting in the light of dawn, Jake jerked his head up, feeling new shock run through him. He wasn't concerned that her death would keep him from completing his mission—he was concerned for *her*. What was happening to him?

His gaze wandered to where Torri slept. He had placed her near enough to the fireplace to be warm, yet far enough away from any wayward embers. Again he felt an unfamiliar ache inside his chest. When she had cried as he held her against him, he had suddenly believed that she was not K'mer's agent. He had no concrete proof. He knew it was simply what he chose to believe. But this new twist in his thinking wasn't logical, wasn't smart. It went against every bit of training and experience he had, and after examining this strange phenomenon, combined with his startling realization, he could come to only one conclusion: He, K'meron, savior of the future, was falling in love with Torri Hamilton.

Jake leaned back against the wall of the cabin where he'd slept, sitting up, his rifle balanced across his knees. He was crazy, insane, even to entertain the thought of love. It had no place in his life. But she was so sweet, so young—damn, so young! He was old enough to be her—well her uncle, anyway. His mouth softened as he continued to watch her. She was quite a trooper, this woman. He wondered how many women caught in a similar situation, blasted back to the past, left at the mercy of an outlaw like him, would survive. Most would have fainted dead away, become hysterical or gone insane. Instead, Torri had fought back, the best way she knew how.

Fought against you, he reminded himself. Fought against a man she considers a murderer, a rapist, a villain. Even if I tried to win her over now, what good would it do? She wouldn't believe me. She'd think it was just another way of getting her into my bed so I can get the necklace.

Fool.

He rubbed one hand across the stubble on his face. What did he think, that after his mission was over he and Torri would retire to a quaint little cottage for two and live happily ever after? If he completed his mission, he would be dead. If he didn't, and managed to get back to the future, he couldn't take her with him. Once there, his life wouldn't be worth an ounce of dychronium. Besides, he could never take Torri into the terror of his time.

Not that she would go, he mused, lifting one hand to his aching head. Dammit! This is crazy! Pull yourself together, man.

A noise from across the room made him look up, instantly on his guard. Torri had rolled on her side, her back to the dying fire, her hair cascading like a midnight waterfall across her torn chemise. He had taken off her heavy dress again before treating her burns. Her face was flushed from sleep, her eyes still half-closed, but even in the dim light, he could see the pain mirrored there.

Jake felt his own burn beginning anew. It licked through his veins and surged through his senses. He wanted her. She hated him. He had ruined any chance he might have had and he had to accept that fact. He had humiliated and shamed her. With a sigh he wondered if the shame she felt could compare with his. He closed his eyes.

Torri stared through the morning light at the man slumped

against the wall. Last night he had stripped her bare, practically raped her. He had threatened her, frightened her, and thoroughly convinced her he was either a madman or evil itself. Then he had plucked her from the fire and saved her. He had gathered a succulent plant whose juice helped to ease the pain of her burns. Jake Cameron had held her, kindly, gently, as years of emotion, held down, stamped down, and denied, had erupted out of her soul. He hadn't tossed her aside and walked away. He had rocked her, murmuring anguished apologies in her ear, stroking her back in slow, rhythmic circles.

Something didn't fit. Either he was an evil killer and a very good actor—or he was a man caught up in something that was, as he said, bigger than both of them. Either he was a ruthless and cold murderer—or a sensitive man trying to camouflage his pain. His compassion had seemed so sincere. Was it real? Or had it all been a well-orchestrated ploy, a way to buy himself back into her good graces? Did he think that he could seduce her into doing what he wanted? She rubbed her eyes wearily as the confusion curled itself around her brain.

Her arms ached. They still felt as if they were on fire. As she turned slightly, the movement grated against her injury and she groaned aloud. Jake stirred on the other side of the room. Torri froze as she watched Jake pick something dark up off the floor, then walk unsteadily across the short distance to her side. She closed her eyes and pretended to be asleep but as he knelt down beside her, his boot leather creaking, she opened her eyes a mere slit, watching him cautiously.

"I know you're awake," he said softly. "Here."

He handed her the second day dress that Hannah had packed for her, a soft blue calico. She gave up her pretense of sleeping, thankfully clutching the garment to her chest. He had on his broad-brimmed hat and it was pulled down low over his eyes. Still, she could see his face was pale, haggard, his hand held to his head as though it throbbed with pain.

"Let's strike a bargain, shall we?" he offered, sounding as if he was forcing himself to say every word.

"What kind of bargain?"

"Let's forget about last night, pretend it never happened. I'll take you back to Dr. Hamilton's and he can take care of your burns. We'll concoct some plausible story." He glanced down at her. Today his gray eyes were darker, like a storm was brewing behind them.

Torri licked her lips, then froze as his gaze followed her gesture. "And?" she managed to say.

"And, I promise I won't touch you again—*if* I can possibly finish my mission without doing so. In return, you must promise me that you'll stay at Dr. Hamilton's, that you won't run away, and most importantly, that you won't talk to anyone outside of the Hamilton household."

"And the necklace?"

"The necklace stays with me."

"So I can't use it, right?" She raised her eyebrow. "Tell me, Lieutenant, what do I get out of this so-called bargain?"

"Well, for one thing, you don't get raped—hopefully." Jake closed his eyes and sighed. For the first time, Torri actually believed his hesitant response was real.

"Torri, listen to me. There's so much you don't understand about time travel. It isn't easy and the TDA isn't always accurate. You might try ten times before you hit the right century, much less the right year. And every time you travel, there's tremendous wear and tear on your body."

Torri frowned. His sincerity was reaching through her defenses in spite of her suspicions and her pain. "What do you mean?"

"I mean, you get tired." He pressed his lips grimly together. With his words, her attention was drawn to the dark circles under his eyes, the fatigue lines in his face. Jake did look weary, infinitely weary. She pushed aside her compassion, but continued to listen. "Every atom in your body is traumatized when you go through time. The scientists call it Molecular Dysfunction. It can—well, it can make you very sick."

"Is that happening to you?" she asked bluntly.

"No." He paused and looked away, then glanced back at her, one corner of his mouth slanted. "But of course, I'm the best. I'm an expert. I can usually get within a few months of my target time period."

His half-smile turned into an actual grin, and Torri realized with a jolt that he was younger than she'd first supposed. Nearer thirty than his mid-thirties.

That smile, one of the few open expressions she'd ever seen cross his face, had transformed Jake Cameron, in her mind, from a killer, into a man she could envision walking with on a beach in the moonlight. Easy, she cautioned herself. Remember what he tried to do to you last night.

That thought was a mistake, for with the memory Torri felt a flush creeping up her neck. How she had struggled not to give in to the delicious way he had tried to make her feel, and how desperately she had wanted to do exactly that. Strangely enough, she had not been embarrassed as they lay together naked, and the thought shocked her. It had seemed—heavens—it had seemed right. Right to lie with a man she scarcely knew.

What is the matter with you, Victoria Hamilton?

"Can't you do something about it," she asked, bringing her thoughts back to the present. "Take medicine or something?"

"Yes, in my own time." He looked away. "And as long as you wear your TDA, it gives you a certain amount of protection."

"But you don't have yours, and now neither do I!" Torri said, alarmed.

"You're in no immediate danger. It takes several trips to weaken your system to the point of illness. But that's what I'm trying to make you see." Jake shifted his glance to hers and the bleakness Torri saw mirrored there was frightening. "You are a totally inexperienced traveler. If you tried it alone, well, you might be lost forever, or eventually die from MD caused by too many trips through time. I couldn't have that on my conscience."

Jake stood, and Torri noticed the stiff way he moved from the crouching position. He's said that he hadn't been affected by this molecular disease, but was that just another lie? Was that the real reason he wanted to bond with her— or was he really going to try to get back to his own time and plead for this innocent man he'd been sent to kill? His last words suddenly broke through her confusion and she rose awkwardly, the pain in her arms causing her to restrain her anger.

"You couldn't have that on your *conscience?* You can say that after trying to rape me?!"

"I didn't try, Mrs. Cameron," he said, as he bent to gather up his tack, "if I had tried, I would have succeeded." The familiar mask slid quickly back into place as he straightened and glared down at her.

"Oh, thank you, Mr. Noble Southern Gentleman," she sneered back at him, holding her arms across her middle. "You graciously decided not to rape me, but instead you did the gentlemanly thing of tying me up and leaving me to burn to death—"

"I saved your life!" he interrupted savagely. "Who told you to stick yourself in the damned fireplace? And if you would just stop being so prudish and provincial, I could take you back to your own time in a matter of hours!"

"And now," she went on, as if he hadn't spoken, "you graciously decide that you're going to keep me here in the past, for my own good, of course! Excuse me, I can see I've been totally unfair in my estimation of you!" She snapped angrily. "Again I tell you, I will not barter my body for your help, Jake Cameron!"

Jake released his breath explosively. "Dammit, that's what you don't—or won't—understand! It's not a barter, it's just physics!" He stomped around the room, his hands thrust into his pockets as he talked. "If we make love I can take you home. Then I can get on with my mission. I cannot let you aimlessly wander through time."

"Of course not," she said sarcastically.

He stopped his pacing and shot her a fierce look, his bearded face harsh in the pale morning light.

"It comes down to this," he said, "either make up your mind to share my bed, or lady, you are likely to be stuck here— forever."

Torri felt her breath leave her as though he had slapped her. He wasn't going to back down on his story, not one whit. Moreover, he had the necklace, and now he was going to make sure she didn't get it. He was no hero, but exactly what she had thought from the beginning—a murdering opportunist.

"I hope you burn in hell," Torri said in a choked voice.

"I probably will!" he shouted. "Believe me, after this it would be an amusement park!" He turned away in disgust. "Get dressed." His voice softened slightly. "Be careful of you.

Chapter Eight

"Jake," Torri said, breaking the silence.

He turned. She had a handkerchief pressed to her nose in an effort to keep from breathing the dust churning up from the horses' hooves. They'd not spoken a word since he'd unceremoniously helped her into the wagon and headed back through the wilderness. He could tell she was hurting. He didn't care. At least, that was what he told himself.

Anger, deep and frightening, churned inside of him, and he knew why. He'd thought himself immune to feelings, to emotions, but he had somehow, in a weak moment, allowed this woman to get under his skin. The truth was, he cared too much, and that caring had interfered with his mission. He'd been too cowardly to take her by force, even though sparing her would mean his own failure and would leave his people at the mercy of K'mer. All because he was too weak to do what had to be done. A sudden rage rose up inside him at the unfairness of his situation.

Why did the Council have to be so implacable? So short-sighted? He had argued with them that there must be another way, an alternative to killing an innocent man. They had called him weak, cowardly, until he'd almost killed two of them and claimed the mission as his own. But why did they have to be so stubborn, so—so bloodthirsty? As far as he was concerned they were almost as bad as K'mer, or could be, with just a shove in the wrong direction.

He had voiced that opinion on several occasions and it hadn't been received too well by the others. That was when they began viewing him with suspicion, and the accusations and goadings had begun. Hot-headed, he had fallen for the ploy. Now he knew that the real reason they had insisted on this plan was simple: they wanted K'meron, son of K'mer, dead too, whether from extinguishing his lineage or from failing in his mission. But could he blame them? He was always suspect, being K'mer's son. How could they ever know if he was really on their side or his father's spy? If he had been in their position he'd have done the same thing.

He ruffled his hair and sighed. What had happened to his honor, his courage? Somehow this woman—this girl—was stealing them both away from him. He couldn't allow it. But how long had it been since he'd felt anything for anyone besides anger and hate?

His lips curved up bitterly. He didn't know. There was no way for him to measure real time anymore. He lived between time and space, where there was no true reality. A shadow, he slipped in and out of history, belonging nowhere, speeding frantically toward his own destruction.

"Jake," Torri repeated his name, more insistently this time.

"What do you want?" he snapped.

"What's a scout?"

"What are you talking about?"

"You told Dr. Hamilton that you were one of Jeb Stuart's men and you went on scouts. What's a scout?"

Torri watched him, gauging his reaction. Since they'd left the cabin he'd not spoken two words to her and the silence and the pain from her burns were driving her crazy. If he would talk to her at least it would help pass the time. The day had grown warm, but a cool breeze was blowing. He'd already shed his jacket and unbuttoned his shirt halfway down the front. At first she could hardly keep her eyes off the sight of his golden-tawny hair curling against his sweaty chest. Catching her gaze, he had slid her a knowing look. Since then she had kept her eyes firmly on the road ahead.

"A scout is when men wear Yankee uniforms and sneak behind enemy lines to get information on the Union's next movements. I'm due to go out next week."

Torri unconsciously lifted her hand to her lips. Jake glanced over at her.

"Worried, Mrs. Cameron?" he drawled sarcastically. He turned piercing gray eyes on her, and Torri watched them soften as his gaze moved to her lips.

Without thinking, she laid one hand on his arm and felt the muscles beneath her palm tighten. A thin bead of perspiration broke out above his lip and he shook her hand off, abruptly pulling a bandana from his trouser pocket and mopping it across his face. Torri pressed her hand to her chest as a trickle of perspiration made its way beneath the blue cotton.

She swallowed hard as Jake's gaze flickered to her movement. It wasn't that hot. No, it was pure, unadulterated unfulfilled passion, burning through both of them like a flame. He knew it. She knew it.

Jake tightened his grip on the reins and swore silently to himself as he watched Torri press her hand between her breasts. A small, damp spot appeared on the cloth and he had to look away before he threw the reins to the ground and took her into his arms. But he wouldn't do it. No, he Lt. Jake Cameron, *K'meron*, self-proclaimed *hero*—he laughed inwardly at the thought—had no intention of burning up in the fire. He knew himself well enough to realize that if he remained near Torri for long, he would throw his good intentions to the wind and make her worst fears come true.

What he had told her last night had been necessary to the fulfillment of his mission. But the noble reason of joining with her in order to protect his time and his people had not been uppermost in his mind as he touched her soft, supple flesh. No, the reasons had disappeared as he became consumed with an uncontrollable urge to become part of her, to be enfolded in her softness, to immerse himself in the sweetness of her innermost being.

He forced himself to focus on the rear ends of the horses pulling the wagon. Control. He was the master of control. Hadn't T'ria told him that again and again, her blue eyes cutting through him like a knife every time he turned down her invitations to what she called sex and he deemed perversion?

"Jake," Torri said, "isn't that awfully dangerous?"

"What?"

"For you to be a scout." He shot her a look. "I overheard you and the doctor," she said wryly. "I remember my history," she went on, "if you're caught behind Yankee lines while wearing a Confederate uniform, that's one thing, but as a rebel caught wearing Union blue, you'd be hanged, or shot immediately. No trial, no jury, just dead."

Jake's mouth tightened, then relaxed. "Yeah, well, we all have to go sometime. Besides, that's a soldier's life, fortune and glory, you know. To go out for the Glorious Cause with a bang, not a whimper." He snapped the reins and quickened the wagon's pace.

"Tell you what," he said flatly, "let's talk about something else, or better still, let's not talk."

"What's it like, being a soldier during the most horrible war America ever fought?" she asked, ignoring his request as he knew she would.

He didn't answer at first. He didn't want to tell her. Didn't want her to know the horror. She was an innocent and he wished, unreasonably, that she could stay, innocent and naive, untouched by the filth of man's inhumanity to man. He glanced over at her and saw her green eyes darken with concern. Maybe she needed to know. Maybe then she would understand a little better why he had to do what he had to do.

"It's like nothing you could imagine." His voice was no longer harsh, but tense, his words barely audible. "Before I came here, I studied the era, but it didn't prepare me for what I've experienced. A man in my company died a few days ago."

"Isn't that what happens in war?" Torri said archly.

He nodded. "But they had to amputate his leg—without anesthetic—the doctors had run out of medicine." His voice turned hoarse. "I had to hold him down." Torri shuddered and closed her eyes. "We had to send his belongings to his brother," he went on. He loosened his tight grip on the reins of the wagon. The horses slowed.

"How awful," she whispered.

"More than awful. His brother was in the Union Army and was with one of the units we had just engaged. He may have killed his own brother." Jake shook his head. "It reminds me so much of the way it is in my time. Afraid to trust anyone, even your own family."

"Who can't you trust, Jake?" Torri asked softly. "Who has hurt you so much?"

Jake looked at her, startled, and quickly willed his face to relax, to slide the mask back into place. "Me?" He shrugged. "No one close to me. You know the story. K'mer. He's responsible not only for my misery but that of uncounted millions."

Torri looked away. She looked tired, Jake thought. He rubbed one hand across his face and felt his own fatigue settle around him like a heavy coat slung across his shoulders. How much longer, he wondered, did he have?

"Have you been in many battles?" Torri asked abruptly.

"A few."

When he didn't offer more she nudged him with her elbow. "Well?"

"Well, what?"

"Well, tell me about it."

"How are your arms?"

"Don't change the subject. Please. I really want to know."

Jake pressed his lips together. "What's to tell?" he said, at last, his voice cold. "Men shoot at each other and sixteen-year-old kids get their heads blown off."

Torri stared down at her hands, then glanced up at him, and Jake was astonished at the look of gentleness he saw in her gaze.

"I knew it," she said quietly. "It can't be so easy for you to kill, Jake Cameron. Not if you feel that way about it."

"Don't kid yourself. It's my job and I'll do it."

"But you don't *want* to do it," she insisted.

"What do you know about it?" he snarled, pulling the wagon to a sudden stop and turning toward her. "What the hell do you know about me—or anything else? Maybe I *do* want to do it. Maybe this is how I get my kicks. Maybe I'm just a murderer, plain and simple like you keep telling me! Maybe I'm counting the moments until I can end another human being's life!" His voice had steadily risen until he was shouting.

Torri shrank away from him and the gentle glow quickly disappeared from her face. Jake felt inexplicably saddened as she turned away from him. "I'm sorry," she whispered.

Seconds ticked by, then Jake reached out to her. Why, he didn't know, but he reached out and brushed his fingers lightly against the side of her neck.

"No," he said sadly, "I am." She lifted hesitant eyes to meet his and the trace of a smile hovered around her lips. With one hand on the reins, he clucked to the horses and the wagon started off again.

Torri's confusion grew with every mile they covered. Jake had left his hand casually lying on the back of her neck, caressing the fine hair there; the electricity between them like a pulsating wave of pleasure. She did nothing to make him take his hand away and admitted to herself that she had never felt so secure in her life as in that single moment. As his fingers began a more direct caress that was pulling her toward him, Torri straightened suddenly and blurted out the first thing that came to mind.

"Do you have any friends?"

Jake's hand dropped away from her and he glared at her in perplexity. "What?"

"The men, in your company," she said hastily, "are they your friends?"

Jake laughed, the sound short and harsh. "It's hard to be friends with sixteen-year-old boys." He sobered. "Hell, Torri, they're all so young. I'll probably make captain in another month just because I'm one of the oldest men left in my company." He turned toward her, and Torri was amazed to see the sudden, stark pain mirrored there. "One boy who rides with me on scouts is fourteen years old. The oldest is twenty-one."

Shakily she drew in a deep breath, aware she was about to shatter the most vulnerable moment they'd ever had in the short time they'd known one another, but knowing she had no choice.

"And the man you're going to kill, Jake," she said, never allowing her gaze to waver from his pain-glazed eyes, "how old is he?"

Jake flinched as though she had struck him, and the slight softness around his lips tightened into their usual grim lines.

"I'm going to tell you this one last time," he said through gritted teeth, "and then I don't ever want to discuss it again. I don't want to hear about morality," he said, "or what you think is right or wrong, or what you think about me. I've got to do what's necessary to save my world—hell—it's your world too, did you ever think of that? Your great-great-grandchildren are probably alive in my time, Torri. What do you think is happening to them?"

"That isn't fair."

"Neither are you!" he exploded. "You come moaning to

me about morality and right and wrong but you yourself are unwilling to make any sacrifices for the sake of morality!"

Torri turned on him in fury. "Why, because I didn't believe that you only want to bond with me in order to go back to your own time and plead for a man's life? If that were true you would've done it to start with! You lied last night and you know it!"

"I told you the truth."

"You wouldn't know the truth if you woke up with it plastered across your face!"

"And you can't *handle* the truth, kitten."

They were nearing Dr. Hamilton's home, and Torri felt a sudden joy at the sight of the white frame house with the cheerful green shutters. There she could feel safe. Even if she was stuck here forever—she swallowed hard—there was at least one place where she felt wanted and safe.

Jake pulled the wagon to a stop and faced her, sliding one arm across the back of the wooden seat.

"Here's the truth: I need to get back to my own time to present reasons, to the Council I work for, as to why I think we can avoid killing the man I was sent to eliminate. Now, as I told you, I can't use your TDA without our joining, so my only alternative is to complete my original mission. If that man dies, it's your fault." His words were very matter-of-fact, his voice composed and calm, like a teacher explaining an addition problem to a not-too-bright student.

Torri jumped down from the wagon and tossed her hair back from her shoulders. She glared up at him, her hands on her hips. "Oh no, Jake Cameron, you aren't going to make this my fault or my mission. It isn't. And don't tell me that malarky again about needing to join with me. You're just hot for me and you know it!"

Gray eyes, like the ashes of a long dead fire, sprang suddenly to life, darkening to smoke. One minute Jake was in the wagon; the next he was beside her, his breath hot against her lips as he cursed her. He didn't touch her but Torri looked up at him fearfully. Gone was any trace of the vulnerable man she'd caught a glimpse of earlier. He glared down at her, his face fierce and foreboding. For a moment, Torri actually thought he was going to kill her on the spot, for he looked as though he'd like to crush the life out of her, slowly, bit by bit, with his own bare hands.

"You conceited brat," he said at last, after using every profane word Torri had ever heard and a few she hadn't. "Here I am, fighting for my friends, my country—the future of your precious United States—and you have the unmitigated gall to flatter yourself into thinking that I've concocted this story in order to have sex with you?"

He turned away from her in disgust. "Believe me, I'd rather make love to a log than you, Mrs. Cameron. I'm sure I could scarcely tell the difference, but at least with a log I wouldn't have to listen to the egotistical ravings of a stupid, stubborn child!" He turned away from her, his back rigid with anger.

Torri was too shocked even to answer.

"You're so worried about losing your precious virginity," he went on, "*if* you really are a virgin—well what about me? I'm going to lose—"

Jake stopped talking. He stood so still for so long that Torri almost went to him. Abruptly he whirled and climbed back into the wagon, his face grim and closed.

"Get in."

The thudding of Torri's heart was suddenly amplified with fear, but no longer fear of him. "What are you going to lose, Jake?" she asked, gazing up, at him, wondering why she wanted to kiss him, wanted to take him in her arms and comfort him. It was crazy. He was a man who needed no one, least of all her, except as he had said the night before, as a pawn in this ultimate game he played.

"Jake," she whispered, "what are you going to lose?"

He looked at her. His eyes were shuttered and closed, like an abandoned house, its inhabitants long dead. Torri shivered in the warm sunlight.

"Nothing. Not a thing. Shut the hell up and get in the wagon."

Torri obeyed, feeling numb and confused. The more she thought about it, the more Jake's words made sense. Why would he concoct this story simply to get her in his bed? Jake had the kind of looks that would send women into catatonic trances. He didn't need to rape any woman. And did she really believe she was such a hot number that he would do all this just because he wanted her body?

Suddenly she believed his story, and yet she didn't know what to do. She *was* a virgin, and what he was asking seemed like a very large sacrifice on her part indeed. But he had been on the verge of revealing that his sacrifice was going to be an even larger one. Yet, he was willing to make it for his people.

Sitting stiffly beside him on the wooden seat, she tried to reach him once more, feeling oddly desperate to break through and somehow touch him—touch the real Jake Cameron.

"If you kill him," she said at last, "something inside of you will die too."

He laughed softly, mockingly, and the sound sent a chill through the very marrow of Torri's soul.

"How true, kitten. How very true."

Chapter Nine

Dr. Hamilton treated Torri's burns and put her to bed. Shaking his gray head as he left the room, he motioned Jake to follow him down the stairs and led the way out to the wide veranda where the old man spun around and glared at him.

Jake pulled a cigar out of an inside pocket, bit off the end of the stogie and spat it out. Lighting the cigar, he tossed the match aside, sending a stream of pale blue smoke over the rail of the porch.

The moon was rising, sending a faint light to illuminate the two of them. Jake met the doctor's glare and watched the scowl deepen on the other man's face.

"Go ahead, Dr. Hamilton," he urged, leaning one shoulder against the porch railing and tipping his wide-brimmed, gray felt hat down over his eyes. "You've got something on your mind. Let's have it."

The doctor stopped his pacing and even in the darkness Jake could sense his animosity.

"I'd like to know what went on up there in that cabin." The words were spoken quietly but the accusation was unmistakable.

Jake chuckled. "Why, Dr. Hamilton, I'm surprised at you. Don't you know that's a private matter between husband and wife?"

"You know what I mean, young man. How did Torri obtain burns on her honeymoon?"

"We told you." Jake's voice was deceptively soft. "Torri tripped and fell into the fireplace when I was out watering the horses. She panicked and ran. Before I could reach her, she had been badly burned."

"And her wrists? Her ankles?" An ominous silence fell between them. "I'm not a fool, Lieutenant. I know rope burns when I see them. What possible reason could you have to tie Torri up? I want some answers!"

Jake flicked the ash off his cigar. "I'd advise you to stick to your own business, Doctor."

His hands clenched together behind his back, Dr. Hamilton paced away from him again. "That girl is my business! I have taken her into my household and placed her under my protection."

"She's under my protection now," Jake stated flatly. "She's my wife."

Dr. Hamilton shot him a disparaging look, then straightened his shoulders resolutely. "You realize, of course, that I have no alternative but to report this—this atrocity—to your commanding officer."

Moving easily away from the railing, Jake placed himself in front of the doctor. Looking down from his height of six foot two, he smiled.

"I don't think you want to do that, Doctor."

"You don't intimidate me! I'm not a helpless woman."

Jake took a slow drag from the cigar and blew the smoke into the shorter man's face. "If I remember correctly," he said, "it was at your insistence that my marriage to Torri Hamilton took place. Now, sir, she is my wife, to have, to hold, to love, to cherish, or to beat black and blue. Isn't that the charm of the Southern culture?"

"Certainly not! No gentleman would ever strike a woman!"

"I have a surprise for you, Doctor." He raised his eyebrow. "I'm not a gentleman. However, I would never purposely hurt Torri."

"You can stand there and say that!" the doctor sputtered.

"Yes, I can. Things are not always as they appear to be."

"I'm aware of that, sir. That's why I requested an explanation."

"I'm not an explaining kind of man. If you want details, you'll have to ask Torri. But let me make myself perfectly clear about one thing. If you go to Jeb Stuart—or to anyone—with this story, I will make you *and* Torri Hamilton sorry you ever set eyes on me."

Dr. Hamilton shook his head, his mouth a grim line. "I'm already sorry I ever set eyes on you, and I can assure you that Victoria feels the same way." He lifted his aristocratic chin which amused Jake. The old man had style, he'd give him that.

"You will leave this house and you will never return here again," Hamilton said solemnly. "Since I was so foolish as to insist that that sweet child marry a man such as yourself, your wife will stay here under my protection until I can have the marriage annulled."

Jake grinned. "A little late for that, I'm afraid."

The doctor paled slightly, but quickly recovered. "If I were a younger man I'd call you out, but as it is, I'll ask you again to leave."

Jake touched the brim of his hat and smiled. "Tell Torri I'll be back to get her later."

Anger filled the doctor's voice again. "You won't, sir! If you show your face here again, I'll have the sheriff on you, have no doubt about that."

"And have no doubt about this, Doctor." Jake's lazy intonations disappeared. "I *will* be back. But right now, I'm due at camp. Tell her I'll be gone for awhile—maybe a month." He turned to go, then stopped and looked back over his shoulder. "In spite of what you think of me, I do want Torri to be safe. That's the only reason I'm leaving her here."

"Safe!" Hamilton snorted. "A lot you care about her safety!"

Jake shrugged. "Well, don't worry, a lot of things can happen. Maybe you and Torri will both get lucky and I'll be killed in battle and that will be the end of it. However, if I make it, I'll be back to claim my bride. If you have the marriage annulled, you won't be hurting me, you'll be destroying her, for she will automatically become soiled goods—not to mention the scandal you'll stir up—and no decent man will have her."

Taking one last drag from the cigar, he threw it to the deck of the porch and deliberately ground it out beneath his boot heel, then headed down the steps from the porch and toward the stable where his horse was tied. Without looking back he knew Dr. Hamilton was standing on the porch, glaring after him. After a moment, the door slammed and Jake smiled grimly as he turned to tighten the girth on his saddle.

Poor old man, he thought. He wished he could put his mind at rest, but what could he have told him? The truth was almost as ugly as the picture the rope burns had apparently painted in the doctor's mind. No, better to let him think the worse of Jake Cameron, than to try and explain the truth. Torri would be safe here, for now, at least as safe as she could be in 1863.

He wished he could say goodbye.

Suddenly, he became fully aware of his own thoughts. Here he was, whining like a little kid over an old man's hurt feelings, and a woman too stupid to accept his help in return for giving up something that didn't matter in the vast scheme of things anyway. He must be getting soft, or else the Molecular Dysfunction was starting to affect his mind as well as his body.

He mounted the golden stallion he had left stabled at the

doctor's home during the honeymoon, and stared into the darkness. No longer were his thoughts crowded with Torri Hamilton. He had a job to do, and by damn, it was time to do it.

Torri opened her eyes. The warm, gentle morning breeze sent the crisp white curtains drifting lazily. Any moment Grandfa would bang noisily on her door and teasingly ask her if she intended to sleep the day away. Smiling, she shifted her gaze away from the sunlight streaming through the windows and realized, with a start that someone was sitting at the end of her bed.

Randolph Hamilton.

With a rush, as if awakening from a bad dream, Torri was aware that she was trapped again in circumstances she could not control. Fighting back the panic that swept over her, she tried to focus on the now familiar face of her great-great-great-grandfather. She was surprised to see deep pain in the depths of his blue eyes and watched as his expression changed to a pleasant greeting.

"Good morning," she whispered, wondering why she felt as though every inch of her body had been bruised or broken. "Where—where is Jake?"

"Gone, thank God," was the doctor's cryptic remark.

Torri glanced up at him sharply. "Gone?"

"Yes." He patted her hand. "Don't worry, he won't be coming back."

A cold chill danced down her spine. "Won't be coming back? What—what do you mean?"

Randolph Hamilton's harsh features darkened. "I told him to leave and not come back." He took both her hands in his. "Forgive me, my dear," he said softly, "I had no idea I was turning you over to such a cold, ruthless individual. We will have the marriage quietly annulled and—"

"What are you saying?" Her panic was back in full force. "You mustn't keep Jake away from me—you don't understand. I must stay with him, be near him at all times!"

"He left you here in my care. He doesn't want you with him, he said as much."

Torri turned away from the compassion in the old man's eyes. Could it be true? Since she hadn't cooperated, had Jake abandoned her? She shivered and drew the coverlet closer around her bare arms. Her nightgown's sleeves had been cut away, leaving easy access to the bandages still swathing her burns.

"Did he—did he leave any message?"

Dr. Hamilton glanced away from her and Torri had the distinct impression that he was struggling with his conscience.

"No," he said at last, "he just told me he was leaving you here and rode away."

He rose from the bed, patting her hand. "Now, you don't worry about anything, Victoria. I've taken you into my household and from this day forth you are my responsibility." He walked toward the door, then stopped and turned back. "And I promise you—you will never have to see Lt. Jake Cameron again."

Torri's protest died on her lips as the door shut firmly behind him. She closed her eyes, letting the anguish settle over her, accepting the truth for what it was.

Jake had abandoned her, and she was forever trapped in time.

Randolph frowned, his brows meeting ferociously above his eyes. His gentle murmuring to his old mare as she plodded up the road toward Richmond was done out of habit. Inside he was bubbling with blistering remarks he'd like to make to his young companion.

He glanced over at his passenger, trying to get a firm

enough grip on his anger to broach the subject hanging between them.

"It's not going to make any difference," he said at last, turning his gaze back to the rump of the horse. "Even if you find him at Jeb Stuart's headquarters, Jake Cameron is not going to allow you to stay there—and neither will Jeb Stuart, for that matter."

"You don't understand," Torri said shortly, blotting the perspiration from her face with a handkerchief.

"No, I don't understand," he admitted. "The man deserts you, not to mention the terrible things he did to you on your wedding night—"

"I do not want to discuss this again," Torri said, more sharply than she intended, and she bit her lip in self-reproach. Dr. Hamilton had been wonderful to her and she felt like an ungrateful wretch treating him the way she had during the past week. First she had tried to reason with him, lying, explaining that she loved Jake and had to be with him, that the doctor had misunderstood what had happened that awful night.

After that didn't work, she had grown angry, fearful that every minute that slipped by meant Jake—and the necklace—was slipping that much further away from her. Anger had finally given way to tears and near hysteria, and with that had come the doctor's grudging agreement to take her into Richmond to find Jake.

Randolph shook his head, taking note of Torri's lifted chin, her defiant green eyes. He could not for the life of him understand her reaction. He'd thought she would be glad for his intervention, that she would hate Cameron for his cruelty to her. Instead, she had been furious when he had refused to try to find the ruffian and bring him back to her.

Oh, he had given in—for a price. He'd agreed to take her to the city to find her husband on the condition that instead of chasing around battlefields with the man, she would wait for him in Richmond—providing of course that she found Jake Cameron at all. Randolph ran his hand over his lined face. In return for his help, Torri had offered to help him tend the wounded. He felt a little guilty about that.

She had informed him, rather coolly, that she had had a lot of experience with sick people, her grandfather in particular, and would be happy to help him. He couldn't bring himself to tell her that the kind of doctoring he did wasn't the kind that allowed for handholding and soothing brows. He shook away the thought. Time enough to prepare her for those horrors later.

He clucked to the mare, half wishing perhaps Jake Cameron's parting remark about dying in battle would prove to be an unknowing prophecy. He flushed with the thought. He was a healer. He wished no man dead. But he couldn't help hoping that the man would soon become just a memory, just an unpleasant part of Torri's past.

Richmond amazed Torri, and she felt the anger that had been her almost constant companion since Jake had abandoned her ebbing as Dr. Hamilton's wagon entered the bustling city. She had expected a sleepy little village, and instead, they had been immediately swept into a whirling mass of people and confusion.

Soldiers were everywhere, walking down the streets in stiff array, or drilling while bystanders watched.

Torri caught herself watching the soldiers, looking for a familiar set of broad shoulders, a head of shaggy, tawny hair, then chided herself.

Think he'll be sitting on a street corner, tied up with a bow, waiting for you? It was going to be harder to find one soldier than she had imagined. Still, camps had to keep records and she had no doubt that she would, eventually, find him, if he was still in Richmond.

But what if his company had been sent somewhere else—

or into battle? How would she ever find him? What if he had been killed? She shook the thought away. Jake Cameron was too mean, too stubborn to die.

In spite of her anger a half-smile lifted the corner of her mouth, then quickly disappeared. Had he really abandoned her, or had Dr. Hamilton misunderstood? The doctor's questions about their wedding night had left no doubt in Torri's mind that he had decided Jake was a monster. He seemed determined to keep them apart and was quietly pursuing the matter of having her marriage annulled.

Torri glanced at him. He was an old, lonely man, she thought. Would he deliberately mislead her about Jake in order to keep her in his home, allowing her to take the place of his beloved granddaughter?

He looked up at her and a warm rush of feeling swept over her. No, he wouldn't do that. After all, it was he who had taken care of her from the beginning, with his kindly thoughtfulness. No, Dr. Hamilton could be trusted. Unlike Jake.

After he had gone, fearing that she was stuck in 1863 forever, Torri had found herself sinking into a deep depression. Now, sitting in the bright sunlight, watching the people passing by, talking and laughing, she felt exhilarated.

She was living in 1863! She, of all the people in the world—excluding Jake—had the unique and unparalleled opportunity to observe and be a part of her own country's past. Instead of mooning around, worrying about Jake, she should take advantage of this whole crazy experience and *live*.

Though she prayed desperately, she had no control over Jake's actions. She couldn't make him come back. She couldn't make another time travel necklace appear. All she could do was try to find him. In the meantime, the only sane thing she could do was to try to adapt to the past. She must accept her situation, at least until she had a fighting chance to do something constructive to change it.

Resolutely, she turned her thoughts away from Jake and back to the sights around her. The doctor had gone to a lot of trouble to bring her here, and she knew he had done it because he was worried about her. Now she was ready to set his mind at ease and erase the worried look on his wrinkled face.

"This is wonderful," she said cheerfully. "Thank you so much for bringing me. I just know everything's going to turn out all right. Please forgive my tantrums and my rudeness to you lately."

The frustration etched into the old man's face eased a little. "It's all right, my dear. I don't profess to understand your devotion to this man, but I must respect your feelings."

"Why are there so many soldiers here?" she asked.

"Richmond is the center of the Confederacy—the capital, the training ground for the army, everything." He glanced around. "Everyone in this city has made some kind of sacrifice to help our Glorious Cause."

He pulled the wagon to a stop in front of the Richmond Hotel, a two-story building that looked as though it had seen better days. They checked their bags, examined their rooms which were plain but comfortable, then left to see more of the sights.

"So, where are we off to now?" she asked as the doctor helped her back into the wagon.

"I need to let the surgeon at the camp know I've arrived. It won't take long, then we'll go back to the hotel and have a nice, relaxing supper." He glanced at her. "You can wear your new dress tonight, all right, granddaughter?" His eyes twinkled and Torri smiled.

"Are you sure you want to pretend I'm your granddaughter while we're here?"

"Why not? Don't want to give the old hens more to talk about than they already have. I can't wait to escort you down to supper tonight. That green dress will knock the boys of Richmond for a loop!"

Torri's smile faltered. There was only one 'boy' she wished could see her in the new dress. She smoothed the soft calico material beneath her hand. Hannah had made several dresses for her journey to Richmond, most of them turned from old dresses left in Amelia Hamilton's wardrobe.

The one she had on now was a blue calico with tiny pink flowers and green leaves scattered across it. It was cut low in the front, exposing a goodly portion of her bosom.

She still hadn't adjusted to the deep decolletage that was accepted as Southern fashion. It was amazing that a society so uptight, so rigid in their conventions, would brook and even condone the sight of a woman's bare bosom!

While at Dr. Hamilton's, Torri never gave a thought to what she wore, but now in this bustling city, she became suddenly aware of how very threadbare the dress was, and how dingy the lace at the neckline. Never a fashion horse, she felt, nonetheless, a little embarrassed at her garb.

Thankfully, Hannah had managed one lovely dress out of some beautiful green material she had found in the bottom of an old trunk in the attic. Her sewing skills were excellent, but Torri wondered, with a little trepidation, if Hannah's homemade creation would stick out like a sore thumb in the formal dining hall of the Richmond Hotel.

Pulling her thoughts away from her meager wardrobe, she looked around. There were so many people, especially women, and as Torri gazed at them, walking together, talking, shopping, she became aware of a startling fact.

They were all just as shabbily dressed as she was. She noted that these women were neat and clean and held their heads high. In fact, it seemed almost as though they wore their remade clothing as a badge of honor.

Torri felt a quick flush of shame. These women were

fighting for their lives, had sacrificed husbands, lovers, sons. Fashion was the least of their worries. Torri thought of Christine and her bulging closet of Paris originals. Any one of her dresses would probably have fed a family of five in Richmond for a week. Solemnly, Torri vowed to be grateful for the clothing Hannah had provided.

The steady clip-clop of the horse's hooves blended into the city noises as the buggy made its way down the dusty street. It was warm, the air still and yet she felt more alive than she had in the weeks since Jake left.

Go ahead, admit it, she told herself. Why do you miss him? *How* could you possibly miss him?

I don't miss him, she argued back. I'm just afraid. If I can't find him, I'll never be able to get out of here.

"Hey, Doc, wait up!"

Torri turned to see a huge, beefy-faced soldier, wearing an outlandish costume, waving at them. He was standing across the street with a group of soldiers. He wore a regular gray jacket, but beneath it were huge, baggy red pants. Atop his head was what looked like a sultan's cap.

Torri stared at him, wondering if someone else had been trapped in time—someone from the Arabian Nights!

The man waved at his companions and then ambled toward them. Dr. Hamilton lifted the reins to move his buggy back into the street, but it was too late. The man blocked their way, leaning one arm across the front of the buggy, one dirty hand almost touching Torri's dress. She inched away and couldn't quite keep from shuddering as he leered at her, his fat lips slipping back to reveal yellowed, rotting teeth.

"Well, well, well, what have we here?"

"Get away from my wagon, Evans, I'm in a hurry," the doctor said.

"Sure, Doc, sure," he agreed, not moving from the spot.

"But I got a hurt place on my ankle; I thought you might take a look at it."

"I'll be over to your company in the morning. Now let me pass."

"Well, now, I don't think I can wait that long, Doc. Especially since you got such a pretty little nurse helping you today." The man laughed, the sound guttural and offensive. Torri hadn't led a sheltered life, but never before had she felt violated simply by another person's presence.

A part of her mind registered the strange fact that even Jake's assault hadn't made her feel the way this man did. Shrinking back against the seat of the buggy, she lifted her handkerchief to her nose as Evans leaned closer and his fetid whiskey-scented breath drifted into her face.

"How 'bout it, honey?" He leered at her, his smile widening. "How 'bout losing the old man so's you and me can play doctor by ourselves?"

Dr. Hamilton's face turned apolectic and he stood, buggy whip in hand. "You, sir, will remove yourself! How dare you accost my granddaughter in this fashion?"

The man guffawed loudly, then spit a stream of tobacco juice into the road. "Wail, just what fashion would you like me to accost her in, old man?"

Soldiers from across the street had watched the encounter and now, gathered behind the obnoxious man, roared with laughter.

Dr. Hamilton raised his whip above his head and Torri cried out as Evans suddenly thrust his big fist into the doctor's stomach, sending him flying off the buggy and sprawling into the street. In terror Torri faced the ugly, bulldog-like face, now only inches from her own. He grabbed her arm in his huge hand, and with the other squeezed her right breast.

"You are some piece of sugar candy," he whispered, pressing

his wet lips against her ear, "and I'm gonna lick you all over before I give you what you're wanting."

Torri shuddered. Suddenly all of her anger at Jake which she'd kept firmly tamped down, came bubbling to the surface. Here, again was another man trying to force himself on her. Well, she was tired of being a victim—and she wasn't going to be one any longer!

With one savage thrust, Torri brought her foot up between the man's legs. To her immense satisfaction, her aim was true. Her would-be attacker stumbled backward, howling as he grabbed his crotch and crashed to the ground. The men around him laughed drunkenly, then sobered as Evans stumbled to his feet and whirled on Torri, murder in his eyes.

Out of nowhere, a slim saber blade suddenly appeared beneath Evans's throat. The man froze, sliding his bulging eyes sideways toward the horse and rider beside him. Then he fled. Torri turned, thankful, and found herself staring up at a man in a gray uniform.

He wasn't handsome, but his face was arresting, provocative.

About thirty, she guessed, though he could have been younger. Square-jawed, his face was slightly full, and when he smiled broadly, as he was doing now, he had wonderful dimples. A thin scar traveled the length of his face on the right side, adding to his rakish air.

His hair was short and a deep, dark brown, rather curly and unruly, a little longer in the back. His brows were thick but they, as well as his clipped, bushy mustache, had a touch of auburn mixed with the dark hair. Torri felt herself melt as he turned his golden-brown eyes to her.

"I—I—" she stuttered, "that is, thank you so much," she finished lamely, feeling absolutely tongue-tied.

As his eyes locked onto hers, Torri felt the power of his gaze. A tingle of excitement shot through her as he swept his dark gray hat from his head. Leaning over his saddle pommel, he lifted her hand to his lips. His lips touched her fingers and she felt as though a jolt of electricity danced suddenly through her body.

Then she realized that Dr. Hamilton was struggling back into the buggy. Ashamed she hadn't immediately thought to help him, Torri turned, her concern for the old man uppermost in her mind.

"Are you all right, sir?" the man on the horse asked, his voice low, his slow Southern drawl sending delicious shivers through Torri. "I am Capt. Lucas Montgomery. I'm sorry this happened." He flashed a smile at Torri. "Although you certainly defended yourself well, miss."

"Captain," the doctor said hoarsely, obviously shaken, "we are in your debt. I am Dr. Randolph Hamilton. May I present my granddaughter, Miss Victoria Hamilton?"

"Enchanted," he said, giving her a look that told her, oh so subtly, just how enchanted he really was.

Torri felt absolutely giddy. She cast about in her mind for something to say—anything to keep him there a moment longer.

"Who was that awful man?" she asked.

His smile turned to an eloquent scowl. "Hiram Evans, a miserable cutthroat if there ever was one. He's a criminal, one of the few remaining New Orleans Zouaves."

"The what?"

"Guess you've never seen one before. Some idiots down in New Orleans went to the prisons and recruited criminals to come and fight for the South. They gave them their choice of serving out their sentences or joining up. Guess which they picked?" His brilliant smile reappeared, tinged with cynicism. "Now they can kill with the government's approval."

"That's the stupidest thing I ever heard of in my life," Torri said indignantly.

"Yes, indeed it is. But that's war for you. The only good thing about the situation is that most of them have either deserted or killed each other in drunken brawls, but there are still a few hanging around, always looking for trouble."

"Why don't they throw them out of the army?" Torri shuddered again at the thought of Evans's leering face.

"Well, Miss Hamilton, right now, I'm afraid the South needs every able-bodied man it can get—even if they are varmints like Hiram Evans. But now, let's not talk about such unpleasantries. How long will the two of you be staying in Richmond? I hope long enough for me to offer my services as an escort around our fair city?"

Torri smiled, feeling suddenly shy, and much younger than her twenty years. "Yes, we're stopping at the Richmond Hotel. Dr. Hamilton is here to help the army with their injured."

"Are you to be his nurse?" he asked, smiling down at her.

"Why, yes, yes I am."

The man leaned back in his saddle and sighed. "I'd keep that information to yourself, Miss Hamilton."

Torri looked at him, startled. "Why? What do you mean?"

He tipped the brim of his hat down and crossed his wrists over the saddle pommel, his brown eyes bright with humor. "Don't you know how much trouble we have with these lazy men reporting for sick call when there's nothing wrong with them? When they learn a beautiful woman is helping the doctor, why, there'll be an epidemic of plagues and diseases, the like of which Richmond has never seen!"

Torri's laughter pealed out merrily and Dr. Hamilton's pale face brightened.

"There, I knew there was a beautiful laugh behind that solemn, but lovely face," Montgomery said. "Thank you for sharing it." He tipped his hat and moved as if to lead his horse away.

"Excuse me, Captain," Dr. Hamilton said, "but would you

mind escorting us back to the hotel? I think perhaps Victoria would like to rest for awhile after this harrowing experience and I believe I would feel safer if you came along. I feel a little weak myself."

Torri turned and shot her "grandfather" an astonished glance. It was obvious that she was no longer shaken by the encounter, but for Randolph Hamilton to admit that he felt weak, must mean he had been more badly injured than he had let on. All at once she realized how much the older man had come to mean to her. She loved him—almost as much as she loved Grandfa. If anything happened to him she would feel as bereft as she had the day Nathaniel had been taken to the sanitarium.

Frowning she reached to take his hand, and saw Dr. Hamilton's stealthy wink. Torri suppressed a grin as she realized his true intent. He was up to no good of course, playing matchmaker to try to get her mind off Jake, but she loved him for trying. And did she really mind an excuse to linger a little longer in the captain's company?

"Yes, Grandfather," Torri agreed, "I think that's a good idea. I do feel absolutely exhausted." She turned back to the other man. "Would it be too much trouble, Captain?" she asked, no longer trying to avoid meeting his gaze.

His smile flashed again, transmitting to her his pleasure. "I would be delighted, Miss Hamilton, and afterwards, I wonder—" he broke off, rotating his hat around in his hands, his eyes lowered.

"Yes?" Torri prodded.

"No, I wouldn't want you to think me bold."

Inwardly, Torri rolled her eyes. Southern rules and etiquette! Would she ever get used to it? She smiled sweetly.

"I'm sure after your gallant rescue I would think no such thing," she assured him.

His smile widened and Torri wondered again at the thrill that surged through her. "Then would you do me the honor of having dinner with me this evening? And you, too, sir, of course," he said, addressing the doctor. "Excuse me, I should have asked you for permission. Forgive me."

Dr. Hamilton waved his hand in dismissal. "Forget that nonsense. Of course, we'd love to join you. It is the least we can do to thank you for your assistance."

Capt. Montgomery lifted two fingers to the side of his hat and brushed it in a light salute. "No thanks necessary, Doctor, just doing my job. But wait just a moment."

He dismounted and Torri had to bite her lower lip to hide the burst of adrenaline flooding through her as he moved to stand beside her. When he leaned across her to address the doctor, she had the craziest urge to kiss his cheek.

"Suppose I tie my horse to your wagon and drive you to the hotel?" he suggested to the older man. "Would I crowd you too much?"

Beaming, Dr. Hamilton assured him he would not. Torri spent the next miserable fifteen minutes wedged between the two men. Miserable because Capt. Montgomery's thigh was pressed tightly against hers, and his left arm, out of necessity, rested against her right breast. Miserable because his touch was causing terrifying signals to saturate her body, signals that were beginning to alarm her. By the time they reached the hotel, and he took her hand to help her out of the buggy, Torri almost swooned.

What was it about this man that made her feel such desire? It was as if she'd been slipped some potent aphrodisiac. Even with Jake she—quickly she cut off the thought. This had nothing to do with Jake. She was just attracted to a very good-looking man. No big deal. Happened all the time.

Taking a deep, steadying breath, she smiled up at the captain, aware her face felt hot, muttered a hasty goodbye and practically ran into the hotel. She thought she heard his deep-throated chuckle behind her and she felt her face flush even more.

What was wrong with her? First she had melted in Jake's arms when he was about to rape her and now, just because some attractive soldier rubbed his thigh against hers she was ready to throw herself at his feet. Or rather, into his bed.

Get a grip, she ordered herself. But later, when she was alone in her room resting, all she could think of was Capt. Lucas Montgomery's warm brown eyes, and the promise of seeing him again.

Chapter Ten

Lying on the clean, white hotel sheets, clad only in a thin chemise, Torri thought about Hannah's and old Henry's arrival that afternoon. Torri had been surprised, not only to see the housekeeper and the elderly servant, but by the mountain of goods stacked in their wagon.

When the doctor had told her of his plans to help the wounded in Richmond, she'd supposed he meant for a week or so. But from what Hannah had said, as she undressed Torri and resolutely told her she had to take a nap like a proper Southern lady, it seemed the doctor planned to stay in the city for several months.

The army had provided the doctor a small, but comfortable, house, vacated these last two years by Union sympathizers, and after Hannah had completed her duties as a lady's maid, she had hurried out of the hotel room and gone with Henry to prepare their temporary home.

Torri took a deep breath and stretched her arms above her head. It felt so wonderful to be rid of the tight corset for a while. The shades had been pulled against the mid-afternoon sun, and while she did feel slightly lazy and languid, sleep was the last thing on her mind.

She did not for the world understand her feelings. Today, when Capt. Montgomery had appeared, it was as though suddenly the sun had broken through the darkness. Torri tossed restlessly on the soft feather bed, her mind racing. And it wasn't just the captain's appearance that had unnerved her, but his touch. Just the slight brush of his lips against her hand, the pressure of his fingers on hers had almost sent her into a swoon.

She sat up in bed. What was wrong with her? Oh, she wasn't stupid—she knew that a chemical attraction between a man and a woman could be intense—her thoughts flew swiftly to Jake and she squelched them immediately—but this was different. His touch had affected her almost like—like a drug. Or was it just that she was ashamed to admit that she could have such wanton feelings for a man?

Torri flung her feet over the side of the bed, her heart pounding rapidly. What was happening to her? Here she was stuck in the past and instead of concerning herself with finding Jake, she was much more concerned over the impression she had made on an attractive man.

She covered her face with her hands. Damn Jake Cameron! she screamed silently. How could he do this to me? How could he just abandon me?

For a brief time, when Jake had taken care of her burns on their wedding night, Torri had seen a side of him that had belied his tough facade. She had been foolish enough to think, for a time, that perhaps he genuinely cared about her. Then he had left her, taking the necklace, knowing that without it, without his help, she would never get back home again.

Torri moved to the long window and raised the shade. She gazed down at the main thoroughfare, then watched as the sun slipped behind the distant horizon, into the hazy twilight. With a sigh, she turned away, resolutely squaring her slim shoulders.

A single tear made its way down her cheek. Silly, she chided herself as she brushed it away. Did you really think Jake was some kind of noble hero? Did you really think he'd come back for you and sweep you up onto his white charger and carry you back to the twentieth century?

Another tear slid unnoticed from the corner of her eye.

"Yes," she whispered aloud. "Yes, I did."

* * *

"Lieutenant!"

The urgent whisper pulled Jake's attention away from the two men standing only a few feet away. The thick brush above him made it difficult to turn his head without making noise, but he managed to accomplish the feat. His effort was wasted. Col. Brent Reed was no longer behind him, guarding his rear.

Immediately, his soldier's instincts came alive. It had taken some doing to get this close to these two giants of the Union Army. He had lain there for two days, had heard a great deal, and had returned this evening, hoping against hope that the men would follow their usual habit of walking beside the river, just before dusk, to discuss strategy and plans. From what he had understood, the night before, Gen. Joe Hooker was solidifying his plans for the next assault against the Confederacy.

Jake glanced back over his shoulder anxiously. Reed wouldn't disappear, wouldn't leave this all important mission unless something was desperately wrong. Still, Jake didn't move. He had to get this information at all costs. But when the muffled whisper came again, this time he dared not ignore it.

Carefully, noiselessly, he inched his way backward across the soft forest floor, hardly daring to breathe. The underbrush scraped against his face, leaving bloody trails in their wake. It was with relief he felt the resistance of the bushes give way to an open clearing.

Cautiously, he moved his body into a position that would allow him to see into the open space without being seen. What he saw sent him plunging out of the brush, a curse on his lips. Col. Brent Reed lay flat on his back, the body of a Union officer sprawled across him, weighing him down.

"Colonel—Brent—dammit, what happened?" he whispered fiercely, checking the Yankee's pulse and finding his wrist cold. He lifted the heavy soldier off the fallen man, then caught his breath sharply.

Protruding from Reed's chest was a knife. Jake paused for a moment, aware that if he removed the knife, a profusion of bleeding, that he might not be able to stop, would begin. However, he could see no practical way to leave the dagger in and somehow get Reed to safety.

Get Reed to safety.

Jake squeezed his eyes shut. All he had to do was walk away and it would all be over. Col. Brent Reed was forty years old, the last of the Reeds. He wasn't married, but he was engaged and would wed on April 14, 1864. He and his wife would head out to Texas and settle there, where they would raise three sons and two daughters, continuing the family line from which K'mer would eventually spring.

He opened his eyes and stared down at the knife embedded in Reed's chest. Just walk away and it will all be over, he told himself. This was why he had come back in time—to this pivotal point in time—because only now could he eliminate, once and for all, the ancestor whose descendants would give life to the future's worst and most dreadful tyrant: K'mer.

He drew in a deep breath. At least this way he would know he had not committed actual, cold-blooded murder. Torri would argue with that, he knew. She would say that murder is murder, and if he let Reed die, when he, Jake, could have helped him, he was just as guilty as if he had plunged the knife into the man with his own hand. He imagined her face when she found out. Never mind that he wouldn't be there to see it, he could see it now, the horror, the disgust, the hatred.

Quickly, before he could change his mind, Jake grasped the handle of the weapon and grunted as he managed to wrest the blade from his commanding officer's body. Blood gushed out of the jagged gash and Jake shrugged out of his jacket, then ripped off the sleeve of his own shirt, stuffing the none-too-clean cloth in to staunch the wound.

Reed was growing whiter by the moment and Jake worked faster. The blood stained the white cloth and dripped onto Jake's hands.

The man would bleed to death, if Jake didn't do something fast. He should've left the knife in, he realized belatedly. Tossing aside the useless cloth, he plunged his fingers into the wound, hoping he could find where the pulsing flow began. As Jake pressed carefully, the injured man groaned aloud.

"I'm done for, Jake," the man said. "Dear God, I kept you from hearing Hooker, didn't I?"

"Take it easy, Colonel." Jake concentrated and felt his fingers slip over a warm, throbbing surge of liquid. "I'm trying to stop the bleeding."

"I—I heard somebody coming up the trail and I slipped back to make sure we weren't discovered." He drew a ragged breath. "He must have already seen me—got the drop on me."

"Don't talk," Jake said, ripping off his other sleeve and stuffing it into the wound, pressing it against the pulsepoint he had located.

"Wait, Jake—look!"

Jake turned. Reed was pointing toward a leather satchel lying on the ground not too far from them. He turned anxiously. "A courier, Lieutenant," he said, lapsing back into more formal language. "Maybe we're in luck after all. Check the pack."

"Sorry, sir, I can't let go yet—you might bleed to death."

"Here, let me hold the cloth. We must know what's in that dispatch. If it's important, you'll have to leave me here and get back to headquarters with the information."

"If I leave you," Jake said quietly, "you'll die."

"If necessary." The older man glanced up at him, the lines in his normal pleasant face deep with pain. "You know as well as I do that we must put our duty first, even at the cost of our own lives."

Jake briefly let the pain flicker through his mind. Duty. Yes, he had to do his duty—but to whom? He jerked himself back to attention to find the colonel groping at the make-shift bandage.

Clenching his jaw with frustration, Jake allowed Reed to stanch his own wound, while he crawled the few feet to the satchel, always mindful that Union soldiers could come upon them at any moment and render his own moral dilemma a moot issue. His hand closed around the leather strap and he twitched it back to him, tucked it under his arm and moved back to Reed's side. There he opened the satchel and took out a sealed packet. It took only seconds to break it open and scan the few pages enclosed. His mouth tightened.

"What—what does it say?" Reed asked, his voice weak.

"Hooker is moving. They're heading for Chancellorsville."

"But Sedgewick has been massing his troops below Fredericksburg."

"A diversion probably, to throw Lee off the track." Jake glanced at the man whose face was now ashen. "We've got to get this information back to camp."

The man shook his head. "*You've* got to take it back. I'd just slow you down. Now, get going, and Godspeed."

Jake felt the struggle within him intensify. If he left Reed here, he would die, Jake himself would never exist, and the message would never reach Lee.

So? The rational part of his brain argued. This isn't your war. All that matters is stopping K'mer.

He turned to go, then stopped, his hand clenched around the smooth leather bag. But how did he know he wouldn't change history somehow if he didn't deliver the message? Or would it change history if he did?

Damn time travel to hell.

"Look, Colonel, I—" Jake stopped. Reed's eyes had slid shut. Quickly, he felt for a pulse. It was there, erratic and weak. Okay, K'meron, he said to himself. This is it. Make up your mind. What's it gonna be—your duty and honor as an agent of the underground in the year 2417—or your duty and honor as a Confederate officer in the year 1863?

A picture of Torri as he had seen her last, her hair unbound, curling past her shoulders, her green eyes snapping with indignation flashed across his mind. Suddenly, he knew he wasn't going to leave Reed to die, knew he was going to take the message to Lee. Not for any noble reasons, but for one simple, selfish one: he wanted to live.

Jake leaned his forehead against the palm of his hand. What was happening to him? He had entered this game with the full knowledge that his success would mean his own death. Now, just because he had met some woman, he was ready to turn coward and save himself at the expense of his own people. Now, because he had somehow gotten caught up in the emotional turmoil of the Civil War, of its people and its pain, he was putting the needs of Robert E. Lee before the needs of the future.

Cursing silently, Jake bent and lifted the still form of Brent Reed, pulling him awkwardly over his shoulder. He would take his commander back to camp. After that, whatever happened to Reed was in the hands of God—not Jake Cameron. He melted into the forest, bowed down with his load, heading south.

Torri stared into the mirror and admired the kelly green dress Hannah had just hooked up the back. It was lovely, even if the dark bodice was extremely low. She tugged at it but couldn't move it even a fraction of an inch.

"Hannah, are you sure this is appropriate for a dinner date?"

The black woman frowned at the unfamiliar phrase. "You don't like the dress, child? I did the best I could, 'course I know it ain't like them fancy seamstresses make, but—"

Torri's laughter interrupted her. "It's a beautiful dress! I didn't mean that at all, you dear, wonderful Hannah!" She pointed to the creamy white flesh above the silky material. "I'm just afraid there's a little more of me showing than I'm accustomed to."

The older woman chuckled. "Honey, what you got don't need to be kept under a bushel. Now, I'm gonna go help Dr. Randolph tie his tie—that Henry can't ever get it right."

Torri smiled as the heavy-set woman lumbered through the door connecting her room to Dr. Hamilton's. She could hear her scolding Henry and grinning, she turned back toward the looking glass. Carefully she rearranged a curl dipping across her forehead. Her long hair had been gathered up at the crown of her head and fell in long curls to her shoulders. She had to admit, she did look exquisite. Except for one thing. She leaned closer to the mirror.

If only she could do something about her face!

The lack of makeup hadn't bothered Torri before. On her wedding day she had had too much on her mind to worry about her appearance. She didn't know why she was now noticing her paleness without blush or lipstick, and although her lashes were naturally dark, they seemed so light without mascara. She wanted so much to look, well, beautiful tonight.

For Capt. Montgomery?

Torri shook her curls rebelliously at the thought, frowning at her image. She had prided herself during adolescence on not being one of those silly, mindless girls who fell in love with every good-looking boy who came along. As she got older, and in spite of her level-headedness, Grandfa had often worried that when she fell in love she would fall hard—and not necessarily for the right man.

When Harry had come along, wining and dining her, charming her with his dark good looks and smile, it seemed that Nathaniel's fears would be realized. Looking back, Torri couldn't believe she had been so foolish, so gullible, so stupid to fall for such a jerk.

As she pinched her cheeks to add a little color to them, she wondered if she wasn't being just as foolish now. What was she doing? Primping like a silly schoolgirl all because her skin had seemed to ignite when Capt. Montgomery touched her.

Her eyes gazed back at her from the mirror. No, perhaps she wasn't so foolish. Maybe she was just lonely. Tired and lonely and aching for someone to hold her in his arms—someone she could trust. Was Lucas Montgomery that man? Time would tell.

She smiled cynically at the apt cliché. Time had gotten her into this mess to start with. She shook away the thought. Just for tonight, she decided, she would forget about her troubles. Tonight she would push away her fears, her weariness, her thoughts of Jake, and try to have a pleasant evening with a pleasant gentleman.

Smiling, Torri tied a dark green ribbon around her curls, gave her coiffure one last pat and went to tell Dr. Hamilton she was ready.

Jake reached the army camp outside Richmond just before dark to find there was no one there who could help Col. Reed. The man was barely breathing, but at least the wound had finally clotted and the bleeding had stopped. Jake checked him over once again and sighed. The man had to have medical attention.

Turning over the dispatches to Lee's adjutant, Jake wolfed down a bowl of beans and wearily told the cook to find someone who knew where in hell a doctor could be found. After a few minutes, a man from his unit appeared and informed him there was a doctor at the Richmond Hotel. Taking a fresh horse from the corral, Jake threw himself into the saddle, and rode for Richmond.

* * *

"Well, this has been wonderful," Dr. Hamilton said in a satisfied voice as he pushed himself away from the white clothed table. "I can't remember the last time I enjoyed a meal so much."

Torri felt her heart sink a little. The meal had consisted of a very small piece of overdone chicken, a baked potato, corn and cornbread. Things must be bad indeed if the Richmond Hotel, known for its cuisine, was reduced to such fare. And it was just like her "grandfather" to treat the whole matter as a frivolous affair. Straightening her shoulders, Torri decided to join in the spirit of things.

She laughed aloud at his remark. "I'll remember to tell Hannah that later," she teased.

Dr. Hamilton rolled his eyes toward Capt. Montgomery who sat staring appreciatively at her. "Do you see what a poor, lone man in a household of women has to put up with, Captain?"

The now familiar smile split the man's face. "All I can say, Doctor, is that I envy you such an existence."

Dr. Hamilton smiled and looked away, trying to catch their waiter. As soon as he was distracted, Capt. Montgomery's brown eyes became suddenly hooded, his gaze sultry as he boldly gazed at her.

Torri blushed and looked down at her hands, feeling quite the demure Southern maid. After Jake's crudeness, it was a joy to experience real Southern chivalry.

Oh yeah? a small inner voice asked cynically. Are you sure it's not the fact that every time he even looks at you, the gold earbobs the doctor gave you start to melt?

Shut up, she told the voice sharply, turning her attention back to the two men. But it was true. Ever since she had descended the hotel stairs tonight on the doctor's arm and seen Capt. Montgomery standing there gazing up at her, his eyes like hot whiskey, and after he had kissed her hand and squeezed her palm, her heartbeat had quickened and her senses seemed to have gone crazy.

She had felt faint when the captain offered his arm to her. When she moved her hand to rest on top of his, their skin had connected with an almost electrical jolt. Somehow she had controlled herself and had even managed to eat most of her meal.

Now, Dr. Hamilton was standing, and roused from her thoughts, Torri frowned. They weren't leaving already, surely? Suddenly the thought of leaving Capt. Montgomery disturbed her greatly.

"I think I'll just excuse myself now," the doctor was saying, "and let you two young people enjoy dessert without me." He patted his vest-clad stomach contentedly.

"Oh, no, Grandfather," Torri protested, feeling both elated and vaguely fearful. "If you don't feel like staying—"

"Nonsense. I didn't say I didn't feel like staying. I really need to get out to the camp. I have several patients already whom I need to check on." He looked around at the crowded dining hall. "I believe you're well chaperoned, my dear."

"Thank you, sir," Capt. Montgomery said, rising and shaking the older man's hand. "I appreciate your trust."

Frustrated, she watched Dr. Hamilton make his way through the crowded room. Sometimes she found Southern customs a vast inconvenience. Now, if she was back in her own time, she and the captain would have enjoyed the entire meal alone, then gone dancing. Perhaps he would have invited her up to his apartment and perhaps she would have gone—perhaps not.

But in 1863, there would be no such choice. They would sit and sip their coffee, eat their cake, and chat for awhile. Then, true to Southern dictates, Capt. Montgomery would escort her up to her room and leave her politely at the door.

Torri sighed, feeling rather wanton at the direction her thoughts were taking.

"Tired?"

Capt. Montgomery's voice brought her back to the present and she smiled at him brightly.

"Tired? My, no, I feel as though I could stay up all night. I guess it must be the excitement of being in Richmond."

He leaned closer and Torri's heart beat slightly faster as he covered her hand with his own. "Do you really want dessert?"

Torri swallowed hard, unaware that her tongue darted nervously across her lips. He was rubbing his thumb back and forth across her wrist. "Wh-what do you mean?"

"Wouldn't you like some fresh air instead?" His smile sent her pulse into a paroxysm that felt like thunder against her throat.

"Yes," she whispered, "yes, Captain, I should like that very much."

"Please, call me Lucas," he whispered back. "After all, I did save you today, did I not?"

"But I've only known you—"

"Ah, the conventions. Yes, of course. As a well brought up young lady, you must adhere to them"—his eyes danced wickedly—"at least in public. Shall we step out onto the veranda where we may enjoy a private moment?"

Mesmerized, Torri allowed him to lead her through the crisp, white tables and out the double doors which led to a wooden platform at the back of the hotel. There were no lights, and the moon was just a sliver in the black night sky. Here and there she could make out large plants which had been placed around the platform to create a tropical feeling. No one else was around.

"I—I really should go upstairs," Torri said, feeling she should at least give lip service to the credos of the day.

"I quite agree," Lucas said softly. He turned her toward him, his arms around her waist. "Go up the front stairs. I'll sneak up the back and meet you in your room in a few minutes."

Torri's eyes widened in genuine shock. "I beg your pardon?"

His hands splayed across her back and he pressed her against his muscular body and Torri felt the torrent hit her as his lips came crashing down on hers. She moaned and the heat in her blood suddenly caught fire.

"Yes . . ." she whispered, her voice seeming very far away as she abandoned herself to the terrifying passion consuming her. "Yes . . ."

Jake burst into the lobby of the Richmond Hotel and headed straight for the desk.

"They told me there was a doctor here," he said to the clerk, his tone brusque and commanding. "Which room is he in?"

The man glanced up at him and raised one brow. "I beg your pardon. We are not in the habit of giving out room numbers to just anyone."

Jake's chin lifted as the man's gaze traveled over Jake's filthy clothes. He was exhausted. Every bone in his body ached to the marrow. The Molecular Dysfunction had been growing gradually worse and the strain of his patrol hadn't helped matters. He didn't have to look in a mirror to know he looked like hell and felt worse. And now this popinjay stood there looking down his nose like some kind of superior being.

A red rage clouded Jake's vision as he reached out and felt his hands close around the man's carefully pressed jacket. With one swift pull, Jake slung the desk clerk over the counter, then slammed him against the wall.

"There's a medical emergency, you twiddling, pompous ass!" he hissed. "I am a Confederate officer and if you don't tell me in the next two seconds where the doctor is, I'm going to shove your blathering tongue down your throat."

The clerk gulped, his mouth opening and closing several times before he managed to stutter his answer.

"R-room t-ten, sir, Dr. Hamilton is in room ten."

"Hamilton?" Jake released the man and he slid, gasping, to the floor.

Torri. He was going to see her. How long had it been? Jake wondered. A month? Perhaps more. He should have sent word to her, he knew. She had probably been frantic with worry, no doubt thinking she had been abandoned—which was basically the truth. Perhaps if she knew he had saved Reed's life by bringing him back to camp for medical attention, maybe, just maybe, she wouldn't hate him quite so intensely. And maybe she would agree to make love to him. There was nothing he wanted now more than the means to travel through time again and leave Col. Brent Reed in peace.

Impatiently he pulled his thoughts back to the present. Reed could be dying, even now. If he died, Torri would never believe he wasn't responsible. He had to get Dr. Hamilton and hightail it back to camp.

Taking the stairs two at a time, Jake rushed down the hallway, his glance grazing over the numbers on the doors as he hurried by. In a matter of minutes he was standing outside room number ten, and without bothering to knock, burst inside.

No one was in the small sitting room, but he could hear muffled voices coming from behind another closed door.

"Dr. Hamilton?" he said, knocking once before throwing the door wide. He stepped back, his mouth dropping open, disbelief racing through his mind.

Torri sat on the edge of a white iron bed, clad only in chemise and petticoats. Her long hair fell in uninhibited glory around her shoulders and down her back. Her face was lifted to that of a man with dark hair bending over her, a soldier, stripped down to his trousers. Jake held himself in check for the instant that the picture registered in his mind. Her face was flushed, her eyes hooded with desire, her lips parted to receive the man's embrace. When Jake heard her moans of entreaty, saw her small hands curl behind the man's neck, something inside him imploded.

A sudden rage coursed through his veins with pulsating power, and just as he had thrown aside the clerk downstairs with little effort, now he grabbed the soldier leaning over Torri, spun him around and sent his fist crashing into the startled man's face. Without giving him a chance to recover, Jake continued to pummel him, using the surprise of his attack to overpower the man and, strategically back him out of the room and toward the door.

He flung the man out, tossed his clothing after him, then locked the door and stormed back into the bedroom. Torri lay on the bed in such a provocative pose that Jake caught his breath. With an iron grip on his emotions, he pulled her into a sitting position and shook her savagely. She moaned, and throwing her arms around his neck, tried to kiss him. Jake threw her back down on the rumpled coverlet in disgust.

Somehow in that moment, a small sense of reason slipped through the fog of rage settling around his mind. Torri lay on the bed, practically writhing from side to side, her eyes closed, low moans rumbling from her throat. Her lover was gone, yet she seemed unaware of that fact. He suddenly realized that she was virtually incoherent.

Drunk? He leaned over to smell her breath and she caught him around the neck with her arms, dragging him down, crushing his lips against hers. She tasted like warm strawberries, but not like liquor. Jake pulled away from her, unable to think coherently himself while her soft lips were working their magic on his senses.

She wasn't drunk, but she was obviously not herself.

Drugged? Jake rose to his feet in fury, intent on running after the man he had so unceremoniously dumped outside the door. He stopped. The man was likely far away by now, and at the moment, Torri needed him more. If this was the kind of drug he thought it was, he knew exactly what to do. In fact, there was only one remedy for Torri's painful malady.

Strange, he thought, he hadn't known this kind of potent aphrodisiac had been available in the 1860s. Very strange.

Jake smiled grimly as he bent over and gathered Torri up into his arms. One thing was for certain, when she woke up tomorrow morning, Victoria Cameron was going to be madder than a wet hen. But by then, Jake would be gone—long gone.

Chapter Eleven

"Can you tell me where to find Lt. Cameron?"

The stiff young soldier standing outside a khaki-colored tent turned and stared at Torri for a full minute, his eyes round with astonishment. Torri smiled and, flustered, the young man drew himself back to attention.

"No, ma'am," he said sharply, "but I reckon he's down with the horses. Jeb's—that is—Gen. Stuart's boys is usually grooming their horses about this time o' day."

"Thank you."

Torri walked briskly through the hodge-podge of the Confederate Army's tents and huts, stepping over the worst of the mud, ignoring the open stares she drew.

She had awakened that morning with a blinding headache and filled with outrage. Although she had little recollection of what had occurred the night before, besides her dinner with Capt. Montgomery, there was one memory that was very clear. At first she'd thought she'd dreamed it, but when she found the pile of soaking wet garments in the ceramic bowl on the washstand, she knew her dream had been real.

Jake—how he had entered the picture she hadn't the faintest idea—had doused her with water, over and over again, until she was soaking wet. She had a vague recollection of him beginning to remove her chemise, but then she must have blacked out again. What had happened after that, she had no idea.

The next morning she had found a note slipped under the door from Dr. Hamilton, obviously from the night before, saying that a medical emergency at the camp would keep him away all night. He had appeared shortly after she found the note and had escorted her down to the hotel restaurant for breakfast. She had tried to eat, but could barely manage a mouthful. She was furious, not only at Jake's effrontery, but at the frustration of not being able to remember what had happened either before the water incident or afterward.

She had reviewed the evening again in her mind. She hadn't been drunk. She hadn't had anything to drink except a cup of weak tea at supper. It didn't make sense. As she pondered her confusion, a servant had appeared at their table and presented the doctor with a card. He had glanced at it then handed it to her with a smile.

Torri had taken it hesitantly and read, "Lucas Montgomery." On the back had been scrawled the message: "Will you attend a ball with me next Saturday night at Mrs. Sloan Merriwether's home?"

"The Merriwether ball," the doctor had said with a chuckle, "that's going to be the social event of the season."

"Yes. But I think I'd rather not go."

"Why not?" he had asked, his salt-and-pepper gray brows pressing together. "Not too fond of the captain?" She hadn't answered and he had shrugged. "Well, I'm not so sure I like him that much myself. I had just hoped—" his eyes had widened suddenly. "Did I do wrong to leave you alone with him last night, dear? He didn't try anything ungentlemanly, did he?"

Torri had smiled and assured her "grandfather" that Montgomery had done no such thing. In truth, she had no idea what the captain might have done. She knew she should have told Dr. Hamilton about her memory loss, but somehow she hadn't been able to tell him that Jake had reappeared in her life.

Instead, she had agreed with him about refusing the captain's offer and expressed her pleasure in having her "grandfather" for an escort. For some reason, the thought of Lucas Montgomery hadn't made her blood rush with passion. Instead, for some uncomprehensible reason, she had felt a terrible fear—almost a revulsion.

Changing the subject, she had asked the doctor if he would take her to the Confederate camp that morning while he made his first rounds. Dr. Hamilton's grin of approval had been all she needed to send a quick flush of shame through her. She wasn't going to the camp for any noble reasons. She had decided to find Jake and somehow, force him to return the necklace to her—and while she was at it, find out exactly what had happened the night before.

Now here she was, watching the mini-city of mud, tents, horses and men in amazement. Dr. Hamilton had refused to let her help him with the wounded until he gave the hospital area a thorough once-over and had given her permission to stroll around. She stared around at the milling people in confusion. How would she ever find Jake?

"May I help you, miss?"

Torri looked up from her thoughts into a pair of quiet blue eyes. The young man was about her age, with a pleasant, freckled face and a bright shock of red hair. He was thin, his complexion pasty. Compassion flooded Torri's soul as she saw he balanced himself on crutches, one trouser leg hanging empty. Biting her lower lip she looked away.

"No—yes—I mean—I'm looking for Lt. Jake Cameron."

"It's all right," he said tightly, "I'll leave."

Torri jerked her head back toward him. "I beg your pardon?"

"I know my leg sickens you—it does all the ladies."

Torri flushed. "Oh, of course it doesn't," she said quickly. "I just felt—"

"Pity?" His nice, pleasant face twisted into a cynical scowl. "Save it." At Torri's shocked look all the color drained from his face and he leaned toward her anxiously. "I beg your pardon, miss. I'm really not fit company for a lady, or anyone else these days. I'll take you to Lt. Cameron."

He started half-walking, half-hopping down the muddy path that ran between the tents and Torri followed.

How old could he be, she wondered. Nineteen? Twenty? And now doomed to live as a cripple the rest of his life. It wasn't right. It just wasn't right at all.

As they made their way through the maze of tents, the man glanced back at her from time to time, his gaze appreciative but shy. "I believe the lieutenant is currying his horse."

Torri grimaced. Did the whole camp keep tabs on when Jake brushed his stupid horse?

"By the way, I'm Cpl. Reynolds, David Reynolds." He smiled. "You aren't Lt. Cameron's sister by any chance?"

"No," she said with a smile, "just a friend."

"Yeah, I figured a man like him would have a woman—I beg your pardon again, miss. I swear army life has just worn away my manners plumb to—" he blushed. "Excuse me."

Torri laughed, feeling suddenly years older than this young man. He seemed like such a little boy. She immediately felt protective of him and her smile softened. "It's quite all right, Corporal. May I introduce myself? I'm Victoria Hamilton and my—my grandfather is Dr. Randolph Hamilton. We're here to help with the wounded."

A shadow passed over his face. "Lord knows they need all the help they can get. We're all afraid we're going to lose one of our best officers—Col. Reed."

"Oh?" Torri said, trying to keep her mind off her coming confrontation with Jake and concentrate on the man's words. "Is he badly wounded? Perhaps my grandfather can help him."

"I hope so. Yes, ma'am, he was wounded bad. As a matter of fact it was Lt. Cameron who brought him in late last night." Torri stopped walking, feeling her stomach tighten.

"They were on a scout," Reynolds was saying as he hobbled along, "and got attacked by a Yankee. Luckily, Col. Reed got the Yank, but not before the Yank got him.

"Miss Hamilton?" He turned, balancing on his crutches, his rusty brows knit together. "Are you all right?"

"What?" Torri shook herself mentally as the young man moved toward her. She waved aside his concern and mustered a smile as she walked toward him. "Oh, yes, yes of course. I just—I had to catch my breath."

"Sure," his chest swelled up slightly, "I can slow down a mite. I make pretty good time around here, in spite of these things."

"I'm sure you do," Torri said, hardly knowing what she was saying.

The corporal, encouraged, began telling her how he often made money just by betting he could outrun two-legged men. As they walked, Torri listened with half an ear, while her mind was running full tilt.

Jake had brought back a severely wounded officer. What was it he had said that time—something about the man he was going to kill being an officer. No—he had started to say that he had to kill a colonel—and then he had broken off before he said the name. Was this Col. Reed the man? Had he tried to kill him and then been discovered? Had he brought Reed back then, to cover his actions, pretending to save the man?

She felt dizzy at the paths her thoughts were taking and had to force herself to stop. Time enough for questions when she found Jake. This time, she would make him answer them.

"Anyway, that's what happened."

Torri refocused her attention to the young soldier, realizing with embarrassment she didn't have the slightest idea of what Cpl. Reynolds had been talking about. He didn't seem to notice, however, as he leaned heavily on his right crutch, and pointed with the other toward a long line of horses about twenty feet away. Several men were brushing them, others sat nearby in front of tents, drinking from tin cups.

"Here you are, Miss Hamilton," Reynolds said, "the elite of the rebel army—Jeb Stuart's pony boys." There was a slight sneer in his voice and Torri glanced up at him, puzzled. The expression seemed somehow out of character with his good-natured attitude. "I'll leave you here, miss," he said. Was there a wistful note in his voice as he turned to go? Torri's heart went out to him again.

"Thank you," she said softly. "Corporal?" He turned back. "Were you—did you ride?" she called after him, hesitantly.

The shadow covered his fair face once more. "Yeah," he said, "I used to ride. That's over." His freckles stood out starkly against his skin and Torri felt hot tears burn against her lashes. His face tensed, and he took a stumbling step backward. "I gotta go," he said brusquely. "It was nice to meet you, Miss Hamilton."

"Thank you, Corporal. Perhaps we'll run into each other again someday."

His somber face brightened slightly at her words, then he disappeared behind a tent.

Sighing, Torri approached the line of horses, craning her neck anxiously, as she looked for Jake. Almost immediately she spotted him, using a currycomb on the mane of a huge black horse. Suddenly shy, Torri circled around the horses, darting quickly behind a large tree, where she could watch but not be seen.

Torri's mouth dropped open. He had lost at least ten pounds since she'd last seen him. He was still bigger than most men, but she noticed his shirt no longer stretched tautly across his muscled back, but hung loose. Jake turned then, and she drew in her breath sharply. Deep shadows made dark crescents under his eyes, giving his face a sunken look. He glanced up and Torri bit her lower lip. His gray eyes, always filled with arrogance or ice, now mirrored a bleak despair . . . and death.

"Jake . . ." she whispered to herself. "What has happened

to you?" Resolutely, she stepped from behind the tree. She knew the moment he saw her, for the bleakness faded from his gaze to be replaced with a sharp, brief pleasure, only to fade into the familiar mask of stony disinterest.

"Jake," she ventured timidly, "are you all right?"

Jake had been expecting her—sure she would want some answers the morning after her experience—but when she appeared, suddenly from behind a tree, she caught him unprepared. He dropped the currycomb he held and as he bent to pick it up, quickly pulled the mask of disdain across his features. When he straightened he closed his eyes briefly, willing the sudden dizziness to pass. It was getting worse, no doubt about it, and his trek with Reed slung over his back, not to mention his fight the night before, hadn't done him any good.

He opened his eyes and met her worried ones. She looked beautiful. Even the worn-out brown dress she wore couldn't disguise her loveliness, and she was looking up at him with something like concern in her eyes—those big, innocent green eyes—as if nothing had happened. As if he hadn't caught her half-naked in another man's arms. He'd had time to think about the whole, tawdry scene and had decided she must have been drugged.

The question was, had she taken drugs for her own pleasure—he'd read a lot about drug-use in the twentieth century—or had she *been* drugged? First of all, he couldn't really imagine Torri using the vile stuff; secondly, it was highly improbable that she just happened to be carrying drugs when she accidently spun herself into the past. No, it was far more likely that she had been drugged by the man he'd seen bending over her bed, half-clothed.

Jake felt white-hot rage at the memory, but brought his emotions under control. He had learned the man's name: Capt. Lucas Montgomery. He didn't know him, but had heard of his reputation for courage under fire, as well as his less-than-gallant reputation for seducing young women. But would the captain really need to use drugs to gain his conquests? And where would he get such drugs? As far as Jake knew aphrodisiacs were virtually unknown in this time. Besides, from what he had heard in his discreet inquiries around the camp, Montgomery had women practically begging for his attention, so why would he feel the need to use drugs on his ladies? Strange. Very, very strange.

Abruptly Jake pulled his thoughts back to Torri. What had she asked? What was wrong with him? Didn't she know that ever since he'd met her his world, his life, his mission had been turned upside-down and inside out and on top of everything else that he was slowly dying because she wouldn't bond with him? He let his gaze roam over her petulant lips.

"Good morning, Mrs. Cameron," he said, turning away from her, pulling the metal comb through the beautiful horse's mane. "So good of you to come to call on your husband."

At his sarcastic tone, Torri tossed her long, dark hair back from her shoulders and lifted her chin.

"I asked you a question, Lieutenant," she said coldly. "Are you sick? Maybe the camp food doesn't agree with you."

"How about you?" he shot back at her. "How are you feeling this bright spring morning?" The picture of Torri in Montgomery's arms flashed across his mind again and he clenched his jaw, fighting for control. Get a grip, schoolboy, he sneered at himself.

"I'm perfectly fine," she answered primly.

"Yeah? Somehow I doubt that."

"I'm sure I don't know what you're talking about." He heard the anger in her voice fade slightly when he turned away and then felt her hand on the side of his face.

"What did you—"

He jerked away as though she had burned him. The Molecular Dysfunction was gaining on him. The bruises had started appearing only that very morning. He knew what that meant. Time was running out.

"What is the matter with you?" she said, suspiciously. "You look like you've been run over by a train."

He didn't answer, just stared at her, as Torri straightened her shoulders, looking ready to do battle.

"You know, you really belong in bed."

"Yes, my love, but in whose?" he sneered.

Torri petulantly stamped her foot. "Are you going to tell me what's wrong with you or not?"

He continued to stare at her, and for a long moment, toyed with the idea of telling her the truth. No. Not yet. He turned back to his horse, running his hand down its side.

"I had a bout of dysentery. It laid me low for awhile but I'm recovering." He bowed slightly in her direction. "I do thank you so much for your concern, Mrs. Cameron."

Another silence stretched between them. Torri moved to stand beside him and patted the black horse.

"Everyone in camp knew exactly where I could find you," she said. "Apparently they can set their watches by the currying of your horse."

He grunted noncommittally. What had she come for anyway? To gloat? To flaunt what had happened with Montgomery? He pressed his lips together. This was ridiculous. In his time people used sex like money. It was a commodity, nothing more. Why should he care if she gave it to every man in camp? The mental picture that evoked turned his face hot with anger, and he ducked down, pretending to check his horse's hoof.

Jake's indifference made Torri want to punch him, but that would only add to the bruises she could see on his pale face. It must have been some fight was all she could figure.

"What's her name?" she asked, indicating the horse, hat-ing herself for asking, wondering why she was trying so desperately to reach out to this stubborn, selfish man. It was obvious he was never going to help her get back to her own time, so why didn't she give up?

Because you care, a little voice said inside her mind, more than you're willing to admit, even to yourself.

"*His* name is Napoleon."

Torri frowned. "Why would you name such a beautiful horse after that ugly little man?"

Jake shrugged. "I liked him."

"Who?"

"Napoleon. Told great jokes."

"You—" Torri stopped in mid-sentence, her eyes widening. "You've met Napoleon?"

"I've met a lot of people," he said brusquely. "I told you, time travel isn't very accurate, Mrs. Cameron."

"Will you stop calling me that?" she hissed, glancing around.

"Why?" he asked, casually wiping away a bead of sweat from his forehead. "Afraid your boyfriend may find out he's making love to a married woman?"

"Boyfriend?" Torri stared at him confused. "What in the world are you talking about?"

"You know what I'm talking about—the soldier-boy you welcomed into your heart, and other places last night."

Torri's eyes narrowed and her voice was a hiss. "You *were* there last night!"

"Oh, so you admit it. That's refreshing. I had thought you might try to deny it, or say you didn't remember."

"Admit what?" she cried in frustration. "Deny what? That you poured a bucket of water over my head? That's all that I remember!"

"Sure it is. Listen, kitten," his voice was seductive and Torri jumped as he moved suddenly toward her. Sliding his hand around her waist, he pressed her against him until their lips were almost touching. "I've decided I don't want you to go out on any more dates."

Torri pushed her fists against his chest and tried to put some space between them, but he held her firmly.

"Oh, you've decided that have you? Well, you can go straight to—"

Her words were silenced as his lips descended on hers, and she felt the slow burn of his mouth ravaging hers, melting her fears, her anger, her defenses. When he finally lifted his head, she felt giddy, then his next words stung her back into fury.

"You weren't so anxious to tell me where to go last night, baby," he whispered against her hair. "Don't you remember how hot you were for me?" He laughed without humor. "Of course I got the distinct impression that any man would do."

Torri tried to pull away, but he held her more tightly. "Too bad I didn't arrive a little later. I bet you and soldier-boy would have put on quite a show. Maybe you could have charged admission. I hear some people like that sort of thing."

Torri jerked out of his arms and brought her hand sharply across his face. "How dare you!" she cried, feeling torn between tears and fury. "I don't know what you're talking about and I don't care. I'm sorry I ever came here!"

"I can beat that," he said softly, a red welt appearing where she had struck him. "I'm sorry I ever laid eyes on you."

"You can be rid of me easily, you know," she retorted, "all you have to do is give me my property."

"Not yet, kitten." He moved toward her again. "Not quite yet."

"Keep away from me," she said, backing away; then she stopped, unwilling to let him see how frightened she really was. Frantically she searched her mind for something that would convince him she meant business.

"I only came out here for the necklace," she said. "I've decided if you won't give it to me I'm going to tell Dr. Hamilton that you have it. I'll tell him you forced me to make up that story and that you were actually the robber all along. He cares about me. He'll believe me."

Jake sighed and folded his arms across his chest. "He might."

"Well?" she demanded after a few moments of heavy silence.

"Well, what?"

"Give me the necklace!"

Jake smiled, the gesture giving his handsome face a decidedly cruel twist. "No."

She stood, her fists clenched at her side. "I hate you."

"The feeling's mutual," he shot back.

"You're a cold-blooded, hard-hearted bastard!" she shouted.

"Right on all counts."

Torri felt like jumping up and down and screaming, but she held herself back, determined to be as rigidly composed as he.

"All right," she said, "don't give me the necklace—but tell me one thing."

"What's that, Mrs. Cameron?"

"If you're so tough—why did you bring that wounded man into camp last night? They say you saved his life."

"So?"

"So—wasn't he Col. Reed? Wasn't he the colonel you were supposed to murder?"

Jake reached out and jerked her back to him, pulling her between the horses.

"Keep your mouth shut!" he hissed. "You want to tell the whole camp?"

Torri tossed her head. "Maybe I do. Maybe I ought to shout it to the world so that the great Jeb Stuart would know that one of his men is an assassin. What happened, Jake?"

she taunted. "Did someone stop you before you could finish him off? Or did you decide to torture him by letting him die slowly?"

"Shut up!" He seized her by both arms, his fingers biting into her flesh.

Torri gazed up at him, terrified by his rage but unwilling to back down. His tawny hair made a bright halo around his head in the sunlight. For a moment, Torri held her breath, half hoping he would kiss her again.

Crazy, she berated herself. You are absolutely crazy.

Slowly, finger by finger, he released her arms from his grip.

"Get out of here, Torri," Jake said softly.

Torri took a deep breath. "No, not until you answer me."

He turned and began attacking his horse's coat with a brush. The beautiful black stallion tossed his head in protest and Jake patted him. "Sorry, ol' boy," he murmured and gentled his strokes.

Torri watched him, wondering irrationally what it would feel like if Jake used that loving caress on her skin. She shook the thought away. She had already felt Jake's touch, and had rejected it.

"How can you do it, Jake?"

"Do what?"

"Kill him. Kill a man in cold blood. I'd like to know what kind of man it takes to do something like that."

To her surprise, Jake didn't turn on her in a fury, but his hand stilled in its smooth rhythm across the horse's back.

"There are plenty of rotten officers around," he said quietly. "Plenty who don't care about their men, or their Cause, only themselves. Reed is one of the good guys and I wish to hell he wasn't. And I wish—" he broke off, shaking his head.

"Wish what?" Torri prodded.

He shrugged. "I've had quite a few close calls since I've

been here. Sometimes I wish a minie ball had stopped me long ago." Jake turned to her, his smile derisive. "You see, Mrs. Cameron, I'm a coward."

Torri felt a brief surge of hope at his words. "Why? Because you don't want to be a murderer?"

"No, because I've allowed my personal feelings to become involved in this mission. I can't any longer. I'm sorry, Torri. That's just the way it is."

"But Jake, listen—"

"No, you listen for a change." He gazed over the top of her head, as if he were looking across time, into his own world. "I've got people depending on me back there. People who will die if I don't do what I was sent to do."

"Then let someone else do it!" she cried fervently.

He shook his head, his gray eyes dark, stormy. "No. It's my job, my destiny." His lips came together in a hard, grim line. "Time is running out."

For the first time Torri saw desperation in Jake's eyes. She also saw shadows painted darkly across his skin, skin that was almost ashen. He looked half-dead. Only his eyes burned with life. Torri averted her gaze from his face.

Above the backs of the horses she could see the camp, men talking, working. She listened to the laughter drifting up from the tents. A bright Confederate flag snapped in the brisk spring breeze. It was true, then, what she had feared and suspected. Jake was ill—very ill.

"That's a funny thing for a time traveler to say," she said her voice trembling slightly, "'time is running out'."

"I don't have access to a TDA that carries my life pattern anymore, remember?" Torri winced at his bitter tone. "I've got to finish my mission, once and for all, before—"

"Jake," she whispered, "are you dying?"

"Lt. Cameron, the colonel wants to see you."

Torri turned to see David Reynolds leading a horse by the reins. He was using only one crutch.

Jake frowned. "I told you I'd take care of the major's horse, Corporal."

Reynolds shot him a resentful look. "And I told you, Lieutenant, sir, that I was still capable of performing some of the duties of a real man."

Torri's mouth dropped open at the man's open sarcasm to a superior officer and she glanced at Jake to see what his reaction would be. To her surprise she saw a flicker of compassion cross his face before he turned away.

"Fine," Jake said shortly. "You can finish currying these horses."

"That's what I used to do, sir," again the emphasis on the word sir was almost a sneer, "before you took me off that duty."

"Consider yourself back on duty, Corporal," Jake said. "I've got better things to do with my time."

"Meaning I don't."

Jake whirled, and Torri stepped hurriedly between the two men.

"What was that you said about someone wanting to see the lieutenant?" Torri asked diplomatically.

Reynolds clung to the gelding, his eyes lowered. "Yeah, Col. Reed wants to see him. The doctor told him he was too weak, but he insisted. He said there was something important he had to tell the man who saved his life."

The last was another sneering jibe and Torri wondered suddenly if Cpl. Reynolds knew Jake's plans. But no, that was impossible. She turned in time to see the blood drain from Jake's face.

"He wants to see me?"

"That's what he said."

"All right. Corporal, finish grooming the horses." He moved away from the man then stopped and turned back, facing him. "And if you ever speak to an officer in that disrespectful tone again, I promise you, I will personally see to it that you are arrested for insubordination."

Torri bit her lower lip as Jake stalked away and David Reynolds glared after him. "Don't worry," she said, "his bark is worse than his bite."

Reynolds turned on her, his face distorted with anger. "I don't need your pity, lady. Why don't you get out of here? Go back where you belong."

Torri felt as though she'd been struck, but that feeling quickly shifted into a sadness for the boy who had lost more than his leg. Without a word she turned and hurried after Jake.

"So," Torri said, catching up with him, trying to match the length of her strides to his long ones. "Col. Reed wants to see the man who saved his life."

"Shut up, Torri."

"Are you going to see him?"

"I guess I don't have much choice, do I?"

"Yes," she said. Jake turned to her and she gazed into his eyes, searching. "Never forget that there are always choices."

"Not for me, kitten," he said wearily, "there's only one. Now, please, go back to Richmond and remember what I said about going out with other men. It could be dangerous."

She shivered, though the Richmond sun was warm, its heat sending a trickle of perspiration down her neck.

"Are you threatening me?" she asked softly.

He arched his eyebrow and Torri thought she saw a flicker of amusement dart through his gray eyes. "Me? Threaten a sweet young Southern girl? You must be joking, Mrs. Cameron."

"You didn't answer my question, Jake," she said harshly, "are you or are you not sick with this Molecular Dysfunction thing?"

He smiled. "Worried about me? Never fear, darling, I've

still got what it takes to satisfy a woman of your, shall we say, unbridled passions?" Jake turned to walk away from her but she grabbed his arm.

"You keep talking like that," she said. "I want to know just what it is you're insinuating."

"What does it sound like?"

Torri searched his face and then stepped back from him. "Oh, I see. You're trying to say that you had your wicked way with me last night while I was—was indisposed."

"Is that what you were?"

"I don't know!"

Jake stared at her. "Are you telling me you don't remember last night?"

She lowered her eyes. "All I remember is having dinner with Dr. Hamilton and Capt. Montgomery. I was—very attracted to the captain, I admit." Jake snorted and Torri's gaze flew upward. "But that's all I remember, Jake, I swear. Please, tell me what happened."

Jake moved away from her and stopped. Then he slowly walked to a log near the horses and sat down, taking a handkerchief from his pocket and wiping his face.

"Jake—what in the world is wrong?" Torri asked, sinking down beside him.

"I'm fine, Mrs. Cameron. Don't trouble yourself."

Torri glared at him. "Fine, Lt. Cameron. Why I would bother worrying about you in the first place I can't imagine."

"Me either. Unless of course you were hot for me." His lips curved up as he repeated the words she had thrown at him so long ago on the way back from their honeymoon.

Her face flamed. It was true, she had been worried when she saw Jake's pale face. Why? Why did she care—other than the fact that he was her only ticket back home.

He reached over and pulled a lock of hair over her shoulder. "Is that it, kitten? Can't resist me after all?"

Torri jerked her head away, and stood, leaving several

strands of hair still clasped in his hand. "Are you going to tell me what happened last night or not?" she demanded.

Jake stood too, his gaze roaming over her flushed face, then lingering on her lips. Then he shrugged. "Not."

Cursing under her breath, Torri glared up at him impotently. "Just tell me if you—if Montgomery—damn you—Jake Cameron!" She turned and without a backward glance, ran back the way she had come.

As soon as she moved out of sight, Jake dropped back to the ground. He pulled off his gray jacket and tossed it aside. Drenched in sweat, he covered his face with his hands.

He was a fool. Last night he could've taken Torri and she would have never known. He could have joined with her physically and then used the TDA to heal himself of this dehibilitating illness. But he hadn't. Why? Because for some idiotic reason that he couldn't understand, he had fallen in love with her.

Now time had run out for him—and for Torri as well. Tonight he would kill a man, save his world, and abandon a woman to the cruel destiny of fate. He tried to smile but the gesture was too exhausting.

Col. Brent Reed had to die. And Torri . . . well, it looked as though she was doomed to wander through time forever, because Jake wouldn't be there to help her find her way back.

Chapter Twelve

Torri almost tripped before realizing that if she wanted to keep from breaking her neck, she'd better lift the long hemline of her dress over the rough stones and potholes of the Confederate camp's road.

She was trembling with fury by the time she arrived at the tent where she'd been directed to find Dr. Hamilton.

How dared Jake treat her this way? How dared he be unwilling to tell her what Montgomery had—or hadn't—done to her? She stopped, fighting for breath. Of course, as naive as she might be, she still had enough brains to know that if Montgomery—or Jake—had taken advantage of her there would have been physical evidence of their sexual encounter. All she'd noticed when the cold water shocked her back to consciousness was the fact that her skin seemed to be on fire. This had to be just another one of Jake's games, but the question remained: what had happened?

Pushing aside the thought, she brushed past the soldier standing guard outside the tent. Ignoring his shout of protest, she hurried inside, almost colliding with a tall, red-headed man whose hair reached to his shoulders. He wore a feather in his gray felt hat, a beautiful silk sash at his waist, a dark cape around his shoulders, and a dashing saber at his side.

Torri felt suddenly as though she teetered once again on the edge of that fine line of sanity, for the man standing in front of her was none other than the Confederate hero, Jeb Stuart.

She wasn't sure how she knew it, (perhaps she had seen his picture in a history book) but she knew without a doubt that this was Jake's commanding officer.

Stopping short, she gulped as she gazed up at him. The soldier from outside the tent had followed her in and made the mistake of grabbing her by the arm. Torri let out a squeal of surprise and protest, and reflexively jabbed the man with her elbow. The soldier yelped and suddenly a familiar, gravelly voice came grumbling out of the center of the tent where several men were huddled.

"See, here," Dr. Hamilton said brusquely, turning away from a man lying on a makeshift table, "I'm trying to do a very delicate bit of stitching here and I'd like to know what in tarnation—" he stopped as he saw Torri standing red-faced between Stuart and an astonished private, wincing, his hand on his ribs.

"I—I beg your pardon, G-grandfather," Torri said hesitantly. "I—I was looking for you. I was ready to leave camp."

"Leave?" Dr. Hamilton turned back to his patient. "Don't be silly, child, we've barely arrived. Now, come over here and help me."

"This is your granddaughter, Doctor?" Stuart said, his voice pleasant.

Torri glanced at him and realized that for all his grand title and reputation he was still just a young man in his twenties.

"How do you do, Miss Hamilton. My name is Stuart."

Torri stared at him, awed by the fact that she was actually meeting a historical hero, when she was jarred by a strident voice.

"Victoria!" Dr. Hamilton snapped. "I need you, child."

Quickly, Torri hurried to his side.

"Here," he said, "hold this needle."

Torri's eyes widened in horror as she looked down at the man on the table. There was a jagged hole in his chest and with every breath he took, it seemed more blood pumped into the already stained cloth pressed against the wound. The man's face was gray, as though his life's blood had already entirely seeped away.

She stepped away from the table. "Oh, Dr.—oh, Grandfather, I can't—I—"

Dr. Hamilton jerked his head up and gave her such an imploring, desperate look, that Torri's mouth snapped shut.

"If you don't, he's going to die," he said bluntly. "Last night I had the bleeding stopped, but somehow it's started again. I don't understand it. Today the wound seems much worse than it did yesterday."

Torri's heart went out to the old man, as he stood there, tired and frustrated.

"Unless someone can help me close this wound," he went on, "someone with smaller hands than I, Col. Reed isn't going to make it." He glanced up at her. "Do you understand?"

Torri's panic suddenly disappeared when she heard the injured man's name. Reed—so this was the man Jake had saved—or had he?

Why had the bleeding started again? And why did the wound seem worse than before? Had Jake's show of saving the colonel been a huge pretense? Had he brought Dr. Hamilton to the camp to help Reed, then somehow slipped back in later and reinjured the poor man?

Torri shook away the thought. No, she couldn't believe that of Jake, in spite of all he had done to her personally. If he was going to kill a man, he would kill him, not leave him to die a slow and torturous death. And there was no way of knowing if this was, indeed, the man Jake had been sent back to kill. Perhaps he just happened to be with Jake when he was shot. In that case, why wouldn't Jake bring him back to safety?

The man groaned and Torri bit her lip. She could rationalize all day long, but the truth of the matter was that just as she had known it was Jeb Stuart inside the tent, her intuition told her that this was the man Jake had been sent back in time to murder.

And the question remained: did she really know Jake Cameron at all?

"I'll help you, Grandfather," Torri whispered, and moved to take the needle from the old man's hand.

"Good girl. Now, just concentrate on what I tell you to do."

The tent flap was flung open suddenly and Torri turned to find herself staring into Jake's cold gray eyes. To his credit, his already pale face whitened even more at the sight of the man on the table, undergoing surgery.

"They told me the colonel wanted to see me," he said, his voice gravely soft.

Dr. Hamilton looked up sharply and glared at him. "Get this man out of here," he said. "I can't work with him in this tent."

Jeb Stuart glanced at Jake, his hand stroking his short goatee, his expression puzzled. Jake's face tightened into granite and without another word, he turned and stalked out of the tent.

Torri turned back to help the doctor, refusing to acknowledge the tears burning in her eyes.

Throwing herself across the iron bed in the house Hannah had worked hard to prepare, Torri felt wearier than she ever had in her life. The housekeeper had managed to move them from the hotel that afternoon while Torri and Dr. Hamilton had worked for seven hours in the makeshift hospital tent at the camp. A skirmish had broken out just across the Rappahanrock and suddenly the tent had been filled to overflowing with injured men crying out for water, for something to stop the pain.

Torri squeezed her eyes shut against the memory. If she didn't think about it, maybe she could pretend that all of it had been a bad dream. She hadn't really seen men clutching their bellies to keep their entrails inside. She hadn't really seen a man bleed to death from a bayonet wound.

The stench of death still clung to her blood-stained dress and exhausted, Torri dragged herself to her feet. The doctor was still at the camp. He had found Torri crying outside the tent and had instructed her to go home and tell Hannah to come back and help him.

The faint glow of the kerosene lamp on the table shed an eerie light across the room. The wallpaper had a pattern of roses between broader stripes. She couldn't tell what color they were in the dim light, and didn't care. Who could care about such things when only a few miles away men were dying—and nothing could be done for more than half who were brought in?

Tears streamed down Torri's cheeks as she peeled off her dress, the hem heavy with mud, the bodice stiff with sweat and blood. She felt ill, nauseous.

No, don't think about it anymore, she ordered herself. Just don't think at all.

She had stripped down to her chemise and pantaloons, and now she shed her last layer of clothing gratefully. Moving to the washstand, she found a pitcher full of tepid water and a small towel.

Dipping the towel into the water, Torri drew the dripping cloth to her throat and sighed as she felt at least a part of the dirt and horror of the day roll away from her. She scrubbed at her skin, her arms, her legs, until she felt almost raw from the rough strokes. Then, with a sigh, she dipped the towel into the water once again and squeezed, allowing the water to trickle over her chest, and between her breasts. It felt so deliciously cool. She dipped it into the water again, and raised it to her face. The coolness was quickly dispelled by a rush of hot, bitter tears.

Dear God, she prayed silently, please, *please* let me go home.

Jake shivered as he crouched beneath the tree outside the stone house. He had asked around and found that Dr. Hamilton and his granddaughter had moved from the hotel into temporary quarters. Beads of sweat formed across his forehead and he wiped them away with the back of his sleeve. His condition was worsening.

After his argument with Torri, and his brief attempt to see Col. Reed, he had managed to make it back to his tent where he had collapsed, then dozed fitfully, feverish, the rest of the afternoon. He had awakened at dark, shivering with chills.

As he had lain there in the darkness, remembering the shock of seeing his commanding officer on the operating table, feeling his own life ebb away, he had known he wasn't going to kill Brent Reed. Suddenly the lie he had told Torri didn't seem so preposterous. Perhaps he could convince the Council to spare Reed if he could give them a good enough reason. He could volunteer to find out the change K'mer had made that brought him to power, and go back and set history aright. Maybe it would work, or maybe they would kill him, but at least he wouldn't die with the blood of an innocent man on his hands.

When had his determination shifted, he wondered, as he shivered now outside the Hamilton's temporary home. When he met Torri? When he fell in love with her? When he had first heard her call him murderer in that scathing tone of voice? Or had it been when he and Brent Reed had sat beside a campfire while on scout and his superior had talked to him as if he were his equal? Maybe it was when Reed had invited Jake to his wedding, to be held next spring. Or maybe it was when he saw that knife sticking out of his friend's body and suddenly realized that he was, indeed, his friend as well as his commander.

"Damn," he whispered to the darkness. Even if he didn't kill Reed, the Council would send someone else back to do it, unless somehow he could convince them otherwise. But to do that, he had to be alive, and he had to have a TDA, which added up to Torri. He had come to tell her the truth and to ask for her cooperation. If she wouldn't give it, then he would die and Reed's chances with him. He would tell her that it was as simple as that.

Simple? Nothing had been simple since he first met Torri. She was so young, so very young. He'd never expected to fall in love at all, but particularly not with a woman like her. But would she even believe him now after being lied to so many times? She was so trusting—or had been in the beginning. He remembered the first time he ever saw her, lying helplessly in the tall grass after his bullet had struck her down.

His mind was wandering, as it had during the arduous trip to Dr. Hamilton's house. He'd ridden silently out of camp on Napoleon, almost falling from the saddle twice before he had even reached the outskirts of Richmond. The nausea and chills had struck him full force when he rode into the yard of the two-story house. He had half-fallen, half-climbed off his horse, thankful that he could trust Napoleon to graze nearby, untended, until he needed him.

Glancing up at the upper story windows, where he suspected Torri's room was, Jake tried to keep his mind from the spasms in his gut. Got to hang on. Got to finish this, once and for all.

Silently, he rose from his hiding place, forcing his thoughts to the task ahead of him. He had waited in the bushes until old Henry had turned out the lamps and the house had settled into darkness. He knew from his information that the doctor wouldn't likely return until long after midnight. The wounded were still pouring in. He, himself, had to report at dawn as the big battle he and Reed had gotten word to Lee about was coming at last.

Jake moved quickly to the window a few short yards away, and found he could hardly stand once he reached it. The world was spinning around him and he clutched the window sill, fighting for his equilibrium. Reaching into his jacket pocket, his fingers closed around the cold necklace. Only one person could bring warmth back to the jewels again. Only one person had the power to bring him back to life so he could save Brent Reed.

But if he were honest with himself, even if he succeeded in joining with her, and Torri's lifeforce restored his, though the jewels, he had no guarantee he could make it back to his own time alive. He wouldn't even try if it weren't for the small impediment of his honor. If it weren't for that, he'd convince Torri to stay in the past with him and together they would live out their lives, happy and content.

Honor. Jake smiled, even though the gesture made his face ache. Somehow, at sometime in the hours after he had seen Reed's chest laid open on an operating table, he knew he had, for the first time in his life, known a man of honor, and known what standard of honor he must now live by.

He gripped the sill more tightly. Much his father had thought of honor when he seized the power of the jewels for his own gain. Little thought K'mer had given honor when he killed his own brother and ordered a bounty placed on his rebellious son's head. Jake straightened, clenching both fists to still their trembling. He'd thought it his duty to undo what his father had done; to destroy K'mer by destroying his ancestor.

The fact that it would end his life as well had made no difference at the time. He was hell-bent on proving himself— and for what? To whom? A bunch of radical militants who, in their own way were little better than K'mer; who were just as bloodthirsty and ruthless when it came to getting what they wanted as the dictator they fought against had ever been.

Since he'd met Torri, for the first time in years he had taken notice of life, of the sweet smell of dawn and the musky odor of twilight. He had begun to hear birds singing again. Before, he had always been able to shut it all out, keeping himself fixed intently, single-mindedly upon his goal. After Torri came into his life, everything had changed. He had changed, and there was no going back.

Jake shook away the thought. He couldn't even think of the possibility of him and Torri together. If she did join with him, he would have to leave her and try to make it to his own time. He would not be able to take her back to her time first. He was too weak. This was the real center of the turmoil. He would have to leave Torri in the past.

If the Council would listen to him—and there were a few, older men and women that he thought might be willing— then he could return for her. But the odds were against them, all the way. Most likely the Council would condemn him on sight as a traitor and coward and kill him. Torri would be trapped in 1863 forever. He closed his eyes as a rush of emotions flooded over him and threatened to swallow him whole.

Cold, he thought. Find it. Find the cold, the ice, the stone. Think of Uncle 'Meros dying before your eyes. Think of the poverty. Think of the children eating refuse from the sidewalks while K'mer and his people grow fat. Think of one man with the power to change history, forever molding it to his own vicious will.

Jake opened his eyes. He had found the cold. The cold had found him. Shivering, he wrapped it around him like a shield, and stealthily rose to open the window above him.

The wood moved stiffly beneath his hand, but at last, with one quick shove, he managed to create an opening a foot wide. Once he would have found it a tight squeeze, but he had lost so much weight recently, it was easy to slip through. Inside, Jake found he was standing at the end of a hallway, near a flight of stairs. Mounting them stealthily, he found himself in another hallway where three doors opened off the narrow, dark corridor.

Soundlessly, he moved to the first door and cracked it open just enough to peek through. Inside was a bed and a dresser with a cracked mirror above it. Two pairs of men's shoes were lined up in front of an ancient wardrobe. Jake pulled the door shut. The doctor's room. Logic would dictate that he would put his granddaughter down the hall to give her more privacy.

Jake felt his heart skip a beat and paused, giving his fluctuating pulse a chance to settle down. The dizziness was beginning again and he had to take several deep, steadying breaths. If he didn't consummate his marriage tonight, he never would.

Curving his hand around the doorknob, Jake turned and pushed. Suddenly, the cold he had sought so fervently, the ice he had hidden in the depths of his heart, melted, dissolved, turned to steam as a new and totally unexpected fire swept through him, heating his blood.

Torri stood naked in the moonlight, her flesh glistening, faint drops of moisture painting a sensuous path between her breasts and down her legs. She turned with a gasp, her green eyes large and sad and luminous in the dim light. Her dark hair curled around her shoulders, and Jake envied the heavy locks their intimacy with her skin. His gaze traveled to her lips, dark and full. They were parted, as if braced for a blow, and she clasped the small cloth she held to her chest.

Torri saw Jake standing there, like a shadow or some unearthly creature who had ventured into her world. His eyes were feverish, the shadows beneath them even darker than before. Her heart began pounding and suddenly the agony of the day was replaced by something much sharper, much more painful.

"Jake," she whispered. The cloth fell to the floor as she opened her arms to him. "Oh, Jake."

He took a step toward her; then his legs wobbled. Torri caught him just as he recovered his balance. She guided him to the bed and he sagged down onto the mattress, turning on his side with a groan. Torri sat beside him, and pressed her hand against his forehead. His skin felt like dry, hot paper. How could she have been so selfish, so blind? He was dying, dying because she wouldn't help him. And she loved him. Gazing down at him lying there so helpless, so dear, she could finally admit it to herself. She loved Jake Cameron.

"Oh, Jake," she whispered, "you tried to tell me, but I wouldn't believe you." Cautiously, she began removing his clothing. Jake helped as much as he could but it was obvious that he was very weak. His jacket came off first and though he was still muscular, his biceps hard and firm she was alarmed at his leanness and the grayish cast of his skin.

Torri's heartbeat quickened. Col. Reed's face had taken on that grayish hue and Dr. Hamilton had said he was dying. Was Jake dying? She took off his shirt, rolling him onto his stomach. She drew in a quick breath. On his back were eight scars—round scars each as big as a fifty cent piece, aligned evenly across the smooth expanse of skin. Lightly she touched one of the scars with her fingertip. What could have caused such a strange wound?

Jake groaned again and she went to work on removing his boots, belt, and trousers. When she was done, she eased him onto his back and he reached out for her.

"Torri?" he murmured. "Torri, is that you?"

"Yes, Jake, I'm here."

"Torri—"

"Shhh," she cautioned, "it's all right, Jake. I'm here. Everything's all right."

His eyelids fluttered open. Incoherent silver-gray eyes stared up at her, then cleared, his awareness returning. He was shivering violently and Torri slipped beneath the covers, pressing her body against him. She flinched at the pain she saw mirrored in his eyes, wondering how much was physical and how much a result of his own, inner torture.

"Torri?" he rasped, lifting his hand to touch her face. "I'm sorry, so sorry . . . I didn't mean to hurt you."

Tears burned her eyes and Torri laid her head against his broad chest. "Oh, Jake," she said against the rough, golden hair curling there, "I know you didn't."

His arms slipped around her now, tightening at her back, drawing her more firmly against him, bare flesh touching bare flesh.

"Oh, kitten, kitten," he said softly, lowering his lips to caress the side of her neck, "you are so very young, so very innocent, so pure."

Torri's reticence shattered as she threw her arms around his neck. "I didn't know—I mean, I didn't believe you about the Molecular Dysfunction. But I do now. Oh, Jake, I don't want you to die." Her lips began to tremble and Jake stared down at her like a man too long without water. "Make love to me, Jake. Make love to me, but don't kill Col. Reed. Please, Jake."

Gently he brushed the back of his hand across the edge of her jaw, his gray eyes smoke-colored. "I won't," he said. Her mouth dropped open and he laughed, though the sound was grating, harsh.

"What are you saying?" Torri said, afraid to hope.

"I'm not going to kill him. I'm going to go back to my own time and find a way to convince the Council that what they want to do is wrong."

Torri leaned her face against his chest, tears burning down her cheeks, her arms wrapped around him. "I knew you wouldn't do it. I knew it."

"But because of my illness I have to go back as soon as I can," he said, stroking her hair with a still trembling hand. "That means, I can't take you home first, Torri."

Torri lifted her head, her chin even with his, their lips almost touching. "I understand," she whispered.

"I'll try to come back for you, but what if I can't?" Torri saw the agonized look in his eyes and it chilled her. "What if I can't ever make it back here again?"

"Then that's the chance we'll have to take," she said, her voice determined. He started to speak again and she covered his lips with her hand.

"Don't you know I'd do anything to keep you from having to do something that I know is completely against your own moral standards? You haven't fooled me one bit, Jake Cameron, now shut up. Don't talk. Don't think." She removed her hand from his mouth and gently stroked it down the side of his face. "Just love me, Jake. For this moment in time, make love to me as though I really were your wife."

Jake looked at her searchingly, then his lips mouthed the words, "You are."

Torri gave herself into his arms, the roughness of his battle-worn hands making hot contact with her skin. As he lowered his lips to hers, Torri felt the fire flow between them as it had the very first time they'd ever touched. Her mouth parted beneath his and the warmth of the union, the sweet surrender they shared, sent a shudder coursing through her.

Jake watched Torri abandon herself to him and could scarcely believe he had, at last, earned her trust.

Lost, he thought as he sank into her embrace. I am lost.

"Torri," he said hoarsely, opening his eyes and dragging his lips away from her, "I—"

"Hush." She brushed herself against his chest and Jake's hands tightened, caressing her back. "Please, don't talk." She gazed up at him and Jake felt himself dissolving into her emerald eyes. "I love you, Jake. For now, for here, forever."

Sudden wonder sprang up inside him, then a quick sense of loss. He took a deep, ragged breath. So this is love, he thought. This is love and life and peace and happiness and everything I ever wanted and everything I ever dreamed. He sighed. And everything I can never have.

Her lips were tracing a hot trail down the side of his neck and Jake groaned, crushing her to him, letting his own mouth reciprocate against the hollow of her throat. A warning rang out in his mind and with effort he dragged himself away from the warmth of her flesh.

"Torri," he whispered, as he forced himself to break the spell. She leaned against him, her eyes half-closed, her lips parted. Jake swallowed hard. "Torri, kitten, look at me."

Slowly, her eyes opened, but that only made it worse. He could see the love in her eyes shining like a beacon.

"Jake, please . . ."

"Listen to me. Will you listen?"

She nodded, rubbing her head against his shoulder like a cat, sending a new wave of fire through Jake's body.

"Dammit, Torri, listen to me!" he hissed through clenched teeth.

The dreamy look disappeared immediately from Torri's face. "Jake . . . what is it? What's wrong?"

"I'm sorry," he said, lowering his voice again, "I just—I have to be honest with you, Torri. I want you"—he drew in a long, shuddering breath—"more than anything in this universe—and not just because of the jewels. I want you, for yourself. But this is all there can be. There can be no tomorrows for us. Even if I make it back to get you and take you to your own time."

Torri smiled, and the gesture almost brought tears to Jake's eyes.

"Did I say I expected anything different?" she murmured.

"Don't love me, Torri," he said, gently brushing one finger down the side of her face. "Whatever you do, don't love me."

She started to speak again and he stopped her, his mouth hot against hers. When he broke away, he knew the fire inside him could not be quenched by anything other than their union.

"Don't love me," he said again, against her hair, his hands stroking her. "But let me love you, Torri. Let me love you while I still can."

Torri moved to meet his magical, feverish touch. Flame seemed to follow his fingers as he taught her, patiently, lovingly, how to ride the wild crest of the fire raging between them, consuming them, burning the imprint of love upon their flesh, until at last, with a cry, Torri threw her last fears, her final doubts about Jake Cameron, into the softness of the night.

Jake was somewhere between sleep and wakefulness, tossing in the confusion clouding his mind. He was back there, in K'mer's dungeon, waiting for his punishment. He had done the unthinkable and opposed his father. No, not his father—for the man had told him he was no one's father, but a god, to be worshipped. To oppose K'mer, was to ask for pain, or death.

Jake had not cried out, not even when they tied him down and placed the electrodes across his back in their most devastating pattern, not even when the pain began, creating indescribable torment. He had not cried out, not until he opened his eyes and found his uncle's dying body hanging a few feet away from him, his features mangled, his flesh torn.

Then the scream had rent him, sent him spiraling into a place so near the edge of insanity, that when he came back, crawling, trembling, horror-filled and hate-driven, the eighteen-year-old boy—Jaco'K'mer—had disappeared. In his place was a man—K'meron—his name boldly declaring his denial of K'mer. There, in the blackness, in the cold, he had vowed that someday, somehow, he would kill the bastard who was no longer his father.

Cold. The cold wrapped itself around him again and he shuddered. He couldn't die—not yet. He had to finish his mission. No matter what. No matter what he had to . . . Jake felt himself slipping away, back to oblivion, when a warmth, slight and gentle, eked down through the layers of ice and touched his mind.

Slowly, he felt himself being lifted up through the lethargy, the stillness, to an awareness of himself as a living being, once again.

He opened his eyes.

The room was small and cold, but the bed was warm, so very warm. His gaze flickered to the woman curled beside him.

Torri.

She was naked, and in the back of his mind he remembered seeing her, shrouded in lamplight, her body glowing like a banked fire. Had that been real, or a dream? Real, perhaps, since he was lying beside her, his own body unclothed. He gazed down at her, wishing for memories that would confirm what he hoped was true. Had they—made love?

Her black hair tumbled in disarray across her slender back and her dark eyelashes lay in crescents against her flushed cheeks. Did she look like a woman who had had mad, passionate love made to her—or like a woman who had been forced against her will?

Surely the latter wasn't true, or Torri wouldn't still be here, lying beside him. He would be facing Dr. Hamilton's shotgun. Jake ran one hand lightly up her arm and she shifted in her sleep. She was pressed so tightly against him, her velvety arms wrapped around his waist, that he feared he was crushing her, and he leaned away. His gaze roamed over her lovely body and suddenly his memory returned in full force. They had joined. Together they had soared to the stars, sealing their love in the age-old way.

Desire coursed through him and he wanted desperately to take her in his arms and make love to her once again, but he closed his eyes, fighting the temptation. It would be better this way, better to leave before she awakened. Carefully, he slid out of the bed and found his jacket where Torri had tossed it on the floor. Reaching in the pocket he took out the necklace—her necklace, and slipped it around his neck.

The jewels seemed to instantly leap to life and with a sigh of relief, Jake felt the warm glow spread through his body, his limbs, his mind. He pulled on the rest of his clothes and made his way silently to the long window at the end of the room. The moon shed a dim light across the night, but its light was overshadowed by that of a fast-approaching dawn. From his vantage point he could see the doctor's wagon. The old man must have unhitched it himself and left it there, near the front porch, then retired without wanting to disturb his 'granddaughter'.

Lucky for me, Jake thought ruefully.

"Jake . . ."

He turned. Torri sat up in bed, clutching the quilt around her neck, hiding her nakedness. Her eyes were large and Jake felt his pulsebeat quicken as he gazed back at her, remembering her warm body pressed to his.

"Are—are you all right?" she whispered, then her gaze fell on the necklace around his neck.

"I am now," he said. He moved toward her and sat down beside her on the bed. "You could've let me die, Torri." Firmly he drew her toward him, and with a soft cry, Torri let the quilt slip out of her hand. Jake ran one finger across her lips, down to her collarbone. Torri brushed her own hand against the rough bristle growing on his jaw.

"No," she said quietly, "I couldn't."

She looked away, and Jake wished he could read her mind.

He'd never had anyone care about him—really care—not since his mother had died when he was ten.

"Why not?" he asked, hoping she would say again that she loved him. Or had he dreamed that part of their romantic liaison?

"I guess," she said, lifting her chin, a little of her old obstinance coming back with the gesture, "that I've just gotten used to you, Jake Cameron."

One corner of his mouth lifted. "Don't hate me anymore?"

She looked away. "I don't think I ever did, not really."

Jake slid one hand up her back and felt a small, singular triumph as she shivered delicately. He pulled her to him but she stopped him, her hand lifting the pendant he wore.

"I wish we could stay here all day, but the doctor will be getting up any time now. Besides"—her green eyes shifted back to his—"you have something important to do. Hurry up and do it, so you can come back to me."

Jake let his fingers trail down the side of her face once again, then nodded. He bent and kissed her, fiercely, and Torri responded with just as much feeling, understanding the desperation she sensed in him.

She pulled away. "Jake—what is it? What's wrong? You're all right now, aren't you? You'll be able to travel back to your own time all right, won't you?" She didn't allow herself to even consider how many times he had warned her of the jewels' inconsistency.

He had risen from the bed and was pulling on his jacket. "Sure, sure I will. Thanks to you."

Torri felt her breath catch in her throat as he turned and pulled her swiftly into his arms. She closed her eyes and melted against him, feeling the necklace bite into her chest as he possessed her mouth a final time. When he pulled away, his gray eyes were warm and filled with tenderness.

"Goodbye, Torri," he whispered, and quickly left her side. Before Torri could cross the room to him, he had raised the window and slipped out. She heard him drop to the ground below. Jumping up, she ran to the window, watching the man she loved moving like a shadow against the dawn.

Torri turned away with a frown on her face. Something was wrong. She could feel it. Something in the tone of his voice, the intensity, the resolute decision. And why hadn't he simply used the TDA right there in her bedroom? Why had he run away from the house, toward Richmond, toward—

Her hand flew to her throat. What if Jake had lied to her again? What if he wasn't going to go back to his time and plead with his Council, but had used her to restore his health and was now on his way to finish the job he had come back in time to do: kill Brent Reed.

Disbelief welled up inside of her. It couldn't be true. Jake wouldn't—her thoughts shifted back to all the times Jake had declared fervently the importance of his mission, the fact that he would do anything to save his world. Anything.

"Damn you, Jake Cameron," she whispered, staring impotently out the window. "But you won't get away with it." She narrowed her eyes in grim determination. "I won't let you."

Chapter Thirteen

Torri had the mare saddled before Dr. Hamilton caught her. It was the sound of a familiar throat clearing that stopped her as she was tightening the cinch.

"And just where do you think you're going, miss, dressed like that?"

Torri glanced down at herself. When Hannah had arrived at Richmond with her load of supplies, Torri had found her jeans, T-shirt, jacket, shoes and underwear in one of the boxes. She had breathed a sigh of relief. Somehow the items comforted her. If nothing else, they had proven to her once and for all that she wasn't crazy.

She turned to face Randolph Hamilton, her face flushing guiltily.

The old man's blue eyes seemed to bore right through her as she stood there, dumbstruck at his next words.

"It's time for some answers, Victoria Hamilton," he said sternly, "or whoever you really are. And this time, Lt. Jake Cameron isn't here to cover for you. I know, because I saw him leave your bedroom early this morning."

His gaze was accusing, but not angry. Torri took a deep breath, and started to speak.

"Now, wait a minute," Dr. Hamilton said, holding up his hand. "No more lies, young lady. This time I want the truth."

Torri swallowed hard, then nodded. "All right, Dr. Hamilton," she said softly. "The truth."

* * *

"I tell you, I'm taking you home," Dr. Hamilton said as he cracked his small riding whip over his old mare's back. The horse picked up her pace only slightly and Torri clenched her fists in frustration. "He could be anywhere and is most likely either in battle with the rest of his men, or has deserted and is halfway to Mexico by now."

Torri didn't believe either possibility for a moment. Jake was biding his time, but he was somewhere close by, waiting for his chance to kill Brent Reed—the chance she had stupidly given him simply because she couldn't control her ridiculous romantic urges.

She slid a glance toward the man beside her, taking in the stern set of his lips. The lie she had told Dr. Hamilton had been pretty lousy, but it was the best she could do on short notice. She had explained that Jake had heard she'd been seen in the company of Capt. Montgomery. Jealous with rage, he had sneaked into her bedroom early that morning, and after they had argued fiercely and briefly, Jake had stormed away, vowing to kill Montgomery. It had taken a good part of the morning to convince the doctor that he had to help her stop her irate husband from carrying out his promise, or at least allow her to go and stop him.

"Let him try it," Hamilton had scoffed as they stood arguing beside the dun colored horse. "What do you think he can do in a camp full of soldiers?"

"But, Doctor, you don't understand—you don't know what he's like when he gets this way! He's irrational! He won't care if he gets caught."

"I believe that," the doctor had grumbled. "But even if he tries, he won't get away with it and then they'll string that no-good husband of yours up by the neck and it'll serve him right."

"No!" Torri had blanched at the thought of Jake swinging from a rope. It was that awful vision that had provoked the sudden lie that popped out of her mouth. "Do you want my child to be fatherless?"

Dr. Hamilton had stared at her, open mouthed, for once speechless. His eyes had shifted to her belly, then his mouth snapped shut, and he had turned and headed into the house.

Torri had flushed with shame at her audacity, and was about to follow and tell the doctor she had only been joking, when suddenly he had reappeared, his suit jacket over his arm, tying his tie around his neck. He had simply jerked his head in the direction of the wagon. With a squeal, Torri had hugged him tightly then run to unsaddle the mare and help harness her to the wagon, with Dr. Hamilton scolding and clucking at her every step of the way.

They had gone first to the camp, discreetly searching it from top to bottom. Torri had made a point of going by the colonel's tent and had seen with relief that the man was still alive and apparently on the mend. No, he hadn't seen Lt. Cameron, Col. Reed had said, but that was probable because Jake's company had been sent along with most of the army massed in the area, to fight Joe Hooker across the Rappahanock.

Torri had refused to give up, but encouraged Dr. Hamilton to stay and talk to the colonel while she conducted her own search.

At sunset, the doctor had dragged her away from searching one of the cook wagons and ordered her into their own. She had argued at first, then realized it would do no good. Now, sitting in the wagon, she realized that she'd just have to return home with her 'grandfather', then sneak out again and return to camp. She had to protect the colonel. She had to save Jake from himself.

Jake watched them leave from his vantage point atop a tall hackberry tree near the colonel's tent. Torri's back was stiff with resolve and even though the doctor was no doubt taking her home, Jake knew she'd be back as soon as humanly possible.

He slid down the trunk of the tree and cheeked the load in his pistol for the third time. His palms were sweating and he wiped them, one at a time, against his worn, butternut-colored trousers, shifting the gun from hand to hand as he did. He had been hiding in the woods all day, even though his company had been called out and was even now marching north to meet Hooker's troops at a little place called Chancellorsville. It was almost dark. It was almost time. He hadn't dared to make a move in the daytime for fear he'd be stopped, but now . . .

He closed his eyes and leaned his head against the thorny branches he was hiding behind, feeling the rapid thumping of his heart against the jeweled necklace he wore beneath his shirt. He was a fool. T'ria had been right all along. This was a job that any other man from his time could have settled in a matter of days, setting to rights all that was wrong. He had insisted that it was his right to kill his own ancestor, avenging his father's wrongs. But what had he done instead?

Gotten involved in a war he had no stake in; fallen in love with a woman who could never be his.

Jake opened his eyes. A pale, translucent moon was rising in the twilight sky. It was full again. He remembered that first night he had climbed into Torri's window at Dr. Hamilton's house. The moon had been full then, too. It seemed like a lifetime ago. Was it possible it had only been two months? He frowned. There was no time to spend on brooding. He sighed, wishing the cool night breeze touching his face in a soft caress was Torri's gentle fingers.

Ah, Torri . . . to think I've crossed time and space and found the one woman I ever wanted to love, the one woman I want to live with forever, and you can never be mine.

Taking a deep breath, he expelled it forcefully, then

squared his shoulders and tightened his jaw with new resolve. Looking quickly to make sure no one was coming, Jake eased from his hiding place and approached the tent where the injured man lay sleeping.

Jake pulled the flap open. A kerosene lamp sat on top of an overturned wooden box next to the colonel's cot. He could see the slight rise and fall of his commander's chest, the paleness of his face. Quietly, he crossed and sat down on the camp stool drawn near to the bed.

He swallowed, feeling the lump in his throat thicken as he gazed down at the man he had followed into battle, the man who had saved his life more than once. He felt dizzy, and reached out to steady himself against the edge of a small table. His gun holster scraped across the wood and the sound seemed to shatter the silence.

"Someone there?"

The voice was a whisper. Jake's eyes sprang open. Reed was conscious. "Yeah," he said softly, "I'm here."

"Is that you, Jake?" Brent Reed asked.

"Yes sir," Jake said, shifting the pistol in his right hand to his left so he could wipe the sweat from his palm again. "It's me."

"They tell me I'm going to make it," his commander whispered. "I'm glad about that. Lillie . . . it would have been hard on Lillie . . ." his eyelids fluttered shut.

Jake stared down at the gun in his hands. Lillie was Col. Brent Reed's fiancee, the woman who would bear Reed's children and begin the family line that would ultimately lead to K'mer and the destruction of the goodness of life.

Reed's eyes opened again and he seemed more coherent suddenly. "Jake? Yes, I thought you were there. You'll have to excuse me, I nod in and out . . . the medicine."

"It's all right, Colonel," Jake said, "just save your strength."

"Did we get the information back in time?" Reed asked "Did Lee—"

"Yes, it's all taken care of. Lee's ready for them. Don't worry."

Some of the anxiety left the other man's pale face. "Not that it will matter," he said, almost to himself, "it's all so pointless, futile."

Jake frowned. This didn't sound like the commander he had come to know. "What do you mean? Lee won't be caught unawares now, and the war—"

"The war will drag on," he said wearily, "until there are no more young men from the South or North left to be sacrificed on the altar of each side's Glorious Cause." He glanced up at Jake. "I'm sorry, you didn't expect me to say that, did you? But it's true. And the saddest thing of all is that even if we do end this war—there will be another, perhaps not in our time, but there will always be another."

Jake stared at the man, then found the words forming on his lips before he could stop them. "But what if you could stop this war? What if by doing one solitary, difficult act, you could change it all?"

Reed's tired eyes shifted back to Jake's face. "One solitary act?" He shook his head. "That's impossible."

"Suppose," Jake said, beginning to feel more desperate by the minute, "you could travel back in time"—Reed smiled and Jake rushed on—"I know it's ridiculous, but suppose you could go back in time and somehow by killing the ancestor of Abraham Lincoln, you could prevent him from ever being born?"

Reed's smile disappeared. "Jake, have you lived to be the age you are and still don't understand? First of all, I believe Abraham Lincoln to be one of the noblest men of our time, and secondly, were I to be able to do such an atrocious thing—it would make no difference."

Jake shook his head, his brows pressed together in confusion. "Of course it would. Without Lincoln—"

"There would be another to take his place. Lincoln is not

responsible for the war. It was the political atmosphere leading up to his presidency, individual situations, individual people using power, sometimes correctly, sometimes not. All of them combined to bring the events of time to the place in which we now find ourselves."

Jake felt the sweat break out across his forehead. The camp was stirring. He had only a few moments to finish what he had set out to do. But he was mesmerized by the words of his commanding officer.

"But what if Lincoln wasn't a good man just trapped by circumstances?" he insisted. "What if he was an evil man who actually did cause all of this bloodshed and calamity?"

"Are you asking me what I would do?" Reed said, his gray eyes piercing into Jake's. Jake could only nod. "If that were true, I suppose I would do whatever I had to do to stop him." Something flickered in the depths of his gentle gaze. "What are you trying to say, Jake? What is this all about?"

Jake looked down at the pistol in his hand. If Reed would cooperate, this would go a lot easier, but first he was going to have to try to make him understand.

"Jake?" Reed said weakly, one corner of his mouth pulled up in the semblance of a smile. "What is this all about?"

Jake didn't hear him. This was his chance, if he wanted to take it. He could still go through with his mission. All he had to do was point the pistol he held at Reed and squeeze the trigger. Then it would be over. For Brent Reed. For K'mer. For Jake Cameron.

"I thought I might find you here, Lt. Cameron. Drop your weapon or you're a dead man."

Slowly Jake turned his head in the direction of the voice behind him. A man stood there, a captain like himself by the insignia on his jacket. He seemed vaguely familiar, but Jake couldn't quite place him. Well, he had committed no crime, was simply visiting his commanding officer. Besides, the captain had no weapon.

"What seems to be the problem, Captain?" he asked. "I was just showing the colonel my new—"

In that instant the man lifted his hand and some invisible force ripped into Jake's chest and burned him with a terrible fire.

Crying in pain, Jake dropped the pistol and fell to the ground, lifting his startled gaze to that of the man towering over him. What had hit him? Who was this guy and how—

Dark brown hair and a reddish-brown mustache. Brown eyes. Lucas Montgomery. Torri's seducer.

The pain laced through Jake's chest, but the memory pierced through the agony. In the moment before he had hit the bastard in Torri's room that night, he had caught a glimpse of his face. It was that face smiling maliciously down at him now. Jake clutched his hand to the aching wound, desperately trying to formulate a plan. A glance at the bed told him Reed was unconscious once again. If he could just reach his gun where it had skidded across the ground he might still be able to make it. He edged toward it.

A low chuckle came from the man above him. "I admire your nerve, Cameron, I really do. Or should I say, K'meron?"

Jake jerked his gaze back to the man and then saw the object in the man's hand. About three inches long and two inches wide, looked the black and silver box like a weapon. The man turned slightly away from him and was adjusting something on the small box. The air left Jake's lungs suddenly. A laser. A laser. The man held a laser-powered hand unit capable of devastating an entire building, probably fitted with a light neutralizer that prevented the burning ray from being seen.

"Permit me to introduce myself, Captain. I am Lucas Montgomery, and just as you have been sent back to this era to kill Col. Brent Reed, I in turn have been sent back . . . to kill you."

"Didn't think my old man would have the brains to figure it out," Jake muttered.

"Oh, we have our sources," Montgomery said enigmatically. "And it was one of those sources that led me to Miss Hamilton, and eventually, to you."

"What sources?"

Montgomery dismissed his question with the wave of a hand. "Unimportant. Suffice it to say that I heard all about the mysterious young lady who had been shot and taken to Dr. Hamilton's house by a man answering to the description of"—he bowed toward Jake—"K'meron. Oh, and the fact that she was clutching a most peculiar necklace at the time. A diamond-shaped pendant set with four stunning gems. Quite a lovely little assistant you have there. Nice of the underground to send her along."

"Torri isn't with the underground. She has nothing to do with this." Jake gasped, trying to hide just how badly he was hurt. He could feel the burn deep inside his chest and as the pain bubbled through him, he realized there was no treatment in this century for such an injury.

"Oh, I think she has a great deal to do with it," Montgomery said, then pointed the phaser at him again. "And you're going to tell me what it is."

A thick haze of blackness shadowed Jake's vision momentarily and he felt faint. His eyelids flickered but he forced them to open again.

"Torri's just an innocent girl. I tell you, she's not involved—and if you try to seduce her again, I'll kill you."

Montgomery chuckled. "Spoken like a true Southern gentleman. It is too bad you had to interrupt us that night. She's a delectable morsel." He lifted his hand to smooth one side of his mustache. "However, after I've disposed of you, I'm sure I can make her eager once again for my touch."

Jake fought the rage swelling inside him. He had to stay calm, stay cool, until he saw his chance.

"What did you give her?" Jake asked through clenched teeth, feeling the pain rip at his chest again. "Why did you even want her? I'd think your tastes run more to whores than innocents."

Montgomery laughed. "Why did I want her? For the same reason you wanted her, I imagine. For the power of the necklace. As for what I gave her, well, that's one of your father's favorite new creations: pheronemepid."

"An aphrodisiac."

"Yes." He walked around Jake to where Col. Reed lay unconscious. He lifted the man's eyelids indifferently, then turned back to Jake. "You know, I'm tempted to let you live long enough to witness the effects—and results—of Miss Hamilton's induced passion. However, I'm afraid you're just a little too dangerous for me to risk that. But rest assured, I will take care of your beautiful bride—oh, yes, I heard about the wedding too—at least until she has outlived her usefulness." His white teeth flashed in the lamplight.

Jake forced himself to his knees. If he was going to make his break it had to be now or never. "But why—why did you want her necklace? You have your own."

Montgomery gave him a strange look and Jake immediately knew that he had touched some sort of nerve.

"You don't have a TDA, do you?" Jake said, lifting one foot to the floor, placing himself in a crouching position. It was agony but he forced himself to breathe slowly. "You're trapped, aren't you?"

A slow smile split Montgomery's face. Using his free hand, he reached inside his coat and withdrew a chain. Dangling from the end of it was a jeweled pendant. "No, Lieutenant, I'm not trapped. But you, however, most certainly are. And now it's time to say, adieu."

"Col. Reed, I brought your—" David Reynolds stopped just inside the entrance of the tent, a newspaper tucked under one arm as he balanced on his crutches. His mouth dropped open as he looked at Jake lying bleeding on the ground.

"Lt Cameron, what—"

Montgomery turned toward him, swiftly slipping the laser into his pocket. "Don't be alarmed, Corporal. This man is under arrest. He stabbed Col. Reed and has now come back to finish what he—"

In that moment, while Montgomery was partially turned, Jake made his move. Springing to his feet, he barreled into Montgomery, sending him sprawling against the other man. Unbalanced, Reynolds went down, taking Montgomery with him as Jake tore out of the tent and ran for his life.

A lantern hung at the front of the wagon, illuminating the area just below the mare's feet. Randolph kept his eyes on it while he tried to organize his thoughts. Now, heading for home, he could concentrate on the day's events. He hadn't believed Torri's story for a minute. He'd been a doctor for thirty years and if she was pregnant he'd eat the wheels on the wagon.

And yet, he couldn't believe ill of her either. She and Jake Cameron were mixed up in some desperate gambit. As far as he was concerned Cameron could hang from the gallows, but Torri—he frowned and clucked to the old mare a little louder. Torri Hamilton was an enigma—and a very rotten liar. But he loved her as though she were his own daughter.

Why, he wasn't quite sure. No, that wasn't true. He loved her because she was kind and warm-hearted and giving. Her help in the camp hospital had put to rest any lingering doubts he might have had about her. No one could care for those boys the way she had, with her heart in her eyes; no woman could have helped him through sewing up one ragged wound after another unless she had character, and courage.

He glanced at her. She was twisting her fingers, her dark brows knit together. Her courage was taking a beating right now, he knew. She was having to fight like everything to keep from flinging him off the seat of the wagon, taking the reins and driving his poor old horse into the ground if necessary to find Jake Cameron. They had searched the army camp to no avail and he had finally convinced her to leave. But the reason for her wanting to find Cameron still remained unexplained. Well, he intended to get an answer, as soon as they reached their temporary home.

"Pull up the horse."

Hamilton cursed himself for his wool-gathering as soon as he heard the harsh, familiar voice ringing with command from the darkness.

"Please," Torri said, her hand on his. "Please stop."

Randolph jerked back on the reins, but as he did, he slipped his hand down the side of the wooden seat.

Jake Cameron's face appeared above the lantern's light, a pistol pointed straight at Randolph. His lips were curved in a tight, grim smile.

"Evening, Doctor," he said casually. "I find myself in need of a lift."

"I don't doubt it." His left hand tightened around the barrel of the old gun he kept hidden there, but he kept talking. "Who's chasing you, Lieutenant?"

Torri watched as Jake threw one arm across the rump of the old mare and aimed the gun at the doctor's chest.

"Probably the whole damn Confederate Army," he admitted.

"Why?"

Jake's eyes slid shut briefly, then sprang open again, as if he were fighting to keep from falling asleep—or passing out, Torri thought fearfully. Was Jake still sick from the Molecular Dysfunction?

"Because they think I tried to kill my commanding officer. Now, move over and give me those reins."

Dr. Hamilton drew the gun suddenly, before Jake could

react. "Step away from the wagon, you cur," the doctor said sternly.

Jake laughed, and Torri darted him a sharp look. The sound was strange, as though he had liquid in his throat.

"I can drop you before you can pull the trigger, Doc." The moonlight turned his gray eyes to quicksilver and Torri involuntarily shivered.

Torri knew if she didn't take action someone was about to get hurt—probably the doctor. She laid her hand across the barrel of the ancient weapon Dr. Hamilton held.

"He isn't going to kill anyone," she said, glaring at Jake, then turned to the doctor. "Please, Dr. Hamilton—Grandfather—remember, you told me I could call you that. Please help him."

The lamplight was flickering across Jake's drawn face and Dr. Hamilton's gaze flickered in that direction too.

"Cameron" the old man said, flinging the reins to Torri and clambering down from the hard seat, "Why didn't you say you were hurt? Get in the wagon."

With a cry of alarm, Torri jumped to her feet and the horse moved nervously from side to side.

"Jake—!"

"Sit down, Torri," Dr. Hamilton ordered, "before the horse bolts. We've got to get him back to the house before the patrols find us, although why I should risk my neck—"

"Thank you," Torri whispered, sitting down and quieting the mare. "Let's get home."

Without further argument, the doctor managed to get Jake into the wagon. He sank onto the hard seat, sagging against Torri on her left side, the gun he held falling uselessly to the floor. Torri put her arm around Jake and tried to help support him.

"Oh, Jake," she whispered, "how could you lie to me?"

"So much for the truth you told me earlier, I suppose," Dr. Hamilton said, taking the reins and actually managing to provoke the horse into a fast trot. "If you want me to help this ruffian, you're going to have to do better this time."

"No, Torri," Jake said, stirring and raising his head. "Keep your mouth shut."

Dr. Hamilton said no more, and the last mile to the house was spent in silence. Torri could feel her fear growing. Would the army think to look for Jake at Dr. Hamilton's? But wait—there was a battle going on. Maybe they wouldn't be able to spare anyone to search for him—or at least it would make things more confusing.

But the thought driving her crazy was one she couldn't stand to examine for more than a moment: had Jake done it? Had he killed Col. Reed? She couldn't bear to ask him, couldn't bear to hear what she feared the answer might be.

"Light that lamp."

Torri took the matches Dr. Hamilton held out to her and turned to the kerosene lamp on the small table in his study. Her hands were shaking so badly that she had to strike three matches before she could get one lit. The soft glow of the lamp seemed to make Jake's ashen face look even paler and Torri whirled away from him, her shoulders shaking with suppressed sobs.

"Here now," Dr. Hamilton said gruffly. "You can't give way to tears now, Torri-girl. You've got to help me." He thrust a round enameled pan toward her. "Go wake Hannah up and tell her to start boiling water. When she gets it ready, put some in this pan and bring it back. And hurry!"

Torri ran from the room, then tore up the stairs to Hannah's small bedroom at the end of the hall. She didn't wait to knock on the door but flew into the room, shaking the startled housekeeper with both hands.

"Hannah, Hannah, wake up! The doctor says come quick, boil some water."

The large woman was oil her feet in a moment, obviously

used to medical emergencies in the middle of the night. She reached for a worn robe and pulled it over her ample form.

"Who is it, child?" she asked groggily, taking time to tie a kerchief neatly over her gray curls. "Who's hurt?"

The sob broke free and Torri forced it back, her voice trembling. "It's Jake, Hannah, and I think he's dying."

Hannah jerked her head up from buttoning her robe. "That boy? No child, the Almighty won't take that boy— He's done picked him out for you—He done told me so."

Torri was too distraught to pay attention to what the woman was saying. "Please hurry!" she cried, shoving the pan into Hannah's hands. "Bring some hot water in this as soon as you can—please! I've got to be with him!"

She dashed down the stairs and into the study. Dr. Hamilton had cleared off his desk and Jake lay on top of it. The doctor had just finished cutting away his shirt. Torri blanched as the cloth fell to the floor, then gasped as she saw the jagged hole in Jake's chest.

"Oh God," she whispered, moving quickly to his side. "Oh God, don't let him die."

Her fears deepened as she saw that even Dr. Hamilton seemed shocked.

"I've never seen a wound like this before," he said raggedly. "It doesn't even look like a bullet wound. It looks almost like he was—was burned, but by an intense heat that was aimed, focused somehow and"—he broke off—"that's impossible."

"Will he make it?" Torri whispered, taking one of Jake's cold hands in her own.

Dr. Hamilton shook his head. "I don't know. I'm not sure I even know how to treat a wound like this." He pressed his lips together grimly. "But first things first. He's in shock. If he comes through and if the wound doesn't get infected, then—we'll see."

"A lot of ifs and maybes," Torri said, smoothing the tousled blond hair back from Jake's forehead.

The doctor nodded. "It's times like these when I want to give up doctoring. Sometimes there is so little we can really do. I hope in the future medicine makes more rapid advances."

In the future! Torri's heart skipped a beat. "Jake," she said, leaning closer to him. "Jake, can you hear me? Jake, you're hurt, dying maybe. Do you want me to take you *somewhere else?* Help me, Jake, tell me how to take you somewhere else."

Dr. Hamilton looked up from his ministrations and frowned. "There's nowhere else to take him. If you take him into town he'll be arrested, and besides, there's not much the hospital can do that I can't do here."

"You don't understand," Torri began, then stopped as Jake opened his eyes and stared around incoherently. "Oh Jake!"

"Torri," he mumbled, lifting his hand toward her. She took it and pressed it gently against her face. "Something hit me . . . burns . . . like fire . . ."

"You were shot, do you remember? Dr. Hamilton says the wound is strange, like nothing he's ever seen before. Jake, what happened?"

"Montgomery . . ." he whispered. "Stay away from that bastard, Torri . . ."

"Jake, listen. Montgomery means nothing to me." She moved closer as the doctor turned away to arrange his instruments on a table beside him. "Dr. Hamilton is going to try to help you, but, Jake, where is the necklace? I can take you to another time if you—"

"Here's the water," Hannah said as she came through the door, carrying the steaming pan carefully in front of her. "Where do you want it, Dr. Randolph?"

"Over here. Put it on this table."

The doctor gave Torri a strange look but she didn't care if

he had heard their conversation. What did it matter? Jake could be dying.

"Now, we'll go in and take a look," the doctor stated.

She had to do something. Every part of her being cried it out. When Jake doubled up suddenly and the doctor held him by the shoulders to keep him from rolling off the table, her mind was made up for her. The spasm passed and Jake lay back, sweat trickling down his face.

"Here, son," the doctor said, holding a small cup to his lips, "drink this." He glanced at Torri. "Laudanum. The last I have."

"Torri . . ." Jake whispered. "Are you there, Torri?"

She stroked the edge of his hairline. "Here," she said softly. "Always here, Jake."

"You've got to . . . get out of here . . . not safe . . . Montgomery . . . K'mer's man . . ."

Torri's blood turned to ice. Capt. Montgomery was one of K'mer's agents. She didn't understand why he had tried to seduce her but now she knew it had to be for some ulterior purpose even worse than simple lust. Some of her memory of that night had come back since her talk with Jake at the camp, and she blushed every time she thought of it. It disturbed her greatly that she had apparently been so consumed with lust for the captain that she must have tried to block it out mentally.

"Do you hear me?" Jake half rose from the table, then sank back with a heart-wrenching groan.

Dr. Hamilton quickly began his ministrations, preparing Jake for surgery.

Torri bit her lip and fought to hold back the rush of tears. "Yes, darling, I hear you, I understand. I'll be careful."

"Kiss me, Torri . . ." he said ". . . kiss me just in case."

Torri leaned to meet his lips, her hot tears mingling salt with the sweetness of the embrace.

"You're going to be all right, Jake," she said fervently. "Don't you dare die on me now."

Jake ran his tongue across his dry, cracked lips and the gesture went straight to Torri's heart. "I've been . . . thinking . . ." he gasped. "We . . . can . . . stay here . . . settle down . . ."

"What, and give up time travel?" she said softly so the doctor wouldn't hear, tears in her eyes.

"For you? In a nanosecond, kitten," his voice was hoarse, faint. Torri swallowed hard. "What do you say?"

As the tears rushed down her face, Torri struggled for composure. "I say you shouldn't say things you'll regret later. Now, just lie still and let the doctor help you."

She laid her hand on his and he squeezed it weakly. "I didn't lie . . ." Jake said, forming the words thickly. "Want you to know—he shook his head "—Reed . . . I was trying . . . thought he should hide . . . if Council sent someone else . . ."

Torri caught her breath at his halting words. Was it possible? Had Jake been trying to help Reed, to hide him from the next assassin the Council would send if Jake failed to convince them to let Reed live?

Jake looked up at her, his gray eyes as warm as the ashes from a fire. "I love you," he whispered, and his eyelids slid shut.

Torri kissed his still lips and felt her tears flow down her cheeks. He loved her. Jake loved her. He hadn't tried to kill Reed—she knew it now without a doubt. He couldn't love her and still try to accomplish his mission.

Dr. Hamilton pushed up his shirt sleeves and dipped his hands in the basin of hot water. Torri was glad that at least the doctor was washing his hands. She knew enough about history to remember that people had often died after surgery in the 1800s due to infection. Jake was unconscious from the laudanum now, but from her brief experience at the camp, Torri doubted it would last that long. The doctor would have to work fast.

Leaning over Jake, examining his wound more thoroughly, the doctor explained to Torri what he was going to do, then abruptly, he stopped talking. She glanced up at him, and felt the panic beginning again.

He was pale, his lower lip trembling. "Dear Lord," he said. "I don't know how he even lived this long. It's as though his chest has been laid open and the insides seared." He shook his head. "I can sew him up, but the damage is really severe. Infection is almost certain to set in."

A sudden pounding on the front door made them both freeze, their gazes locked on one another.

"The patrol!" Torri said in a hushed voice.

"Stay here, I'll see who it is." Dr. Hamilton turned to go, then glanced back. "I'm sorry, Torri. He was a scoundrel, but I know you loved him." He walked out of the room.

"He isn't dead *yet!*" she whispered, feeling her anger blaze. He couldn't die. She wouldn't let him die. Quickly, she searched the pockets of his trousers. The necklace wasn't there. Then she spied his jacket. She grabbed it and something heavy fell from the pocket with a clunk and Torri scooped up the necklace, feeling hopeful again.

"It's David Reynolds," the doctor said from behind her. "I told him to wait, he—the necklace."

She turned. Dr. Hamilton stood in the doorway, his face reflecting a mixture of confusion and betrayal. "My family necklace."

Suddenly Torri felt something inside her snap. "This is *my* necklace," she said. "My grandfather gave it to me." She pointed at it, the chain dangling from her fingers. "And it isn't just a necklace—it's a time travel device," she said boldly, "and I, dear great-great-great-grandfather, am from the future."

She met the doctor's widening eyes and wondered if he thought she was crazy.

"And right now," she went on, "I'm going to use it to take Jake to another time—a time where he can get help."

Dr. Hamilton was shaking his head in disbelief. "When my father was about to die he talked about crazy things—about traveling through time. I supposed it was the rantings of a delirious mind," he said softly. "Can it be true?"

Torri took a deep breath and smiled at him. "I am one of your descendants," she said, "and very, very proud to be."

The old man stared at her for a long moment. "I don't know what to say, what to think. You say you can take Jake through time—to a future time where he can get more advanced medical care?"

Torri hesitated. "I've never done it before. My getting here was, well, sort of an accident. I'm not sure . . ." her voice trailed away.

Dr. Hamilton placed his gnarled hand on her shoulder. "Torri, dear, he's going to die. What other chance does he have?"

She nodded and hugged him tightly.

"None at all, Doctor," a voice said from behind them. "Not one chance this side of hell. Step aside."

Torri turned slowly. It couldn't be David Reynolds, not talking in that cold, snide tone of voice, not holding a gun on them, a sneer on his freckled face. But it was. The boy took a rolled up cigarette out of his pocket and stuck it in his mouth.

Torri saw his hand was shaking and spoke quickly. "David, don't do this. Jake didn't really try to kill the colonel."

"Maybe he did, maybe he didn't. I don't know."

"He didn't!"

"I don't care about the colonel."

"Then why—"

"You said you can take someone into the future with you, right?" he asked.

"I can take Jake," she said cautiously.

"Then that means you could also take someone *back* in time, doesn't it?"

Torri tossed her hair back from her shoulders. "David, what *are* you talking about? I've got to get Jake help, and you stand there and—"

"I'm talking about this." He pointed down at where his leg used to be. "I'm talking about you taking me back in time, before this happened, and letting me relive that day again." He smiled but his eyes remained stony. "You can bet this time I won't be anywhere close to Shiloh, Tennessee or the Confederate Army."

"It's not that easy, David," Torri said, feeling frantic at the delay.

"I don't believe you!" He raised the gun. "You could do it if you wanted to—you were going to take Jake."

"Yes," she said, "because we're—we're married and that gives us a special bond. I've got to go—now!"

He lit the cigarette dangling from his mouth and sent a stream of smoke between them. "You'll take me first."

"David, listen. I can't take you. I understand how you feel." She moved toward him and he stepped back. "You aren't a bad person, I know you aren't. You can't let Jake die when I could help him. In the future there are medicines that will help him live. Here"—she faltered, then plunged on—"here he'll die."

"I'll take my chances," David said.

"*Your* chances?" Torri said angrily. "What about *his* chances?"

David glanced down at the unconscious man. "I'm sorry, but I don't want to be a cripple the rest of my life," he said, the cigarette trembling between his fingers. "I want my leg back."

"I understand," Torri said, "but we can't just play God with history. What has happened was meant to be, for some reason we can't understand."

"Please, spare me," he sneered, "you sound like my pastor spouting about God's will."

"I don't claim to understand it," Torri said quietly, "but I know it's true."

"So maybe it's God's will that the two of you came back to my time so you could take me back, did you ever think of that?"

"Look, there are things I wish I could change about my life," Torri said. "Everybody feels that way, but time travel is dangerous and changing history can be disastrous."

Suddenly she knew what she was saying was true and that it applied to her grandfather and his situation. I'll have to sort that out later, she thought.

"What if losing your leg inspires you to be a great doctor and you discover penicillin or something?" she asked, turning her attention to David.

"Discover what?"

"It doesn't matter. What I'm trying to say is if losing your leg somehow is used to shape your destiny in the future, and you go back and change it—you'll not only change your future but your descendants' futures as well."

"But that's what Jake is here to do, isn't it? Change the future by changing the past?"

Torri stared at him, stunned. David looked at Torri triumphantly. "You can save your platitudes, ma'am. I'm afraid they no longer hold any water." He turned the gun toward her. "Now I'd be obliged if you'd give me the necklace. If you don't want to help me I'll do it myself."

"You can't use it," Torri said. "It's tuned only to my body—and—Jake's."

"That's not what I hear. Now, hand it over."

Suddenly, Torri understood. "Oh, David," Torri said, her gaze softening, "Montgomery's been talking to you, hasn't he? He's using you, David, to get the necklace. He tried to use me—"

"Give it to me, ma'am or I'll have to hurt you."

Torri shook her head. "Then you'll have to hurt me. And I don't think you will."

"Why?" His blue eyes narrowed and his smile widened. "Think the crippled boy is too chicken?"

"No, David," she said, "I think you're too kind."

His hard gaze wavered, then he took the cigarette between his thumb and forefinger and flipped it away. He stared down at the gun and back at Torri, then shrugged.

"Well, it was worth a try I guess." He lowered the gun. "I guess I was just bluffing. It's just that . . ." he looked down at his leg. "Well, I guess I don't have to explain."

"No," Torri said, "I just wish it could be different."

"Thank you, Cpl. Reynolds," a voice behind them said. "Once again you have served your country well."

Torri's heart began thumping wildly as she watched Capt. Montgomery take his place beside David. David grinned and Torri realized his pitiful act was just that—an act. She glared at David, then shifted her gaze to Montgomery.

He smiled, his lips cruel and mocking beneath his mustache. "And once again, I will serve the best interests of my country as well." He cocked the gun and pointed it at Jake. "Goodbye, Lieutenant."

Chapter Fourteen

"Torri," Jake groaned. "Get away from me."

"I won't! If the captain wants to kill you he'll have to go through me to do it!"

Montgomery's smile widened. "And you think that will deter me, my dear? I think not, since I intend to kill you as well. He almost had me convinced that you were nothing more than a simple country girl, but now it's quite obvious that you are one of the underground as well."

"Leave her out of it!" Jake shouted, and Torri gathered him into her arms as a spasm seized him. The seizure passed and she turned, furious, toward their assailant.

"Now wait just a minute," Dr. Hamilton said, his gray brows knit together angrily. "You're a Confederate officer—how dare you come in here and threaten my granddaughter?"

"She isn't your granddaughter. And *if* I were only working under the authority of the Confederate States of America you could most certainly report me to my superior, however, my authority comes from a somewhat higher source."

"What do you mean a higher source?" Dr. Hamilton asked. "And what possible authority could you have to take an innocent girl's life?"

"He's from the future too," Torri told the doctor, lifting her chin and glaring up at Montgomery haughtily. "He's been sent back to stop Jake from defeating an evil man."

Montgomery smiled rakishly. "You misunderstand, ma cherie," he said. "I don't intend to stop the death of Col. Reed, in fact, as soon as I get the chance I will eliminate him myself. Now, please step away from Lt. Cameron."

"Torri, get out of here," Jake said weakly. "You can do it."

She knew he meant that she could use the TDA and escape, but she tightened her grip on his hand and looked up at Montgomery defiantly.

"I thought you were K'mer's agent," she said, stalling for time. "Why would you want to kill Col. Reed?"

"Why, to advance my plan to overthrow K'mer and take his power away from him, of course. That pompous ass is no more able to rule than a snail. K'mer sent me back to stop the underground's plan, but my dear friend didn't know that I have my own visions of grandeur."

"Then why did you stop Jake from killing him?"

Montgomery laughed. "I didn't stop him. I knew Cameron wouldn't go through with it. I've been watching him for days, wrestling with his honor and his conscience. I've come in contact with too many like him to believe he would cast aside his accursed principles." His even teeth gleamed beneath his mustache. "I, on the other hand, have no such principles. I will kill Reed and eliminate K'mer, then I shall rise to power, with the help of these."

He held out two necklaces identical to the one Torri now clutched, hidden, in her hand.

Torri was startled. "Two necklaces?

"Yes, my dear. You see, the scientists in our time have made even greater advances in the field of time travel science since the first devices were created. As I'm sure K'meron has told you, the TDA is a rather unreliable little invention. Doesn't always take you where you want to go, although my own has been adapted and is vastly more accurate than your outdated ones, and it can also transport more than one person at a time—if that person is in physical contact with the other."

"However," he paused importantly, "our scientists have

theorized that if the properties of several devices were combined, the person in possession of those devices would be able to transport himself with pinpoint precision and accuracy to any time period—without the worry of Molecular Dysfunction."

Dr. Hamilton sank down into a chair. Torri darted him a quick look and saw he was completely overwhelmed.

"Where did you get the necklaces?" Torri asked, stalling for time.

"One of them is my own. The other I discovered when I was searching the field after a battle for any men still alive." His gaze flickered to Jake. "I can only assume that it belongs to our courageous lieutenant."

Jake was struggling to sit up and Torri turned to help him. "If it is mine," he gasped, "how can you use it? It's tuned to my lifeforce."

Montgomery's smile broadened with pleasure. "Only until you're dead. Then I will take your TDA and your lovely wife's—along with her lovely self—and we will return to the future where I will use my newly acquired power to rule the world."

He moved toward Torri and brushed his fingers down the side of her face. She shivered. "Remember, Torri?" he said, leaning over until his face was against her hair. "Remember how it was between us? And so unfortunate that we were interrupted, don't you agree?"

Torri shoved him away and turned to Jake who was trying to stand. "Jake, no—"

"That bastard isn't going to take you with him—" Jake doubled over.

"I'm afraid you aren't in a position to dictate what anyone will do, Lieutenant. Now, my dear, I will need your necklace as well. I don't quite trust your having it any longer."

"Are you sure you aren't making a big mistake?" Torri said, stalling for time. "You really have no way of knowing how the changes you make in the past will affect the future. It could destroy you along with K'mer."

"I shall take my chances. Now, I'm afraid our little conversation is at an end. If you will be so kind as to give me your TDA and then move away from the lieutenant." He gestured with the gun but Torri stood her ground.

"You're crazy if you think I'll let you kill him."

"Ah, I begin to understand." His brown eyes glittered with humor. "This is obviously a case of true love, but as you know, in all great love stories true lovers must meet death together. I'll be more than happy to send both of you on to your just reward."

"Torri!" Dr. Hamilton took a step toward her and Montgomery nodded at Hiram Evans, who had entered the room. The big man grabbed the doctor, his leering face breaking into a vicious smile.

"Leave him alone!" Torri cried.

"You didn't say nothing about killing anybody," David Reynolds interjected anxiously. "You just said we'd get Jake and then they would have to use that thing to take me back and fix my leg."

"You don't understand, dear boy," Montgomery said. "This is necessary if you want your leg back."

"But—"

"Do you want to remain a pitiful cripple for the rest of your life?" Montgomery's cruel words stopped David's protest and the man moved sulkily to stand beside K'mer's agent.

Torri's fingers curled around the smooth diamond shape in her hand and she put her arm around Jake. She hoped Dr. Hamilton would be all right, that Montgomery wouldn't hurt him after she and Jake disappeared. All she needed was a chance, a second of diversion. She glanced up and her gaze met David's. He winked at her. Torri caught her breath and stared at him. The rest of his face was perfectly deadpanned. He winked again, then looked down at his crutch and back up at her again. Torri blinked to show she understood, or at least thought she understood, and David smiled.

"And now that chivalry has been served," Montgomery was saying, "it's time to say goodbye."

"My leg!" David cried, suddenly falling, his full weight coming down against Montgomery's shoulder, his crutch crashing down on Montgomery's wrist. Startled, the captain staggered, then dropped the pistol he held.

Torri lunged for the gun, beating Montgomery to it by a split second. She jumped to her feet and pointed the weapon at the captain's middle as he stood, his face volcanic with anger.

"Funny how quickly things can turn around, isn't it, Captain?" she said.

"Yes, isn't it?" He smiled and held out the necklace he had displayed moments before.

"Drop it," she ordered, just as the captain twinkled and glistened and finally disappeared into thin air.

Dr. Hamilton stood staring after him, his eyes wide with shock. Torri too stood gazing at the empty space where he had been only seconds before. She recovered quickly, however, and turned the gun on Hiram Evans.

"Let him go, you filth," she said, feeling a small triumph as he dropped his hands hastily from the doctor. She handed Dr. Hamilton the gun. "Here, Doctor. I can't waste any more time. I've got to get Jake out of here."

The doctor took the gun and forced Evans to the floor, his hands over his head. "But where—where did Montgomery go?"

"Who knows? And there's the horror of it. He could be anywhere in time, doing anything. That is the danger, the danger Jake tried to tell me about." She looked over at David who was struggling to his feet and went to him.

"David, thank you."

He shrugged. "I guess there's worse things than being crippled in your body—like maybe being crippled in your soul."

The doctor patted him on the shoulder. "You've made a good start back to a full life, David, leg or no leg."

Torri nodded and reaching up, kissed his cheek. "I knew you had a good heart, David Reynolds, from the very start. Thanks for proving me right." She turned to Dr. Hamilton. "Doctor, if I never see you again—thank you for everything. I love you as though you were my grandfather."

"Be careful," he whispered, leaning over and kissing her. "Come back to me, Granddaughter."

Torri nodded and tried to smile. She turned to Jake and wrapped her arms around him, suddenly struck by the fact that she didn't know where to take him. If they went too far forward in time, they might end up in Jake's time where there would be no help at all for him, but not far enough would leave them without the medical expertise they needed. Torri made up her mind quickly.

"Think of 1994," she said to Jake. Better the time period she knew than an unknown time. She only hoped doctors in 1994 could deal with this kind of injury. She slipped the necklace over her head and pressed herself against his side. With a gasp, she felt the awful, whirling, spinning vortex suck them downward into a terrifying cacophony of color.

Torri paced along the hospital corridor, then glanced up as a nurse in a crisp white uniform walked briskly by, toward the nurses' station.

"Excuse me," Torri said, rushing over to the woman who looked up from her clipboard, mildly irritated. "Can you tell me if my friend is still in surgery?"

She had bright yellow hair arranged in stiff her bangs that puffed out from her forehead. Torri thought it not only unattractive but out of style, along with her eyebrows, which looked painted on, and were pressed together now into a frown. "Who?" she said impatiently.

"Jake Cameron. I—I brought him here a few hours ago with a—a gunshot wound and they took him to surgery." Torri drew the back of her hand across her eyes, half afraid that she might burst into tears any moment. She took a deep breath and tried to sound as composed as possible. "I haven't heard anything since."

The nurse's gaze swept over her, taking in the grubby jeans and the weariness in Torri's face. Her voice softened slightly.

"I just come on duty so I wouldn't know. Sorry." She turned back to her clipboard.

"Please," Torri said, "I've been waiting here so long! The doctor said—" her mouth went suddenly dry and swallowing seemed a monumental task. She couldn't help the way her voice was cracking and plunged on. "The doctor said he might not make it, and that was two hours ago."

"I'm sorry," she said again, then patted Torri's shoulder. "I'm sure the doctor will let you know something as soon as possible. Why don't you go down to the cafeteria and get a cup of coffee?"

Torri stared after her as she turned and strode briskly back down the hall. She turned away, no longer trying to blink back the tears. She felt half-crazy. Living in 1863 now seemed like some incredible dream. Did Jake feel that way after traveling through time?

Jake.

Torri paced up and down the corridor and let the tears come. How could she bear it if Jake died? How could she ever bear it? In those few moments when he told her he loved her she had known such joy, such hope. If he died . . .

She walked back into the waiting room and sank down on the stiff plastic couch. As her head bobbed and her eyelids drooped, somewhere in the back of her mind she realized she didn't know where in time she was.

When they had appeared in downtown Richmond it had been dark. The town had looked different, somehow, just like the cab which had taken them to the hospital. Summoned by a passerby who had stumbled over her and Jake, the cab driver had been extremely helpful. She was so worried about Jake that on the way to the hospital she hadn't paid much attention to Richmond, but figured it had to be relatively close to her own time. The taxi had looked weird, out of date, though how many years out of date she didn't know.

Torri lay down on the plastic couch and closed her eyes, drifting into a deep sleep.

Her grandfather was dying. She stood in the room where he lay, his breathing raspy and harsh, but as she moved forward, something stopped her from reaching him. Again and again she pressed against the invisible wall holding her back. Finally she beat against it with her fists, crying out his name. He stared up at the ceiling, oblivious to her presence, but Torri could see his lips moving, forming her name: Torri, Torri, Torri. Over and over he called for her, over and over she cried out in response, but he never heard.

Torri awoke bathed in sweat. She sat up from the position she had slid into during her sleep and hugged herself, suddenly cold. It's just a dream, she said, trying to believe it. It's just a silly dream.

"Are you the one who brought the gunshot wound in?"

She looked up at the sound of the voice and the blood drained from her face. A policeman. Of course, gunshot wounds were always reported to the police. And she'd better have a good explanation ready or it might mean a lot of trouble for both of them.

"Y-yes," she said, running her hand through her tangled hair, "I brought him."

He sat down beside her and his gaze roamed over her, sizing

her up. "Well," he said, taking a notebook from his pocket, "the law states that gunshot wounds have to be reported to us. I'm here to to find out what you know about it, since the man himself can't answer."

Torri nodded. "It-it was all a terrible accident," she began. The door to the waiting room opened and a man clad in a white v-neck cotton shirt and pants, with what looked like a shower cap on his head, walked in. Torri stood up as she recognized the doctor who had taken Jake into emergency surgery. He had been kind and compassionate and she moved toward him eagerly.

"Is he all right? Why did it take so long? Is he going to live? Why wouldn't anyone tell me anything?"

"Take it easy, young lady, one question at a time." He smiled down at her, his blue eyes warm with compassion. "I'm Dr. Gallagher. You brought him in, didn't you?" She nodded, unable to speak. "Well, you probably saved his life. I would have liked to have waited a day or two before going into his chest, but we couldn't wait to stabilize him. There was too much that needed repairing."

"Is he all right?" she whispered.

"I think he will be, in a few days. They'll be taking him first to the recovery room and you can see him in a little while. But first I have a few questions to ask you—"

"Excuse me, Doctor," the policemen interrupted, "but I've got a few questions of my own."

Dr. Gallagher glanced at him, an amused expression on his face. "Well, Officer, perhaps the young lady can answer both of our questions. They're probably very similar."

The policeman debated for a moment, then nodded his head begrudgingly.

"I've never seen a wound quite like that one," the doctor said. "How did the accident happen? I couldn't find any trace of a bullet—not even a place where it could have exited the body."

Torri drew in her breath quickly and decided to bluff it

out. "I don't know," she said, "I mean, actually I just found him, on the street."

"I thought you told me he'd had an accident," the policeman said, "like you were there or something."

"Well, I mean, obviously he had been in a terrible accident," she stumbled through the lie. "That's all I meant."

"He was wearing a copy of a Civil War uniform wasn't he?" the doctor asked curiously. "It was so bloody and tattered I wasn't sure at first, but I'm sort of a Civil War buff and after a second look I was pretty sure. It was, wasn't it?"

"I—I don't know. I told you, I just found him."

"Strange thing about that wound," Dr. Gallagher went on thoughtfully. "It looked more like a burn than a gunshot wound." He glanced down at Torri. "Was it you who told the nurse he'd been shot?"

"Yes, I—I assumed he had been, because he said—yes, he said, 'I've been shot,' just before he passed out."

The doctor rubbed one hand across his chin. "I suppose it's possible he had an old weapon, since he had the old uniform, and it misfired."

"I really don't know," Torri said, feeling near panic. "Look, I was just trying to help. I don't think it's fair for everyone to question me like I'm a criminal or something!"

"I've got my job to do, young lady," the policeman said, "and of course in cases like this, where there's a gunshot wound, well—"

Torri began to tremble, either from reaction or the trip through time or the harshness of the policeman's voice, she didn't know.

"Take it easy," Dr. Gallagher said, noticing her discomfort. "If you aren't involved in this, you won't have to go through this again, will she, Officer?"

The policeman shot him a look that said plainly, 'Oh yeah?' and Torri felt another surge of mounting panic as the officer turned toward her.

"You seem pretty concerned about a total stranger," he said, his dark eyes piercing her.

"Well, I—I guess anyone would feel concerned if they'd fallen over a poor guy on the sidewalk, hurt and in pain and—and—" her voice broke and the doctor patted her shoulder again.

"Of course," he said kindly, "anyone with a heart would be concerned." He looked at the officer pointedly. "Is that all?"

"I'll need your name and address, young lady," the policeman said.

Torri hesitated, then gave her right name and her grandfather's address.

"You live alone?" he said, scribbling.

"No," she said, "I live with my grandfather."

The policeman shot her a doubtful look. "Mind if I call him up?"

Torri realized her mistake immediately. She opened and closed her mouth several times. "He—uh—he isn't home right now."

"Oh, yeah?" the cop said suspiciously. "And just where might he be?"

She swallowed hard and grabbed at the first thought that filtered into her brain. "He's gone to Hawaii!" she blurted.

"Hawaii?" the doctor and policeman said, almost in unison.

"At a time like this?" Dr. Gallagher asked, lifting his eyebrow.

"Yes," she said, wondering why they were so astonished. "He left two weeks ago." She frowned. What did the doctor mean when he said a time like this?

"You poor kid," the officer said, "You must be worried stiff, and then to have this happen to you, today." He waved the little notebook. "I'll be getting along, now. Thanks for the help, little lady. I doubt you'll be needed again."

He walked off down the corridor and Torri breathed a sigh of relief. She didn't know why he'd stopped pressing her for answers but was grateful just the same. Slipping her hand in her pocket, her fingers brushed against the pendant. We can leave anytime, she thought, trying to comfort herself, anytime at all. Just remember that and don't get shook.

"When can I see him?" she asked the doctor who was looking at her curiously again.

"I'll send the nurse around to tell you when you can see him," Dr. Gallagher said. "It shouldn't be too long."

With another comforting word the doctor left and Torri suddenly felt like dancing down the bleak hospital corridor.

Jake was all right, he was going to be all right! She did do a little jig in the waiting room, then collapsed into the plastic chair, feeling happier than she had in a long time. A sudden growling from her stomach turned her thoughts to practical needs. She had a little change in her pocket—was there time to run down to the snack bar she'd seen at the end of the hall and get a candy bar or something?

When did she last eat? She couldn't remember. An orderly with bright red hair walked by and suddenly she thought of David. Poor David. What had happened to him, she wondered. Was he somewhere with Montgomery—or dead?

Dizziness swept over her and Torri realized she was faint from hunger. Thinking about David would have to wait. Jake needed her right now and she had to be strong. She hurried down the hallway to the small snack bar and bought a sandwich. She was walking away from the register counting her change, sure the girl had undercharged her, when her foot collided with metal. Torri looked up to find she had snagged a newspaper stand near the doorway. Her eyes widened as the change in her hand fell to the floor.

In giant, bold-faced type the headline proclaimed:

JAPANESE BOMB PEARL HARBOR! AMERICA TO ENTER THE WAR!

I'm in the wrong time, she thought, suddenly understanding

why the nurse's hairstyle and the cab had looked so strange. It also accounted for the policeman's backing down when she'd said her grandfather was in Hawaii. *I'm not just a little bit in the wrong time either. It's 1941 and I'm right back in the middle of another war!*

She walked back down the corridor, dazed, trying to sort things out. A nurse, a different one this time, came up to her and jarred her from her reverie by touching her gently on the arm.

"Miss? Are you the one waiting to see the man who was shot?"

Torri nodded, too numb from her discovery to do anything more.

"If you'll come with me, I'll take you to him."

Torri followed her, feeling like a sleepwalker, but she snapped back to reality as soon as she saw Jake. She rushed to his side, trying not to see the tubes in his mouth, his nose, his arm.

"Jake . . ." she said, taking his hand and feeling the tears well up in her eyes. "Oh, Jake."

The nurse discreetly left and Torri leaned closer to him. Would he be all right? He looked so pale. Thank God she had brought him back. If they'd stayed in the past he'd be dead now, she was sure of it. She was slightly amazed that he had made it anyway. 1941 wasn't the most modern of times.

His eyelids twitched and he opened and closed his mouth several times as if he were thirsty, then ran his tongue across dry, cracked lips. Torri saw a glass of water with a straw in it on the little table next to his bed. She gave him a drink from the glass, watching him tenderly, brushing a wayward lock of blondish brown hair from his forehead as he struggled back to consciousness.

"I love you," she said aloud. "I love you even though it's stupid. I know we can never be together. I don't even know that you'd want us to be together. But it doesn't matter. I love you and I know that you love me."

His eyes flickered open and Jake stared at her, disoriented and confused. Then the cloudy look in his eyes cleared, and he looked down at the IV tube in his arm, then back up at the rack holding the life-giving blood.

"Torri?" he croaked. "Where—where are we?"

"We're safe, Jake," she said, feeling the truth of the statement seep inside her. "We're safe, and you're going to be all right."

His eyes flickered shut and Torri sank down on the chair beside him and leaned her head against his bed. Within seconds she was asleep.

Jake's thrashing jarred Torri from her sleep. One look at his agonized, blue-tinged face sent her flying to her feet. She rushed to the nurses' station in the front of the room.

"Something's wrong!" she shouted to the nurse sitting at the desk. "Hurry!"

The nurse moved quickly to Jake's bed, glanced at him and immediately bolted and ran from the room. In seconds, she and another nurse burst back in and began to frantically work over Jake's now still body.

"What's wrong?" Torri cried. "What are you doing?"

The nurse nearest the door turned and gently pushed her back out the door and into the hall, in time to see Dr. Gallagher taking long strides toward her. Without glancing her way, he hurried into the room, leaving Torri standing alone, blinking back tears.

Stop it, she told herself brusquely. You can't help him if you fall apart.

Gathering her courage, Torri slipped inside the room. She couldn't see past the bodies grouped around the bed but she didn't move any closer.

"All right," Dr. Gallagher was saying sharply. "Begin heart massage now."

In horror, Torri realized that Jake's heart must have stopped and they were trying to get it to start beating again. She felt a distinct pain in her hands and realized she was gripping them together so tightly that her fingernails were digging into her flesh.

The moments seemed an eternity as they worked over Jake. When Dr. Gallagher turned around, the relief in his blue eyes apparent, Torri breathed in relief.

"Dr. Gallagher, what—"

"Not in here," he said in a low voice. He led her out of the room.

"Did his heart stop?" Torri asked.

He nodded. "Yes, which isn't uncommon in cases like these where a wound has come so close to the heart."

He rubbed the back of his neck in a gesture that reminded her suddenly of Dr. Hamilton and she smiled, in spite of the seriousness of the situation, wondering in some other part of her mind if all doctors employed similar gestures of frustration.

"Will he be all right?"

"I think so. I have to admit I'm a little surprised it happened, even though, as I said, it isn't unusual. But at his age, with his strength, well, it just surprised me, that's all. From now on, though, I'm going to order a nurse to stay at his bedside at all times until we move him to his own room."

"When will that be?"

"Probably not until tomorrow morning, now." He patted her on the shoulder and frowned, his voice curious. "I have to admit also that I'm surprised to still see you here. Why don't you go home, and then if you're still concerned about this person you just picked up off the street, come and see him in the morning."

He grinned down at her and Torri knew, as the blood

rushed to her cheeks, that she wasn't fooling him a bit. But if she admitted it, he might call the policeman back and she wasn't ready to deal with any more questions right now.

"Okay," she agreed, "I'll do that, but may I see him first?"

Dr. Gallagher gave her a searching glance, as if he wanted to ask her something, then thought better of it and shrugged. "Of course, but don't stay long. See you in the morning." He strode off down the hallway.

Torri hurried into the recovery room. A nurse was sitting beside his bed and she glanced up sympathetically as Torri moved to stand beside the bed.

"Jake?" she whispered, leaning down until her lips almost touched him. "Jake, everything's going to be all right. I'll be back soon, I promise." She looked back at the nurse, but the woman was studiously reading a medical journal. Torri brushed her lips against his cold face, against the edge of his stubborn jaw that she loved to see clench in determination, or even anger.

Jake. Tears flooded her eyes and Torri straightened, forcing herself to think positively. They had escaped from Montgomery, that was all that mattered. Torri brushed an unruly lock of hair back from Jake's face.

"I love you," she said softly.

Torri left the room, emotionally exhausted, physically a wreck, wondering what to do next. She walked down the corridor, her hands in her jeans pockets, frowning in concentration. I don't have much money, she thought, mentally counting the change in her pocket, and I'm not in a time when I know anyone, except—

Torri had been walking without paying any attention, and looked up to find she had walked all the way to the main waiting room. She had spent most of her time in the small waiting room closest to the operating room, and hadn't noticed that there was an old-fashioned phone booth tucked into a corner across from the nurses' station. Impulsively she crossed the room and entered it, closing the narrow hinged doors carefully behind her.

She picked up the Richmond phone book and began flipping through the Hs until she reached the listing for Hamilton. Quickly Torri ran her finger down the page.

"Nathaniel Hamilton, Nathaniel Hamilton, Nathaniel—Nathaniel Hamilton!" There it was in black and white! Nathaniel Hamilton! The same address and everything!

"Then he's living in our house right now!" She did some quick mathematics in her head. "He's about twenty-seven years old. He told me once he'd gotten married very young, at age twenty. And his wife is alive too! She didn't die until 1970!"

Torri dropped the phone book from her trembling hands as the meaning of what she was saying sunk in. All she had to do was find a way to her grandfather's land and she could meet her grandmother! She couldn't count the number of times Grandfa had told her about Martha, his adored wife. How she liked to go for brisk walks in the wintertime, how she loved birds and always made sure the ground was covered with seed for them, summer and winter. She loved children too, he had said, and how she would have loved Torri, if only she had lived that long.

The little empty place in Torri's heart that her mother's love had once occupied suddenly ached to have that kind of love again. She leaned her head against her arm and let a few tears slip down her cheeks. Then her head snapped up and a new determination appeared in her eyes.

"Why can't I?" she whispered. "Why can't I go out there and meet her? I can pretend I'm lost, or—or—something! But I could meet her and I could see Grandfa too!"

What about Jake? was the thought that came immediately to challenge her decision. I'll wait until they take him to his room, she finally decided. It's only a few hours more, and then I'll tell him what I'm going to do and that I'll be back soon to visit him again.

That settled, she headed for the small waiting room where she tried to make herself as comfortable as possible on the stiff plastic couch. Jake was okay, and in a few hours she was going to meet her grandmother. Torri closed her eyes and hoped that this time her dreams would be sweet.

"You can go in now."

Torri walked anxiously into the hospital room. Jake lay in the hospital bed staring at the ceiling, the look on his face one of listless despair. That expression didn't change, even when he caught sight of her.

"Hello, Jake," she said, so happy to see him awake and alive she could hardly contain herself. She moved to his side and kissed him gently on the forehead. "The nurse said for you not to try to talk much."

"You look like hell," he whispered, his gray eyes shifting away from her face.

Torri flushed. She'd spent the entire night on the hard plastic couch, hadn't bathed since she couldn't remember when, had no comb, no brush and no make-up with her, and had been worried sick about Jake. She didn't doubt she looked a wreck.

"Thanks," she said, trying to keep her tone light, "you look pretty miserable yourself."

He turned his gaze back to hers and Torri was disturbed by the pain she saw mirrored there.

"I wasn't trying to kill him, Torri."

"I know." She walked to the end of the bed, then began smoothing the sheets, tucking them in on the side, her eyes averted. "You were mumbling something about it while you were unconscious."

Jake ran one hand through his tousled hair, his brows

knit together in frustration. "I thought if I could tell the colonel the truth, make him understand, that maybe even if I failed to convince the Council and they sent someone else back to kill him, he would at least be forewarned. I was even going to take him to Jeb Stuart's cabin and get him to lay low there for awhile."

"Why didn't you tell me?" Torri asked, looking up from her intense concentration on making his bed. "I thought—" she broke off and looked away, her face flushed.

"You thought I had lied to you again and used you so I could kill Reed." She nodded and Jake reached up to capture one of her long curls between his fingers and pulled her toward him. She sank down on the bed and leaned into his arms, careful not to touch his injured chest. "I don't blame you for thinking that, Torri. I've lied to you so much—"

Torri stilled his words with a quick, fervent kiss. "It's all right, everything's going to be all right. You'll get well and we'll go to your time and—"

"I've got to go back to 1863," he said, brushing his finger down the side of her jaw. Torri caught his hand in hers and pressed his palm against her face.

"Jake, you're too weak, you can't go anywhere."

"Montgomery has to be stopped before he kills Reed," he reminded her, kissing her hand and bringing it to rest on his thigh. He looked around the room, his gaze disoriented. "Where in time are we, anyway?"

Torri bit her lip. "Well, I didn't quite reach the mark. I was trying to get to my own time. This is 1941."

"Ah," he said thoughtfully, "World War II. Hard times." He seemed to consider the matter for a moment, then gestured with his hand, the one that wasn't attached to the IV. "Get me my clothes."

Torri laughed. "In your dreams, buster."

"Don't argue with me, just do it." Jake's voice was soft but determined and suddenly Torri felt that WWII might be a picnic compared to the fight that was about to take place.

"Are you crazy?" she demanded, sliding off his bed and facing him, her hands on her hips. "You're lucky to be alive. The doctor said you ought to be dead!"

His eyes slid shut and he sighed, deeply, then caught his breath in pain. "Yes," he whispered, "I ought to be dead."

Disregarding his remark, Torri went on angrily. "If you think you're going to get out of this bed and go traipsing back through time to fight Montgomery, you are sadly mistaken." He glared at her and Torri sighed. "Look, Jake, I know that I was the one who wanted to save Col. Reed, but I'm selfish. I don't want to save him if it means losing you."

Jake's eyes flickered slightly and Torri wondered at the wry smile that curved his lips.

"You don't understand. I have to stop Montgomery."

Torri brushed aside his words. "Jake—you said yourself the TDA is inaccurate. We might not even be able to get back to 1863 and you're too weak to chance it."

He turned his head slowly and looked at her, his eyes like steel. "Give me the TDA, and get my clothes."

"No."

Jake shot her a startled look.

"You are too weak to do any time traveling at all and you know it!" She glared at him with as much fierceness as she could muster. "I just came in to tell you that I'm going to be gone for a little while. A policeman may come in to see you because the doctor had to report your gunshot wound. "So," she tossed her hair back from her shoulders with a flippant shake of her head, "if I were you, I'd start working on a story instead of trying to figure out a way to kill yourself!" She turned and stalked toward the door.

"You don't understand. Torri—Torri— Dammit—wait—"

Jake punched the bed in helpless rage as the hospital door

swung shut behind her. He struggled to roll out of bed and found to his utter frustration that he was too weak to sit up, much less stand and go after her. She was gone and the necklace with her, before he could bring himself to tell·her the truth—that K'mer was his father. Now he would pay the consequences for his fear of admitting his loathsome lineage. If Montgomery killed Reed, Jake would die too, and every minute that ticked by without returning to 1863 brought him that much closer to death. Jake closed his eyes and prayed Torri would return in time.

Torri walked down the hospital corridor through the main waiting room to the elevator. She took great pleasure in punching the down button with her fist. She rode the elevator to the first floor and walked out the front door, feeling overwhelmingly relieved to get away from the hospital and Jake. After walking for awhile, she slowed down and realized she was heading in the general direction of her grandfather's house. If there were still buses, there was enough change in her pocket to get her to the Hamilton mansion.

The bus stopped just outside the city limits and Torri had a long walk ahead of her, at least another five miles, but she didn't mind. She needed the time to think, to try and sift through the big mess in her mind and figure things out. Pulling her jacket closer she suddenly realized it was late fall.

Torri stopped in her tracks. Not only had the TDA taken them to the wrong time, it had put them into a different season. Well, why not? If the device was as unreliable as Jake said it was—anything was possible. She started off down the road, glad that the sunshine streaming through the trees on either side made the walk fairly pleasant, even if the air was a trifle chilly.

It was hard to believe that only a month or so ago she had watched Grandfa go to the sanitarium, and thought if the worse thing that could ever happen to anyone. And it was terrible, there was no doubt about that, and she still intended to do something about it, once she got back to her own time.

But something had changed inside her. It had happened back in 1863, while she had helped Dr. Hamilton care for the wounded. It had happened, she thought, when she saw David Reynolds' missing leg. Then she had realized that war was the worst thing that could happen, to a nation, to a people, to a world. Individual problems faded and paled beside the all consuming effort of humanity to simply survive the odds of man trying to destroy man.

Was that how Jake felt? Was that feeling what had driven him to try to kill Col. Reed, even though he didn't want to? America in his time was involved in a different kind of war—a war of the underground. But weren't their goals and their dangers the same as those in open warfare? Weren't they taking the same risks?

Suddenly she understood why Jake was so angry. He was more than just a soldier in a cause. He was the only hope for his America and his people and he thought he had failed them.

She remembered the scars she had seen on Jake's back the night they made love. What had happened to him? She'd never had the chance to ask him. The Civil War had been filled with atrocities caused by battles. Was Jake's time filled with the same kind of horrors, with his people unable to fight back?

Torri started walking again, her thoughts flying almost faster than she could keep up with them. Slavery. She'd seen some of it back in 1863, during her trips into Richmond and at the hospital, seen how the blacks were treated. Even though Lincoln had declared them free, they were still property in the eyes of most Southerners. A lot of them had been treated well, she knew, but still most were considered inferiors, menials, animals. Was that the way it was in Jake's time? And worse?

Torri touched her aching head. How she wished her grandfather had never given her the necklace and she had never been swept into this living nightmare!

The sound of a cow mooing made her lift her eyes from the road and Torri saw she was only half a mile or so from her grandfather's land. She recognized the curve in the road up ahead, and quickened her pace, her heart quickening also at the thought of seeing her grandparents.

She almost passed right by the old home place. There was no huge iron gate, and no mansion. Torri crossed the road and stared at the torn up ground where she remembered the big house standing and realized work was just beginning on its foundation. No workmen were around, so she walked over to the mounds of dirt, feeling slightly dizzy as the knowledge that she was actually in her grandfather's past sunk in again.

"Here, chick, chick, chick," a voice called from the woods behind her. It was a pleasant, feminine voice and Torri started toward it. When she came out on the other side of the woods, she saw the familiar sight of Dr. Randolph Hamilton's frame farmhouse, now old and dilapidated. With a rush, Torri remembered her grandfather telling her that he and Martha had lived in the old house until he built the new one—the house Torri had grown up in.

A woman stood in the backyard, throwing corn to a bunch of clucking chickens. She looked up as Torri appeared, and brushed a wisp of auburn hair back from her forehead. The rest of her hair was pinned in a neat bun. Torri recognized her on sight, from the photograph her grandfather always kept next to his bed. It was Martha Hamilton, her grandmother.

"Hello," the older woman said, waving one hand, "I'm glad to see someone enjoying this lovely day." She turned up the collar of her thick sweater. "Even if it is a little brisk."

Torri walked toward her hesitantly, but didn't miss the opportunity to explain her presence. "Yes, I went out for a walk and I guess I got sort of turned around. I didn't mean to trespass."

"Oh, don't worry about that!" Martha said, scattering the last of the corn around her feet. "You're welcome to tramp these old woods anytime. A lot of history out there, you know, a lot of history."

"Yes," Torri said softly, "I know."

"Here I stand talking and I haven't even introduced myself. I'm Martha Hamilton, and you must be the Jacobses' niece, Trisha. They told me I could expect a visit sometime this week, but I'd forgotten all about it until I saw you come through the woods."

"W-well, it's an odd way to pay a visit, I suppose," Torri stuttered.

"Not at all." She set the enameled pan down on the step and walked over to Torri. "You see, you just thought you were lost. You came to exactly the right place. Come in, dear, and we'll have a nice talk."

Torri hesitated again. She didn't like letting this nice, sincere woman think she was someone else, but neither did she dare tell her the truth! And coming up with her own story was just another lie in the long list of lies that traveling in time seemed to demand. Might as well let her think she was this Trisha person. At least that way she was guaranteed a chance to talk to her grandmother.

The kitchen was just as she remembered it from 1863, except it was more cheerful and at the same time, more run-down. The high ceilings made the room look bigger than it was, and crisp white curtains at the windows looked mellow against the pale blue walls.

"I'll miss this old place," the woman said wistfully, "but my husband has his heart set on building me a fancy new house and I haven't the heart to say no."

"This is a very old house, isn't it?" Torri said, gratefully drinking the glass of milk Martha set down in front of her, trying not to gulp. The sandwich from the hospital was just a faint memory to her starving stomach.

Martha turned to the old-fashioned oven behind her and opened the door. "Yes, my yes. If this old house could talk, what stories it could tell!"

Torri smiled. "I bet it could. My grandfather told me it was built before the Civil War."

The woman turned, a pan of gingerbread, from the smell of it, in her two mitted hands. She looked at Torri strangely. "Your grandfather? I don't guess I know him, do I?"

"Oh," Torri said, flustered. She had already forgotten she was supposed to be Trisha somebody. "I—don't know."

"Well, anyway, he's right." She looked around the kitchen lovingly. "This old house was built in 1855. My Nathaniel's grandmother died here and his father was born here. I'll miss it, yes I will."

"Why don't you just stay here and not build the new house?" Torri said, eyeing the gingerbread hungrily. Martha smiled at her, and for the first time Torri noticed the freckles on her nose. It gave her a homey, happy look.

"And spoil Nathaniel's fun?" She cut a big piece of gingerbread and put it on a plate, then placed it in front of Torri. "Why I wouldn't dream of it. And he's right, of course. I'm a sentimental fool, but this old place isn't going to stand up much longer. It's just that we've had a lot of happy memories here."

"I shot you first!" Two little boys came barreling into the room, firing cap pistols at each other. The bigger, who looked to be about six years old, ran up to Martha and threw his arms around her skirt.

"Mama, Mama, I shot Jeremy first and he won't fall down!"

"Now, Nathan, he's smaller than you. Maybe he doesn't understand the game."

"He understands all right," the boy said, glaring over at his brother. "He just cheats."

"Here now, enough of this," Martha scolded. "Don't you see we have company? Come and say hello to Trisha, Mrs. Jacobs' niece. These are my sons, Nathan, he's six, and Jeremy, he's four."

Torri could only stare at them, her mouth hanging open as the two little boys said a begrudging how-do-you-do then scrambled for a piece of gingerbread before flying back into the other room.

My father! Torri thought in amazed silence. I just met my father and my uncle, Jeremy!

"Boys!" Martha exclaimed. "I swear I should take a switch to their backsides but the truth is I'm just an old softy when it comes to children—especially my own."

"Do you have any brothers or sisters?"

Torri heard the question through the fog around her brain and shook her head, too flabbergasted to speak.

"An only child? Well, that can be nice too, never having to squabble with the others." She smiled and Torri suddenly forgot the strangeness of it all and only felt her grandmother's loving spirit.

"Where is—is your husband home?" Torri asked, hoping Nathaniel would be, wishing she could see him and her grandmother together just once.

"No, he's in town at his office. This war has kept him busy. He owns the *Richmond Chronicle*, you know, and then with him being Civil Defense Chairman for this part of town, I hardly ever see him anymore." Her voice was wistful, then she offered Torri another piece of gingerbread. She accepted gratefully. Her stomach was so empty it was knocking a hole in her side. As if in conjunction with her thoughts, a knock sounded from the other room.

Torri jumped, remembering another knock on that same door one hundred years before, only a few nights ago. She shook her head to dispel the thought and wondered if time travelers ever went crazy.

"I'll get that, it's Lavida, dropping Christine off," she explained, then headed through the kitchen door.

She was gone before Torri understood what she had said. Christine. Christine? Grandfa had told her that Martha used to take care of her aunt when she was a child until her mother, Lavida, had sent her to a boarding school when she was about six years old. Was it possible she was about to meet the woman—child—that would someday grow up to ruin her grandfather's life?

Chapter Fifteen

The door to the kitchen opened again and there stood the most beautiful woman Torri had ever seen. She had honey gold hair, swept up in an elaborate coiffure, her eyes were dark-lashed and a startling aquamarine blue. Only her haughty expression kept her face from being truly lovely, and Torri felt an immediate dislike for the woman.

Martha hurried in next, holding a little blond-headed girl by the hand. The girl had her eyes downcast, her lips puckered into a pout.

"Lavida," Martha said, "this is Trisha, Mrs. Jacobs' niece. And this, Trisha, is Christine, Lavida's daughter."

The woman swept Torri a disdainful look and drew her mink coat a little closer as if fearing Torri might damage it just by her presence.

"How do you do?" she said coldly, then turned back to Martha. "Martha, I do appreciate you're being willing to take Christine for such an extended time, but the doctor says I simply must get away. The divorce was so stressful—"

"Yes," Martha said, looking down at the little girl still standing beside her, "I know it was hard on all of you. But it's just fine with me for Christine to stay here." She knelt beside the girl. "We'll have a lot of fun, won't we, Chris?"

The little girl's pout disappeared and she looked up hopefully at Martha. Her face was a younger copy of her mother's, her eyes the same blue, her hair the same honey blond. She started to smile, then lowered her eyes again, the pout reappearing as her mother spoke, her tone harsh.

"Please, Martha, don't call her by that terrible nickname! Now, Christine," she shook her finger at the little girl, "you will mind Mrs. Hamilton won't you? And Mommy will be back before you know it."

With that, Christine threw herself around her mother's legs and set up a howl that Torri was sure could be heard for miles.

Lavida frowned in annoyance. "Christine, really! Stop this behavior at once!" She pulled the little girl away from her and gave her a shake. "Now, I'll be back soon and when I come I'll bring you all kinds of wonderful things from the islands." She bent down to the little girl's level and her voice softened. "You'll like that, won't you, darling?"

"I d-o-o-on't w-a-a-ant y-o-o-ou t-o-o-o g-o-o-o!" Christine wailed.

Lavida straightened. "Well, I'm going!" she snapped. "You'll be just fine here with Martha. Now, give me a kiss, I've got to go before I miss my train."

The trembling little girl reached up and planted a kiss on her mother's face then dissolved into tears again. Lavida pried the loving little arms from around her neck and picked the child up, depositing her in Martha's arms.

"I don't know what's wrong with her. Goodbye, Martha, you have the address where I can be reached. Goodbye, Christine, be a good little girl."

The cold woman then swept out of the house, leaving the little girl weeping as if her heart would break. Martha held her close and patted her comfortingly.

"There, there, Chris. Mommy will be back before you know it. You and I are going to have a lot of fun together, and Jeremy and Nathan have been waiting to play with you."

"Don't want to play wif' them," came the muffled reply.

"Well, would you like a piece of gingerbread and a glass of milk?" There was a sniffling moment, then a brusque nod from the blond head. "All right. I'll get it and you can sit in the playroom and just watch the boys play for awhile, how about that?"

Torri watched as Martha led Christine into the other room. She came back shaking her head and began to cut a piece of gingerbread.

"That poor child," she said, "to have such a selfish mother. The only reason I'm a party to any of it is that I know if I didn't keep her, Lavida would hire a stranger to babysit her. This is the second time in the last six months she's gone off and left that little girl for more than a month at a time!"

"What's her last name?" Torri asked, almost afraid to hear the answer.

"Lavida?" She paused to think, then placed the piece of gingerbread on a plate and handed it to Torri, before cutting another wedge. "Let me see. It was Nelson first, and then Connors, now it's Humphreys, that's the girl's father."

Christine Humphreys! She *was* her aunt! Torri sat deep in thought as Martha poured a glass of milk. She carried it into the next room and Torri could hear her talking to the little girl in quiet, gentle tones.

No wonder Christine was such a witch! was the first thought that came to Torri's mind. With a mother like that, who wouldn't be? Torri thought back to how her mother had been, sweet, funny, a little hot-tempered, but quick to say she was sorry first. How would it have been to grow up with a mother so selfish that she dumped you every few months then went off to find another husband?

"Lavida never did want that baby," Martha said after coming back in from the playroom. "She's not a relative but her mother and I were very good friends when she was alive." She sighed. "Lavida's mother was a kind woman but her father was a monster. I suppose that's why she turned out this way."

"My grandfather always said that the things that happen to a person as a child can follow him throughout his life,"

Torri mumbled around a huge bite of gingerbread, then flushed and apologized. "I'm sorry, it's just so good."

Martha smiled. "I'm glad you like it. Well, I suppose that's true. Lavida has even hinted around that she'd be willing to give me and Nathaniel custody of Christine, but I don't know if that's a good idea. I'm afraid I'd just get attached to the little darling and then Lavida would swoop down and carry her off."

"Excuse me for saying so, Mrs. Hamilton," Torri said, brushing the crumbs from her lap, "but you already seem pretty attached to her."

Martha nodded and set a cup of hot tea down in front of her, then sank back into her own chair. "Yes, that's true of course. But is it right to take someone else's child? Maybe I've misjudged Lavida. Surely she must love Christine in her own way."

Torri stared down at her hands. It was strange to feel such empathy for Christine, but she did.

"You know, my parents died when I was six years old. I went to live with my grandfather, and he was wonderful." She lifted her gaze to her grandmother's puzzled one. "But I had an aunt—an aunt who was very selfish and mean. I've often wondered what would have happened to me, how it would have changed my life if she had been my guardian instead of my grandfather."

"Your parents died when you were six?" Martha said, perplexed. "But I met them last fall when they came to the County Fair. They said you were staying with a friend."

Torri almost dropped the gingerbread plate off the table. "Yes," she said, thinking quickly, "those were my adopted parents. I—I was adopted." She flashed Martha a bright smile. "I really ought to be going."

"Oh, must you go?" Her grandmother looked genuinely disappointed and once again Torri got a glimpse of what it would have been like to have had a mother. "Well, I've enjoyed talking to you, dear, and you come back any time."

"I enjoyed it too," Torri said sincerely. "And thank you for the gingerbread; it was really delicious. I wonder—" she hesitated.

Martha smiled. "Would you like one for the road?"

Torri laughed. "Well, actually, I've got a friend in the hospital. I was going in to see him and I'd like to take him a piece."

"Of course!" Martha got up and started immediately cutting a huge hunk of gingerbread. "Is your friend very ill?"

Immediately, Torri regretted saying anything about Jake, but she answered the question as best she could, getting by with saying he had had an appendectomy. More lies, the honest part of her whispered. Shut up, she hissed back. In a matter of moments she was on the front porch with a piece of gingerbread in her hand.

"Now, come back, anytime," Martha was saying, "I'd love for Nathaniel to meet you—well, what do you know? Here he comes now."

Torri looked up, startled, and saw a tall, thin man walking up the dirt driveway. He had dark brown hair and she had to look twice to recognize her grandfather.

"Grandfa . . ." she whispered as he walked up the steps, a newspaper tucked under his arm, a weary but pleasant look on his face.

"How's my favorite girl?" he asked, pausing beside Martha to peck her on the cheek.

Torri's heart leaped at his words, then sagged again as she saw he was talking to his wife, not her. But that's what you used to—I mean—what you'll say to me too, every day after school. Oh, Grandfa, how I miss you! she thought.

"And who's this lovely young lady?" He turned to Torri and she could only stare. This young, young man was her grandfather. How handsome he had been, how much like her own father.

"I—I'm—" she started, only to be saved by Martha's intervention.

"This is Liz Jacobs' niece, Trisha. She came by to see me today."

"Is that so?" He looked at her sharply and Torri could see the keen mind of a newspaper man at work. After a moment his rather stern face relaxed. "Well, that's great. Martha doesn't get a lot of company out here."

Suddenly Torri wished she hadn't said she had to go so soon. How she wanted to talk to her grandfather, even—her heart began thumping rapidly—tell him who she really was. Could she, was it possible she could warn him, tell him about what was going to happen forty or fifty years in the future? Or would that be doing what she accused Jake of doing? Trying to control destiny?

Her palms were sweating and she was glad her grandfather didn't offer to shake hands. There was an awkward moment as they all stared at each other, then Torri broke the silence.

"I've got to be going," she said, unable to keep the wistfulness out of her voice, "it was nice to meet you."

"Don't run off on my account," her grandfather said, "come on in and stay for supper."

Torri felt torn, but the image of Jake alone in the hospital overshadowed her desire to accept the invitation. "No," she said, "I've got to go into Richmond and visit a friend of mine who's in the hospital."

Nathaniel Hamilton glanced around. "I don't see a car or a bicycle."

"I'm going to walk."

Martha threw up her hands. "All the way into Richmond? Why I wouldn't hear of it. Nathaniel, you can run her into town, can't you?"

"Oh, no," Torri said quickly, even though a part of her hoped he would insist, "I wouldn't want to put you out."

"I know the Jacobses haven't gotten their truck fixed yet," Martha said, "but I could switch Liz Jacobs for letting you walk all the way out here—and this close to dusk too!"

"Please don't get mad at her," Torri said, thinking that poor Liz Jacobs was going to have a lot to explain after Torri left. "I'm used to it, really." She went quickly down the steps.

"Wait a minute!" Her grandfather's authoritative voice stopped her and she turned back, anxiously.

"Now, there's no reason for you to walk. I just remembered I left something in my office." He gave Martha a hug, then pointed to his car. "Come on, Trisha, is it? I'll run you to the hospital. Glad to do it."

Torri looked up at Martha on the porch and wished she could hug her goodbye. By tomorrow her grandmother would have discovered she wasn't Trisha Jacobs at all and Torri wouldn't be able to come back again. Now she wished she had corrected her at the beginning and just given her another name, told her she was on vacation, out for a walk, anything—but now it was too late.

"Goodbye," she said to her grandmother, "I'm glad to have met you." She hesitated, then plunged on. "I know you won't understand this, but today has been very special to me. You've—you've helped me."

Her grandmother's brow puckered a little, as if trying to understand what Torri meant, then she smiled. "I'm glad, dear, and anytime you want to come and see me, you're very welcome."

Torri turned quickly away and climbed into the car beside her grandfather, fighting the tears welling up in her eyes. Thankfully Nathaniel didn't seem to notice and he didn't speak until they were well on their way into Richmond.

"Now," he said, giving her a sideways glance, "who are you really?"

Torri stared at him, her mouth wide open. "W-what do you mean?" she asked, trying to think of what to say.

"I mean, I met Mrs. Jacobs' niece yesterday in town and she's short, plump and has short dark hair." He cocked his head at her. "You seemed sincere—that last little conversation with Martha—so I don't think you meant any harm. But why pretend to be someone you aren't?"

"I—I—wish I could tell you," Torri said, staring down at her hands. "I just don't think you'd believe me."

"Try me."

Torri swallowed hard and opened her mouth. Don't do it, the little voice in her brain said. You'll either end up in a straitjacket or blurt out what's going to happen in the future. Either way you could get yourself—and your grandfather— into a lot of trouble.

Quickly she thought up a convincing lie, feeling again the sharp pang of guilt for having to tell yet another fabrication.

"The truth is," Torri said. "My fiance and I were in a car accident. He's the one who's in the hospital. I went out walking— to think about things—and I ended up at your house."

"So far out in the country?" He gave her a doubtful look.

"Yes. I love to walk. I get tired of the city." She glanced at him, her eyes round, and she hoped, full of sincerity. "When I met your wife and she thought I was someone else, well, it just seemed easier to play along."

"Why?"

Torri looked out the window and when she spoke again she tried to sound sad—which wasn't difficult. "I—I don't know. I guess I needed someone to talk to. I—I've been trying to decide whether or not to get married and there she was and seemed so nice and open and—and I'm not making much sense, am I?"

Not any sense at all! she thought miserably. She was just rambling, making up more and more lies and the best thing to do was to just keep her mouth shut. There was a long silence and Torri felt the sweat break out across the back of her neck. Inside she was screaming. Grandfa! Grandfa! It's me! I want to tell you so much, I want to warn you of what lies ahead! But if I do—

Torri lifted her head and stared out the window. If I do, how do I know I won't change something that shouldn't be changed? She looked at him.

He was rubbing his hand across his chin in a gesture so familiar it brought a lump to her throat.

"I don't really understand," he said, "but no harm done I suppose. Will your fiance be all right?" His slightly bushy brows were pressed together in concern and she quickly averted her eyes.

"Yes, thank God."

Her grandfather nodded, obvious relief on his face. How kind you are, Torri thought suddenly. You don't know who I am and yet you care. And Martha will care too, when you tell her. She won't even be angry, I know. I wish I could stay here with you. Stay here and not go back to the mess I left behind.

Torri closed her eyes and leaned her head against the window. When I get back home, she thought, I'm going to ask Grandfa if he remembers this, and I'm going to ask his forgiveness for lying to him so completely.

"Here we are," Nathaniel said, pulling the car up in front of the hospital entrance.

Torri didn't move for a minute. This was her last chance, if she wanted to tell him the truth, if she wanted even to drop him a hint about who she really was. Would it hurt to tell him her name?

"Thank you," she said, opening the car door slowly. "And I want you to know, I didn't mean any harm."

"I believe that. Would you—when I tell Martha, I think it would mean a lot to her if I could tell her your real name."

Torri smiled, glad the decision had been taken out of her hands. "It's Victoria, Victoria Hamilton. My friends call me Torri."

Nathaniel frowned. "That's odd. My name is Hamilton too." The frown disappeared. "Well, I guess it's a common name." He handed her a card. "Here's my business card. If you stay in town longer than you think you might, give us a call. I think Martha took a shine to you."

Torri felt the tears smarting at her eyes again and blinked them back. "I liked her, too." She climbed out of the car, then turned. "Thank you, Grandfa," she said without thinking, then gasped and slammed the door, running quickly up the steps and into the hospital.

Inside she leaned against the door and closed her eyes tightly. The desire to go home rushed over her with an intensity she had not felt in many weeks. She had to get back home and save her grandfather.

A familiar voice caused her to look up in sudden disbelief. In the hallway she saw Dr. Gallagher in conversation with— Lucas Montgomery! Montgomery no longer wore his Confederate uniform, but dark trousers and a white lab coat, and he held a clipboard.

Torri swallowed hard and took an involuntary step backward. How had he found them? He'd bragged about all the advances the scientists had made, had they devised a way to track the other devices through time? Suddenly, she wondered if Jake's heart failure *had* been an accident. Even the doctor thought it had been unusual. A cold chill ran down her spine. Was Montgomery posing as a doctor to try to get rid of Jake?

I've got to get to Jake, she thought, her back against the door. I've got to get us out of here.

The long lever to the entrance door pushed down with her weight, and before she knew what she was doing, Torri found herself running down the front steps of the hospital, down the sidewalk and into the alleyway beside the building.

She dodged garbage cans and leaped over old boxes until she reached the back of the hospital. Crouching down behind the last garbage can in the alley, aware Montgomery could have more men with him, watching the place, she cautiously peeked over the top. No one was in sight. Quickly she ran up the few back steps and into the hospital.

The sound of her footsteps rang out in the silent corridor and Torri switched to her tiptoes, ducking into a closet marked LINEN. She sank down behind a pile of folded towels and leaned her head against her hands, trying to think.

Torri's fingers sought out the comfort of her necklace, still around her neck beneath her shirt, for a moment. Then she edged toward the door and opened it a crack. The hallway appeared deserted and she slipped out, moving soundlessly through the corridor, darting a cautious look over her shoulder from time to time. She reached the stairs without any problems.

Jake was on the fourth floor and she knew that there wasn't much chance that his door would be unguarded now, but still she headed up the first flight of stairs, her feet barely touching the steps as she flew quickly up them. Torri stopped on the second landing to catch her breath for a second, then started up again.

"In a hurry, Miss Hamilton?" said a deep voice from behind her on the landing.

Torri stopped. She had reached the fifth step above the landing and turned back, her heart pounding as she faced her enemy.

He stepped forward, out of the shadows. In his hand he held a small black box. "How lovely to see you again," he said smoothly.

Torri made a sound that was a cross between a laugh and a snort of derision. "Sorry I can't say the same. What do you want?"

"I think you know what I want. Your necklace and your cooperation, in that order."

"Go to hell," Torri said, backing up a step.

His low, malicious chuckle sent a shiver of fear up her spine. "Hell is a fascinating place, lovely one. And you may find that dancing with the devil is preferable to dying."

Torri took another step up the stairs. "You tried to kill Jake in the recovery room, didn't you?"

"Yes, and I would have succeeded if you hadn't woken up and alerted the nurses. You are decidedly becoming a nuisance, my dear."

"Well, just to satisfy my curiosity, what did you do exactly?" Torri only hoped if she kept him talking perhaps she could find a way to escape this deadly madman.

"I just injected a substance into his I.V. which would cause him to have a heart attack. And he did! How marvelous drugs can be! But then again, you already know that, don't you, my beauty?"

Ignoring his insinuation, Torri's glance darted to the object in his hands, as she tried to stall for more time. She took another step up. "What's that?" she asked, remembering old episodes of *Star Trek*. "A phaser or something?"

Montgomery laughed. "As if you didn't know. You're good, you are very good, I'll give you that."

"That's what you used on Jake in 1863," Torri said, remembering Dr. Gallagher's comments about Jake's injury.

"Yes, and unless you join me now, it's what I'll use on you."

Torri ran her tongue across her dry lips, wishing her heart would stop thudding in her ears.

"Except," he went on, "this time I'll set it on the highest setting and you, my dear Miss Hamilton, will simply disappear into oblivion. K'meron will never know what happened to you. He will simply think you deserted him and disappeared into time."

"How did you find us?"

"Oh, yes, that's an interesting little bit of information you may not be aware of. When a TDA is being used within a space of one hundred years, it enables someone else to use one within that same space with a much larger degree of accuracy, rather like the currents of a river draw debris into its undertow."

"What a fitting comparison," Torri said.

"Clever. But you understand what I mean. The power of your necklace drew me to you. All I had to do was open my mind and allow the jewels to home in on your signal. And now, Miss Hamilton, we have dallied long enough."

As Montgomery glanced down at the weapon he held and twisted the dial to change it to a more lethal setting, Torri seized the moment and propelled herself off the step and into the startled mans arms. Wrapping her legs around his waist, Torri knocked the weapon from his hand, and as the two of them fell backwards, Torri heard Montgomery's shoulder blades crack as they hit the floor.

Montgomery howled in agony and his grip loosened long enough for Torri to wrench free. She turned and took the steps by threes. She knew she only had moments before Montgomery alerted the hospital or made it to Jake's room himself. Torri dashed down the hall, thankful that for the moment it was blessedly empty. She barreled into Jake's room and as he looked up, startled, threw herself against him, thrusting the necklace into his hand.

"Take us to 1863, Jake," she ordered. "Now!"

Jake didn't waste time asking questions. The door to the room burst open, but not before the kaleidoscope of watercolor started, blending and fading, sending the two of them far away from Lucas Montgomery.

The colors swirled around her and the old panic surged up inside of Torri until a gentle pressure on her hand reminded her that Jake was with her, no matter where they ended up, Jake was with her. Goodbye, Dr. Gallagher, she said silently, I liked you. Goodbye, Grandmother. Goodbye, Grandfa— again. The colors stopped and the blackness pulled her down into infinity.

Chapter Sixteen

"You'll be just fine. All you need is rest now and your body will heal itself." Dr. Hamilton leaned back after examining Jake's chest and shook his head. "I can't get over the technique the doctor used to close the wound. Amazing."

"What's amazing is that we made it back here," Torri said. "I expected to end up with dinosaurs or cavemen." She turned to Jake. "What do you think made the difference this time?"

Not only had they reached the right year, but they had arrived only a few days later than when they left 1863. According to the doctor, the search for Jake had stopped during the battle of Chancellorsville, the battle that had taken place on the day Jake was shot.

Jake raised up on his elbows, his dark eyebrows pressed together. "I've been thinking about it and I'm not really sure, but maybe the fact that both our life energies were combined and we were mentally concentrating on the time period had something to do with it."

Their eyes met and his gaze was hot, liquid. Torri felt a similar fire ignite inside her as she remembered combining her life energy with Jake's. How, she wondered, could she have ever let Montgomery touch her? After their return to 1863, while Dr. Hamilton was out of the room, Jake had explained to her that Montgomery had given her a strong aphrodisiac to try to get her into his bed. She had been vastly relieved to know that she hadn't acted of her own accord; however, it still was rather disturbing to realize a drug could make her behave so wantonly, and with such a horrible man. Her thoughts returned to the discussion at hand.

"But when I tried to take you to the future when you were dying, we were both thinking of 1994," Torri reminded him. "And we ended up in 1941."

His mouth quirked. "Sorry, kitten, but I passed out before that ride ever started. So this trip was the first time we used our ability together." He eased back against the pillow and glanced around the plain room where the doctor had insisted he rest ever since they arrived the night before.

They had appeared in downtown Richmond, at the same location where they had arrived in 1941. Luckily, it was an empty lot in 1863. It hadn't been far from there to Dr. Hamilton's temporary home, although they had both held their breath, afraid of being recognized before they reached safety.

Explaining the TDA in more detail to Dr. Hamilton—Torri's being given it by her grandfather and his being committed to the sanitarium, as well as the story of K'mer and Montgomery—had taken most of the night. Dr. Hamilton had then related a story about his father. It seemed that on his deathbed the elder Hamilton had told his son a disturbing story about Randolph's spinster aunt traveling through time, and about her diary. He'd told Randolph to read the diary when the time was right. But Dr. Hamilton had chalked it up to a dying man's ravings.

To Torri's intense relief, once the doctor had heard the entire story and had promised to read the diary soon, he did an abrupt about face on his attitude toward Jake. He even understood the things Jake had desperately done on their wedding night, which made Torri more than a little angry at the two of them, nodding at one another like old friends.

She'd gotten over it, though, too happy that Jake was alive to be angry at anyone for long. But was his theory about their accurate trip through time true? Or had Jake just been lying to her all along about the inaccuracy of the device to keep her in 1863 until he was able to use her TDA himself?

Torri lifted her hair from her nape and sighed. She was hot and tired of thinking. She had to choose to trust Jake. If she didn't, it would make everything they had shared a charade.

Torri turned to find him watching her, his expression guarded, his gray eyes wary. Did he suspect she doubted him?

"Is he really going to be all right?" she said abruptly to the doctor. "I mean, he'd barely been out of surgery for more than a few hours before we had to take a chance on traveling back here again."

"He'll be fine," he reassured her. "If he'll take it easy for a while."

"Will you two stop talking about me as if I'm not here?" Jake said in a cross voice.

Torri shot Jake a quelling look. "You won't be here at all unless you stay put. Now, is that clear?" She folded her arms over her chest and tried to look stern.

Jake stared at the ceiling for a moment, then asked for some water. Torri brought him a glassful, watching him suspiciously. Jake drank it down, with Torri supporting him, then lay back, his face pale, his expression determined.

"I've got to stop Montgomery," Jake said. "I can't wait until I'm better."

Torri shook her head. "We aren't going to let you, are we, doctor? You can't help the colonel if you're dead!"

"You don't understand." His gray eyes shifted to hers and were so glacial that suddenly Torri felt frightened. She moved closer to him, and picked up his hand, squeezing it gently. He returned the pressure and his gaze softened slightly, even as the lines in his face grew deeper.

"K'mer is my father," he said.

Torri's mouth fell open. "Your father!" She stared down at him in horror. "Then your own father tortured you."

"Yes."

She dropped his hand and paced across the room, her mind reeling with the implications of what he had said. "Your father!" Torri whirled around. "But that means—that means that if Reed dies . . ." her voice trailed away.

Jake nodded. "I die. Simple, eh? It's very tidy, really. The underground gets everything they want in one neat package. K'mer is gone forever, and K'meron—his untrustworthy son—is dead too, after proving himself by his noble sacrifice."

His voice was bitter and Torri felt her eyes burn from her tears as she realized what he must have endured, first at the hands of his own father, then from the very people he was trying to help.

"Oh, Jake, what did he do to you?" she whispered. "Those scars on your back . . ."

"Yeah," he cut her off. "But the scars on my soul are the ones that torture me. He killed my uncle, his own brother, right in front of me. He told me that if I wouldn't help him, wouldn't stand at his side as some kind of prince, then I wasn't his son. Which by that time, was just fine with me." He took a deep breath. "The funny thing is that when I escaped from him and found the underground, they wouldn't trust me. For five years I did everything I could think of to prove myself. Then, well, they knew my uncle had given me his TDA, before we were captured and he died, so—"

"So they asked you to commit suicide!" Torri said, pacing the room again, her hands clenched behind her back.

Jake closed his eyes. The memories of his father and his torture were painful, but the memory of T'ria and her people—their refusal to accept him—hurt almost as much.

"Whether I killed Reed or not, the result would be the same: I'd be dead, along with the rest of my family. Or rather, we would have never existed. I decided I didn't want to sit around and wait to disappear from existence. At least when the time came I'd know it was by my own hand. Maybe I was trying to prove to myself I wasn't afraid to die, that I wasn't a coward." He laughed without humor. "All I've ended up doing is proving that I am."

Torri stopped her pacing and sank down onto the bed. She leaned over Jake, one hand on either shoulder. "Why? Because you refuse to murder an innocent man?" Torri asked, leaning toward him. "Because you want to live? Don't be ridiculous." Tears flooded her eyes. "You aren't a coward!"

"I didn't have anything to live for before." Jake reached up and smoothed her hair back from her face. "That doesn't make me any less of a coward now."

"Jake Cameron, you can never convince me that you wouldn't have come to this same conclusion with or without me. You aren't saving Reed because you want me. You're saving him because you aren't a murderer." She leaned down and kissed him gently, then repeated, "You are not a murderer."

Jake pulled her to him and Torri felt the gratitude in his embrace and when their lips met again, she knew that Jake had started back on the long road toward believing in himself.

Dr. Hamilton cleared his throat abruptly and they both looked up, startled to find another person in the room.

He chuckled, and winked. "I'll head out to the camp and check on the colonel." He shot Torri a stern look. "I'm taking Henry and Hannah with me, so it's up to you, young lady, to keep this man in bed. And that's an order."

Dr. Hamilton walked out of the room and after a few minutes they heard the front door close, followed by the gentle hoofbeats of the horse pulling the wagon into town. As soon as it was obvious he was gone, Torri moved to the door, shut it, then turned around, cocking her eyebrow provocatively.

"Well," she said, her hands moving to the back of her dress, "he did say it was an order."

* * *

After making sure that Torri was sound asleep, Jake swung his legs over the side of the bed. He brushed one finger down the side of her face. She stirred and he dropped his hand away. Their lovemaking had been like a slow flame, steadily stoked from a seemingly unending supply of fuel. They had burned with it the rest of the afternoon and into the night, then slept, exhausted.

Torri had asked him several times if he was in pain, and even though he was miserable from the burning in his chest, he denied it. He knew it would be the last time he would ever make love to heir.

Jake dressed as quickly as he could, although he had to stop often to catch his breath. He donned trousers, shirt and boots, provided by a thoughtful Hannah for when "Mr. Jake is feeling better," since he'd left his own clothing in 1941.

The room was shadowed, but lit by moonlight. He moved cautiously around until he found what he was looking for. The necklace lay on top of Torri's blue jeans, crumpled on the floor. During their lovemaking she had worried about the pendant pressed into his chest, so she had tossed it on top of her clothes. He picked it up and gazed down at the sparkling jewels.

Love. Yes, he loved her, for all the good it did him. Talking about his father, about his uncle, the resistance, had brought it all back to him, made it all real again. He had lost touch with his mission and as a result, had lost himself in Torri's love. His gaze raked over her sleeping form. She was so beautiful, and so young. He closed his eyes. He had to go. Had to stop Montgomery. He had no illusions about his own invincibility. It could easily be he who lost in this final battle. He had to find Montgomery and put an end to this game. His only fear was that it might mean leaving Torri trapped in the past. He closed his eyes.

Give me the strength, he silently begged a God he had long ago stopped believing in, to do what is right.

Torri opened her eyes and saw Jake sitting on the side of the bed, his face buried in his hands. She'd been dreaming about her Grandfa. She lay there for a moment and thought, with a kind of fear, how far away and dreamlike her Grandfa had become, even when she was awake. Coming back to 1863 had felt like coming home, and the memory of her grandfather's face on her mind seemed more and more like a photograph, flat and indistinct. It was a frightening feeling.

"Jake?" she whispered. "Are you all right?"

His head jerked up with a snap and Torri saw the old mask—the mask she hadn't seen after the night they first made love—settle over Jake's features.

"What is it?" she said, sitting up and moving to his side. "What's going on?"

"You've got to get out of here," he said, extending his hand toward her. The other rested on the necklace.

A cold chill swept over her and Torri flung herself away from him, practically falling out of the bed to the floor. Jake circled the end of the iron footboard, his purpose written clearly on his face.

"No!" Torri said, moving quickly to the other side of the room, the sheet she had clasped around her trailing. "I'm not going back to my time before I know you're all right. After you stop Montgomery—"

"Montgomery may stop me—has that ever occurred to you?" Jake said, still relentlessly pursuing her around the room. "If I die, you're going to be stuck here forever." His expression grew even harder, if that were possible. "I told you, Torri, remember? I told you there could be no future for us. We've both known it all along. You belong in another time, another place."

"You said that you loved me." She moved toward the door

but Jake blocked her way. She backed away before he could touch her.

"That has nothing to do with this."

"It has everything to do with it!" she shouted from the other side of the bed where she had circled to escape him again.

"We can't be together."

"I won't accept that, Jake."

Jake stopped and stared at her, an incredulous expression on his face. "What? You knew—"

"I don't care what I knew—I'm in this for the long haul," she said defiantly. "Once I know you've defeated Montgomery then maybe I'll go home. But not until then—not until I say!"

"Will you stand still!" Jake said, lunging for her.

Torri neatly side-stepped him and he sprawled across the bed, groaning. Torri moved toward him then caught herself.

"Are you all right?"

"Please, Torri," he said, gasping, "let me take you home. I've got to know you're safe."

Moonlight drifted through the window, casting strange shadows around the room. Torri could hear Jake's labored breathing and her own heart pounding rapidly in her ears. If she went back to her own time, she would never see Jake again. She knew it as surely as she knew she loved him.

"Then you should understand how I feel," she said from across the room. "I want to know *you're* safe."

He pulled himself to a sitting position and Torri felt a pang as she saw how weak he still was.

"You don't understand, do you? Suppose I stop Montgomery, suppose I make it back to the Council. What if they don't buy my little speech about letting Reed live?" He ran his hand raggedly through his tawny hair. "If they don't kill me on sight first, of course." He shook his head wearily. "Either way, I could be a dead man. We have no future."

Torri moved around the end of the bed and faced him, still keeping her distance. Her voice was hushed. "If you take me back against my will it will be as much a violation of my person as if you had raped me that first night we spent together." Her words were sharp and decisive as she took a step toward him. "I want our time together, Jake—however long or short that time may be."

"What about your grandfather? And Christine? What about changing history so that you can help him?"

She caught her breath. "That's changed." Torri turned away from him. "I've seen what meddling with time can do—how dangerous it is, and I have no intention of trying to manipulate it to my bidding. My grandfather. . . ." She swallowed hard. "My grandfather will be all right."

"Rather callous of you, don't you think?"

"Damn you, Jake!" Tears ran down her cheeks as she stood with her fists clenched, her chest heaving with anger and fear. "I love you! That may not mean anything in your time, but it means a hell of a lot in mine! Can't you understand that I'd rather die with you than live without you?"

Jake stood and walked toward her. Torri didn't move this time, but stood poised for flight as she gazed up into his eyes. They were dark with pain, tender with love. He held her spellbound until at last she felt him take her hand. She jerked away but his hold tightened and Torri realized he was pressing the necklace into her palm, jewel side up.

"Yes," he said softly, "that, I understand."

Torri released her pent-up breath with a sob and threw her arms around his neck. "Hold me, Jake," she whispered. "Hold me and never let me go."

The Confederate camp was quiet in the misty hour before dawn as Torri and Jake approached stealthily through the dense woods surrounding its perimeter.

They had agreed—after Torri convinced him to let her

stay—that their first priority was to protect Col. Reed. Montgomery was the random element in this equation and there was no telling where or when he would turn up. They couldn't take a chance on sending Reed a message warning him. It was too likely he might dismiss it as a prank or a joke. Their best bet was to get him out of the rebel camp and into a hiding place—with or without his cooperation.

They stopped in their slow push through the dense underbrush, and conferred in low voices as to how they could best take out the sentry outside the colonel's tent.

"I'm going to make a reconnaissance of the area," Jake whispered. "Stay here." He slipped into the blackness.

Torri sat back on her heels and waited, realizing that she was tired, dirty, and hungry. When this was over and she was back in her own time, she was going to take a long, hot bath, go to her favorite restaurant and then sleep for a week.

Without Jake. She covered her face with her hands. Could she really bear to leave him? But what choice did she have? He'd made it very clear there was no future for them together. If they succeeded in saving Reed she knew he had to go back to the future. He had made it clear that under no circumstances would he take her with him to that place of horror. No, when this was over, it would really be over. She would go her way and Jake his, and their love would become just a distant memory.

Her throat tightened and Torri quickly turned her mind toward Mrs. Merriwether's ball the next night. It was there they intended to trap Montgomery. Hannah would spread it around town that Torri would attend the gala affair with her grandfather, Dr. Hamilton, and that she was going to wear the doctor's heirloom necklace. If Montgomery had indeed come back to the past, he would surely show up at the ball.

The plan was simple but dangerous, especially for her, since she would be the bait and K'mer's agent was unpredictable. She and Jake had argued about it for almost two hours before he finally agreed—on the condition that Torri was never left alone with Montgomery.

She shifted in her cramped position and glanced over her shoulder. Dr. Hamilton was waiting with the wagon a half mile down the road that led through the woods. Jake would carry Reed to the wagon and then the doctor would take him to his home outside Richmond. Hopefully, if Montgomery had returned to the past, he wouldn't have any idea how to find Dr. Hamilton's home.

Torri released her breath in a quiet sigh. She hadn't wanted the doctor involved any further, but when he heard their plan, he was determined to help them.

"Okay," Jake whispered, after appearing soundlessly at her elbow. "I knocked out the other sentry and this guy is the only one we have to take care of now."

Torri shivered. "I know we have to do this but I wish it could be with less violence."

Jake smiled and reaching inside his jacket, took out a small, metal canister and a rag. "No violence, well, very little. The doc gave me some chloroform. The sentry is sleeping like a baby. It was easy to get the drop on him. He was alone in the woods." He gestured toward the remaining sentry. "The problem with this one is going to be getting close to him before he sees me."

"Jake," Torri said, as a sudden inspiration struck her, "let me create a diversion. I'll keep him busy while you sneak up behind him."

"What kind of diversion?" he whispered back.

"Don't worry, I know what to do."

"I don't think—" Jake broke off as he realized she was already moving out of the brush and into the open. "Torri—get back here! I told you—" he stopped talking aloud and instead swore roundly beneath his breath as he drew his saber from its sheath. A gun would make too much noise, but if he could get behind the man—the train of thought ended abruptly as Torri moved into his line of vision. His eyes narrowed and his mouth dropped open in astonishment.

She had unbuttoned the top three buttons of her shirt—borrowed from him—and had tucked the edges into her bra. The shirttails were tied together above her belly button. Now she was walking toward the sentry, in tight jeans, swaying her hips seductively. Jake smiled with grim determination and resheathed his sword. He knew what she was up to and it was clever, though dangerous. Sliding soundlessly through the bushes, he circled the tent, ending up in a thicket ten yards away from it. He took a deep breath and willed the pain in his chest to subside. Now it was up to Torri.

Torri leaned over and scooped up a handful of dirt, then, closing her eyes, rubbed it on her face. On the off chance that one of the soldiers she had helped tend in the hospital was the sentry, it would be wise to at least try to disguise herself. She'd seen the women who hung around camp after nightfall, dirty-faced, pitiful women from the brothels in town, hoping to entice some off-duty soldier into parting with a few coins.

Torri straightened and started walking again toward the sentry, her heart throbbing in her throat. Her adjustments to her clothing had been crude, but she hoped, effective.

She'd tousled her hair, and with her exposed cleavage and tight jeans molding her legs—something unheard of in this era—she thought she had at least a fighting chance of luring the man away from his post and lowering the odds of Jake being reinjured. The doctor had cautioned them before they all left that Jake's wound was far from healed and he was taking a great risk with this undertaking. Of course, as far as Jake and Torri were concerned, he would be taking a greater risk if he didn't.

Taking a deep breath, she swiveled her hips and walked directly into the sentry's line of fire.

"Who goes there?" he said, pointing his gun in her direction. "Give the password."

"Why, nobody," she said in her best Scarlett O'Hara voice, "just little ol' me. And sugah, I don't know no password."

"Hold it right there." In the shadowy moonlight Torri could just make out the man as he bent down and lit a lantern at his feet. He put a bucket over it, leaving only a circle of light. "Okay, now just move forward slowly."

Torri obliged, her hands on her hips, and was rewarded by seeing the man's chin sag suddenly to his chest as she moved into the light. "Hi, darlin'," she said in a sultry voice, "I seem to be lost and I was hopin' you could help a poor helpless female find her way home."

The man lowered his gun and Torri saw a dumbfounded smile cross his face. As she moved nearer, she saw he was young, about seventeen, and she was glad it was too dark for him to see the flush of shame spread across her cheeks.

"Say," he said, his Southern drawl thick with dialect, "is you one of them bad ladies?"

Torri was only a foot away from him now and she draped her arm over his shoulders. He stared down at her exposed bosom and the rifle slipped to the ground.

"Oh, honey," Torri said, pulling him toward her, "I am one of the baddest of the bad ladies."

She felt him tremble against her, then suddenly she found herself seized in his wiry, young arms. She pushed him back, laughing softly. "Not here, honey, not here. Someone in the tent might hear."

"Ah, it's just the colonel, and he's so full of laudanum that he wouldn't hear if Gen. Grant walked in." He bent his head to hers and she narrowly avoided his wet, urgent kiss.

"No, no, sugah. Not here. I can't show you a good time out here in the open." She fluttered her eyelashes at him. "But you come with me into the woods and I promise you, you'll be glad you did."

He took a step toward her then stopped. "I—I can't. I can't leave my post. I'd be shot if the colonel found out."

Torri felt a brief stab of guilt. The boy would be court-martialed if it was learned he'd deserted his duty. But maybe there was a way she could help him out, afterward. She leaned against him, and knew he didn't have a prayer of resisting her.

"That's too bad," she said, running her hands across his chest. "You're such a big, strong soldier-boy too. But, if you can't, then you can't. Guess I'd better go." She turned away from him and began walking away.

"Wait," he whispered urgently. Torri glanced back at him, careful to keep that languid look in her eyes. "I guess it wouldn't hurt none if I took a little break." He licked his lips nervously. "I mean, if I wasn't gone long."

Torri moved back to him, lifting her hands to caress his face. "Oh, it won't take long, sugah, not long at all."

She led him toward the woods and showed him a narrow path toward a clearing. Just as she was about to follow, she glanced back and saw Jake's shadow slipping behind her would-be customer. In a moment the boy was on the ground.

"I'm going after Reed," Jake said. "You keep watch."

Thirty minutes later Torri was back at the wagon, with Jake close behind, carrying an unconscious Col. Reed.

"Is he all right?" Dr. Hamilton asked anxiously, moving to help Jake with the injured man.

"He was asleep but he roused when I picked him up. I had to use the chloroform."

"The sentry said he had already taken laudanum," Torri whispered. "Is there any danger from mixing the two?"

"How much did you give him?" Dr. Hamilton asked even as he checked the colonel's pulse.

"Just like you showed me, just a capful onto the cloth," Jake said, starting to help Torri into the wagon; then he turned her toward him and ran his gaze over her provocative outfit. He wiggled his eyebrows suggestively as he drew her to him.

"One of the baddest, eh?"

Torri felt her face grow hot, then lifted it for his kiss. "If that's what it takes, sugah," she said shyly.

They hid Reed in the doctor's attic. Hannah had already prepared the low-ceilinged room, asking no questions, just moving silently to fulfill the wishes of the employer she trusted implicitly. Jake lowered the colonel to the makeshift bed—a cot layered with blankets—and frowned down at him as he groaned and turned restlessly in his sleep.

If they could keep Reed sedated and hidden, Jake thought, then maybe he still had a chance. For what? he asked himself honestly. To stay with Torri? Impossible. His only chance was to convince T'ria and the others that there had to be a better way to end K'mer's reign than by killing an innocent man. That was the first argument he intended to present. If, by some miracle he pulled that one off, the second was going to be even harder.

While he had been in the hospital in 1941, in those few short hours—the first semi-peaceful ones he'd had in years—he'd done a lot of thinking and had come to an important conclusion.

The necklaces had to be destroyed.

Time travel was a weapon, and even if they defeated K'mer there was always the possibility that the TDAs could fall into the wrong hands. He had to convince the Council that the devices were too dangerous to keep in existence. He didn't delude himself that his voice would carry much weight with them—unless—

He turned away from Reed's bedside to stare out the tiny attic window as the thought raced through his mind. What if he could bring K'mer's agent back with him instead of killing him?

Montgomery had said his device had the capability to transport more than one person through time at once. If

Jake could get his hands on Montgomery's TDA and use it to abduct him, he would prove to the resistance once and for all that he was loyal to their cause—and they would have an important hostage. He leaned his head in his hands. Getting Montgomery's TDA could be tricky, not to mention dangerous. He'd have to come up with a foolproof way of taking the agent prisoner.

"Jake?" He felt Torri's hand on his back and he turned, schooling his features not to reveal his inner turmoil or the constant pain he endured from his healing injury.

"We need to talk," he said quietly.

"It's too dangerous to try to capture him," Torri said, then took a bracing sip from the cup of tea Hannah had given her only moments before. "I thought you were going to kill him."

She and Jake and Dr. Hamilton were seated in the small parlor. Hannah had produced a very nice tea for them, including some wafer thin cookies.

Jake laughed without humor. "My, how bloodthirsty you've become, Mrs. Cameron. I thought you said I wasn't a murderer."

Torri lowered her eyes, feeling a sudden shame. "I'm not. I just—" her gaze flickered back to his. "I just don't want you to get hurt."

The curves around his mouth softened slightly. "Well, there's no question of the danger, kitten, but no matter what we do from this point on we're taking a chance." He picked up his own cup and stared into it, then put it back on its cream-colored saucer.

"You aren't telling us something," Torri said, quick to pick up now on Jake's shifting moods. It was true then, that the two shall become as one. Since their joining, Torri had felt so close to Jake that sometimes she felt she could almost read his mind. Right now he was wrestling with some weighty problem, a problem that concerned her. "What is it, Jake?" she prodded.

He stood and paced across the room, his hands thrust into his pockets, his head down, his face etched in stone. Dr. Hamilton watched him and shot Torri a look of warning. She was alarmed as she rose from the table and moved toward Jake.

"What is it?" she repeated, laying her hand on his sleeve. He looked up at her and the pain in his eyes made her heart leap suddenly with premonition. "You're hurting—sit down and I'll—"

"Torri." His quiet voice stopped her more effectively than if he had shouted.

Suddenly she knew what was coming. She lifted her chin defiantly and one corner of Jake's mouth eased up slightly, acknowledging the light of battle in her eyes.

"We're changing the plan," he said. "You aren't going to that ball to risk your life with scum like Montgomery." He turned away from her. "I'm going to take you home, Torri."

"Like hell you are."

Jake whirled, his eyes shards of ice. Torri knew then that she was about to fight the battle of her life.

"I'm not leaving. We've already discussed this and I've made my position perfectly clear."

"I'm not giving you a choice any longer," he said. He sat back down and picked up his cup of tea, then grimaced. "Haven't you got anything stronger, Doc?"

Dr. Hamilton looked from Jake to Torri and back again, then rubbed the lower part of his face. "Well," he said, rising, "I guess a small amount of medicinal whiskey wouldn't hurt you. Might kill the pain a little."

Jake shot him a sharp look. "I'm fine," he said flatly.

"Sure you are." Dr. Hamilton shook his head. "I know you're hurting. Chest wounds are very painful and you've sorely tested the limits of both your endurance and the skill of the doctor who sewed you up." He patted Jake on the shoulder and cocked his eyebrow in Torri's direction. "You might want to reconsider this strategy though. It might be wise to save your strength for the real skirmish that's ahead."

"I know what I'm doing," Jake growled.

The doctor shrugged. "Just remember, women have been outmaneuvering men since the dawn of time. Always thought if the Confederacy had a few women generals they'd have already licked the Yankees." He winked at Torri and left the room in search of the whiskey.

Torri folded her arms across her chest. "I'm not going."

"You are."

"I'm not."

"You don't have a choice."

Furious, Torri pressed her hands, palms down against the table between them. "I *do* have a choice, Lt. Cameron—or are you back to playing caveman again and going to chase me around the room? This time I'll scream for Dr. Hamilton and he'll stop you."

Jake shoved his chair back and circled the table. He grabbed Torri by the elbow and spun her against him. Torri caught her breath as she looked up into eyes that were no longer a cold gray, but had shifted to warm charcoal, and the fire in them burned into her heart and her soul. His hands gripped her arms tightly, then moved with gentle skillfulness to cradle her face.

"I love you," he whispered as he gazed down into her eyes. "That's something I never thought I would ever feel—not for anyone ever again. Do you think I would risk your life for anything—even saving my world?"

Torri stared up at him, lost in the impact of his words, the flood of incredible joy encompassing her heart. "But Montgomery—"

"I'll stop Montgomery," he said and a flicker of coldness

anced back into his eyes, "but that doesn't mean I have to
ut you in danger again. I was foolish to let you come with
1e to the camp, but even then I was still trying to deny
"hat I felt, what I knew."

Torri touched his face, letting her fingers trace the tiny
nes at the corners of his eyes and around his lips. "I never
hought I'd hear you say it—when you weren't under anethes-
1c, that is."

He grinned, and Torri's heart flipped over as she caught a
limpse of the happy, carefree man Jake might have been if
hings in his time had been different.

"I never thought I'd say it," he admitted, sliding his hands
own to her shoulders and lifting a curl from her shoulder to
"rap around his finger. "As hard as I tried not to, I fell in
>ve with you, Victoria Hamilton." He released her hair and
>oked away. "And even though there's no future for us, to-
ether, I want to know that I took care of you, that I didn't
:ave you stranded in time."

"Why are you so sure we can't have a future together?"
'orri asked, feeling overwhelmed by his unexpected confes-
1on. "You could come back with me to my time or—or we
ould stay in 1863. If you take care of Montgomery, we'll be
afe here. Dr. Hamilton will help us."

Jake stared down at her, an emotion she couldn't define
urning in his eyes. "I can't," he said at last. "There's too
1uch to be done in my time. I can't just—run away."

"Why not?" Torri pulled back, breaking away from him,
er chin jutting out angrily. He said he loved her more than
is cause, but now, once again he was proving that wasn't
rue. "Because the world can't survive without the great
`;meron there to make everything right again? Because you
ave to keep proving yourself to people who don't care if you
ve or die?"

Jake released his breath raggedly. "Torri, try to understand.

I love you, I want you safe, and there's nothing I'd like mor‹ than to spend the rest of my life with you, but it's not pos‹ sible."

"Take me with you to your time then."

He shook his head. "That's something I'll never do."

"Why not? I could help you—we'd be together and—"

"You don't know what you're talking about!" Jake sai‹ savagely, pushing her away from him.

It was possible that when he returned to his own time th‹ Council would be pleased that he had captured Montgom‹ ery and accept his new plan, but there were no guarantees‹ It was more probable that he would be summarily execute‹ by the Council for they might believe he had allowed Ree‹ to live so K'mer could continue to rule. In their eyes, h‹ would have proven he was truly his father's son. The though‹ of Torri trying to make it alone in his time sent a cold chi‹ through his soul. If he wasn't there to protect her, she'd be a‹ the mercy of T'ria and her ruthless band.

"This is how you prove that you love me?" Torri said furi‹ ously. "'Gee, it was great, kid, but it's over. Can I drop yo‹ somewhere and see ya around?'"

Jake shook his head in exasperation. "We both knew‹ deep down, that one day we would have to leave each othe‹ so let's not make a production of it." He moved to the doo‹ and opened it as Torri sputtered with indignation.

"Production!"

"Get some sleep. You need it and so do I." He closed hi‹ eyes from the pain and fatigue; then his eyes flashed open‹ "When we wake up, I'll take you back to your time—tha‹ will ensure you get there safely. Then I'll use your necklac‹ to return here."

"But what if you can't get back here?" she protested, stalk‹ ing across the room, grabbing him by the shirtfront an‹ shaking him passionately. "Without my life energy you won'‹ have the same accuracy. Jake, we've already been over this!‹

"It's decided," Jake said, his voice like steel. "I'm taking you home." He gently disentangled her hands from his shirt. "It's decided," he repeated wearily.

The door closed behind him with unarguable finality.

Torri stared unseeing at the door. Jake was determined to get rid of her, to keep her safe while he went after Montgomery. He would either die in the attempt or capture Montgomery and return to his own time. Torri buried her face in her hands. She should be happy he was going to take her home. Wasn't that what she'd begged him to do all along? Her grandfather needed her much more than Jake Cameron. He could take care of himself.

But she loved him.

The thought was a sharp knife piercing her soul. Torri clenched her fists behind her back and spun away from the door to cross the room. If he really loved her he would take her with him to the future. She knew there were dangers there, but they'd be together and that's what counted—why couldn't he understand that? And why couldn't he see that their plan for her to attend the ball and lure Montgomery into the open was by far the best way?

Torri paced. If only the TDA were more accurate, she wouldn't fight so hard against returning to her own time. If she knew for certain that Jake could make it to his own time in one piece, and then be able to come and get her after all the turmoil was over, she'd be willing to wait—galling as that waiting would be. But there were no guarantees of anything, except Jake's stubbornness. Torri stopped pacing and a slow smile spread suddenly across her face.

Torri left immediately. She didn't stop to change her clothes or take that long-dreamed-of bath. She did take time to leave a note, one she felt sure would eventually result in disastrous consequences, but it couldn't be helped. She had to protect Jake. She had to make sure there would be a future for them. Once out of the house she took to the woods, hoping she could make it to the camp before Jake decided to seek out Montgomery himself.

If she could find Montgomery and take his TDA, then Jake could take her home and she would feel assured that he could return to 1863 and then pick her up eventually. If he would only go along with their original plan it would all be so simple! He could defeat Montgomery, take her with him to the Council, convince them of their stupidity, then they could both go to her time and live happily ever after. Why did men have to make things so complicated? she wondered.

As she trudged through the woods, heading for the dirt road that would lead her into Richmond, she pieced together a plan. Montgomery wanted her TDA. What if she pretended that Jake had died in their last journey through time and she was stranded in 1863? Would he believe that she was panic-stricken and willing to do anything in exchange for getting back to her own time?

She thought it over carefully. He could kill her, of course, and then be able to use the power of her necklace, but wouldn't he more likely take the pleasurable way of using her body first? Besides, she hadn't brought the TDA along. That was part of her bartering power.

If she could get him into a vulnerable state, perhaps she could somehow turn the tables on him. It was a risky venture at best, she knew, and the thought of having any kind of intimate contact with the evil man again filled her with disgust, but if it would save Jake—if it would stop him from forcing her to leave him and give him the leverage he needed with the resistance in his own time—it would be worth it.

Torri reached Richmond just before dawn. As the city stirred from slumber, she realized that her jeans and shirt would draw attention to her and that was the last thing she wanted. She ducked down a side street and wrestled with he problem, wishing she'd had enough presence of mind to grab a dress before she bolted from Dr. Hamilton's. As if in answer to her prayers, she looked up and saw a sign in front of a dilapidated building: Laundry done 5 cents a tubful.

Torri looked up and down the deserted street before trying the front door. It was locked. She started to turn away in frustration, then saw that one of the front windows was slightly open. Triumphantly, Torri lifted the wooden frame, hoping its screeching protest would not be heard by any early-risers. Inside there were several neat stacks of clothing, but to Torri's growing apprehension, they were all men's clothing.

She was about to admit defeat when she saw, in the corner, a crumpled wad of material. It proved to be a dirty skirt and blouse, probably left by the washerwoman herself. Torri turned her nose up at the less than fragrant odor permeating the clothing, then smiled. The camp officers had their laundry done in town. She knew it because Montgomery had made some comment during their dinner about having too much starch in his shirt. Now all she needed was a gun. Her smile faded into determination as she began to undress.

Jake stared down at the note in his hand with disbelief. She was gone. Without a word, without a farewell. Gone back into the dark void that had brought her into his life.

"What is it, Jake?" the doctor said.

They had come downstairs together. After his argument with Torri, Jake had fallen asleep on her bed, too exhausted to wait for her to get over her anger and join him. The doctor, too, had pleaded fatigue and gone to his own room.

Jake had awakened, rested, but still determined to convince Torri that she would be better off in her own time. It would seem she had come to that same conclusion herself. But she hadn't waited for him to take her there, insuring her safe arrival, she had disappeared into time alone, and there was no telling where in the universe she'd ended up.

"Jake? What is it?" Dr. Hamilton said insistently.

Jake handed him the paper. "She's gone. She's used the necklace to try to reach her own time."

"What? But why?" He scanned the words on the paper, his gray brows knitted with fear. "She says she can't take a chance on your not being able to come back here from her time to defeat Montgomery, that the inaccuracy of the TDA makes it too risky." His head jerked up. "But she's taking the same risk—trying to make it back on her own, isn't she?"

Jake nodded and leaned his face into his hands. "I just wanted her to be safe. She could wander forever through time. If she misses the mark and keeps on trying, her molecular structure will start breaking down like mine did."

"But she has the necklace—won't that keep her safe?"

"Only through a certain number of trips through the time vortex. After that—" he shook his head and felt the despair engulf him. "Torri—what have I done?"

Torri walked into camp dressed in her washerwoman-garb, the bandana disguising her dark hair, dirt on her face. No one seemed to notice her at all. Apparently the sight of a slovenly washerwoman was a common sight at the camp. She'd lugged along a basket full of clean clothes she'd found in the laundry and luck of all lucks—Capt. Lucas Montgomery had three shirts to be delivered.

Finding a gun had been fairly simple. She just watched in her slow, ambling trek around the camp until she saw a soldier place a pistol in a saddlebag, then hurry away as the mess call sounded. She'd slipped the gun out of the leather bag and hidden it at the bottom of the basket, under her bundle of clothes.

Now, after asking directions from a soldier who'd wrinkled

up his nose at the rank smell of her clothes, she shuffled along, her head down, toward Capt. Montgomery's tent.

She paused outside the entrance and took a deep breath. As she'd dressed, she'd gone over the worst-case scenarios in her mind. If Montgomery didn't buy her story, her best bet was to first disarm him of his nasty weapon, then turn the lethal lasar on him in order to persuade him to give up his TDA. She would then tie him up and hotfoot it back to Jake. The question was, could she overpower the man even with the threat of a bullet through his brain?

Taking another deep breath, she stuck her head through the tent opening.

"Laundry," she called out in a heavy drawl.

A low voice muttered for her to enter and she shuffled inside. Montgomery was standing by a table, glaring down at some papers. She ducked her head, leaning over the basket, pretending to straighten the top shirts.

"I hope these shirts are laundered properly," Montgomery said coldly, tossing the papers to the table. "Last time I—" he stopped as Torri straightened and met his gaze squarely. His familiar, nasty smile spread across his face. "Miss Hamilton, why as I live and breathe."

"Hello, Capt. Montgomery," she said coolly. "I do hope you'll excuse my appearance. I didn't want anyone who knows the doctor to see me in the camp."

"Ah, but why not, my dear? Surely you aren't hiding from your precious "grandfather" and your beloved husband? Where is Lt. Cameron anyway? There's the little matter of a general court-martial awaiting him."

"He died when we made the trip back from 1941," Torri said, without hesitation. "He—he was too weak." She looked away as if overcome by grief. "And now I'm trapped here in the past."

Montgomery picked up a pair of gloves on the table and put them on, taking his time as he adjusted each finger.

"I—I thought he was going to help me," she went on, feeling the situation slipping further out of her control. "That's why I stayed with Jake—he promised to take me home. Now I realize he lied to me."

She tried to look distraught but he wasn't watching her. He was checking something in an inner pocket of his jacket. Torri stiffened, expecting him to pull his laser. She bent casually over the basket of clothes where she could grab the gun if she had to.

"Indeed?" he said, his gaze speculative. Torri relaxed as she saw his hands were both at his sides, and he held no weapon. "What about your own TDA? Why don't you simply use your necklace and return home?"

Torri jerked the bandana from her head and let her hair cascade down her back. She didn't miss the quick gleam of interest that lit Montgomery's eyes.

"I'm afraid to use it," she said, taking a step toward him. "I know you've suspected me of being an agent, but I'm not. I didn't mean to travel through time, it was an accident."

"Do go on."

Steeling herself she moved to his side and placed one hand on his arm, fighting down the revulsion she felt. "I need your help."

"Why of course, my dear," he said silkily, drawing her into his arms. He ran his thumbs down the side of her neck. "You know I will help you—for a price."

He bent his head to hers and Torri shivered as he brushed his lips against hers. His kiss burned into her as he shoved his hands into her hair and molded her body against his. When he finally released her, Torri turned away, gasping with the intensity of his embrace as well as her own reaction. Instead of being repulsed she had felt a surge of answering passion just like—

Torri spun around to face him, her hand flying to her throat as a familiar languid feeling swept over her.

"You—you used that on me again—" she said, horror-stricken. "That drug!"

Montgomery chuckled and opened his hand. His gloves were marked with a yellowish stain. "It does ruin gloves, but fortunately they protect me from this drug, which is absorbed through the skin. But it's not quite the same drug, my dear. That drug is fortunately colorless. They're still developing this one."

"What is it?" Torri whispered, almost afraid to hear the answer.

"K'mer's scientists have developed quite an assortment. While this one does slightly increase sexuality, it is more widely used as a truth serum."

Torri felt the blood drain from her face. She spun and ran to the basket of clothes where she frantically plunged her hands into the laundry. Her fingers closed around the barrel of the gun even as she felt Montgomery's blow to her wrist. She cried out and fell to her knees. Montgomery captured her arms and shook her.

"K'meron isn't dead. You're here to trick me—foolish as that attempt has proven to be. Now, tell me—where is he?"

"No!" Torri cried, fighting the lethargy coursing rapidly through her veins, thankful that she'd at least had the foresight to leave her necklace at Dr. Hamilton's. "Jake is dead! I want to go home—that's the truth!"

His hands moved into her hair again and he tightened them there, the pain ripping into her skull as he dragged her to her feet. Her wrist was throbbing and she sobbed aloud as his hot breath touched her lips.

"I want the truth. You cannot resist answering. Even now the drug has made its way to the part of your brain that controls decision making. In another moment you will willingly tell me anything I want to know—and do anything I say. Col. Reed has been kidnapped. It is obvious that you alone couldn't have managed that little disappearing act, nor do I think the doctor capable of engineering such a feat. Now, tell me where K'meron is."

Torri shook her head trying to clear her hazy brain. She ran her tongue across her lips. They felt numb, swollen, as if a dentist had given her novacaine. She frowned and looked around. Everything was blurred and distorted and she felt so sleepy, so very, very sleepy. Then, all at once, like the closing of one window and the opening of another, everything seemed very simple, and she felt very calm.

She smiled. Peace and contentment permeated her spirit. Her bones felt watery, yes, like water flowing through her innermost being. But water couldn't hold her body up and she felt herself sinking. Now she was being held in strong, warm arms. She snuggled into them, nuzzling her head against the broad chest beneath her fingers.

"Jake?" she asked softly. "Hold me, Jake."

"Of course, darling," a voice said soothingly, "but first tell me again what our plan is, our plan to stop Montgomery."

She leaned against him dreamily. "I'm going to trick him," she whispered through thickened lips. "I'll go to Mrs. Merriwether's ball and dance him onto the terrace where you'll be waiting." She sighed. "You'll take care of him and then you and I will be together, always." Torri lifted her face to his, her eyelids half-closed. "Won't that be wonderful, darling?"

"That, my love, will be almost as delicious as you yourself," Lucas Montgomery answered, as he lowered his mouth to hers.

Chapter Seventeen

"Jake."

Jake was on his feet instantly. He'd stretched out on the floor of Col. Reed's makeshift room three hours earlier to rest for a moment and mentally go over the sketchy plan he had worked out to capture Montgomery. But instead, he had lain there thinking of Torri.

What was happening to her? Had she made it back home or was she lost somewhere in time, fighting for her life? And what if Montgomery had some way of tracking her? With his new advanced techniques of time travel there was no telling what he could do. Maybe that was how he had followed them to 1941 and then back to 1863. Maybe even now Montgomery had found Torri and had taken her to the future as his prisoner.

That thought had made a cold sweat break out on Jake's forehead and he had turned fitfully on the hard floor, fighting the panic that threatened to undermine his control.

Why had he warned her that he was going to take her back to her own time? Because he needed her cooperation, he reminded himself, her thought energy to make sure they reached her time.

Exhausted, he had finally fallen asleep. Now he looked up into Dr. Hamilton's frantic face and in one quick movement came to his feet.

"What is it?"

The old man ran his tongue across his lips and for the first time Jake saw real fear in the doctor's eyes.

"Doctor—what's happened?"

"He—he has Torri."

Jake drew his breath in sharply. "What? Who has Torri?"

"Montgomery—he has her." The doctor clasped his hands and wrung them together. "He visited Mrs. Merriwether today and told her that he was coming to the ball tonight with my granddaughter. I—I had stopped by to treat her daughter's cold. When she brought it up I almost fell out of my chair."

"But that's impossible!" Jake spun away from him, his fists clenched at his side. "Torri's gone—she used the necklace to—" He turned back. "Or did she? Maybe instead she left the note to cover her tracks while she went running to Montgomery."

"Why on earth would she do that?" Dr. Hamilton rubbed the back of his neck in perplexity. "Why would she seek out such a dangerous man—especially when she knows that he plans to destroy you?"

"That's a very good question, Doctor," Jake said, his lips pressed together grimly. "Maybe our innocent little Torri isn't as innocent as she pretends."

"What do you mean? You don't think—"

"I don't know what to think," he said, cutting him off. Jake bent over to pick up his belt with the long saber attached, then buckled it around his waist, his thoughts racing too fast to separate. Torri with Montgomery. Her note. Her anger at their last parting.

"You know Torri loves you," Dr. Hamilton said, his voice hushed and unbelieving. "She wouldn't do anything to help Montgomery."

Jake's gaze shifted to meet the doctor's concerned one then flickered away to rest on Col. Reed, who lay still unconscious on the cot in the corner of the room.

"Unless," he said quietly, "she's been helping him all along."

* * *

"You're awfully quiet, my dear." Lucas Montgomery's voice was as obtrusive as the hand he kept proprietarially around her waist. She shifted away from him but the hulking body on the other side of her made it impossible to keep from touching either man.

"If you're expecting clever repartee Captain, I'm afraid you brought the wrong date."

Torri rubbed her eyes with the heels of her hands. The aftermath of the drug he'd given her was worse than a hangover and had left her with a dull ache behind her eyelids and constant nausea in the pit of her stomach.

After his inquisition, Montgomery had revived her with spirits of ammonia and hot coffee, and her fuzzy memory of him touching her intimately had made her immediately lose the contents of her stomach. Montgomery had simply laughed and offered her a canteen of water.

Now he squeezed her waist then ran his hand up her side. "I do wish I'd had time to do more than simply taste of your favors, my dear. But then, there is always later, isn't there? After all, I have all the time in the world."

His laughter rang out, chilling her and Torri huddled miserably in her seat. They sat, crushed together in a hired buggy, Montgomery on one side, holding the reins, Hiram Evans on the other. The stench of the soldier was almost overpowering and Torri unconsciously drew the hem of her dress away from his dirty boots.

"What's wrong, my dear?" Montgomery asked, feigned concern on his face. "Is Hiram a little too coarse for your refined Southern ways? Better get used to such men, for if you don't help me capture K'meron I will make good on my threat to take you to the future. Once there, bedding Hiram will look like a garden party in comparison to what I have in store for you."

Torri swallowed hard and didn't answer, but looked down at the gloves she was twisting in her lap. Montgomery had provided everything: a room in a private hotel that she suspected was actually a brothel; a bath in hot, steaming water, and last of all, a beautiful dress made in the latest, almost unobtainable Paris fashion.

How he had acquired it she had no idea and would rather not know. It was bad enough to be treated like some prize racehorse being readied for the show. Torri steeled herself against the despair that threatened to overwhelm her.

Oh, Jake. Why did I do this? Why didn't I listen to you and make you listen to me? Now we don't have a chance.

She lifted her hand to her throat. She was truly trapped and at the mercy of this madman and his assorted henchmen. The magnitude of what he might be able to accomplish if he had enough jewels to power an accurate TDA was frightening. If only to stop this tinkering with time it was imperative that K'mer be stopped. Torri suddenly understood more than ever Jake's desperation to destroy his ruthless father—and others like Montgomery. She stared down at her hands. Somehow she had to get Montgomery's TDA. But how?

"Is your TDA like mine?" she asked, with sudden inspiration.

"I have an original like yours, however it has been adapted with new functions."

"Do you always wear it?" she blurted.

Montgomery lifted both his auburn eyebrows. "Why, Miss Hamilton, is this your oh-so-subtle way of finding out if I am presently in possession of my amulet?" When she didn't answer he shrugged. "Do remember when we arrive at the ball that you are to behave as a typical Southern woman. To do otherwise is to seal your own fate."

"It's already sealed, isn't it?" Torri shot back at him. "The only reason I'm going along with you is because of the threats you made against Dr. Hamilton's life."

"Ah, yes, dear Dr. Hamilton. I did ask around and the doctor is telling his friends that his delightful little grand-daughter went back to her home out West. But I made sure the doctor will be in attendance tonight. I'm sure the sight of you will bring a glow of joy to his face—especially when he sees your escort."

"How did you make sure he'll be there?" Torri asked suspiciously.

"I have many circles of influence, my dear, in many different times and places. Here in Richmond I discovered the dowagers of the old South are really in charge of society. I have complimented and petted and bribed every old crone in this town, so when I ask for a favor, they comply—or they know I won't bring them bonbons from my next trip to Charleston, the dear little things."

"You really are a bastard."

He pretended to gasp. "Such unladylike speech. Hiram, I do think our Torri needs a reminder of the strict obedience that I demand."

Evans turned toward her, his ugly face leering with pleasure as his hand slid up the front of her bodice.

"Stop it!" Torri cried, shoving his hand away. "I understand—just keep him away from me!"

"And if Hiram's reminder isn't enough, perhaps this will be." Montgomery took a small vial from an inner pocket and held it up. "This contains the pheronemepid that you fear so much. You would hate to shock the delicate sensibilities of the ladies at the ball with your wanton display of sexuality that would no doubt result if I used this on you again. However if it is necessary to make you compliant . . ."

"No," Torri said, the defiance draining out of her. "I'll behave, I promise." Just the thought of Montgomery using the drug on her again, forcing her sexual feelings to surface, spiraling out of control for his pleasure made her stomach roll with nausea.

But if he takes me to the future, she thought dismally, that will probably be the least of the depravities he inflicts on me.

As if he could read her mind, Montgomery chuckled and lifted his hand from her waist to curl around the back of her neck. Torri gathered the velvet cape Montgomery had provided more tightly around her shoulders, and tried desperately to turn her thoughts away from her fear.

She was glad that she had left the note. At least this way Jake wouldn't take crazy chances trying to rescue her. Of course, if the doctor came to the ball and saw her, he would tell Jake, which was just what Montgomery wanted. She released her breath in a long, trembling sigh. Montgomery's intent was to let Jake know she was under the agent's control. Tonight was just a prelude to what lay ahead. Torri shivered and closed her eyes.

The plantation where the party was to be held was a few miles outside of Richmond, and the quiet sounds of the horse's hooves had almost lulled her to sleep by the time they arrived in front of a large, brightly lit house.

Torri gazed up at the white columned mansion, feeling once again as though she was lost in a scene from *Gone With The Wind*. There were at least two dozen other buggies and wagons in front of the great mansion and Torrie swallowed hard, feeling an odd foreboding. A black man appeared, dressed in evening clothes, and took the reins.

Montgomery jumped down and reached both hands up to encircle her waist. He lifted her bodily out of the buggy and lowered her slowly to the ground. Torri almost gasped out loud. It reminded her too sharply of another time she had been swept off a wooden seat and into strong arms. But this time the arms were not Jake's and Torri held herself stiffly away from Montgomery. He bent his head to hers, his mustache brushing against her ear, his breath warm.

"Remember everything I've told you," he warned.

Torri drew in a quick breath then nodded. He released her suddenly, extending his arm with a pleasant smile. Torri placed her hand on his forearm and watched the satisfied smirk on his face as he noted she was trembling.

The sound of fiddles drifted out across the warm spring breeze as they strolled up the stone walkway to the front porch. At a signal from Montgomery, Evans stopped at the huge front door, nodded to the captain and disappeared into the night. Magnolias scented the air, and as Torri walked up the steps, she lifted her chin to meet Montgomery's challenge.

As they entered the hall servants rushed up to them to take their cloaks before Torri and Montgomery walked into the large, candle-lit ballroom. Torri gazed around at the room, filled with men and women. Her plastered on smile quickly faded. Many of the men were on crutches, or wore bandages around their heads, arms and legs. Others seemed to be whole, but weary. Torri wondered about the sanity of men who made war on their own brothers.

They greeted Mrs. Merriwether, who gave Torri a knowing perusal. She flushed as she realized that her new gown was out of place amid these Southern women who had turned their old dresses so many times they were almost threadbare. Silently she cursed Lucas Montgomery.

"It's so nice to meet you, my dear," the overweight woman said graciously in spite of the touch of anger Torri saw flashing in her eyes. "I've heard so much about you from your grandfather. And where is the dear man tonight?"

Torri glanced up at Montgomery, unsure of how she should answer.

Mrs. Merriwether gasped. "You don't mean to tell me that Capt. Montgomery brought you here unchaperoned!"

Torri could see that the confirmation of such an action might very well result in finding herself burned at the stake, or at the very least ousted from this social event. She smiled and opened her mouth to tell her genteel hostess that she had, indeed, traveled alone with the captain.

"Why, my dear Mrs. Merriwether," Montgomery said smoothly, effectively stopping Torri from speaking. "Would I do anything that wasn't the height of propriety? Dr. Hamilton came with us of course, but as we were coming inside he was detained by someone asking medical advice. I'm sure he'll be along any moment."

The dowager nodded, satisfied, and turned her attention to the next person waiting to greet her. Montgomery guided Torri across the room to the banquet table where an adequate variety of food and drink were available. He shoved a glass of wine into her hand and Torri glared at him.

"I'm not thirsty," she said through clenched teeth.

"No?" He took the glass from her hand and set it on the table. "Good, then let's dance, shall we?" His perfect smile gleamed down at her. "What better way to attract your dear grandfather's notice?"

Without waiting for her answer, Montgomery swept her into his arms and swung her onto the dance floor. As he spun her dizzily around the large ballroom, Torri searched the crowd for Randolph Hamilton or Jake. She prayed fervently that neither would be there. It was possible that if his plan failed, Montgomery would simply take her and return to his own time—though knowing the man's determination that seemed unlikely.

After the third dance Torri pleaded exhaustion, and Montgomery steered her out of the crowd onto the French veranda that stretched behind the house.

There was only one other couple outside, walking and gazing up at the few stars just beginning to come out in the fast encroaching blackness of the sky. A low stone wall surrounded the large, flat stones sunken into the ground to create the patio. The mansion was built on a hill overlooking the Rappahannock and the river glistened blackly in the bright moonlight.

"Now," Montgomery said, leaning one muscular thigh on top of the wall and crossing his hands in front of him. "Isn't this lovely?"

"Look," Torri said, "there's really no need for this. I told you if you'd help me I'd give you my necklace. Let's get out of here."

"And miss the party?" Montgomery asked in feigned astonishment. "Why I wouldn't dream of it, my dear. I know you want to get me alone again, but your insatiable appetites will have to wait until later."

Torri steeled herself. Maybe she hadn't tried hard enough to win him over before. Her natural revulsion to the man had influenced her better judgment, but now Jake's life hung in the balance. At the very least she could try to distract him in case Jake did miraculously show up. She moved toward Montgomery and put her arms around his neck. His eyebrows lifted in surprise.

"You know, everything your truth serum pulled out of me was true, but what you didn't ask me was how I felt about Jake. How I felt being used by him and being stranded in time, waiting until he decides to help me out." She lifted the fan she held and tapped his chin lightly. "What makes you think I still want to help Jake Cameron?"

Montgomery's brown eyes gleamed in the moonlight. "I'm willing to be convinced," he said, sliding his hands around her waist.

Yes, I just bet you are, Torri thought, keeping her smile locked in place.

"So convince me," Montgomery taunted.

Torri glanced around. The other couple had gone inside and she and Montgomery were alone on the veranda. Trembling, she lifted her hands to cup Montgomery's face and brought her lips down to his. He pulled her roughly against him, devouring her mouth; then he moved his lips lower to grind against her collarbone. Torri gritted her teeth and suffered the feel of his slimy lips against her skin, his hand tugging at her bodice.

"What a touching scene."

Torri whirled around. Montgomery immediately pulled her back against his chest, but she didn't care. She was so happy to see Jake she could have wept. He stood there, his tawny hair curling around his head like a lion's mane, his gray eyes as steely as the gun he held pointed at them. His gaze flickered over her, lingering on the cleavage revealed by her low-cut bodice.

"Nice dress. There's one thing for certain—Montgomery's whores always get the best of everything."

"Jake." Torri whispered. "It's not what you think."

Jake stared at her, wishing more than anything he could reassure her, take away the fear in her eyes. One look at her face as she walked onto the veranda with Montgomery had been more than enough to convince him that she was there under duress. He'd been hiding near the wall and overheard all of their conversation.

For a moment he'd really thought perhaps she was on Montgomery's side. Then the scum had grabbed her and buried his face in her neck and Jake had seen the revulsion and terror flicker again across her face. What she was doing, she was doing for him. He believed that, because for the first time in his life he believed in someone besides himself. But he had to make her think otherwise, and convince Montgomery she was nothing to him. He had to somehow get Torri out of the line of fire.

"No?" Jake lifted his eyebrow. "What is it then, dear wife? Just a little goodbye kiss between old friends?" His eyes narrowed. "You've played me for a fool, Torri, and you're going

o die for it." He cocked the hammer of the pistol. "Move
way from him. I'm going to take care of you one at a time."

"I don't think so, Lieutenant," Montgomery said. "Please,
drop your gun."

One corner of Jake's mouth eased up. "You don't believe
'll take a chance on shooting you because of her? I'm
through playing the sap for the two of you, Montgomery. I
now she's one of K'mer's agents and like all the rest of his
cum, she is totally expendable—woman or not."

"I'm not in the least interested in your sad tale of betrayal.
'm simply telling you to drop your gun before my man drops
ou. On second thought, carefully place the gun on the
round. I don't want to take a chance on its going off acci-
lentally."

Jake went cold as the sound of a rifle being cocked sounded
ehind him. Slowly he released the cocked hammer of the
istol he held, then knelt and placed the gun on the stone
eranda. Hiram Evans, standing behind him, took advan-
age of his vulnerable position and shoved Jake forward,
ending him sprawling to his knees. Torri tried to reach him
ut Montgomery yanked her back.

"Gently, Hiram, gently," Montgomery cautioned. "We
lon't want to alarm the party-goers, now do we? Get up Lieu-
enant. You and I and the lady are going to take a nice, long
valk down by the river."

Jake dragged himself up and they were forced at gunpoint
o crawl over the wall. Torri caught the hem of her long
lress twice before Jake picked her up in his arms and helped
ler over. They walked down a narrow path that led from the
eranda down the long hill to the river. The captain stopped
lear a natural rock formation that jutted sharply downward,
creating a waterfall.

They were quite a distance from the house and Torri real-
zed with a chill that the distance, combined with the sound

of the rushing rapids below them would certainly cover the sound of a gunshot or two. But that wasn't even a consideration. Montgomery's laser could effectively eliminate the two of them soundlessly, and leave no trace of their bodies.

"Well, here we are at last," Montgomery said. "Four fellow travelers in time." Torri glanced at the hulking figure of Hiram Evans and the captain nodded. "Oh, yes, Hiram's one of us. One of my best men and actually a lot smarter than he looks, aren't you, Hiram?"

Hiram grunted in response.

"And now, Miss Hamilton, do join your beloved." Montgomery instructed.

Torri hurried to Jake's side and was surprised when he gathered her into his arms. She wrapped her own around his waist and gazed up at him fearfully. "Oh, Jake, I didn't—wasn't—"

"Shh, kitten," he whispered. "I know. It was just part of the game."

"Did you really think I would believe that you suspected your precious little wife of being K'mer's agent?" Montgomery asked, sounding perturbed. "Really, Lieutenant, I gave you more credit and I hoped you at least respected my intelligence. Even during your little performance, the simpering love you feel for the woman was unavoidably obvious."

Montgomery sighed loudly. "But you are correct. It was all part of the game and the game is over. A pity, but it can't be helped. At least you can comfort yourselves in knowing that in the midst of this vale of tears you both found true love." His lips spread in a deadly smile. "After all, isn't that what counts? Or is it?"

As Torri had feared, he reached into his pocket and withdrew the small black laser.

"I didn't want to take a chance on anyone walking up from the party and seeing two people simply disappear into thin air."

Torri glanced up at Jake, her mind racing. There had to be a way out of this—there had to be! It couldn't end like this, not now when she knew that Jake truly trusted her. She saw his brow knotted in concentration. Surely he would think of something, he wouldn't let them die.

"You still don't know where Col. Reed is."

"My dear Lieutenant, your lovely wife has been a fountain of information during the time we have spent together, so please don't trouble yourself further on my account."

Jake looked at Torri and she flushed, gripping his hand more tightly.

"He gave me a drug—some kind of truth serum," she whispered.

Jake's fingers tightened around hers in comfort and understanding. Torri felt a rush of love toward him. Even now, at the end, he was protecting her, willing to sacrifice himself for her.

Torri squeezed his hand in gratitude when suddenly, Jake turned and pushed her into the river. She went under almost immediately, but fighting to reach the surface, she broke free in time to see a burst of light shoot out and hear another splash. She had no more time to think as her sodden clothes pulled her down under the churning waters of the Rappahanrock.

Gasping, Torri struggled, fighting the tangled skirt around her legs. Just when she didn't think she had the strength to fight to the surface one more time, strong arms encircled her waist, dragging her upward. She drew in a ragged breath and began coughing and sputtering as water rushed out of her lungs; then the cold and the shock reached her senses and she felt herself slipping away into unconsciousness.

Jake kept one arm around Torri and swam in strong, powerful strokes to the shore. He had thrown himself in after her before Montgomery or Evans could get off more than a wild shot. Unfortunately that shot had caught him in the back of his thigh. He was losing blood rapidly, but that was the leas of his worries.

The momentum of the river had carried them hundred of yards away from Montgomery and Evans, but it wouldn' be long before they would find Jake and Torri. Jake had t get Torri out of the water, to safety. He heaved himself an her onto the dry ground, forcing weight on his injured leg a he picked her up in his arms. He made sure she was stil breathing. Her pale, bloodless face gleamed against his arm in the moonlight and once again he cursed himself for no taking her to her own time when he'd had the chance Wincing, he shifted the slight burden of her weight and dis appeared into the blackness of the night.

"He'll head straight for the doctor's house," Jake said throug gritted teeth, as Torri bound a strip of her petticoat aroun his thigh. A close examination had shown that the lase had hit a glancing blow to the side of his leg and the woun wasn't serious. Lucky, Torri had said under her breath, ther burst into tears. She was calm now, working rapidly to ban dage his wound, and jerked her head up at his words.

"Because of me."

"Don't be ridiculous," he said sharply, leaning back agains the tree that grew in the center of the thicket where the were hiding. She was shivering and he pulled her down be side him. "I'm sorry."

"For what?" Torri said, leaning her head against his chest her teeth chattering. She was drenched and so was Jake, bu even soaking wet she could feel the heat of his arms aroun her, and their comfort. After a moment her teeth stoppe knocking together and she sighed contentedly.

"For snapping at you. For not taking you home the minut I laid eyes on you," Jake said. "For dragging you into this. Fo scaring you into trying to fight Montgomery on your own."

"It's not your fault."

"You're right." He tilted her face toward his, smoothing his thumb against her jaw. "It's your fault." Torri started to speak but he cut her off with a burning kiss that left her breathless when they finally moved apart several minutes later. "It's your fault," he repeated, "because you made me love you, Victoria Cameron. And once I started loving you, I got selfish. I started wanting crazy things like—to live and not die, to have a wife, a family, a home. Yes, it's definitely all your fault."

"Guilty as charged," Torri whispered against his lips, then kissed him gently and laid her head on his shoulder. "And not a bit sorry—for making you love me, that is, or for keeping you from throwing your life away, not to mention Col. Reed's. But I am sorry for messing things up by confronting Montgomery alone. I just couldn't bear to leave you, Jake." She rested her chin on his shoulder and gazed up at him. "I thought if I could get Montgomery's TDA it would be more accurate than yours and at least you'd have a chance."

"I know, kitten, I know. It's all right."

They lay there together, not speaking, until at last Jake released his breath in an explosive sigh. "Okay, rest time's over. We've got to get going." He pulled her to her feet and for a moment they leaned against one another, each feeling the embers of desire smoldering between them.

"Later," he said softly, bending to touch his lips to her forehead.

"Will there be a later for us, Jake?" Torri asked.

He cradled her face in his hands and gently kissed her. "I don't know," he said. "I only know that there will be a forever, because that's how long I'll keep loving you, Torri Cameron. Forever." He turned and led her by the hand out of the thicket.

They approached Dr. Hamilton's borrowed house from the rear, Jake's limp becoming more pronounced with every moment. Torri had to bite her lip to keep from expressing her concern. If they didn't stop Montgomery, Jake's leg wound wouldn't matter. He would no longer exist.

The moonlight was so bright the yard was lit almost as brightly as noonday. "Now what?" Torri asked. "We can't just knock." In answer Jake tossed a pebble at the kitchen window.

The back door opened and Hannah appeared, yawning, a bucket under her arm as she made her way sleepily out to the little shed where the doctor's milk cow was housed.

Stealthily, the two skirted the edge of the woods that bordered the doctors property until they reached a spot behind the shed where they couldn't be seen from the house.

They could hear Hannah humming loudly in the shed, banging the pail down and grunting as she squatted down beside the old jersey.

"Hannah!" Torri said in a hoarse whisper.

The humming stopped, then Hannah began to sing in a low, singsong voice. "Yea, Lord, nobody knows what troubles they be," she warbled. "My house, Lord, you got to see the troubles dere, oh yes, Lord the troubles there be."

"Is it Montgomery?" Jake hissed through the thin boards of the shed. "Is he here?"

"Oh, Lord, yes, you ain't seen the troubles I seen, yes, the troubles." Her voice trailed off again and Jake gripped Torri's hand tightly.

"Has he found Col. Reed?" he asked urgently. He was rewarded with yet another verse of a Negro spiritual, skillfully adapted.

"But the good Lord, He done had some mercy on my soul, oh, yes, some mercy, but de devil, he be wanting to climb dem stairs up to de heavenly places, oh yes, Lord, to de refuge of the Lord."

"He's going to the attic. Stay here, Torri."

"No, Jake, I'm coming with you."

Jake spun on her furiously. "Dammit, Torri, for once do as

I say! Stay here and stay the hell out of the way." Before he got ten feet away from her Jake heard her rapid footsteps behind him. He whirled and grabbed her by the wrist. "If I had time I'd haul you across my lap and give you the spanking you desperately need. Do you want to get me killed?"

Torri paled. "No, of course not."

"Then stay out of the way."

"I will," she agreed, licking her dry lips. "But I'm not going to let you go in there alone." She clutched his arm fiercely. "I love you, Jake—and whatever happens in there it happens to both of us."

Jake closed his eyes and shook his head in exasperation, then unexpectedly pulled her to him and hugged her tightly. He dropped a kiss on her forehead. "There isn't time to argue, but listen, kitten, if you love me, do what I tell you."

"I will. I promise."

"Let's go."

They entered through the back door. The house was silent, still, and for a moment Torri thought they must have misinterpreted Hannah's strange song, when suddenly they heard footsteps overhead.

"They're in my room," Torri said, listening to the sounds. "No, they're going down the hallway, toward the attic stairs."

"Okay, listen. We're going to go up there, but I want you to wait at the bottom of those steps. I'll go in, and as soon as I get up there, you make a noise, any noise, and I'll try to take advantage of the distraction."

"That's the plan?" Torri said in disbelief. "Are you kidding me?"

"You got a better one?" he asked tersely. When she didn't reply he shrugged. "Just stay behind me," he growled, and then went into action. He moved through the kitchen first, grabbing a carving knife from the table and tucking it through his belt.

Then, gesturing to Torri, he moved toward the stairway with the grace and silence of a jungle cat, and slipped up the steps. Torri was amazed that he could move like that with his leg injured. She hurried after him but couldn't move as fast, as quietly. Jake was standing outside the open door to the attic as she reached the top of the stairs. He held up one finger and she slid to a stop.

Carefully, he moved inside the doorway, then motioned for Torri to follow. She did, positioning herself at the bottom of the stairs as he cautiously crept up the stairwell.

They could hear voices, that of Montgomery and Dr. Hamilton—and was that David Reynolds' voice? With a terrible sense of impending disaster, Torri watched Jake enter the room, counted to ten, then cut loose with the most bloodcurdling scream she could manage. Then she didn't wait any longer. She took the stairs two at a time and burst into the attic.

Jake was struggling with Montgomery for possession of his phaser, while it appeared Dr. Hamilton had just broken a chair over Hiram Evans's head. The soldier was sitting, a dazed expression on his face as she came in, then he clambered to his feet and turned on the doctor with a roar. David Reynolds was lying in a heap on the floor.

Torri looked desperately around the room for a weapon. There was nothing, with the exception of a glass pitcher in a basin on a small washstand. She grabbed up the pitcher and brought it down over Evans's head. This time he went down and didn't get back up.

"Hold it."

She turned to find Lucas Montgomery holding his laser on her. Jake was doubled over, his knife on the floor, stained with blood. Torri took a step toward him, but Montgomery motioned her back. He pulled Jake to his feet and flung him toward Torri and the doctor. Torri caught him and helped him to stand. He was breathing heavily and Torri could see blood staining his chest.

She ripped his shirt open and saw that his barely healed wound was bleeding again, and bruises were appearing around the still puckered stitches.

"You bastard!" she shouted at Montgomery. "You hit him in the same place you hurt him before!"

For the first time Montgomery wasn't smiling and Torri suddenly noticed that a dark stain of blood was spreading rapidly across his abdomen.

"I'm afraid that will be a rather moot issue in a moment, dear Miss Hamilton," he gasped. "As soon as I kill Col. Reed, K'meron will disappear as though he never existed. But don't despair," he coughed and a sharp look of pain crossed his face, "you'll soon be joining him."

"Drop it, Lucas."

Montgomery froze, then spun in disbelief to face the bed, and Col. Brent Reed who was holding a gun.

"I said, drop it."

"But, you were unconscious," he said, staring dumbly at the man. "I checked you myself."

"I haven't been unconscious since yesterday." Reed slipped out of the bed and took the laser from Montgomery's hand. He was still pale, but Torri noted that he seemed to be much stronger than he appeared. "The doctor stopped sedating me and allowed me to regain consciousness. He told me the whole story, hoping I would believe him."

He smiled and the gesture immediately endeared him to Torri. "Well, I did. It's crazy but I believed him. He gave me a gun yesterday, afraid you might try something like this, and when I heard you downstairs, I slipped it under the covers." His smile faded. "Now, Captain, give Lt. Cameron your time travel device and I'll allow the doctor to check what damage has been done to you."

Montgomery's hand snaked toward his jacket pocket and Jake limped across the room, catching him by the wrist.

"Hold it right there." Jake jerked both of Montgomery's arms behind him. "Reynolds, give me your belt."

The crippled man struggled to his feet, then took off his belt and handed it over. Jake bound Montgomery's hands together and shoved him down to the floor, then searched his pockets. After a moment he triumphantly held up two jeweled pendants.

"Which of these is yours, kitten?"

"Neither." She shot Jake a superior look. "You didn't think I'd be stupid enough to take it with me when I tried to take on Montgomery, did you? Mine is downstairs in my dresser drawer."

"Go and get it," he ordered.

Frowning at him, Torri did as he asked, returning a few minutes later with the TDA in her hand.

"Then these two are mine and Montgomery's." He turned to Torri and took her necklace from her.

"What really happened to my necklace?" Dr. Hamilton asked suddenly as he straightened from examining Montgomery. "I know now that you took that one from my safe, but what happened to mine?"

"This is yours," Jake said, "and, I'm not sure, but I'm afraid if we don't leave it here with you, it will never be passed down to Torri and none of this will ever take place."

The doctor raised one gray eyebrow. "Would that be such a bad thing?"

Jake reached out and brought Torri closer to him, his arm around her shoulders. "I don't know about you, Doc, but I'm extremely glad that Torri had that necklace." He leaned down and kissed the tip of her nose. "Otherwise, I would have never met her, never known love, never known life."

Dr. Hamilton smiled. "Yes," he murmured as he took the

necklace Jake was handing him. "My own life would not have been the same, my dear, without you."

Reed spoke up from his corner of the room. "I, too, Miss Hamilton, find myself greatly in your debt. Lt. Cameron has told me that it was your influence that actually saved my life."

"Maybe in the beginning," Torri said. "But Jake would've made the right decision, sooner or later." She watched Dr. Hamilton tuck her necklace into his pocket and suddenly felt strangely bereft. "But how will I get back?" she asked Jake. "If the doctor has the necklace—"

Jake turned and put his arms around her, stilling her anxious words. "I'll take care of you, Torri. Trust me." He smiled down at her and kissed the pucker between her brows, then moved to touch his lips to hers. Torri felt her qualms slip away as he held her.

"Harrumph!" Dr. Hamilton cleared his throat just as Col. Reed began coughing fitfully, and Torri broke away from Jake, flushed with love and embarrassment.

"How—how is Montgomery?" she quickly asked.

"He'll be all right," the doctor said gruffly. "Jake hit him a glancing blow across the ribs. I've stanched the flow of blood. I'll get my medical kit. I want to look at Jake's chest, too. David, you come with me."

"Wait a minute," Jake said, the tone of command in his voice stopping the doctor at the door. "How do you know you can trust him?"

"Jake, David helped us." Torri protested, even as the red-haired man shook his head.

"I don't blame him, Miss Torri," he said, his ruddy face flushed with color. "He ain't a man who trusts easy, but the doctor's been hiding me here, 'cause ever since I helped you escape, Montgomery's been trying to kill me."

"He can be trusted," Dr. Hamilton said softly, then

gestured for David to follow him. David started after the doctor, then turned back to face Jake.

"I thought I'd do anything to get my leg back—and I almost did," David said. "But when it came down to having to kill innocent people—even if it seemed the only way—well, I couldn't do it. You can understand that, can't you, sir?"

Torri's glance darted to Jake and with a pang she saw the brief flash of sorrow cross his face.

"Yes," Jake said, the animosity suddenly gone from his voice. "Yes, I can understand that. Thank you, David, for your help."

Torri moved to Jake's side and slipped her hand into his, signaling her pride in his generosity by gently squeezing his fingers.

"So that's the cause of all this trouble," the colonel said, his eyes on the necklaces Jake held. "May I, Lieutenant?"

"Of course." Jake crossed to Reed, glanced at his ashen face and gestured toward the bed. "But first I'd suggest you sit down." He took the gun from the trembling man's hands and turned it on Montgomery, sitting slumped against the wall. He handed Reed one of the necklaces. "And until we sort these out, be careful to hold this by the edges. Montgomery's device can transport anyone and I don't think you'd like it in my time."

The colonel's gaze flashed back to his. "Do you like it there, Jake?"

Jake laughed without humor. "Hell, no."

"Then why go back at all? Take Montgomery's device and leave him here for me to deal with." He glanced at Torri. "You have a chance for happiness. I suggest you take it."

"Pretty generous coming from a man I've been trying to kill," Jake said, looking away.

"A wise man once said desperate times call for desperate measures." Reed smiled and handed the TDA back to Jake. "It would seem that you live in desperate times, Jake. But this is your chance to escape that desperation. To find a new life."

Jake turned away and found Torri staring at him. He gazed down into her emerald green eyes and ached at the sight of the love he saw mirrored there. Don't look, he thought as his own love for her seized him in earnest. You can't stay with her. You have to convince T'ria and the others not to kill Reed and then to destroy the TDAs. You have to stop the insanity.

"I can't," he whispered. "My work isn't finished."

The expression in Torri's eyes changed from tenderness to pain, and she turned away.

Jake walked over to Montgomery and hauled the captain to his feet. "I'll take you home, Torri, then I'll take our friend here to face the people he's helped to enslave."

The doctor reappeared, medical bag in hand, David close behind him.

"Grandfather—I mean," Torri smiled up at the older man, "Dr. Hamilton, after you look at Jake's chest, please check his leg. He was shot again."

"Don't you ever know enough to duck, son?" the doctor said good-naturedly as he knelt beside Montgomery. "I'll see to it, and Torri," he glanced up, his blue eyes bright with love, "I will always be your grandfather, never forget that."

Too choked with emotion to speak, Torri leaned down quickly and planted a kiss on his head, then turned to Jake. She stared at him wordlessly, then took a deep breath.

"When the doctor's through taking care of you I want to talk to you," she said, trying not to tremble. "In my room. Be there." And without another word she turned and hurried down the stairway.

Torri opened the door to her bedroom and suddenly found herself reliving the first night she'd spent in 1863—the first she remembered anyway. Jake had come to her by moonlight, through the window like some kind of overgrown Peter Pan. He had educated her about time travel and then and forever irrevocably stolen her heart. She sank down on the bed and buried her face in her hands. Now he wanted to leave her; wanted to return her to her own time and disappear into his own as though they had never loved, never been together, never existed.

Torri lay on the bed and closed her eyes. It was more than she could bear. It was more than anyone should have to bear—to find her one true love and be told he could never be hers—could not even exist in the same time as she. It wasn't fair. There had to be a way to convince Jake, to force him—

No. She would never want to force Jake to do anything. If he came with her it had to be because he wanted to be with her as much as she wanted to be with him. There could be no coercions, no manipulations, no deceit. Only love.

The door opened and she looked up. Jake stood there in the doorway for a moment, then slowly moved inside and shut the door behind him. He had drawn his dark blond hair back in a queue and had changed his filthy shirt. He didn't come to her but walked the length of the room until he stopped in front of the long window at the end of the room. Suddenly Torri had a dizzying sense of deja vu. He had stood by her window once before, gazing up at the moon as he told her he was a time traveler, trapped by forces he couldn't control.

His eyes were quicksilver gray in the moonlight, like some unearthly creature. Again.

Full circle, she thought. We have come full circle at last.

"Sit down," she said, when she could push the lump out of her throat. "I want to check your chest wound myself."

Jake grinned wryly and moved to sit in the chair beside her bed. She unbuttoned his shirt and saw the fresh bandage showed only pink traces of blood. Satisfied that he was all right she started rebuttoning his shirt, but Jake caught her hand and brought it to his lips. Torri looked at him. The moonlight had turned his face to porcelain, his eyes to their truest silver, his hair to gold. Jake bent to touch his lips to hers and Torri met his embrace hesitantly.

"Torri," he whispered hoarsely. "I don't have the right to ask, I know that better than anyone. But I love you and I want to spend this night loving you and making memories that we can take with us to warm us on the lonely nights ahead."

"Jake," Torri said, pressing her cheek against his, "please, stay with me, or, if you can't do that—come back to me." She leaned back and gazed into his silver eyes. "Take Montgomery back to your time, but then come to me in mine. Don't throw our love away."

"Oh, kitten," he shook his head helplessly. "You don't understand. When I return to the future not only do I have to find a way to convince the Council not to kill Reed—and me—but once that little thing is accomplished I have to convince the Council to destroy the TDAs!"

Torri eyed him sharply. "But if you do that, then you can never—"

"Never return to you. Never again travel through time."

"No." Torri's fingers twisted tightly in the fabric of his shirt. "Don't do it, Jake. You have to be able to come back to me."

He shook his head. "Don't you see, it's the only way. The TDA is not just a device—it's a weapon! We've seen firsthand what havoc it can wreak in the lives of innocent people."

"Yes, but—"

Jake laid a finger across her lips. "I'm sorry. There's no other way. Now, I love you and I want to spend what's left of this night with you. Do you want to spend it with me?"

Torri's mind whirled with doubts. How could she make love to him again, knowing it would be the last time? How could she bear to take him into her arms, into her soul, knowing that all she would have afterward would be the memories—for the rest of her life?

"No," she whispered, rising and walking to the window.

She steadied herself against the sill. "I don't think I could bear it." She heard Jake cross to the door.

"I understand," he said. "I'll—I'll come and say goodbye as soon as I'm ready to go."

She nodded, her back to him, her gaze fixed on the bright moon she could see above the treetops, as her mind traced over the agonized future that would soon be hers.

Never to see him again. Never to hold him. Never to talk and laugh and help one another again. Ever. Forever. She closed her eyes and hot, angry tears brimmed against her eyelids. She heard the door close and with a cry, she turned and ran to it, wrenching it open. Jake stopped and looked back at her, his eyes hopeful, his fists clenched at his side.

Torri shook her head wordlessly, watched the sorrow flicker back into his gaze, then with a sob, held out her arms to him.

Jake closed the space between them in two long strides, sweeping her up into his arms, clasping her to him.

"I love you, Torri Cameron," he whispered, "and I will love you throughout eternity."

Torri cradled his face between her hands and her heart contracted as she saw the solitary tear slip down his cheek. "There is no time in eternity," she reminded him gently.

"Then that's where we'll meet, my love," Jake said hoarsely, "where time can no longer separate us."

Torri met his burning lips with her own anguished passion and as Jake carried her back into the room and shut the door behind them, as he lowered her to the comfort of the four-poster bed and eased his body beside hers, Torri knew that somehow, during these last hours left to her, she would find a way to make him stay.

Chapter Eighteen

Torri stood in furious silence beside Jake as he shook Dr. Hamilton's hand, talking in low tones.

Their night together had been wonderful, more than just physical union. Torri had felt as though they were truly joined, in spirit as well as body. She closed her eyes as she remembered the last time he had possessed her, the last time they had melted together, defying the forces that had brought them there, defying the insanity that threatened to separate them. They had soared together, the two becoming one, reaching inward, upward and over the highest star.

Torri opened her eyes but couldn't see as the tears blurred her vision. She'd thought Jake would change his mind, but as soon as he awakened he'd acted as though he couldn't wait to take her home and leave her forever. He'd pulled on his clothes, practically commanded her to do the same, then went out to find Dr. Hamilton.

Now they were saying goodbye to Dr. Hamilton and Col. Reed. Montgomery stood on the other side of Jake, his expression sullen and angry, sporting a long, red welt across his forehead, and a black eye. The captain had needed a little physical persuasion to force him to reveal how his new TDA worked, and since there was always the chance that Montgomery could've given Jake the wrong information, Jake had explained that he was going to return Torri to her own time, but bring Montgomery with them. Jake was convinced the man wouldn't jeopardize his own life. Then Jake would jump from her time to his own.

"Torri?" Jake was asking her something and she shook he self back to reality. He frowned at her and brushed the tea from her face.

"I'm all right," she said, stepping back. Jake's concer shifted into that hard mask she hated so much.

"Aren't you going to tell the doctor goodbye?" he aske stiffly.

Torri turned to Randolph Hamilton and he held out h arms. She hurried to him and buried her face against h chest. "I'm going to miss you so much," she whispered. " love you just as much as I love my grandfather."

"And I love you, dear one," he said, hugging her tightl "I'll miss you every day for the rest of my life."

"I'll never forget you," Torri promised, choking back h sobs. "Thank you for everything you've done for me—an Jake."

She kissed his leathery cheek and turned away before sh broke down completely, then walked over to Col. Reed. H sat in a chair near the window and, fighting tears, Torri hel out her hand to him. He took it between both of his an smiled up at her. Torri looked down into his gray eyes tha looked startlingly familiar.

"I'm glad Jake didn't kill you," she said softly.

He chuckled and patted her hand. "I'm glad too. Than you for helping him reconsider the matter."

Jake was suddenly beside her, and he too thrust out h hand toward the colonel. Reed kissed Torri's and winked her, then stood and clasped Jake's hand, enfolding it in hi They gazed at one another for a long moment, then Jak cleared his throat.

"Meeting you has helped me more than you can imagin Brent," he said. "To know that there are—were—men of hono in my family tree, well it has helped to offset the knowledge what my father is. I also want you to know that I'm sorry I trie to kill you."

"You saved my life, Jake." Reed released his grip and put his hand on Jake's shoulder. "Don't kick yourself for what you planned to do. The fact that you found the courage to do what was right is what matters."

Torri watched the quick flush of color stain Jake's face and realized for the first time just how much Jake had not wanted to kill an innocent man.

Their goodbyes to Hannah had already been said, privately, as well as to David Reynolds. Hannah was thoroughly confused by the actions of her young friends and had been told they were leaving to go and live in Texas. She had shed a copious amount of tears and had baked fresh biscuits for them to take with them. David Reynolds was another matter. Jake had closeted himself with the boy in the doctor's study and when they both emerged an hour later, David was pale and nervous.

Torri had questioned Jake and learned he had told him some things about the future and time travel that had convinced the young man to take the secret he carried to the grave.

"I feel like Dorothy in the *Wizard of Oz*," Torri said, looking at the doctor. "I've wanted to go home for so long, but now it's so hard to say goodbye." Jake and the doctor exchanged confused looks and she laughed. "Never mind." She glanced up at Jake. "Well, this is it, isn't it?"

"Yes." He gazed into her eyes for a long moment, then, taking a deep breath, turned to the doctor and Reed. "Will you excuse us a moment?" Jake asked, then without waiting for their answering nods, he took Torri by the hand and led her into the study.

Spending one last night with Torri had been a mistake. When he had awakened that morning, her warm body pressed to his, her dark hair like a shimmering curtain across his chest, he'd almost wept. He didn't want to leave her behind. He wanted them to have a life together, forever. Was it such an impossible proposition? Wasn't there any way on earth that he could make it happen?

"Torri," he said, "don't be angry. I'm sorry if I seemed—callous this morning after what we shared last night. It's necessary."

"Why?" Torri demanded. "Why do you have to treat me like I never meant anything to you? Or is that the truth? You had your last fling and now it's over and you're ready to dump me?"

Jake sighed and ran his hand through his hair. "You know that's not true. I love you and—"

"Then take me with you!" Torri's fingers bit into the flesh of his arms. "Don't do this to us, Jake! Don't separate us forever. I want to go with you."

"What about your grandfather?"

Torri squeezed her eyes shut, then they flashed open. "You use that against me! You purposely try to make me feel guilty if I want to go with you instead of helping my grandfather! Of course I want to help him, but couldn't I go and help him, then go with you?"

"We don't have time."

"Time!" Torri laughed harshly. "We have all the time in the world!"

"You know what I mean." Jake said, turning and walking away from her.

"Yes, I know what you mean," she said. "You mean that you don't want to be with me. All right, Jake, take me home."

Jake spun around, and for one agonized moment suspended in time, their gazes locked. He looked away first.

"Come on, then," he said, opening the door. "It's time to go."

The doctor and the colonel were melting, their shapes shifting, sliding, colliding with one another and the suddenly spinning background of color. Torri felt the awful sensation of time travel begin, but this time she had the added emotions of grief and despair to contend with as well. She was leaving a dear, dear friend in Randolph Hamilton, and in a matter of moments she would be leaving the love of her life.

She should be happy she was returning to her grandfather, should be grateful, but the truth was his image had faded until he seemed so unreal, so like a distant memory that even though in her mind she knew who he was, in her heart he was now as Randolph Hamilton had once been: a picture hanging on a wall, someone who had lived long ago who had no relation to her.

She felt the shame overwhelm her even as the black vortex of the time/space continuum shifted around them. Jake's hand was solid and warm in hers and she clung to him desperately as unconsciousness seized her and flung her once again into the dark void from which she both hoped and feared to emerge.

"Torri! Torri, for God's sake, wake up!"

Torri opened her eyes and came to her senses all at once. Jake was struggling with Montgomery. Somehow his bonds had come loose and he had managed to free one hand. Jake had him under control but it was obvious that if he didn't do something soon Montgomery would be free.

"I've got to transport now!" Jake cried. "I love you—"

Torri felt suddenly paralyzed, then as the figures of Jake and Montgomery began to twinkle and dissipate in front of her, she sprang to her feet and with one desperate lunge, threw herself against the two men.

The emptiness sucked them down, twisted them around as the kaleidoscope of colors surged and swirled, sending them forward into another time. Torri clung to Jake, feeling as though any moment she might be bucked off by the pitching currents of time. Then the nothingness consumed her once again. When she awoke the blackness still consumed her, and yet she was conscious.

"Jake?" Torri groped around in the darkness until she found his hand.

"I'm right here."

"Where's Montgomery?"

"I cold-cocked him just as the transition started." He jerked his hand away from hers and even in the darkness she could feel his fury. "What in the hell have you done?"

"I—I—had to come with you," she said, choking back her own anger. "I couldn't let you just leave me!"

"I had to leave you!"

Jake felt the sweat break out across his upper lip and wiped it away, his mind racing. He had made a grave error in judgment. He had planned to leave Torri near her grandfather's home and then walk the two miles or so up the road until he reached the spot where he had first appeared in 1863. They had to be in the right location in order to reach the underground's headquarters, but in the heat of the moment, in his fear for Torri's safety, he had gone ahead and transported them to 2417. Now he had no idea where they were.

"Jake," Torri said, her voice tense, "where are we?"

"I don't know, but you do exactly as I say, understand? No arguments."

"I understand."

Sudden, blinding light filled the area and Torri ducked her head, covering her eyes with both hands.

"I should've known I'd find you in the dark with another woman," a sarcastic female voice echoed around them.

Torri opened her eyes, keeping them narrowed until she could adjust to the light. Jake was already on his feet, and once her vision cleared, she could see the hesitant look on his face as he waited for whoever had found them to approach.

Torri stood and moved to Jake's side. He put his arm protectively around her shoulders, and she felt a certain calm in knowing that whatever they were about to face, they were facing it together.

A woman, about twenty-five years old, stood a few yards away from them, clad in a tight, iridescent jumpsuit that showed her well-rounded figure off to advantage. A low slung holster at her hip carried some type of weapon, and she rested her hand on it, as if it were an old friend. She was flanked by two men who had their own weapons, strange rifles that seemed to be made of plastic.

Her hair was short and curly, and she had blue eyes. The woman stared at them for a long moment, then descended the stairs, walking directly to Jake. "Welcome back, K'meron," she said, ignoring Torri. The woman slipped her arms around his neck and kissed him passionately. Torri felt a slow burn beginning in her solar plexus, but tried to look as unconcerned as possible.

The woman leaned away from him then and smiled, the gesture giving her face the appearance of a dangerous animal.

"Failed again, eh, K'meron?" she purred, then abruptly dropped her arms and turned away, nodding curtly at the two men standing behind her. "Search them," she ordered.

Torri cried out as one of the men grabbed her roughly. Jake responded by slamming his fist into the belly of his own assailant, then turned to help Torri.

"Freeze, K'meron."

Jake stopped in mid-action, his breath coming hard.

"I see you haven't forgotten your training," the woman said as the two men seized Jake, one on either side and she moved in front of him. She lifted her weapon and displayed the tiny flashing red light on the mechanism. "It was set to kill, darling," she warned, "so please, let's not have any more of this nonsense or I'll simply get rid of your little friend.

Now, my men will search you both and you will not resist, is that clear?"

Jake nodded, and Torri was terrified as she realized just how close Jake had been to dying. These people were desperate—and ruthless.

"Where are we?" Jake said as the men went through his pockets and patted down his clothes. He winced as their hands made contact with his injured thigh. "How did you find us?"

"We're in a warehouse near headquarters. Since you've been gone we managed to kidnap one of K'mer's scientists and forced him to tell us some of the new advances they've made on the TDAs. One of the new features is a way to track the person using the TDA by picking up the electromagnetic waves that emanate from the jewels themselves. A kind of homing signal, if you will. When you activated yours and arrived here, it registered on the new equipment the scientist created for us."

"Where is this scientist, T'ria?" Jake asked. "I'd like to talk to him."

T'ria's delicate features hardened. "He's dead. You didn't really think we'd let him live, did you?"

Jake cursed under his breath. "Of all the stupid, short-sighted, vicious—"

"That's quite enough. I should kill you right here and now, K'meron. I certainly don't have to listen to your insults." The men searching Jake handed her the two jeweled necklaces they'd taken from his pockets and her dark eyebrows shot up. "Another TDA. Does it belong to your girlfriend or to that?" She indicated the still unconscious form of Montgomery on the floor.

Jake spewed his breath out in exasperation. "For once in your life will you listen first and shoot later? I have important information."

T'ria nodded, then her eyes narrowed and moved to Torri,

ppraising her even as she answered him. "I'm always willing
o listen—not that it's going to do you much good this time.
Search her."

Torri gritted her teeth as the men grabbed her and ran
heir hands over her body. To their credit they performed
heir search professionally, then stepped away and to her
stonishment, held up another TDA.

"Where did that come from?" she asked Jake. "I gave it
ack to Dr. Hamilton before we left."

Jake frowned. "It must have happened when we appeared
n your time. For a moment you were there, and the neck-
ace reappeared, because you did give it to the doctor and it
vas handed down in your family."

Torri put one hand to her forehead. "This is too mind-
oggling."

"If you're through explaining Basic Physics 101," T'ria
nterrupted dryly, "perhaps you'd like to tell me who your girl-
riend is and all about this lovely specimen who has no
oubt been on the receiving end of your fist."

Jake answered her coolly. "That is M'tgomery, K'mer's
ight-hand man. He was sent to kill me. I captured him and
rought him here from 1863 to use as a bargaining weapon
gainst K'mer. This"—he gestured to Torri—"is Torri Ham-
lton." He squeezed Torri's shoulder. "Torri, this is T'ria,
)'vid, one of the leaders of the underground."

T'ria smirked and turned to Jake, running her hands across
is chest. "Why did you bring her here? I—" she stopped as
he felt the bandage beneath his shirt. "Why, Jake, darling,
ou're hurt." She stepped away from him, her blue eyes like
hards of glass. "The question is—why aren't you dead?"

"I need to talk to the Council."

T'ria folded her arms across her chest. "They won't be any
appier about things than I am. Answer me. Why are you still
live, K'meron? Why is K'mer alive? Why didn't you complete
our mission?"

"Because I found Colonel Reed's existence to have significant importance."

"Oh, really? What significant importance?"

Jake glanced down at Torri, then took a deep breath. Here was his chance. If he could convince the Council of his reasoning they might let him live—and Torri along with him. And they might realize that the dangers of using the TDA far outweighed the benefits.

"The importance of being a good and kind human being."

T'ria's face registered disbelief. "Would you mind repeating that? Are you telling me you didn't kill Reed because he is a good and kind human being?"

"T'ria, listen," Jake said, taking a step toward her. "I've thought this through—the killing has to stop, and it has to stop with us. With M'tgomery we can find a way into K'mer's inner sanctum and reach him—without having to take innocent lives."

Torri watched the byplay as T'ria lifted her chin, her blue eyes hard and unyielding.

"Really?" the leader said, her tone languid. "Now, why do I doubt that your concern is for innocent lives, K'meron? Could it be because you've dragged your sweetheart along with you?" she sneered. "You just don't want to die. You are, after all, a coward."

"How dare you?" Torri blurted, her pride in Jake overpowering her fear. "He's risked his life for all of you—captured one of K'mer's most trusted men—"

T'ria whirled on her, her blue eyes aflame. "But he didn't kill Brent Reed—and why? Because of you." She waved one hand dismissively in Jake's direction. "It's obvious he's in love with you and just as obvious that he's chosen to save his own skin and let the rest of the world go to hell!"

T'ria placed her hands on her hips, her chin lifting defiantly. "Or perhaps what we've suspected all along is true—

Perhaps K'meron isn't a coward at all, but a traitor; a willing puppet who serves his father"—she spat out the word—"K'mer."

"And are you any better than K'mer?" Torri said.

T'ria gave her a cool glance. "I beg your pardon?"

"You and your—people." She said the word derisively. "Are you any better than K'mer? He murders innocent people. Isn't that what you want to do? Kill Brent Reed—and K'meron—two good, innocent men?"

"Yes, for the sake of the rest of the world."

"That's enough, Torri," Jake said, pulling her away from T'ria's fiery gaze.

"It isn't enough!" Torri cried, jerking away from him and turning on T'ria in fury. "You say you're fighting for the sake of the rest of the world, but from what Jake tells me, none of you even trust one another." She paced the room, glancing at the two men with T'ria who had not yet said a word. "Look at the scientist you killed in cold blood! You're willing to sacrifice anyone in order to free the world from K'mer— in fact, you're willing to *be just like him*."

"You don't know what you're talking about," T'ria snapped.

"Don't I?" Torri walked back to Jake's side. "Well, I know this. You're jealous—jealous of the love you see Jake has for me, a love he never had for you. I think that's why you sent him back to kill Brent Reed. I think that after all, you're nothing more than a woman scorned, T'ria."

T'ria straightened and fire burned again in the depths of her blue eyes. Torri felt a small triumph that she must have hit a nerve with her last jab. But how would the woman react?

"I do not put my own personal needs or feelings above those of the resistance," T'ria said at last, her face flushed. "Unlike some others."

"I'll admit that I want to live," Jake said, folding his arms across his chest and glaring at her. "And I want Brent Reed to live. He was a good man and he raised his children to be good men." He stepped forward, his fists clenched. "And you know what else? I'm a good man." He looked down at Torri who stood beside him. His voice softened. "I deserve to live."

T'ria stood in stony silence staring at them, her gaze flickering from Torri to Jake and back again.

"Ridiculous sentimental nonsense," she scoffed.

"No doubt to someone like you who only sees love as a way to manipulate or satisfy her own base needs, it is ridiculous," Jake said savagely. "But I've changed, T'ria. I've discovered something that no one—not even K'mer can take away from me."

"The love of a good woman?" T'ria said with a laugh. "How droll." Her gaze raked over him, as though taking inventory of his obvious assets. "What you call love is simple lust, K'meron, and if you'd ever been willing to take me up on my offer to assuage that need in you, you wouldn't have fallen prey to such a weak emotion. Now, you are truly no longer of any use to us."

"Wait a minute, there's more. We have to destroy the TDAs," Jake said.

First incredulity then amusement flashed across T'ria's face. "Are you joking or insane? Either way it's sure to get you killed."

"I mean it. T'ria, the TDAs are a weapon and in the wrong hands could destroy everything!" He pointed at M'tgomery's inert figure. "He used his TDA to try to subvert K'mer and put his own regime into power."

"He can be eliminated."

"But can you eliminate everyone? We have no idea who has access to the devices. We must use him to infiltrate K'mer's palace and confiscate the TDAs—then destroy them to make sure that no one can ever again circumvent time or history."

T'ria studied him for a long moment and Torri saw a slight flicker dart across the woman's perfect features. "While there is truth in what you say, I doubt the sincerity of your motives. You are either one of your father's agents after all, or simply trying to serve your own interests. It will be up to the Council to decide which."

She snapped her fingers and the two men, standing behind her, hurried forward to seize Jake by both arms.

"No!" Torri cried, throwing herself against the nearest one.

T'ria grabbed her by the hair and with one vicious tug, flung her to the floor, then knelt beside her and pointed her weapon at Torri's head.

"No! Leave her alone!" Jake shouted, struggling against his captors. "She has nothing to do with this. Just let her go back to her own time, T'ria, and I'll go with you quietly."

Torri's heart was pounding against her chest as though it would burst. She craned her neck to look at Jake. Panic was written on his features and suddenly she knew a sorrow that pierced more deeply than any bolt of energy T'ria could put through her.

All her doubts about Jake had been foolish. He loved her. He hadn't wanted her to come with him because he'd known the dangers here, even from his own people. He'd tried to tell her but she hadn't believed him and he'd been trying to protect her all along. Fool that she was, she'd thought he was trying to abandon her.

"Jake, I'm sorry," she said, tears streaming down her face. "I understand now."

"Take her home, T'ria." Jake said softly. "Give me your word you won't harm her but will take her back to her own time. You can use M'tgomery's TDA. It has a special feature that allows two people to transport at the same time." He took a deep breath and released it quickly. "Then you can do with me as you will and I won't resist."

T'ria considered his words for a moment then stood and replaced her weapon in its holster. "Very well. If I have your word that you will cooperate fully with the Council and accept our ruling on your mutinous actions."

Jake closed his eyes briefly. "I promise—if you'll give me just a moment with Torri before you take her back."

T'ria snorted. "You have changed." She signaled the guards to release him. "Keep your weapons on him at all times and don't let him touch her."

Anguish and despair swept over Jake like a tidal wave as he moved to Torri's side. He'd been crazy to come back here. He should have done as Col. Reed had said and left Montgomery in the past, then grabbed his one chance at happiness by returning with Torri to her own time. He would gladly leave behind his mission, his precious fight for right. He knew now that the Council would never listen to him. They were hell-bent on K'mer's destruction and he had no doubt that they would bring their own about as well. But now it was too late.

"Torri," he said in a low voice that he hoped wouldn't carry to the others. "I'm sorry. You were right. I should have listened to you and gone with you."

"Jake." Torri took a step toward him and T'ria hurried to her side, jerking her away from him, digging the weapon she held into Torri's back. Torri struggled, but finally stopped in defeat. She was two feet away from Jake and it was apparent that T'ria didn't intend for them to get any closer.

"Never forget that I love you," she whispered.

"Listen to me Victoria Cameron," he said, leaning toward her as far as the two neanderthals on either side of him would allow. "Neither time, nor space, nor even death can separate us forever. We will be together again one day."

Torri gazed back at him, her heart aching at the thought of never seeing him again. She stretched her hand toward him.

"How sweet," T'ria's sarcastic voice shattered the moment, as she shoved them apart, thrusting her body between them. "Now, say goodbye, Mrs. Cameron. You must tell me about the wedding, Jake," she said with a malicious smile, "after the little wife is gone. Which of the devices is Montgomery's?" Jake pointed to one of the two she held. She tossed the other to one of her men. "Ready?" she glanced at Torri, her gaze challenging.

Torri lifted her chin slightly. "I feel sorry for you," she said.

T'ria laughed. "For me? Whatever for?"

"You've lost your capacity to love—to feel," Torri said. "And losing those things are even worse than losing your freedom, because your feelings are something that no one can ever take away from you—except yourself." She and T'ria locked gazes and for a long moment Torri thought maybe she had made the woman understand; then the leader of the underground whirled around, dragging Torri with her.

"Jake!" Torri cried. "I love you!"

"Remember," he called, his steady voice moving farther and farther away as T'ria clasped Torri's arm firmly and pressed the jewels in the necklace. The kaleidoscope began, separating them with time and space and infinity, yet she could hear his words.

"We hold time in the palm of our hands . . . and our hearts. We'll be together again, Torri, I promise we'll be together again."

She watched his face fade from sight as the vortex sucked her into the watercolored mist, T'ria's fingers digging into her arm. Torri closed her eyes and felt the tears on her cheeks dissolve, along with her consciousness.

* * *

Torri trudged across the countryside, a trickle of sweat coursing down the back of her neck. True to her word, T'ria had
brought her back to her own time. They had appeared in
the middle of a woods near the same field where she had first
disappeared. She had begged T'ria to be lenient with Jake—
to search her heart and find one ounce of compassion for
the two lovers. But she feared she had only made matters
worse. T'ria had become angry and, shoving Torri to the
ground, had disappeared into time.

Torri had sat there for awhile, unwilling for a moment, to
move. She had lost Jake. No matter what he had promised,
she knew that she would never see him again this side of the
grave. Trying to turn her thoughts away from him, she hurried on, scarcely noticing when her foot struck something
square and blue and sent it flying. Torri shot a casual glance
back and ground to a sudden astonished stop. She moved
quickly and looked down at a small, tattered book lying in
the grass and picked it up.

The diary. The diary her Grandfa had given her those
many days ago. Or had it been? Had she returned only a day
after she had been swept back into 1863? T'ria had assured
her that with Montgomery's new device she would have no
trouble getting her back to her own time. She smoothed one
hand over the cover of the diary and stood, clutching it to
her chest like a shield.

Jake had his war to fight in the future; she was about to face
her own. Nathaniel Hamilton would not live out his days
in Sunnyside Sanitarium. She would get her own lawyer—
somehow, someway—and she would battle Christine, the
courts, the judges and the psychiatrists, until she made them
see reason.

She would bring her grandfather home and she would tell
him all about her amazing trip through time. She would tell
him how sorry she was for not believing him when he'd first

ntrusted the necklace to her. She would hold him in her
rms, and he would hold her, and together they would re-
uild their lives, together.

Unafraid, Torri took a deep breath and squaring her
noulders, headed up the hill toward the Hamilton mansion.
'he battle was about to begin.

Epilogue

"You've got to breathe, Torri! Don't push, breathe!"

The sound of the nurse's voice echoed through the mi[st] of pain surrounding Torri's mind and body. Obediently sh[e] pushed the breath out of her mouth instead of trying [to] force the baby out of her body.

As the contraction passed, Torri lay back limply again[st] the pillow, her hair slicked away from her sweaty face, an[d] stared at the pattern of tiny roses on the wallpaper. Sh[e] sighed. She was glad she had decided on the comfortabl[e,] homey birthing room instead of the sterile delivery roor[m,] but it still wasn't her own cozy room at Grandfa's house. A[t] this moment she wanted to go home more than anything i[n] the world.

Torri turned to the nurse, her voice weary. "I've change[d] my mind," she said. "I don't want to have a baby. Pack m[y] bag. I want to go home."

"I'm afraid it won't make a bit of difference, Mrs. Cam[-]eron." The face of her obstetrician. Dr. Mitchell Pric[e] bobbed cheerfully in front of her bleary eyes. "I think one [or] two more contractions will bring your baby home. Just han[g] in there." He patted her hand and walked away to examin[e] a chart.

The nurse fiddled with the sheet on her bed for a m[o]ment, then glanced up at, Torri, a hesitant look on her fac[e.]

"What is it?" Torri asked, suddenly anxious. "Is the bab[y] all right?"

"Oh, of course, of course," she said hastily. "I was ju[st]

wondering if there isn't some way we could get in touch with your husband."

Torri released her pent up breath in a rush. Jake. How she wished there was some way to find him. She had waited, sure he would return to her; waited for seven long months to no avail. When she had learned, a month after returning to her own time, that she was pregnant with Jake's child, she had been ecstatic. She had felt again their deep bond of love, and had begun to hope that Jake would, somehow re-turn to her. But eventually she had resigned herself to the fact that Jake was either dead or imprisoned in the future. Otherwise he would have come to her, he would have found a way, she knew. She had picked out the wallpaper for the nursery, bought sleepsuits, knitted little booties, and finally picked out names, all without Jake.

Torri closed her eyes against the sudden wave of loneli-ness that had become her constant companion.

"No," she said, softly stroking her rounded abdomen. "His work for the government keeps him in very odd places. I'll—I'll send a telegram after the baby is born."

The pain ripped through her again and Torri cried out with the intensity, panting as hard as she could in response to the nurse's terse orders. The doctor walked over to check her progress and immediately smiled.

"The head's crowning," he reported.

"Does that mean—" Torri asked breathlessly.

The nurse hurried to snap plastic gloves on the doctors hands. Torri squeezed her eyes shut and pushed, but it was no use. She was too tired, too weary from the long hours of labor.

"Come on," a deep voice ordered, "push, Mrs. Cameron, and that's an order!"

Torri lifted herself up again, supported by the nurse. She was so tired. Sweat dripped down into her eyes and blurred her vision as she tried to bear down and bring Jake's child into the world. She squeezed her eyes shut. Jake. If only he could be here. If only he hadn't stayed in his own time. She opened her eyes, hearing the doctor and nurse encouraging her to give one last push and suddenly, Torri saw Jake. Blinking, she tried to dispel the apparition by scrubbing the back of her hand across her eyes.

It *was* Jake—and T'ria! Torri tried to sit up but another spasm seized her. The baby was coming. She concentrated on one last, incredible push and somewhere between conscious and unconsciousness, Torri felt the terrible pressure of the past eighteen hours give way to sudden relief.

"Torri, Torri darling, open your eyes!"

Torri's eyes shot open and tears streamed down her face to mingle with perspiration as she saw the most precious miracle of all . . . her daughter. So enraptured by the sight of the tiny, red, squalling face, and so tired after the long hours of labor, she didn't even question the strong arm around her, or the voice that had ordered her to open her eyes.

"Isn't she beautiful?" she breathed, as the nurse wrapped the baby in a blanket and handed her to Torri. She held out her arms to accept the precious bundle. "Isn't she absolutely beautiful?"

"Yes," the nurse said softly. "Torri, dear, did you know you have a visitor?"

Torri followed her smiling gaze to the man who was sitting beside her, supporting her, smiling down at her with warm, gray eyes.

It took a few minutes for the doctor to tend to Torri and for the nurse to make her more comfortable, but soon she was left alone with her husband and their child.

"Jake." She lifted her hand to touch his face, then smiled. "You're real."

"Sorry for the delay, kitten," he said softly, brushing a strand of hair back from her face. "It took a little longer than I hoped to sort things out." He cocked his eyebrow at her and tried to look severe. "Do my eyes deceive me or did you forget to tell me something important before you disappeared out of my life forever?"

He touched the baby lovingly and smiled in wonder as one little hand curled around his finger. Torri saw the awe and love mirrored in his face.

"I didn't know. Really I didn't," she answered, feeling suddenly, ridiculously shy. "Do you mind, very much, I mean, that we have a child?"

He pulled her close again, his breath warm against her hair. "Oh, kitten, I'm only afraid I'll let the baby down, the way my father did me."

"No!" Torri turned and pressed her fingers against his lips, then caressed his jawline. "Don't say that. Don't think that. You are nothing like your father."

"No, not anymore." He drew a deep, ragged breath. "My father is dead."

"What happened?" Torri asked. "Did they listen to you? I mean, I guess obviously they listened to you."

"Not at first. They were going to kill me but surprisingly enough T'ria convinced them to hear me out. I was finally able to win a few of the Council over to my way of thinking, and eventually the others came around as well. They really are good people."

Torri found her attention wandering as she looked down at her daughter's tiny face, so perfect, so beautiful. She'd thought she could bear having her child alone, but suddenly she knew how bereft she would have been if Jake had not arrived. She stirred herself from the powerful lethargy beginning to fog her reasoning. "But if they agreed, where have you been?"

"It took time, if you'll pardon the pun. We used M 'tgomery to infiltrate the palace and T'ria—" he broke off, gently touching the tiny scrap of dark hair curling on the baby's head.

"T'ria killed your father," she finished for him.

"Yes. I'll tell you all about it, later." He kissed the baby's forehead, then hers. "Right now we have more important things to think about. She's beautiful, Torri."

"Jake," she whispered.

"Yes, kitten?"

"Don't ever leave me again."

He chuckled. "I can't. T'ria brought me back and dumped me here. I wanted her to bring me back to when you first returned, but she wouldn't. I don't know why she waited to deliver me at this particular moment, but I'm glad she did. She's promised to round up and destroy all of the TDAs." He stroked the side of her face lovingly. "No, Mrs. Cameron, I'm afraid you're stuck with me, forever."

Torri smiled up at him. "I can live with that." She gathered the precious bundle in her arms more closely. "What shall we name her?"

"I was thinking . . ." his dark eyebrows knit together ". . . what do you think about Tamara?"

"Tamara? Why Tamara?"

He tightened his arms around her and Torri felt quick tears at the sudden passion she saw in his. "Because that's what we have waiting for us, my love—all the tomorrows that life has to give."

Torri nodded her agreement, just as the door to the birthing room opened and a tall, older man walked in, his hazel eyes dark with worry.

"Victoria Hamilton!" he said sternly. "I thought I was going to get to hold the baby first!"

Torri smiled. "Sorry, Grandfa, but I'm sure you don't mind letting your great-granddaughter's father hold her first."

His wrinkled face split into a wide smile as he gazed down at the bundle in Torri's arms.

"A girl," he breathed, in a tone of adoration. "A baby girl. Good job, Torri," he said softly, his gaze shifting to rest with pride on her flushed face. She nodded her understanding, then looked up at Jake who was frowning at the two of them, obviously feeling out of place.

"Jake," Torri said, "this is my grandfather. Grandfa, this is my husband, Jake Cameron, the one I told you about."

"Oh, yes, you mean the one *I* told *you* about, don't you, at the very beginning of all this nonsense?" He chuckled as he reached out and shook Jake's hand over the baby's head. "Welcome to the present, young man. Now, let me hold the baby. At least I get to be the *third* to hold her, even though I was the one who had to run to the store for pistachio ice cream in the middle of the night for seven months!"

Laughing, Torri held the baby out to him and he sank into a chair next to the bed, his face wreathed in gentle amazement.

"Thank you, Lord, for letting me live to see this day," he said reverently.

"Yes," Torri echoed, "thank you." She reached over and squeezed his gnarled hand affectionately. "You know, if you had been my coach like I asked you, then you could have been in here for the whole experience."

"Be your coach? At my age?" He placed his hand over his chest. "Even this tough old heart couldn't have stood up to that!"

"It's stood up to a lot worse in the last seven months," Torri reminded him. "But we finally won, didn't we?"

His hazel eyes twinkled back at her with warmth. "Thanks to you, Torri-mine, only thanks to you."

"And a cracker-jack attorney, don't forget that!"

"I take it you won the war with Christine," Jake said into Torri's ear as he wrapped one of her curls around his finger.

"Yes," she said with a sigh of contentment, "I won." She glanced at her grandfather. "We won."

"Here, sweetness," her grandfather said suddenly, handing the baby back to her. "I've got to go call a few of my old cronies and brag about my beautiful great-granddaughter." He paused at the door, his face bright with unashamed tears of joy, and winked at them both. "Congratulations, Mr. and Mrs. Cameron."

Torri leaned back against the curve of Jake's arms and turned to meet his kiss. As their lips touched, Torri felt the warmth of his love wrap itself around the three of them, more precious than jewels, more lasting than time itself.

The baby in her arms stirred and they both turned to watch life's tiniest miracle yawn. In that heartbeat of a moment, for Jake and Torri Cameron, at last, time stood still.

INTERACT WITH DORCHESTER ONLINE!

Want to learn more about your favorite books and authors?
Want to talk with other readers that like to read the same books as you?
Want to see up-to-the-minute Dorchester news?

VISIT DORCHESTER AT:
DorchesterPub.com
Twitter.com/DorchesterPub
Facebook.com (Search Pages)

DISCUSS DORCHESTER'S NOVELS AT:
Dorchester Forums at DorchesterPub.com
GoodReads.com
LibraryThing.com
Myspace.com/books
Shelfari.com
WeRead.com

There was little of joy and beauty for Tessa LaPrelle, a scullery maid in 1903 London, but for a painting called

The Bride of Time

The nude raised eyebrows and speculation that Tessa had posed. Impossible! Even if some man could make her so wanton, even if the subject had Tessa's thick chestnut hair, the work had been commissioned a hundred years previous, at the start of the Regency!

What drew Tessa was a small window in the painting's corner, a seeming portal to that wild Cornish wilderness. Sometimes she dreamt she had been running all her life—from what and to whom, she was about to discover.

DAWN THOMPSON

ISBN 13: 978-0-505-52728-8